The Boy in the Emerald Fire

C.A. Jackson

Hardback ISBN: 978-1-967257-00-3
Ebook ISBN: 978-1-967257-06-5
Paperback: 978-1-967257-13-3

First Edition

Cover design by Cassandra Ritter

Library of Congress Control Number: 2025945060

For permissions or inquiries, please contact
hello@booksbyjac.com

Dedication

I dedicate this book to my wife, Emily. Without that fateful walk we went on, the idea for this book, for Lorian, and for all the magic and gods and myths that followed, none of it would exist. Thank you for your patience, your strength and your resilience. Words can't describe the influence you've had on me, and this book. You are my Naivety, my world. My everything. I love you.

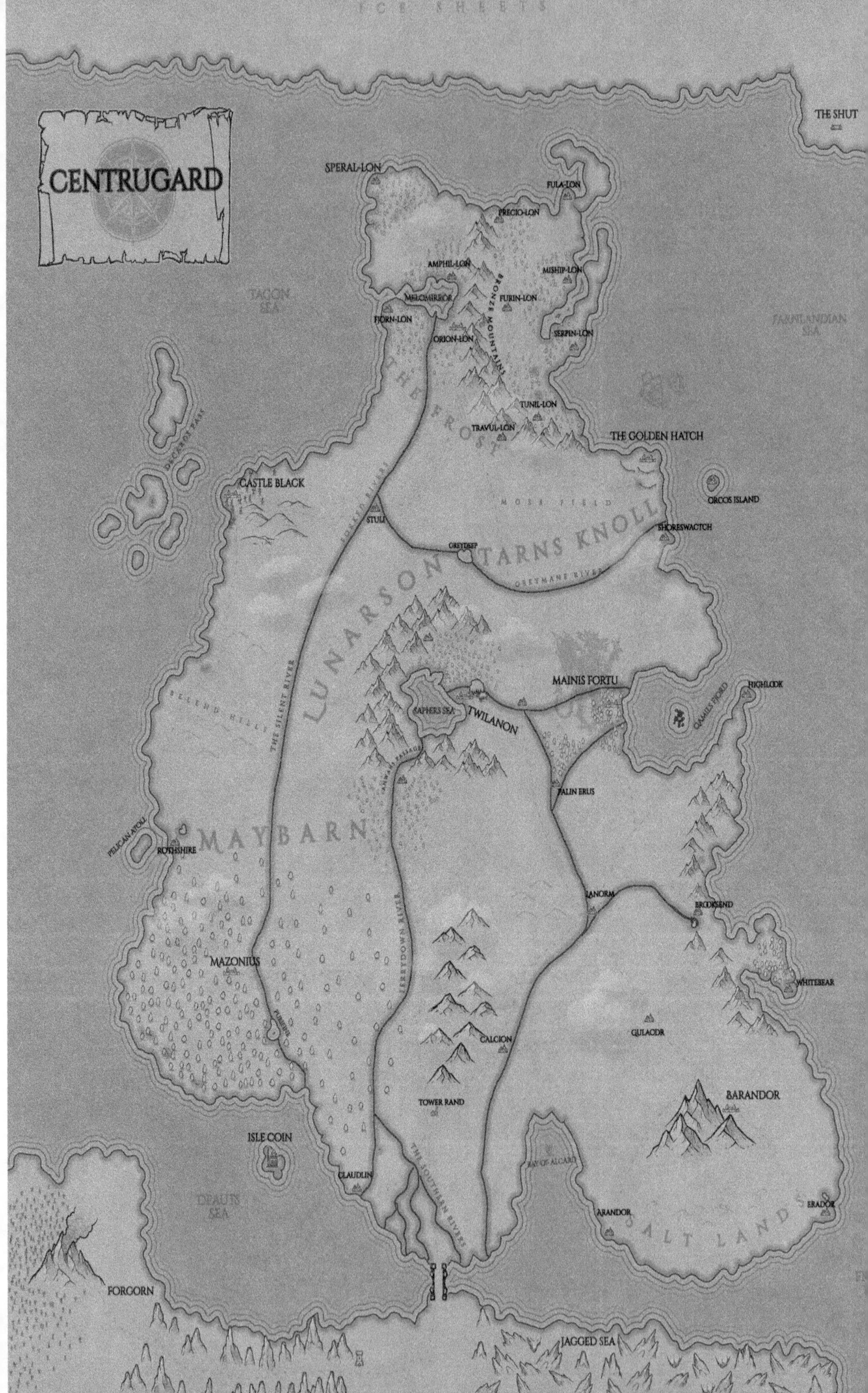
ICE SHEETS
CENTRUGARD
THE SHUT
SPERAL-LON
FULA-LON
PRECIO-LON
AMPHIL-LON
MISHIP-LON
MELOMIRROR
FURIN-LON
FJORN-LON
ORION-LON
SERPIN-LON
TAGON SEA
FAUNLANDIAN SEA
TUNIL-LON
THE FROST
TRAVUL-LON
THE GOLDEN HATCH
MOSS FIELD
CASTLE BLACK
ORCOS ISLAND
STULI
SHORESWACTCH
OREYDEEP
TARNS KNOLL
LUNARSON
OREYMANE RIVER
MAINIS FORTU
HIGHLOOK
SAPHERS SEA
CRAMILS FIELD
BELEND HILLS
THE SILENT RIVER
TWILANON
PALIN ERUS
PELICAN ATOU
ROTHSHIRE
MAYBARN
LANORM
BROOKSEND
FREETOWN RIVER
WHITEBEAR
MAZONIUS
GULAODR
PELISIRE
CALCION
BARANDOR
TOWER RAND
ISLE COIN
DEAUN SEA
THE SOUTHERN RIVER
BAY OF ALCARI
CLAUDLIN
ARANDOR
SALT LAND
ERADOR
FORGORN
JAGGED SEA

Table of Contents

Chapter 1: An Opportunity for More

"The horror of the situation was that, in the small hours before they were executed, the children were under the impression that their fathers and mothers had collected them to finally claim them as heirs. The brutality of the event will forever stain the parchment of our histories."
—Magistrate Ryeson's personal account of the Bastard Crusades

The small town of Amphil-Lon lay nestled between towering mountains and the vast lake of Melomirror, its houses huddled together like old friends seeking warmth. Smoke spiraled into the crisp morning air from chimneys, signaling the city's awakening. The snow-covered thatch of its dwellings shimmered brilliantly as the warm rays of the infant sun settled atop them. In the outskirts of the port stood the blacksmith's forge, a haven for sparks and the rhythmic pounding of metal on anvil.

Lorian wiped fresh sweat from his brow, and the coals in his wicker basket nearly spilled over as he balanced it on his knee.

Dealing with coal was his least favored chore, and the task his father most often assigned. It wasn't hard work; he was a man now, after all, and he found this was much less strenuous than shaping steel, but the grime of the blackened fuel was exceedingly difficult to wash off.

He wondered if noble magic would make the job easier—if it was even capable of washing clean a filthy pair of hands, or if it was only meant for keeping the masses in order. Those without power. Those like him.

"Forge is getting cold, son. Fill the ol' girl up!" his father shouted from inside the workshop. It had been just the two of them for as long as he could remember, as his mother had passed from the pox when he was still a babe.

He hated thinking of his mother. He was branded with the surname Night instead of Oslison because of her. She was a whore, a lady of the night, and while he knew it wasn't her fault, it was all he could associate her with when the thought arose.

Lorian smartly carried the basket into the workshop and began fueling the fire with the hardened shards of coal. He loved watching the flames dance back to life, observing them grow and breathe as if they, too, lived and held thoughts.

"You'll need to be heading out soon," his father said as he oiled a short sword the two of them had recently finished. Lorian watched his father coat the blade before binding it in thick leather for delivery. "You're to deliver this to Lord Varios' estate. Drop off the parcel, give your thanks for his business, and return home. Nothing more. Do you understand?" he ordered, a subtle plea for Lorian to obey.

Tonight was the twenty-second anniversary of the Bastard Crusades, and his father always grew more protective during this time. A few years prior to his birth, the collective nobles from across all lands of Centrugard signed forth a law. This legislation gave them the right to secure their magic by eliminating any children sired outside their direct family lines. This precedent was used to kill any and all illegitimate offspring who carried or potentially harbored noble blood. Thousands died, all for the sake of purity.

Since then, the crown had prohibited the killing of bastards, nobility or not, without just cause. This alone could not end the crusades; it merely hid the barbarous act under political shadow.

Most days, Lorian wondered why the royals refused to interject themselves and hold those who participated accountable, but today wasn't one of those days. He was smart enough to know holding a lord culpable was just as impossible as getting them to stop fucking whores and having illegitimate young.

Regardless, he knew his father would be on edge until the anniversary was over. He had spent over two decades protecting him and hiding him from any nobles who may have been overly cautious and deemed him one of their misbegotten seeds.

Lorian clenched his jaw and steadied his breath. Anger always grew when he pondered the cruelty of the ruling class. "Father, I'll be all right. I'm more than old enough to avoid suspicion. I am your son, and my eyes bear no glow of magic. We are safe, as we have been for years."

"I know, my boy. I'll never not worry for you," his father began as his words turned tender. "When you have your own babes one day, you'll understand." He pushed the blade into Lorian's arms and patted his shoulder. "Take care on your journey, and wear my nice silks if you're to speak in front of a lord. Remember your lessons, Lorian. One stray glance or sour word, and you may come home with fewer fingers. I've got Sebastian ready for you. Damn beast is huffing up a storm outside. Gets antsy when stabled too long."

"I'll be back soon!" Lorian replied in haste as he made for the door. If he was quick enough, he could return before nightfall and avoid a cold bowl of stew, though he knew his father would keep the pot hot until he returned.

He was thankful to have a caring father, yet the love could feel smothering at times. No law forced the father of a child branded Night to raise and care for him, nor was there any benefit to doing such a thing. He knew his father faced many hardships for taking him in—poverty, harassment—but none of these stopped him.

He could never repay his father in a hundred lives, but he was determined to try if the chance ever arose.

"Oh, one more word, lad," his father said after following him out the front. "The order said to inform Lord Varios the sword is a gift from Lord Handall of the Whale-tooth. Best not forget; not often a noble sends us work," he finished before handing Lorian a leather pack.

"Aye, I'll tell him," Lorian said as he watched his father return to the workshop. He waited a moment and then left for the journey to Varios' manor—purposely leaving behind his father's silks out of distaste for the flashy garments.

The sun had risen since he awoke, and the whole of Amphil-Lon now sprawled out beneath him from the hill on which the shop sat. A lively scene unfolded—a small sea of homes and shops fully animated. Chimneys pumped smoke into the air, and inhabitants engaged in busy conversations, offering discounts and friendly greetings. Lorian had never been fond of this city, mostly due to the scorn he felt as a bastard in a place that held station and name so preciously. However, the beauty of the port town could not be ignored. It was nestled alongside the northeastern bank of the lake, standing in stark contrast to the otherwise thickly forested landscape.

The nearly still surface of the water mirrored the morning sky—a streak of fading red fire dancing under the bright yellow blanket of sunlight. The gentle rays smoothly settled into the frigid waters of Melomirror, distorting light as the sun's beams scattered through sections of newly formed frost and ice. The mesmerizing morning rainbows would soon be disrupted by the ripples of fishing and cargo ships making their way around the harbor. Yet, for now, they thrived, and Lorian wished to savor them for as long as time would permit.

After absorbing what he could from the scenery, he sucked in a chilled breath and continued down the hill toward the city. Lord Varios' manor was on the opposite side of the town from his father's shop, perched alongside the coast a few miles west. He would need to traverse through the busy streets and out the Western Gate to make the best time.

Luckily, his father had allowed him the use of Sebastian, a white and gray spotted horse. He had heard his father refer to the steed as a Ledani, which apparently meant the beast had blood roots to a Ledanomere, or an elven-steed, though he knew such things were fairy tales.

Lorian was not what one would consider well-studied, but his father had gone through a lot of trouble to educate him in the ways of the world. Politeness and decorum in the face of those with higher station. Brief histories of Centrugard so he may hold a proper conversation. Basic reading and writing to learn and communicate through more than spoken word, and arithmetic so he would know the value of himself and his possessions.

Lorian approached the stable, which sat slightly downhill from the shop, and untied Sebastian. After securing his pack to the saddle, he led the beast down to where the land stood flatter and more solid.

He knew from experience anyone attempting to straddle the animal on uneven footing would risk finding themselves with injury, like he did when he was younger—a scar on the backside of his head existing as proof.

After ensuring the ground was safe, he leaped onto Sebastian's back, and together, they trotted south toward the city.

"Good boy, Sebastian," he said as he patted his horse's neck. "I think today should be a good day despite the chill in the air. First, we'll deliver the sword; then, if time permits, we can visit the Canary for a pint—and a carrot for you, of course," he finished as he chuckled at himself.

The horse gave a series of foggy exhales, which he took as confirmation for their after-journey treat.

"Lorian!" resounded a familiar voice from down the footpath. A friend of Lorian's, Feln, trotted forward on a dark gray steed. She was garbed in red and black satin, which stretched tightly about her waist and covered part of her braided head—the robes of a merchant. The ensemble made her seem very dignified; he grinned, as he knew how rough around the edges she could be. She stopped her horse beside his, and the two clasped hands.

Her porcelain face was pink near the tip of her nose, and her blue eyes sparkled under the light of the rising sun. "Thought you could sneak off before saying goodbye to me, did you? Well, think again. I left early just to catch you before Nord sent you on another delivery. Surprised he let you leave the shop this time of the year."

He raised his chin and lifted an eyebrow smugly. "He's starting to see me for the man I am!"

"Oh my!" Feln reacted with an exaggerated breath, her hand pressing against her chest in practiced sarcasm. "I see you now for the man you are, dear Lorian. Perhaps I'll forgo my apprenticeship with the merchant's guild, and you can take my hand and make an honest woman of me!"

Though he knew she preyed upon his pride, he couldn't help but blush at the thought of it. She snickered at the redness of his face and, to his relief, granted him the mercy of changing the topic. "Where are we off to now, Blade Apprentice Night? Another delivery to Sergeant Ironson and his garrison of drunk gate guards?"

He went silent for a moment, hoping to add tension to the grand reveal of his newest client. He gave a grin and said, "Actually, Feln, I'm to deliver this sword to none other than Lord Varios. At his estate, to be precise."

Against all odds, her white face seemed to lose a shade, and she furrowed her brow in concern. "Lorian, Varios is a high-born noble. Watch your words and stay vigilant. Men with such powerful magic could scorch the skin from your bones and not think twice about it."

He rolled his eyes in response, doing his best to exude annoyance. "I know, Feln. I wasn't born this morning; I'm just delivering a sword."

"Nothing is so simple when nobles are involved. Especially for bastards. You must take great care, or else," she replied coldly.

Her words stung, and he was sure his face portrayed his pain. He watched as she averted her eyes in momentary guilt. Affecting his tone to sound sarcastic, he decided to lighten the mood. "O! How fortunate!" he began in a sing-song rhythm. "To be spared the ire of a noble for behaving properly! What a world! Perhaps I should try my hand at cards down by the Canary with how fortune smiles at me!"

She sat staring at him with a grin, which threatened to break his composure. "What a revelation you've made today, good Lorian. To discover the unfairness of society at the ripe age of twenty is a gift in itself. If you've time later, you could write a song on the wetness of water or the starch taste of dirt."

Lorian eyed her playfully and replied, "I think I shall, Feln! Though the dirt always tastes sweeter with you around."

Laughter broke between them, and for a moment, he was glad. "So, leaving for your understudy, correct? Soon, you'll be a full-blooded merchant, and you can finally open your own shop."

"Yes, I'll be off shortly," she said with a stifled breath.

"Well, I'm sorry I couldn't make a day out of seeing you off. Father requires my help, per usual, and we can't afford to turn down business. Though wish it I may," replied Lorian with a half-smile. "You've been a good friend, Feln. I'll not forget your kindness."

"Nor I yours, dear Lorian," she said. A melancholy moment seemed to pause time between the two friends as neither could be sure when they'd reunite again.

Breaking the silence, he reached out and grasped Feln by the forearm, and she grabbed his in return. They smiled as they gave each other a proper goodbye. "Going southward toward the capital, yes? Traveling by sea out of Fjord-Lon, or braving the Powdered Roads?"

Feln released her grip, as did he. "By sea, I'm afraid. I'd risk bandits before I'd give the ocean a chance to swallow me, though the decision was out of my hands," she said as she chuckled nervously.

"Then the twelve gods be with you, friend. Travel well, and may your future be lush with coin."

"And may they see fortune upon you as well," she replied.

Lorian watched his only companion take leave for possibly the last time. He felt a change within himself as she left his sight. The environment seemed to shift as well: the wind was harsher, the cold nipped harder at his exposed face, and the sun seemed only a mirrored and distorted version of itself. Though he was inclined to stay rooted in place, gazing at the space she had disappeared from and hoping for one last glimpse of her, he knew he must continue on his own path.

Sebastian and Lorian made good time as they traversed the dense woods surrounding the city. The tall pines formed a natural barrier, restricting their view into the foliage. Morning sunlight flickered through the trees, creating a pulse of light that irritated Lorian, prompting him to draw his hood forward.

Despite the frozen climate, the foliage was alive with the chittering of animals. He knew these creatures had adapted to the environment over many years, with only the larger creatures choosing to hibernate and sleep through the cold. Watching them go about their day—searching for food, keeping an eye out for predators, and frolicking when they felt safe—was therapeutic for him.

He admired their freedom and envied it. Birds, in particular, held a special place in his imagination. As a boy, he would daydream about soaring high above the treetops, wings propelling his feathered body higher than any bird had gone before, reaching heights over the stars. He often wondered about the unseen realms beyond his vision, contemplating what might exist above the heavens.

Feln used to tease him about this fantasy, saying if he were a bird, the only freedom he would find would be freedom from thought, which was already the case. He didn't think he would miss her so soon.

He soon approached the tall northern entrance that filtered entry into the city. Two guards stood watch on the ground, while a slew of others marched along the topside of the reinforced wall that cradled the buildings within.

Narrow slits in the stone revealed another layer of defense: they acted as ports through which archers and crossbowmen could fire if ever needed.

Lorian always felt a daunting sensation creep alongside his skull when he entered through the Northern Gate. The gates were enormous, and he could hardly believe man could construct such a fortified thing, whilst nature alone could not.

On approach, a guard stopped him—as was customary—and asked him to show his identification papers. Reaching into the pack he had fastened to Sebastian's harness, he removed a small leather-bound booklet that held his important documents and handed them over.

"Lorian Night, eh?" spoke the guard roughly. The soldier had a certain inflection to his words that made him believe he was not from the north but rather one of the eastern provinces, where they stretched their words and rolled their R's. "Very well, bastard. Pay the entry fee, and you may pass."

Lorian's eyes widened with surprise. He had never needed coin for entrance, but it had been some time since he'd last entered the main city, and he was uncertain if this man spoke the truth. "My apologies, sir; I was unaware of the new cost. Would it be possible to speak to your sergeant so I may ask for more details?"

The soldier removed his helm to better see Lorian; his tanned face scrunched in disgust. "Are you giving me orders, bastard? Do you believe me to be a liar?" barked the guard, his free hand grabbing the handle of the blade he had fastened to his waist. "Consider your price doubled, boy."

Lorian knew he was being swindled now. He began to feel dread's embrace, certain the man was being false but unable to do anything about it. *The curse of a bastard*, he thought. The guard began to unsheathe his sword. Before the blade could lift even halfway from his sheath, a voice ordered him to attention.

"Reynolds! About face."

The guard spun on his heel, his helmet swiftly returning to his head.

"Why have you stopped this man, soldier?" spoke another armored individual Lorian knew as Malcom Ironson.

Reynolds began to stumble on his words, clearly attempting to think of an excuse clever enough to warrant the unlawful detaining of Lorian.

"Because I could not pay the new entry fee, Sergeant Ironson," Lorian supplied.

A grim color set itself onto Reynolds' skin, a dull shade of gray as blood drained from his face and limbs.

"Is there truth in this, soldier?" barked Sergeant Ironson. Lorian fought back a smile—he knew he had forced the guard to confess his wrongdoing. "Five lashes for extortion. If those don't suit you, how about removal from the gate watch and a court appearance with Magistrate Lawson?"

Reynolds shivered at the sound of the magistrate, and what blood he had left in his face escaped back into his heart.

"I'll have the l-lashes, sir," stuttered the guard.

"A wise choice, soldier. Report to the whipping pole immediately," ordered Sergeant Ironson.

As Reynolds marched toward a door set into the side of the wall, Sergeant Ironson strode toward Lorian until they were a few paces from one another. "Lorian," said Ironson.

"Sergeant."

"You could have lied, you know. Saved him from suffering a few lashes in the blistering cold. Why didn't you?"

"Because." He straightened his back upon Sebastian and raised his chin. "What if the next time he attempted his deception, it wasn't me but an innocent woman with her children? I believe after those lashings, he'll think twice about abusing his power," he finished, a stern look set on his face.

"An answer wise beyond your years, bastard," replied the sergeant, a cunning smile on his lips.

"And because I didn't like him, but that's beside the point."

Ironson burst out with laughter, his foggy breath blinding him for a few quick moments. "An even better answer, I should think," Ironson said as he reigned in his laughter. "Tell your father he's raised a very wrathful young man. And give him my thanks for repairing my chainmail last harvest. I'd be out a pretty coin if he hadn't done me the service."

"I shall pass on your message, sergeant. For your assistance today, I should say you both are very much even in deeds now," he said with a smile.

"Aye, we may be. Careful going forward, Lorian. A storm is supposed to be blowing through soon. Best to get inside before it does. The bite of winter is always full of surprises. Travel on now," said the sergeant, giving Sebastian an encouraging slap on the rear. He lifted a hand to a soldier beyond view, and the Northern Gate began to whine and creak as an unseen device lifted it.

Lorian took heed of the sergeant's warning and hurried through the crowded street of Amphil-Lon toward the Western Gate. The streets were packed with vendors displaying an assortment of fishing-related goods—carp, red eye, blue-gill salmon, and a variety of tools meant for catching, luring, descaling, and more.

The smell never grew dull in the nose; a new variety of spoiled fish guts seemed to arrive every day. Even as one who was more than familiar with the foul scents of the city, inhaling the noxious fumes of waste this early was enough to rattle Lorian's stomach.

Lorian yanked upon Sebastian's reins in time to avoid a bucket of waste tossed into his path by an older woman, the near-black liquid peppering a passing wagon instead.

He rapidly made his way through the remainder of the city and out of the Western Gate in what he would consider record time. He had never visited the lord's manor and was anxious to see what true luxury looked like.

The trees on that end of the lake were far less dense and offered a view of the water as he traveled. He had always loved the smell of the lake when it wasn't tainted by fish or piss.

When he was a boy, he used to sneak into the lake for a swim until he was caught by a dock worker who had beaten him for scaring off the fish. One day, he'd swim in those waters again, without worry, without hesitation.

Lord Varios' manor came into view after he and Sebastian made a hard left toward the shores. It was a beautiful estate and made the rest of the buildings in Amphil-Lon seem dull in comparison.

The manor was two stories tall and seemed to be carved from marble. It had a series of tall columns supporting a large triangular overhang and a set of large glass windows that offered a look at both the lake and the city. A tall stone wall surrounded the manor and terminated at a single entry point. A thick cast-iron gate had bars bent and shaped to match the Varios family emblem: a twin-headed snake with a tail coiled behind it in knots.

Lorian brought Sebastian to a stop just before the gate and led the horse to a station where he could be secured. He would go on foot from this point.

"What business do you have here, commoner?" a voice from beyond the gate said. It was a man wearing a powdered wig and garments identifying him as a servant.

"Good day, sir," Lorian said. "I am to present a gift to Lord Varios on behalf of Lord Handall of the Whale-tooth."

The servant eyed him for a hard minute before responding. "And where is this gift now?"

Lorian reached over the saddle and unlatched his pack. He had tied the sword and its leathers to the pack before leaving the shop so as not to forget the gift. "Here it is, sir." He showcased the sword to the servant, holding the blade in front of him with outstretched arms.

"Very well," replied the servant in a deadpan voice.

The gate opened with a gentle whine, a sign of well-oiled metal, and Lorian marveled at the meticulous care of the lord's property. The landscaping drew his eyes in with a cobblestone path leading to the front doors, surrounded by perfectly trimmed hedges and hand-carved statues.

Guided by the servant who granted him entry, he made his way to the front entrance, passing a small encampment of men stationed on the side of the lord's manor—a personal unit, he assumed. As he approached the manor's foyer, a scream pierced the air, shattering his daydream.

Glancing toward the encampment, he saw a shirtless man tied to a pole, his back bearing deep cuts from whipping or flogging. Another blow fell, prompting a wince from Lorian. Flooded with guilt, he remembered condemning another man to a similar fate earlier in the day. Unable to ignore the distressing scene, he couldn't help but ask, "Why are they beating him?"

"Thievery," replied the servant flatly.

Assuming no further explanation would be offered, Lorian continued into the foyer through large double doors.

The interior of the manor surpassed the exterior in extravagance. Walls were adorned with fine paintings, velvety drapes covered every window, and busts of unknown figures filled the spaces between. Chairs were plentiful; he estimated there were enough for every commoner in the city, with some to spare. Twin stairs curved alongside the front of the home, leading to a large balcony where the manor continued.

At the base of the stairs, in the space between them, sat a large painting of the lord. His dark, slick hair met his forehead in a widow's peak. Though appearing to be in his late forties or early fifties, his slender face and wide build made age estimation challenging.

Lorian found himself enamored with the lord's eyes, a telltale sign of magic. Lord Varios' left eye was chestnut brown, contrasting with the whitish-blue hue of his right eye. Even in the painting, the magical blue eye stood out, emitting a subtle glow.

"The lord of the manor is preparing for a journey this afternoon and will see you in his study when he has finished so he may receive the gift. You are to wait here until you are called on," instructed the servant as he disappeared into a service entrance nearly indistinguishable from the rest of the carved marble wall.

Lorian soon found himself alone, and his nerves unsettled further. His father's lessons never covered the formalities of presenting a gift to nobility. He doubted his father was aware of such formalities in the first place. The lessons only explained how to respond to a noble or gentleman if first spoken to. He did not know how long he was to wait, or if he was allowed to relax in one of the many chairs decorating the room.

Would I be punished for sitting? he thought to himself. Not willing to risk it, he began to pace instead.

Adjacent to some of the chairs were desks and stands displaying the wealth of the lord. Trinkets of silver and gold sat atop the tables and came in all forms—from candlesticks to plates, decorative pieces, and vases. He stared at a particular fork, which shone brilliantly—gold cutlery atop a silver plate—and thought how something so small could be worth enough money to give him a life of luxury and peace.

His thoughts snapped back to the present as he remembered the man outside, split in half for the exact same crime, and he suddenly felt an itch originate from between his shoulder blades.

After an unnerving amount of time, the servant appeared before Lorian, seemingly out of thin air. "The lord will see you now. Follow me," he said in his now familiar dull voice.

The servant led Lorian through a series of doors into a variety of rooms, each more lavish than the last. One room even contained a framed sword that looked to be made of pure gold. Finally, the servant arrived at a door that forced them to stop and wait. After a moment, the servant knocked upon the door three times and promptly left Lorian to handle the rest himself. He looked around wildly, unsure what to do. No command came from beyond the door, so with his heart beating in his throat, he opened the door and let himself in.

The walls of the lord's study were lined with more books than he had ever seen. Manuscripts, encyclopedias, scrolls of correspondence, and more dressed the walnut shelves from top to bottom. A fireplace on the far end of the room was roaring with fresh logs, and the marble floor was covered with an intricate rug of unknown design. In front of the fireplace was a large wooden desk scattered with paper and other objects.

Behind the desk, sitting in an armchair, was Lord Varios. He fettered through loose papers with one hand and held a bloodied whip in the other, laying the object gently upon the desk.

"And who said you could enter without permission?" asked Varios, his tone as posh as his station. Lorian felt too stunned to speak. He knew the gaps in his knowledge would fail him one day, though he didn't expect it to come this soon. Annoyed at the lack of response, Varios looked up from his writings to examine the individual who lacked respect. "Ah, a commoner. Tell me, boy, why have you come?" he asked as he returned to his work.

"A . . . A gift, my lord. Crafted by my father, Nord Oslison, and gifted to you by Lord Handall of the Whale-tooth." A nervous stutter intruded into his words. Lorian walked forward with the sword and bowed before the baron with his arms forward as he presented the gift.

Varios jumped from his desk with force, his brow furrowed in anger, and he gave the entirety of his focus to Lorian. "Does your disrespect have no limits? You offer me a sword crafted by a commoner on behalf of a gentleman. Tell me, who ordered you to come here?" demanded the noble, his tone calm in contrast to his body language.

Lorian kept his head down out of fear when he replied, "Lord Handall, Your Grace. I was not aware—"

"Raise your head when you speak to me, boy. Or are you so above me that meeting my eyes in conversation is beneath you?"

Lorian flicked his head up at the lord's orders, fighting against his fear. Lorian's eyes kept darting from Varios' magic blue eye to the bloodied whip upon the desk, and he began to wonder if this was to be his fate as well.

The baron noticed this, and, for a moment, Lorian thought Varios seemed ashamed.

"Worry not, boy. This whip is not meant for you. I have a rule in this estate: If I command the punishment for a crime to be a beating of any sort, then by my hand shall the punishment be carried out. I do not believe violence to be an answer in most situations. But when violence is needed, it is only right I be the one who acts as its arbiter."

"Yes, Your Grace," was the only reply Lorian could make, his fear keeping his thoughts from forming critically.

Varios seemed to soften greatly, perhaps noticing the fear he had unwittingly instilled in Lorian. "Forgive me. I have startled you with my words. Take a seat, and we shall discuss your reason for being here. You're telling me Lord Handall has ordered this sword gifted to me?" asked the lord as he returned to his chair.

Lorian followed suit and was relieved not to stand any longer; his legs were weak from the interaction.

"Yes, Your Grace."

"I see. I know you wouldn't understand, but Lord Handall seeks to insult me. To bring me a gift of this quality, as fine as it is, and not have the nerve to present it himself is a dishonor to me."

Lorian shrank before the noble. "My apologies, Your Grace. I wasn't aware. Please forgive me."

Lorian's heart dropped as he realized he had lowered himself in the very same manner everyone did before the might of nobility. He had relinquished all sense of self-respect and decency in the name of appeasing the imaginary rules of conduct, and he felt ashamed.

Anger replaced the shame, and then he felt nothing. No fear of the noble or any reprisal he may face. No fear of the difference in their station or of the mighty power the noble commanded, and no fear of the ridiculousness of the world and the hierarchy in which he existed. Lorian's face turned to stone in reaction to this new awareness. If Varios noticed this change in his demeanor, he kept any acknowledgment of it to himself.

"What is your name, boy?" asked the lord.

"Lorian Night," Lorian responded with an unfounded sense of authority.

A smile grew upon the Lord's face, which he made no attempt to conceal. "Well, Bastard Night, I have a job for you. You see, I'm to set off toward the mines of Orion-Lon. Part of my duties as baron is to inspect the mines from time to time, ensure smooth operation and relatively safe working conditions, as well as keep order within the city. As it so happens, I am out a squire," the Lord said as he pointed to the bloody whip upon his desk. "You will come in his stead. For your reward, I shall pay you ten gold coins, and I shall gift you this necklace the thief saw fit to take."

Without thinking, Lorian accepted the job. Ten gold coins were more money than he had ever seen. It could keep him and his father fed through the next two winters if they spent it wisely. It was too precious an offer to refuse, nor could he when ordered by a noble, but willingly accepting it gave him a sense of control. "Yes, sir. I shall accompany you. I am not trained as a squire but will learn quickly."

"I'm sure you will, Lorian Night. Meet with Rikard and prepare yourself. We leave at the top of the hour. And don't forget your pay," the noble added as he tossed a leather purse and a trinket to him.

The pouch contained more than ten pieces of gold, which Lorian hoped the Lord wouldn't notice, and the necklace was a dirty silver chain that connected a small sphere to a larger, opaque ring. He wondered why, in a house full of treasures, someone would steal something not even the lord himself wanted to keep.

Lorian left Varios' study. Outside, to no surprise, the servant he now knew as Rikard was waiting. He stashed the pouch in his pocket and, with no room left to stow the necklace, simply placed the trinket around his neck for safekeeping.

Chapter 2: Beyond the Safety of Home

"While the validity of previous races inhabiting these lands is in great debate, the simple presence of artifacts and written languages, from which our own derives many linguistic elements, is clear and present. If common logic and rationale are applied, the existence of these ancient races is evidenced by these discoveries."
—Matron-Scholar Annalese Spearsdottir

From ten, he counted in reverse, the motions new and foreign to him. Lorian followed Rikard's orders as well as he could, considering the disparity in his experience, but the physical motions of this maneuver were too alien to his commoner's feet.

"Blast it, bastard! If I were to close my eyes right now, I'd surely mistake you for a drunken hog! You have no grace about you!" Rikard chastised, his deadpan voice swinging in pitch to match his frustration.

"My apologies, Handsir Rikard. I'm fairly new to this, as I'm sure you've noticed," replied Lorian with as sarcastic a tone as he could summon. The title of handsir was new to Lorian. It was given to the head servant of the lord and, despite the oddity of the name, gave Rikard power over all the other house servants.

"Again, from the top, boy. Before the day's end, I shall have you fully memorize the proper way to greet your lord. Three steps, then bow! No! Incorrect again! Stay off your heels, you clunky mule!"

Lorian and Rikard were covering the forms of formal interaction in a small clearing adjacent to the servants' tents. They were a day's ride east, toward the mines of Orion-Lon, when Lord Varios' company was brought to a halt.

The company had set camp a stone's throw from the Powdered Roads, as those in the frost called them, and cleared what foliage they could before unloading their travel wares.

The snow fell softly that morning, leaving everything thinly veiled in the white powder. Horses neighed alongside the clattering of the soldiers' armor, and small clouds of breath formed throughout the camp where soldiers and servants spoke.

Apparently, the lord wasn't a fan of traveling in the dark, so to offset the time lost, they would leave at daybreak, marching all throughout the day and evening. Of course, to leave at daybreak meant Lorian and the other servants and guardsmen were to have the company prepared for travel well before first light.

This was Lorian's first time away from home without his father. They had often spent the summer nights hunting in the forests north of Lumer-Lon, having to take a ferry across the mouth of the river from which the great lake flowed. Lorian had heard of the river called the Weller-man's Pass before. When asking his father why it was called this, he scoffed at the name and insisted man always had a way of perverting the true and beautiful names of things and places.

According to his father, the river was once called Foren-Dell because it ferried the refugees of the ancient world into the sea, from which they never returned. Lorian's reminiscing made him miss his father, who, in complete fairness, was likely more than furious with him. Lorian had only time to request a letter be sent to inform his father of his new employment and subsequent journey.

He had sent the letter with five of the twelve gold pieces, hoping the riches would soften the blow of the news, though he knew he would be in for quite the verbal lashing when he returned.

After fumbling the greeting maneuver another dozen times, he finally managed to perform a satisfactory step-and-bow, catching Rikard off-guard. Instead of complimenting him as he had hoped, Rikard simply rolled his eyes in a fashion that seemed to portray annoyance.

"Very well," said Rikard, "you may head to the stewpot and fetch yourself some breakfast."

Not waiting another moment for fear of more instruction that might interrupt his chance to eat, he made for the stewpot, salivating. Lorian found Rikard's instruction to be just as brutal as working metal, the heat of the forge replaced by the fury of a handsir's disapproval.

En route to the stew he would happily lap up, Lorian took note of his surroundings as best he could in the cold hour before daybreak.

Several servants had been brought along, including himself, Rikard, several handmen acting as polishers, pack mules, and Varios' valet, who dressed the lord in cloth and armor.

An ironically thin cook had been brought to serve the lord his meals, though the servants had to endure the cooking of an appointed guardsman, who seemed to be unaware of the existence of spice and seasoning. Still, Lorian was never one to complain about a hot meal when his stomach was empty. In total, twelve guardsmen were included in the company and were stationed in separate watches—some guarding the front, some on the rear, and two outside the lord's tent.

Daybreak was almost upon the company, and the small outcropping acting as their temporary campsite was already well and busy. The thick pines lining the lake's perimeter, or the Silver Coast, as the people of Amphil-Lon called it, began to grow shorter and scarcer as they approached the Bronze Mountains, which cradled the ore-rich town of Orion-Lon at its base.

The thinly veiled, snow-covered trails grew thicker with powder as they traveled, a sign their destination was growing ever closer. The large mountains carried much humidity, and, paired with the fumes and gases released from the mines, created a thick layer of moisture in the summer and dense snowfall in the winter.

Lorian approached the stewpot, which sat centered within the camp. The flame beneath the large cast-iron vessel flickered, casting shadows that jumped around the edges of the light. The warmth of the fire was pleasant and second only to the smell of the food bubbling within the pot. Several logs were used as makeshift bench seats and placed uniformly around the pot.

Two hand servants removed themselves when they saw Lorian and vacated their place beside the warmth of the fire. "Perhaps there is some benefit to being a bastard," he murmured. After his morning with Rikard, he was more than happy to warm his frozen hands and eat his fill in peace.

"Try not to underestimate companionship, squire. We're all just lonely creatures seeking the warmth of kindred souls," spoke a voice from beyond the makeshift hearth.

Squinting to see better, Lorian could not tell where the words came from until the man approached him, his identity revealed by the flames.

Lord Varios came forward, his heavy coat and hood slightly obscuring his face. Lorian, who had already grabbed a bowl, dropped the dish in an impromptu attempt to show the progress he'd made when greeting the lord. Stepping thrice and bowing, he waited for his lord to acknowledge his gesture and free him from his stance.

"By the gods, have you learned the formal greeting in a day?" asked Lord Varios.

"Yes, my lord," replied Lorian, who remained in the bowed position.

"I can tell. Your form is awful," said the lord. "You may rise."

Slightly embarrassed, he stood upright and waited for further instruction.

"You came here to eat, did you not? Then eat. Fill a bowl for me as well. The damned cook tried to feed me venison and sprouts for breakfast. I need something lighter for the journey."

Lorian grabbed the bowl he had dropped and filled it to the brim with stew, burning himself in his haste as the ladle splashed hot broth onto his wrist. He set the dirtied bowl on the stump as he did not wish to offend his lord by offering him an unclean dish. To Lorian's surprise, Varios sat himself next to the bowl and began to eat the stew without hesitation. Lorian sat as well, after pouring himself some food, and tried his best to avoid speaking unless spoken to.

"So, Night, how do you find the life of a squire?" asked the baron between bites.

"I am honored you chose me, Your Grace. Though I am not sure how a squire should behave or what duties I am to assume," he admitted, his honesty catching him by surprise. He nervously wondered if he was being too informal with his liege.

"You are a squire only in the title, Night, as you are not one of noble birth, and you do not possess land. To your fairness, I am no knight, so perhaps squire isn't the best title to give you. For now, you are an aide, though the title matters little. Your duties are what I tell you they are. For now, you are to accompany me and handle my correspondence, manage my personal items, and perform the tasks I order, should they arise," spoke the baron, his eyes never rising from the bowl he so eagerly emptied.

"Understood, Your Grace," replied Lorian. After a few moments of thinking, and a few spoons full of well-needed nutrition, Lorian's thoughts got the better of him and he asked the lord a pertinent question. "Why have you chosen me for this role, Your Grace? Surely there were others who would have filled this position better. Someone within your estate could've replaced the thief. I suspect my position is given to me to mock Lord Handall," surmised Lorian, his fear spiking as he realized he may have been too bold with his words.

Varios, finishing the last of his bowl, set the spoon and dish on the log next to him and turned to face Lorian. "And how would I do such a thing?"

"He used me to insult you, and you believe instead of responding in kind, making me your personal aide can be used against him in some fashion."

"You are cleverer than your station would suggest, Lorian Night. But you needn't be worried. Not all nobles are monsters. I find myself not able to trust much of my staff at present, and you were a convenient solution to a temporary problem," said Varios, his tone authoritative and proud.

"And I like the look in your eyes," he added. "You're a boy who believes his worth, his value, is more than what the circumstances of his birth should dictate. And you'd be right and wrong. We cannot escape fate, bastard. No more than we can rewind the hands of time and wed your parents before you were sired."

Lord Varios rose from his seat, prompting Lorian to rise as well in respect. "We leave within the half-hour. Grab your steed and ride with me. I have letters I must read, and I don't wish to do so whilst riding. Upsets my stomach, you see."

With haste, the company settled its temporary affairs with the outcropping and resumed its journey toward the Bronze Mountains and to its final destination of Orion-Lon.

The next two days consisted of the same rigorous exercises in formality, both in the evening and early morning, and when requested, the reading of the lord's various political affairs via his correspondence. Lorian had learned a great many things about the lord this way.

Most of the letters were from other nobles discussing the goings-on of high-born society such as upcoming balls, bills of intrigue from the capital, the status of taxation and how it's never high enough, and so on. The most intriguing letter was from an unknown sender, the envelope standing unique amongst the rest, sealed with dark blue wax in contrast to the usual red.

The lord forbade Lorian from opening this letter and others like it, as it was what he referred to as unfit for the eyes of a commoner.

Lorian was able to glean from other letters that Varios was at one point married, but after the death of his spouse, he spent his time as a widower and refused to marry again. He couldn't tell if his wife had borne children before her death, and the letters didn't indicate if the lord had ever taken it upon himself to sire an heir.

After a day of long and uncomfortable travel, Lorian dared to ask a question most nobles would hang him for, though, in private, he found Lord Varios quite casual.

"Why don't you have an heir, Your Grace?"

Lord Varios stared at him for so long that Lorian began to question if he'd live through the night. Then, in a curious tone, the lord replied, "Because I feel no need to forfeit my magic or to let it slowly dwindle until I find myself old and powerless."

A look of confusion slowly encompassed Lorian's face. He knew most children of Wielders could also wield, but he didn't understand why the lord would have to forfeit his magic to have children.

Noticing his confusion, Lord Varios took the opportunity to elaborate. "This is relatively common knowledge, bastard. Your father has failed in this respect. When a noble sires children, each child inherits a portion of their noble parents' magic. Over time, the connection to magic wanes and, at the end, vanishes completely. Have you ever heard of the Bastard Crusades?" asked the lord.

"Yes, Your Grace. The kingdom wanted all the bastards dead and gone many years ago."

"Correct. He hasn't failed you completely, I see," replied the lord. "And why did the great nobles of our precious kingdom want these bastards gone?"

"I thought it was to keep their names and legacies clean, Your Grace?" asked Lorian, a sliver of realization breaching his confusion.

"Yes, I suppose that was one excuse they used. In reality, the nobles wished to control the flow of their family's magic. With unnumbered bastards running around fathering bastards of their own, control of this magic would be impossible. To resolve this issue, an order was carried out every few years to cleanse the bastards, returning the nobles' power back into the hands of their respective families and returning control," answered the lord, his face turning grim as he spoke.

"The truth is usually worse than the assumption, I'm afraid. To sire too many children is to lose the very essence of what makes a noble *noble*. Many lords, such as I, wait until their later years to sire, and even then, some only sire a single child. This keeps the power strong and untainted in their eyes."

"Are there not issues which stem from this, Your Grace?"

"Ah, yes, there are, indeed," replied Lord Varios. "Having a single child can lead to the potential fall of a house. Even as nobles, we are not immune to sickness, disease, or fatal wounds. If a noble's only heir were to perish, an entire line of magic would vanish as well."

"But would the line of magic not return itself to all the other nobles, making you all more powerful, Your Grace?"

Lord Varios called a stop to the entire company with a raised fist. All the horses to the rear and front screeched to a halt as hooves and wagon wheels fought against the friction of gravel, dirt, and snow.

"Listen to me, Lorian Night. Never speak those words out loud. Ever. There is a shared idealism within this world of ours. Noble must never turn on noble. Any mention of what you just inquired about is a death sentence. Do you understand? Not just for you. For your family. For your friends and their families as well. It will not be tolerated." The words from Varios were as intense as his glowing blue eye.

"Forgive me, Your Grace," replied Lorian in a defeated tone.

"My lord!" shouted a guardsman from the front. "Orion-Lon is fast ahead!"

Chapter 3: For Whom the Bells Toll

The Bronze Mountains stood tall against the white blanket of snow-covered earth before it. Jagged rock snaked both north and southward, illustrating an insurmountable obstacle nature had wrought forth.

Several peaks of the mountain range stretched so impossibly high that even from where Lord Varios' company had camped, they could not be seen—a dark amalgam of clouds obscuring them from Lorian's lustful eyes.

Thanks to his father's lessons, Lorian knew the Bronze Mountains were named thusly due to the enormous amount of tin and copper available within their depths.

The mountains contained other raw metals, but to reveal these would require one to excavate deeper than any had before, and Orion-Lon was a town that came to be specifically for this purpose.

At first, bronze was the main export due to the easily accessible nodes on the surface. Recently, iron and silver were struck and, due to popular demand, replaced bronze as the main export, causing a mighty increase in the town's population.

From all over the world, individuals and guilds flocked to Orion-Lon to find fame and fortune, and as a consequence, those who wished to steal these new fortunes also appeared. Reports of bandits and thieves continued to increase, forcing Lord Varios to make an appearance every so often to restore order and facilitate the punishment and execution of captured bandits and thieves. Lorian had never witnessed a man die, and he had no wish to ever witness such a thing if the choice was his to make.

In the distance, just before dawn, a series of chimes rung aloud.

"The countdown has begun," spoke Handsir Rikard, his usually monotone voice now low and full of dread. Rikard had shared information with Lorian before light fall after yesterday's long ride, and to his dismay, informed him of the events in which the lord would have to participate. He knew the duties of a lord were sometimes undesirable, but he felt this was too much. Further dismay came to him when he discovered through Rikard's instruction that he too would have a hand in the events to come.

"I cannot be expected to execute a man, Handsir Rikard," he pleaded.

"He almost never calls on us for such tasks, but it is not for us to decide, Night. We follow the orders of our lord, and if instructed, we shall swing the blade or pull the lever. Your actions are never your own. Take comfort in this, son," said Rikard, his tone overly soft.

His use of the word '*son*' made him feel a mixture of contempt and sadness. He thought of all the orders Rikard might've had to carry out in the past and how those actions may have imprinted themselves upon the servant.

Lorian knew that whatever was to happen today would be life-altering. Why else would the servant who normally treated him so poorly try to comfort him? Dread and woe crept into his heart.

The morning sun had begun to rise, and so did the angst within him. The company behaved as normal—tents were packed, food was consumed, and horses and wagons were loaded as efficiently as they had been throughout the previous week of travel. He had overheard some of the guardsmen saying Orion-Lon was still a few hours' journey toward the Bronze Mountains, which struck him with surprise. He could see the faint outline of the city, the structures obfuscated by light snowfall, and wondered why it would take so long to reach its gates.

"The distance is greater than the eyes believe, squire," spoke a guardsman from behind him. This guardsman was dressed in mail and bore the crest of House Varios upon his chest plate. A red cape stretched across his back and was outlined with thick white wool, which, to Lorian's assumption, would be better suited to lining the inside of the armor for warmth.

"Orion-Lon is not only downhill from this position but slightly uphill from the small plain in between here and there. Factor in a few bridges needed to cross the streams and a slower pace needed to traverse the thicker patches of snow, and we should arrive at the Western Gate within six hours," finished the guardsman.

"I thank you for the information, sir," Lorian replied with gratitude.

The tall, armored man raised his chin high and swelled his chest. "I am no sir, bastard. But I am the captain of this company. Captain Bowers, or Captain, will suffice."

"My apologies, captain. Are you not an officer, then? Or are officers not considered to be 'sirs'?" He wished to know the order of things within Varios' company. He would need to if he was to excel in this new position.

"The appropriate title is 'sir.' But I won this position through blood and effort, not by being born with a silver spoon so far up my ass it could make my words sweet," Bowers said in a playful tone. "So, you shall speak to me using my earned rank, not my imaginary title."

"Understood, captain," said Lorian, trying to sound confident and informed. As Captain Bowers mounted his horse, a steed as black as night, Lorian did the same. "Captain, if I may ask a favor of you."

"You may ask; doesn't mean I'll oblige," replied the captain.

He steadied his breath and braced for rejection. "I was raised as a blacksmith. My skill with the sword only goes as far as forging them. I'm afraid I have no skill at wielding one in combat. Is there anyone under the lord's command who could teach me in their spare time?"

Bowers replied with only a laugh at first, then a look of intrigue. "And why would our bastard squire wish to take up the blade? Isn't the lord's cock the only blade you'll need to wield? Or does he have a servant for that one, too?" he said in a fit of laughter.

"Afraid not, captain. I've been charged with only handling the balls," replied Lorian, trying his best to keep from breaking into a fit of laughter.

"By the gods, you are witty!" roared the captain, his laughter sending a charge of foggy breath forward. "Very well. I shall find you a tutor, bastard. Instruction will be given when it's convenient, but it shall be on your personal time to train, of course. The duties of my men come first."

In an attempt to not sound too elated, Lorian simply thanked the captain and started to wonder what the training would consist of. Tales of heroism and valiant deeds began to swirl around in his mind as he imagined his future. He remembered the daydreams he used to have as a child, adventure and mountains of gold just out of reach. Bowers heeled his horse and strode alongside Lord Varios, near the front of the company. With a wave of the hand from the lord, the formation leapt into motion to finish the remainder of their journey.

The next few hours proved tiresome for Lorian. The winter winds had grown more intense as the company traversed the plain that stood before the base of the mountains.

Without many trees or hills blocking the gale, the formation of a small vortex peppered the group with thick flakes of frost, and the occasional hail formed. The horses had the most trouble as their hooves began to lose traction when encountering the iced-over sections of the bridges that stretched over the streams and divided the large field into uneven sections.

The bells of the city chimed orderly as the company pushed forward, the number of chimes decreasing each time. More than once, Lorian and other servants had to dismount their steeds and pull them by hand, even pulling the lord's horse at one point when it refused to carry on.

He and the other servants fell on several occasions, the impact caking their clothes and exposed skin in cold mud, forcing Lorian to change and wash while on horseback afterward. He was no stranger to forcing a steed uphill in poor conditions, though the ordeal left him greatly exhausted.

In total, the predicted six-hour journey stretched into eight, and when the sun was well past its zenith, the company arrived at the Western Gate of Orion-Lon.

True to Captain Bowers' word, the city was slightly uphill, eventually tapering off into a flatter region that kissed the base of the mountains above. The sun, to their luck, had yet to fall behind the towering stature of the Bronze Mountains, providing them with some warmth.

The whirlwind that terrorized the plains below withered as they approached the city, the mountains acting as a natural shield from the elements. As Lorian drew closer, he could see the streams below, likely formed due to runoff from the mountain. A larger stream bent around the perimeter of the city, acting as a natural moat.

A drawbridge hung open from the walls and sat nestled into a groove that connected the opening of Orion-Lon to the rest of the mountain base. Several dozen people, some independent of one another and some traveling in larger groups, stood outside the drawbridge as guardsmen inspected them for the proper documentation and any goods they carried.

Lorian made note of the other travelers as Lord Varios' party pushed through to the front of the line. Those who were forced to wait shook bitterly from the cold; most were clearly underdressed for the weather.

He saw mostly men, dirt-covered and ungroomed, and assumed them to be miners and ore workers looking for work. Others appeared to be transporting goods and other stock, such as cattle and grain. A few travelers consisted of families whose intentions in the city he could not glean, though their miserable faces made his gut twist with anger.

How could the city not prioritize women and children who shivered in the cold?

Upon seeing a mother and her babe with nary a cloth to cover their bodies apart from thin, ragged dressings, he grabbed an extra blanket from the pack fastened to his horse and broke formation, riding to their shambled wagon and gently tossing the blanket at them.

"Thank ye, m'lord," shouted the mother as he trotted back to his position.

"You should not have done that, bastard," chastised Handsir Rikard as Lorian recovered his spot in the company.

"But she carried a babe, handsir. They could freeze to death out here!" he said in protest.

"It is not for you to decide. Lord Varios' presence here is meant to establish order and remind the would-be criminals of the consequences that come with breaking the laws. His laws. They cannot mistake his presence for charity. Prepare yourself; you'll likely be whipped for this transgression." Rikard sighed.

A coldness similar to the frost covering the mountains entered Lorian's veins. He had never been whipped before, despite his station. He did not regret helping the poor woman or her babe, though he knew he would regret the pain he would face later. "Very well, handsir. I shall accept any punishment for my mistake."

"Damned fool," spat Rikard as they approached the checkpoint into the city.

Ahead, Captain Bowers spoke with a few of the guardsmen, undoubtedly telling them of the company's identity. A hand jumped into the air and summoned Lorian up front. It was Lord Varios. He heeled Sebastian and made for the lord's side. "Your Grace," said Lorian, who now awaited his orders, "my apologies. It was not my intention to harm the purpose of this visit." It was a weak attempt to get ahead of any trouble coming his way.

The lord's eyes were distant in thought, and his jaw was clenched. "We shall speak of this later. It seems we are being stalled at the gate for some reason, and I need you to discover why. I am going to send you into the city, as you appear the least recognizable. Seek out Lord Aaron and report back to me. Something is wrong here." Without further explanation, Lord Varios snapped his fingers, and a guardsman leaped from his horse and grabbed Sebastian by the reins, leading him and Lorian to the front.

Panic welled within Lorian's chest. *What does he mean by 'least recognizable'? Is it because I'm not a soldier, or because I'm young? I don't understand why he would send me!*

"And I'll not tell you again," spat Bowers to the guards on watch. "Lord Varios' presence has been requested, and to refused us entry into the city is an open act of defiance from your lord."

"My apologies, sir. No entry to the city is permitted until all is deemed safe—not even for Lord Varios," said the guard in a trembling voice.

Lorian, now adjacent to Bowers and his horse, waited for orders from the captain.

"Very well. We are escorting a royal tribunary from the capital, on behalf of the crown. This is Sir Bramsey, and to deny him entrance is an act of open rebellion against his majesty," threatened Captain Bowers, his hand already on the pommel of his sword. "Will you allow him passage, soldier?"

With the threat of treason hanging over the nervous soldier, a call of judgment was made.

"L . . . Let him through! But only him." Turning to Lorian, the soldier said, "A thousand pardons, sir, but I must ask you to head directly to Lord Aaron and go nowhere else."

Lorian was in a panic, unsure what to say. In his best attempt at impersonating a high-born, he simply nodded; he didn't believe a tribunary would waste words on someone beneath his station.

To Lorian's surprise, it worked. The guards seemed too nervous at the mention of treason to verify his identity, lest they be hung or quartered. With no resistance, Lorian heeled Sebastian, and together, they entered Orion-Lon.

The city before Lorian was a marvel. Buildings and temples were constructed into the side of the mountain, starting at the base and continuing up at least three dozen stories, by Lorian's measurement.

Most buildings were constructed of stone and appeared to be carved out of the very mountain itself. Three rings in total embodied the whole of the city, each ring smaller and higher-placed than the last. Large tunnels were constructed into the mountain, with mouths at each ring extending deep into the stone and out of sight. Numerous sets of stairs connected the rings in uniform locations, facilitating travel between the rings.

Lorian could see that ramps were paired with most sets of stairs, suitable for medium cargo, and there were pulley systems as large as entire shops for heavier cargo and cattle.

Most buildings were uniform in appearance, sharing the mountain's pale gray texture and color, save their green-tiled roofs, which contrasted sharply with the dull stone. Each ring within the city had a canal carrying small vessels and goods in a semi-circle fashion. The streams terminated at a controlled exit point, allowing water to flow down to the next ring, and so on.

The streets were carved from stone as well, etched with rectangular pieces of varying sizes. Oil-fueled lanterns hung from metal poles to illuminate the city at night, and metal grates lined the edges of the carved road, carrying wastewater to unknown locations. It was the most spectacular thing he had ever seen.

A loud chime of a bell shocked him out of his gawking. He noted the bell tolled only once this time. Searching the city for the bell tower brought Lorian's gaze to the second ring. From where he stood, he could make out a cluster of buildings, temples perhaps, forming a square around a courtyard. As he was unsure where he would find Lord Aaron, the bell tower became a central location of interest. He heeled Sebastian with a heavy foot, and together, they raced forward, eager to bring this search to an end.

Lorian forced his way through the streets of Orion-Lon, taking care not to seriously injure anyone as he went. Sebastian was a broad-shouldered steed, and not much seemed to scare him from where he steered.

Coming upon the first wall leading to the second ring, he noted the pulley system was already in transit, carrying a handful of sheep, cargo, and other various items. Time was too precious to wait for it to unload and travel back down. Pulling hard on Sebastian's reins, he pointed the beast at the stairs adjacent to the lift shaft.

Three total flights made up the distance between this ring and the next. As he forced his way onto the stairs, Lorian became thankful they were wide enough for his horse with space to spare. The stairs were also secured by a metallic handrail he hoped would keep others from falling off as he passed.

Heeling Sebastian several times encouraged the horse to begin the climb. Orion-Lon must have had servants who cleared the steps of snowfall periodically because he noticed the steps were only thinly covered in powder, which made the climb less hazardous. In just a few minutes, the horse had climbed all three flights, leaving only a handful of citizens alarmed, save two men who were slammed harshly into the railing. He had no time to consider their safety but would make amends later if time permitted.

With little time to delay, Lorian took a moment to absorb his surroundings and get his bearings once he exited the stairwell. The bell tower stood tall amongst the other buildings, and with the location now set, he spurred Sebastian to dash forward.

Sebastian whined painfully as Lorian again gave the horse a heavy heel, cursing the situation he found himself in. He loved Sebastian as a family member and did not wish the animal to suffer this abuse.

Forcing more citizens to the edge of the pathway, he pushed into the heavily crowded streets of the second ring. His destination fast approaching, he heeled Sebastian for what he hoped was the last time, and with a few heavy breaths and strong strides, they found themselves standing at the base of the bell tower.

Lorian's original observations were correct: The tower seemed to be a single piece in a squared grouping of temples. Within the center of these buildings was a large stone courtyard surrounded by tall metal fencing. Guards stood watch just outside the perimeter of the gate, blocking him from fully seeing what was hidden behind them.

What he could glean of the yard showed a small crowd of people huddling alongside a stage, though who or what was upon the stage, he couldn't see.

A guard standing outside two doors leading into the bell tower approached him. "Who goes there?" demanded the soldier as he drew a short sword from the sheath fastened around his hip.

Lorian was unsure if he should continue with his disguise as a tribunary from the capital or be more forthcoming, and decided on the latter. His heart beat loudly in his chest, and he feared it might give him away. "Lord Varios of Amphil-Lon wishes to speak to Lord

Aaron immediately! I am to bring Lord Aaron to the Western Gate without hesitation."

The guard seemed suspicious of him at first but relented and walked through the doors he was guarding. Lorian, taking this moment to prepare, dismounted Sebastian and tied his reins to a tether jutting out from the corner of the bell tower's base. The guard returned within moments and approached him again. "Magistrate Strawman wishes to have words with you."

"I am not here for the magistrate, guardsman. I am here for Lord Aaron," Lorian replied authoritatively. He watched as the guards eyed one another, a silent message passing between them. A still moment passed, and his skin tightened as if his body was telling him to flee.

He recoiled in fear as the soldier brandished his sword. "This is no request, messenger. You will speak with the magistrate!" the guard bellowed. With no weapon to defend himself, Lorian felt trapped as the imposing figure cornered him. The guard seized him by the shirt and pushed him toward the bell tower doors. From inside, another soldier swung the doors open and propelled him forward with a forceful shove.

The bell tower seemed larger on the inside, with rows of pews flanking a central aisle.

Each pew faced forward, leading the eye to a stone altar adorned with cloth and books at the pathway's end. Illuminated by small oil lamps, the room exuded a solemn ambiance; a grand chandelier hung from the ceiling, gently swaying in the breeze. Dominating the space behind the altar was a sizable metal symbol depicting a mountain merging into the form of a man, his arms outstretched in what seemed a triumphant gesture.

It dawned on Lorian he was standing within a temple devoted to the worship of Gan, one of the natural gods.

An effeminate voice resounded from behind the altar. "You must forgive the lack of decorum my guards have shown you, messenger. They aren't the most intelligent, and I promise to have them properly educated." A small, heavy-set man emerged from a door set into a wall adjacent to the symbol of Gan.

His flushed, plump cheeks rested above a small chin, and his black, beady eyes were bordered by heavy wrinkles, giving his face a permanently smug appearance. He wore purple robes decorated with golden lace around the cuffs and neck. Two black stripes ran down the center of the robes, and white tassels flared out from the bottom of the garment.

"Magistrate Strawman," Lorian said as he took three steps and bowed. Normally, this greeting was reserved for lords and other nobility, though Rikard had mentioned it showed great respect when performed for a magistrate.

"Oh, you honor me, messenger. Tell me, what news does Lord Varios bring? I was under the impression he wasn't to arrive for at least two more days."

"Magistrate, Lord Varios requests the audience of Lord Aaron at the Western Gate immediately. He has been denied entrance to the city and wishes to know why."

"Oh, I'm terribly sorry. Lord Aaron is overseeing a small expedition within the mines right now and is unable to attend. We've temporarily barred entry to the city until the hanging ceremony finishes. We have a few criminals whose mere presence could start a revolt, and our nobility must be protected from such violence."

Lorian felt uneasy at the explanation provided by the magistrate. A noble should be present at an execution of this magnitude, he assumed. Lorian wondered why Aaron would be absent for something so important. And why would a noble like Varios be safer outside the walls, instead of within them? Lorian was not prepared for a situation like this.

"I understand the circumstances, magistrate. I'm sorry to say, but I'll still need Lord Aaron to be summoned to the Western Gate as ordered by Lord Varios," Lorian explained, trying his best to not sound disrespectful.

The magistrate stroked the ends of his lace collar with engorged hands. "Persistent, aren't you?" he replied. "Very well. I shall have you wait within the courtyard while we request Aaron's presence. My guard will escort you." He walked toward the door he'd entered through.

The same guard who'd cornered Lorian gave him another shove as they made for a door that led to the courtyard. As the guard opened the door, Lorian finally realized what the stage was for.

Three prisoners were shackled by their wrists and ankles. A noose swung gently in the wind. A group of finely dressed lords and ladies crowded near the stage yelling slurs and throwing stones at the prisoners. They laughed with one another, celebrating wherever they successfully stuck a prisoner.

Two of the captives were men in their thirties, their skin pale and bruised as if they had been held for weeks without care. The last prisoner was a child of ten or younger who stood adjacent to the others in nothing but a loincloth. The child shivered terribly against the cold, and his whimpering was audible despite the manic shouts of the crowd before him. His long blond hair was unkempt and stretched toward the nape of his neck.

Lorian's eyes widened in shock as he realized the boy bore the magic eye of the nobles. One hazel eye was partnered with an eye glowing red like an ember. The boy's face was scrunched together in fear and pain.

Lorian watched as a rock struck the boy in the head, sending a stream of crimson blood down his face. The boy wept more intensely and tried to cover his face in vain, his shackled wrists forcing his arms into a straight, rigid position. Cries from the crowd revealed the truth of this execution. "Kill the bastard!"

Lorian, furious with this display of cruelty, turned toward the guard but hesitated. *Will I be punished for this too? Will every injustice I call out be rewarded with a whip on my back?* he thought as fear froze him. He remembered the shivering mother and her babe, then the subservient look upon his father's face in the presence of nobility, and his fear melted away. *So be it.*

Lorian sucked in a breath and steadied himself. "What is the meaning of this? What is this bastard's crime, and why does he stand postured before a hanging noose?"

"His crime is being a bastard, messenger," spat the guard, his face twisted in pleasure.

"Release him at once! The killing of a bastard has been outlawed by the crown. Release him!" shouted Lorian.

Blurred vision and searing pain engulfed his face, quickly replacing his anger. Lorian had been struck harshly with the handle of the guard's blade.

Regaining his vision, Lorian struck wildly at the guard with a closed fist, his hand catching no purchase but air. The guard slammed his gauntlet-covered forearm into Lorian's nose, sending sharp flashes of pain deep into his skull. Tears and blood trickled down Lorian's face as he fell to his knees. Before he could regain his composure, another swing of the sword handle struck him in the temple, sending him violently to the ground.

Hot liquid drained down Lorian's face and ear. A profound disorientation overwhelmed him, and waves of nausea surged through him, forcing him to retch uncontrollably. The thick, acidic liquid caught in his throat, suffocating him, while his weakened state left him unable to even tilt his head to rid himself of the vile contents.

Two guards forced Lorian to his feet. With blurred vision, Lorian watched as a guard forced the young bastard forward, looping the noose around his neck and tightening it.

"I demand . . . to stop," gurgled Lorian, his words slurred and unintelligible.

The guard shouted something that, to his dulled senses, was incoherent and indecipherable as the magistrate joined the guard, addressing the crowd. All Lorian could hear was the pounding of his own heart and the disorienting screech of his eardrums.

The magistrate seemed to finish his speech after a moment, and with a hand signal, the boy was hanged. Lorian was forced to watch for ten minutes as the boy convulsed violently against the rope, the weight of his small body too light to break his neck. He watched as the child's pale skin turned purple and his eye vessels burst within his skull. Foam bubbled from the boy's mouth, and with a final set of twitches, the child was dead. His tongue hung from his lips, swollen and bloodied from the boy biting deep into it during the struggle.

Lorian wanted so badly to be back home with his father and away from this madness. He no longer wanted to gaze upon the evidence of man's barbarity, choosing instead to shut his swollen eyes and pray to the natural gods that this would end soon.

Chapter 4: Prometheus

"Magic is as perplexing to both those who wield it and those who do not. The laws and properties that bind our feet to the ground are the same that bind magic to a Wielder: absolute. While there are those who seek to understand magic at its most fundamental levels, there are those, such as I, who wish to simply abide by its laws, lest we welcome its wrath."
—High-Gothic Anders Dinivy

Lorian attempted to rise to his feet but dropped immediately, his weak arms taking the brunt of his weight as his legs betrayed him. The bitter taste of iron and bile filled his mouth, and his head rang like the bell above.

The audience of gentlemen before him yelped in excitement, shouting foul remarks at the body of the child, whose innocent life they had taken. For the first time in his short existence, Lorian truly felt what it was like to hate. Rage and grief acted only as a precursor to the bottomless, cold feeling of malice that roiled within him. It felt mindless and without reason, a void within one's soul that could only be sated with violence, and not even he believed that would be satisfactory.

Would hanging each of these men in the same barbaric way they had hanged that innocent boy be enough to atone for their animalistic treatment of those beneath them? Lorian did not believe so. Suffering, many magnitudes greater than what they had wrought, would be the only justifiable course of action against these wretched creatures before him.

Hate made his pain fade as he imagined himself morphing into a tool of vengeance, his feelings becoming weapons of slaughter that would rend the men before him into piles of lifeless meat. After all, they were better suited as fertilizer than the sentient creatures they currently were.

"Natural gods of the world . . ." Lorian began to plead, a faint whisper amongst the toil of voices and the clattering of boots on stone. "I give my soul unto you. In exchange, all I ask in return is to be made more than what I am. I beg you, o' lords of forces beyond what we see, give me the strength to kill these men and all like them. Please." Tears fell to the dirt-crusted stones beneath him. A silent sob escaped from his mouth.

A flash of light struck Lorian in his left eye; he ignored it in his grief. Twice more, his vision was blinded by the light until he bothered to inspect what tried so desperately to grab his attention. The soldier to his left, who, until recently, had held Lorian by the arm to force him to watch the execution, had hidden in his right boot a dagger.

For a moment, Lorian was unsure if a sign had truly been sent to him or if it was by chance alone that he noticed the weapon, though it did not matter as he felt it would be useless in clumsy, untrained hands like his. Perhaps, if he was quick enough, he could take his own life.

Surely that would spare me the further torture that will undoubtably follow these executions, he thought.

As if thunder itself had been birthed forward, a noise unlike any Lorian had ever heard rang loudly, forcing an uneasy silence among the crowd gathered within the courtyard.

Screams of men coupled with the clanging of metal followed shortly. Lorian could smell the burnt remains of meat and charred wood as ash descended upon him, mixing gently with the timid snowfall. In a panic, Magistrate Strawman descended from the stage, holding his purple robes above the ground with both hands to keep from tripping, and ran toward a building opposite the bell tower where the noise seemed to travel from. His short, fat legs moved with surprising quickness as he fled from this unknown calamity.

The guard to Lorian's right drew his sword from its sheath, as did the guard opposite him, and ran for the bell tower door while the other pointed his blade at Lorian, keeping him from rising from the ground.

Swinging the closed door open, the guard attempted to enter the tower, sword at the ready. A hand from within the tower smartly flung forward, grasping the guard by the face and taking him by surprise.

Lorian watched as a stream of fire spilled forward from the hand and interrupted the guard's scream, forcing its way down the guard's open mouth.

Tendrils of flame danced along the armored guard, peeling the flesh from his body in large, wafered chunks. The armor around his limbs grew red hot, like iron left in the forge too long, and began to collapse inward as if a vacuum had formed within his chest. His eyes charred then melted—viscous liquid running from his sockets before sizzling into nothing.

Within moments, the guard was a husk of ash and searing metal, the thick black smoke of his flesh wafting away in the cold air above.

Lorian felt the glimmer of the dagger as it reflected the waning sun and forced himself to look away from the spectacle before him. Noticing his captor's astonishment at what had befallen his comrade, Lorian made for the dagger with speed he was unaware he had. As he rose to his feet, a clarity befell him that seemed to move time in small increments. A calm unlike any other washed over him as his objective became clear.

Devoid of any feeling, Lorian plunged the dagger deep into the guard's neck, catching him unaware. The red spray of blood showered Lorian as the guard swung wildly in his direction. Lorian found that simply taking a pace backward was enough to avoid any harm as the dying man desperately tried to free the dagger from his neck.

Falling to his knees, the guard threw his sword to the ground and pulled the dagger from his flesh, and bright red blood squirted in rhythm with his ever-slowing heartbeats. Now with the advantage of higher ground, Lorian grabbed the guard's short sword, fumbling the heavy metal as his blood-soaked fingers strove to find purchase.

With the weapon now steady in his hands, he pointed the tip at the guard and lurched the blade forward, finding resistance when the blade met the man's eye. Lorian forced the man to a horizontal position and jammed the blade deeply into the man's face. The guard grabbed the blade with one hand, and with the other, he desperately reached for Lorian's neck, his wound releasing more of the thick crimson liquid with every movement.

With every ounce of strength he could muster, Lorian forced the blade deeper. He could feel the crunch of bone as he pressed in, hear gargling as the guard choked upon his own life essence, then nothing as the blade sailed easily through his gray matter, ending his life.

Unable to remove the blade, Lorian released the instrument of death. A hand grabbed him by the shoulder, the same hand that had spewed fiery death just moments before, forcing Lorian to spin around, swinging wildly.

Two hands caught him by the wrists, bringing his poor defense to an end. In his state of panic and adrenaline, Lorian could only see two eyes staring at him, their colors familiar but unidentifiable in his confusion.

The hands forced Lorian to a kneeling position, a sad look stretched upon his mature face. "You are safe now, Lorian. Steady yourself. Breathe."

Relief came over Lorian as he realized it was Lord Varios' hands that held his own, and he collapsed into his lord with a sob that was no longer silent.

The gentlemen who found themselves too frightened to flee were directed to a corner of the courtyard and forced to sit upon the cold stones below, their fine silks and satins absorbing the filth and grime they had trod upon earlier.

At the request of Lord Varios, the men present had their hands bound by rope, and the women—whose hands were also bound—were given chairs from surrounding buildings to sit upon. Even when making arrests, Lord Varios showed a modicum of respect and politeness.

Lorian sat opposite the detainees and tended to his wounds with the help of Handsir Rikard. The old servant thoroughly scrubbed the dried blood from Lorian's hands and head, applying a handkerchief filled with snow to the throbbing wound on his nose to lessen the swelling. Lorian was grateful for the cold when Rikard had to stitch the small gash upon his temple, as it made the pain less intense.

Lord Varios, between commanding his men, saw fit to cut the hanged boy from where his body was perched, handling him ever so delicately, as if life still flowed within his body.

Sadness blanketed the noble's face, his sharp features shadowed in grief. He pulled linen from the dressings upon the pews within the bell tower to cover the boy's body and neatly prepared him for travel by securing his legs and arms with rope.

Lorian watched as Varios carried the young boy away, through the church, and out the front doors of the tower, setting him gently into the back of a wagon he had commandeered.

Lord Varios replaced his grief-stricken look with one of alertness, his eyes wide and unflinching. Lorian was unsure of how the lord could keep his composure amid the chaos and turmoil but let his assumptions lie, as he knew the lord couldn't react in any other way lest he show weakness.

A loud squabbling came from the building opposite the bell tower. Its source was revealed when Magistrate Strawman fell less than gracefully through the doors, his face catching the rest of his round body as he slid through the courtyard. His purple robes billowed upward as he fell, revealing the magistrate's naked body beneath, his bluish skin fighting desperately against the cold to force blood into his misshapen limbs.

"How dare you treat a magistrate of the crown like this!" he screamed, his mouth and eyes layered with dirt and frost. "I shall have your head for this disgrace!" he continued as he made several unsuccessful attempts to lift his heavy body off the ground.

The magistrate crawled forward, looking for a sturdy object to help leverage some of his weight, when he found himself at Lord Varios' boots.

"Hello, Strawman," said Lord Varios, his tone steady and unrelenting. Lorian watched on curiously, unsure of what Varios planned to do with the coward at his heels.

"Lo . . . Lord V . . . Varios. A pleasure to see you, old friend," the magistrate replied, either fear or the cold forcing a stutter into his words.

"Captain Bowers," barked Varios, "secure the prisoner's hands and hold him in the bell tower for interrogation. I shall join you thereafter."

He kicked the magistrate's hands from his boots as if the overweight politician were a bug.

"Aye, Your Grace," replied Bowers, who had apparently been the one to kick the magistrate through the doors earlier. He quickly bound Strawman's arms and lifted him from the courtyard floor with ease. Forcing him forward, Lorian could hear a series of shouts and the clatter of objects falling into one another as Bowers secured him for interrogation within the bell tower.

Lorian watched as Varios made his way over to where he and Rikard sat. The handsir assumed the formal bow, as did Lorian after a moment of hesitation. Upon the customary "Rise" from the lord, Rikard gathered his things and left to attend to others who were injured.

"You're looking better," said the lord. "I'm going to need you to tell me exactly what happened here, Lorian. I'll need a damn good answer to justify arresting a magistrate and killing these men," he continued, his tone as stern as his face. And so, Lorian did just that.

"They hung the boy, Your Grace." he replied softly, the event threatening to replay itself in his mind.

"I saw. What was his announced crime?" replied the lord.

A moment of confusion came over Lorian. *Did he not see the boy when cutting him from the rope?* he wondered. "Your Grace, it was an unlawful execution of a bastard. Did you not see his eye? He was a Wielder of magic."

For a moment, Lord Varios lost the rigidity within his posture, and a look of rage overcame him. "I see," he replied. "His eyes were ordinary, so I was unaware. When a Wielder of magic perishes, so too does the spark within their eye." The familiar rigidity returned to him.

Confusion consumed Lorian's face. "Why would a magistrate order the public execution of a Wielder, bastard or not? Nobles don't turn on each other, right?"

"There are many reasons, unfortunately. I must speak with Lord Aaron immediately. I'm assuming you never had the opportunity to meet with him?"

"Magistrate Strawman said he was away, leading an expedition within the mines."

"How convenient. Wait here and aid Rikard if you're able. I must have words with the magistrate."

Lord Varios promptly made for the bell tower doors, shutting them behind him.

Lorian began to assist Handsir Rikard with bandaging those who required help, even stitching wounds that were small enough for him to manage. Lorian knew his way around a needle thanks to his father. Without a mother or any other woman in this house, it was his duty to mend tears in garments and other fabrics to prolong their life. A small piece of him missed his father at that moment.

Lorian was stitching a small cut within the forearm of a guard as horrid screams emanated from the bell tower. Soon after, the rancid smell of seared fat, not too dissimilar to the scent of overcooked beef, permeated the air as Lord Varios left the building, securing gloves to his hands as he did.

"Lorian, grab a sword and follow me. Bowers, keep things moving along here. I want these prisoners in cells before the hour ends. Oh, and send for a doctor. The magistrate will need someone with more skill than our faithful handsir, I'm afraid."

Captain Bowers replied with a fist slamming firmly on his chest in salute. "Understood, Your Grace."

Lorian followed his lord back into the bell tower as they made for their horses. The smell within the tower was more potent than outside, forcing Lorian into a silent gag.

Just beside the altar lay the magistrate, half his face seared from chin to brow. The once smooth skin was now a melted mess of flesh, uneven ripples of meat cascading about his head like the surface of a lake whose still waters were disfigured by the skipping of a stone.

The sight repulsed Lorian, and for a moment, he felt pity. He wished to the natural gods he could rip whatever empathy he had for the magistrate out of him and burn it the way his lord had immolated that guard, yet he found himself victim to its pull.

Lord Varios and Lorian mounted their respective steeds, a breath of relief escaping Lorian as he saw Sebastian unharmed, and together they rode toward the mouth of the second ring's carved tunnel that snaked into the rocky depths before them.

Leaving the bell tower at a steady trot, Lorian took note of how the commoners of Orion-Lon desperately threw themselves out of his lord's path, as if Varios himself towed death incarnate.

Fear laid heavy in the eyes of the city's pedestrians and merchants as recognition of his lord spread forth. Lorian began to wonder what deeds Varios had accomplished in the past to give his very presence an air of unbridled fear.

"Why do they cower from us, Your Grace?" asked Lorian between the heavy sounds of hoof striking stone.

"Because my arrival only beckons misery. This is by design, Lorian Night, and it's a testament to the hard work I suffered in my previous visits. If the common man fears me, think of how the guilty criminal feels. I do not relish being looked at as a monster, but the resources this city provides are paramount to the capital, and the capital is paramount to the survival of society. We all have a part to play," Varios replied, his chin held high and his eyes piercing each man foolish enough to return his gaze.

"Your Grace, would Lord Aaron not be more suitable to that role? Is this not the city in which he operates and resides?" asked Lorian, who wished to keep the conversation steady. He feared that should it stop, he would be left to thoughts of recent events.

"I see the chaos of battle has done nothing to dull your wits, bastard," commented the lord, a hint of sarcasm in his voice. "Yes, this is Aaron's city; by all rights, it is his to rule as he sees fit. This issue lies with the lord himself. He is lazy in his duties and is not learned in the ways of ordinance or litigation of criminals. I was asked by his majesty, King Marcus of House Dinivy, to act as arbiter of justice in multiple cities, Orion-Lon taking priority."

Lorian noted how 'arbiter of justice' fell off the lord's tongue with disgust.

"Your Grace, why you of all the lords available?"

"Why not me?" Varios said with a laugh, his rigid scowl returning as soon as it left. "The king and I have history. Before you were born, there was a war in the Southlands that threatened to split the country in twain. I acted as lord commander of the king's main force, a large company of nobles restructured as cavalry. Apparently, I impressed him, though my deeds aren't what I'd consider impressive more as much as they were horrid. I was appointed arbiter a few years after the war, after the banning of the Bastard Crusades." The lord finished speaking as they came to the mouth of the carved tunnel that stretched and twisted out of sight.

"Here is where we enter. Orion-Lon has multiple entrances into the mining shafts that spread deep into the mountain like roots beneath an iron tree. From outside the city, each ring seems to terminate after only half a rotation, but we call them rings for a reason. The second half of each ring extends into the mountain and completes the full circle before emerging back into the open. Halfway through the inner portion of the second ring is where we'll find the lift that descends into the mountain. Let's move by foot going forward." Varios descended from his steed, tying the animal to a set of rails adjacent to the mouth of the inner ring.

Lorian followed suit and tied Sebastian next to his lord's mount.

"I promise there's a bag of carrots coming your way after this, Sebastian," Lorian whispered to his horse, petting his brow as he did.

Together, Lorian and Lord Varios ventured forth into the inner ring. Lorian immediately knew why Varios recommended they go on foot, as certain sections of this ring became too narrow for a horse to fit comfortably with a rider.

The quality of this side of the ring paled in comparison to its exterior. The buildings carved into the stone were smaller and layered with filth. The commoners here were covered in soot and grime that undoubtedly came from the mines. The unevenness of the stone below suggested they were carved with less care or had been maintained poorly.

Lorian realized, based on the contents of the dwellings and the residents' attire, that both foreigners and mine workers were segregated to these areas.

As the pair moved forward, the natural light from outside dimmed enough that a certain blackness enveloped their vision. Before long, all light from outside had dwindled, forcing them to rely on the glow of the oil lanterns to guide them.

Lorian's eyes adjusted to the darkness after some time, and he was better able to absorb the details of the dwellings within the ring that saw no light.

The deeper sections of this ring were inhabited mostly by miners and their families. The abodes were small and cramped, and nearly everything was covered in a thin film of algae from the dampness. Sickly children coughed loudly from within their homes, no doubt a sign of some infection from the poor living conditions.

"Why would anyone choose to live like this?" Lorian asked aloud, not expecting an answer.

"Because it's all they know. Workers come from all over the country; the Saltlands, the Squelch south of the capital, even our people from Speral-Lon and Fula-Lon travel here for work. It pays decently, and comes with free housing and even the promise of fortune should a miner come across a rare garment during their excavation."

Lorian spat, "A gamble. The wager being the lives of your family."

"We're here," said Lord Varios. Though the ring continued on, the pair came to a halt in front of an archway that was carved out of the exterior of the second ring's walls.

It led to a large opening that ferried workers from each ring down into the depths. A platform rested within the middle of the room with large anchors jutting from each corner.

Chains thicker than Lorian had ever seen weaved through the anchors and disappeared into a shaft of darkness far above them. Small metal railings acted as the only source of security and encompassed all but the front gate of the lift.

Workers present on the shaft quickly fled upon realization that the lord was present. "Get on," ordered Lord Varios, and Lorian obeyed.

Once both men were on the lift, Lord Varios swung the gate shut, its hinges hissing in protest, then grabbed a lever that Lorian had not seen from his previous vantage point. The long lever protruded roughly from the front-right anchor and contained a series of gears that intertwined with one another intricately.

Lord Varios yanked harshly on the lever, and the lift groaned loudly. The sound startled Lorian. The lift moved in a quick jerk, then descended smoothly as it climbed its way down the shaft and into the heart of the mountain. A single oil lamp lit the lift poorly, and Lorian had to rely on the shadows that danced around him to guide his way.

"How deep is Lord Aaron, Your Grace?" asked Lorian, eager to remove himself from the lift.

"As deep as the lift will carry us, if the magistrate is to be believed."

"And do you? Believe him, I mean."

"Not many men have the heart to lie after losing half their face. Not when the remaining half stays unburnt," the lord replied harshly.

Lorian wondered to himself about the many reasons Lord Aaron would have for being absent today. He began to think that Lord Aaron was in danger and needed rescuing.

Who could take a Wielder prisoner? Lorian thought. After seeing the raw power that Lord Varios displayed, Lorian figured each noble could take on an army if pressed.

Maybe his inability to bring order to his own city was a reflection of his character. Perhaps Lord Aaron is indeed a weak man.

The sudden braking of the lift cut Lorian's mental wandering short and threatened to buckle him at the knees. Oil lamps within the mines lit the lift's exit much better than the single lamp they rode with, calming Lorian's nerves. The bottom of the shaft was carved crudely; uneven chunks had been removed from the walls and a disproportional archway led to an adjacent pathway. Without speaking, Lord Varios made for the pathway, rounding a corner as he did. Lorian hurriedly followed for fear of being left behind.

The pathway ahead of them stretched farther than their eyes could see, rooms branching off in random intervals that led to ore nodes of varying types.

The dampness seemed to increase as they traveled farther down, and dew droplets soon began to form on Lorian's skin and clothes. Lord Varios' dry skin was an exception to the otherwise wetness of the stale air. Looking closer, Lorian could see steam rising from the lord every so often, as if he was using his magic to flash away the condensation that clung onto him.

The acrid smell of ancient stone forced Lorian to plug his nose when it became too unbearable. *A mixture of eggs and wet grass*, he thought.

The faint pounding of hammer on stone echoed from a room not much farther than where they stood, causing Lord Varios to draw his sword.

Lorian clumsily drew his too.

The blade felt foreign in his hand and swayed unsteadily, as he was unaccustomed to its weight. His recent altercation played a heavy part in his lack of balance too, he assumed.

Moving in relative silence, the pair crept forward.

A hollowed-out room to their left glowed brightly, illuminated by many lanterns. A muttering noise could be heard, as if two strangers were speaking with near-silent voices. Preparing his sword in one hand, Lord Varios removed the glove from his other, using his teeth to pry the leather off.

When they were close enough, the lord jumped around the corner, forcing a sharp scream from the unsuspecting victim.

As Lorian rounded the corner to aid his lord, he found an older woman who had fallen backward in shock.

The strange woman was dressed in red garments that wrapped around her like robes. A tool belt hung from her shoulder to her hip like a stylish sash; it bore a variety of tools—chisels, brushes, small hammers, and a spread of objects Lorian could not identify.

By appearance, the woman was nearly fifty years old, indicated by her softly wrinkled eyes and sparse gray hairs that contrasted with her walnut locks. Her gentle eyes sat behind thick glasses blanketed by a thin layer of dust from her fall.

"My apologies, child-scholar. I thought you to be a threat. Forgive me," said the lord with an apologetic tone.

"Oh, my lord! No forgiveness is necessary!" she said in a hasty tone while awkwardly forcing herself into a standing position. She immediately gave the lord an introductory bow and waited for his response.

"Child-scholar, that is not necessary. Please stand," replied the lord.

Lorian was shocked at his response. *What was a child-scholar, and why didn't they need to bow? And why did this one feel the need to do it anyway?* Lorian wondered.

"It is the least I can do for worrying you, my lord," she said as she lifted her head.

"I was unaware there was a mission to the mines, let alone this far north," Varios said.

"This visit is less than official, my lord. I am here on my personal time to study some scrawlings that were reported to my sect by some miners. History hardly waits for permission, so I figured I shan't either! Please excuse my lack of formality."

"All is forgiven. I shall be on my way," replied Varios in a hasty tone as he attempted to continue on.

"Oh, please don't leave yet! You have to see what I've discovered! Look here at these inscriptions!" she said with an enthusiasm Lorian didn't know existed. Without hesitation, the child-scholar grabbed Lord Varios by the hand and forced him a few feet into her alcove. Lorian was taken aback by how casually she treated the lord, especially one who was clearly a stranger to her.

She pointed to a wall she had excavated, revealing an obsidian-colored material with large hexagonal patterns that created a grid-like surface. It was reflective and shone brilliantly in the light of the many lanterns. Odd symbols decorated the wall in certain sections, completely indecipherable to Lorian.

"Look here!" she pointed, a smile stretched happily across her face.

"The stone is very beautiful, child-scholar, but I must take my leave now," said Varios. He slowly inched backward.

"Wait, no! Did you not see the writing? If what we know about the ancient world is true, this section says 'Stovir was here!'" she said with another smile eagerly painted on her face. She stared at Lord Varios in a way that forced him to reply.

"That's . . . very good," Varios replied awkwardly.

"Isn't it?" she yelled exuberantly. "This may be the first written evidence we have of a race more ancient than us! This could shatter society as we know it! Think of the implications! And what is this material on which it was written? For what purpose was it chosen? Could it be a fuel source of some kind? Perhaps a new metal for machinery or armaments? No hammer or chisel I have can break it! What if we found a substance harder than diamond? Can you imagine an arrow with this as the head? Or even better than savage weaponry, think of the technologies we could invent! New mechanisms and trinkets to bring wonders to this world! This could rewrite our understanding of mathematics and the physical sciences! Imagine a world where communication was instant, or the flight of man was no longer an impossibility, but a commodity!" she said, her visions of the future making her lose focus.

She continued her lecture, unaware that the audience had fled halfway through.

"Your Grace, was it rude to sneak away from her? Could there be truth in what she was saying?" asked Lorian, who felt more than guilty for fleeing.

"First child-scholar you've met, I assume? No surprise. They hardly ever leave their sanctuary in the capital. Always buried in those damn books. Each of them is no less insane than my mother. For all she knew, that was a petrified chunk of cow shit that the miners placed there for amusement. Lunatic," spat Varios, who showed no attempt to hide his dislike.

"Why are they called child-scholars? She was well into grayhood," asked Lorian.

"*Child-scholar* is a title, not a description. A child-scholar dedicates their life to learning what they can of the ancients, abstaining from all the pleasures of the world. They have political immunity, to a degree, and are exempt from taxation. In exchange, they forfeit the right to own land, marry, or bear and sire children. I will agree with you, though. She is quite old to still be a child-scholar. By her age, she should be running a sect as a matron-scholar. I suppose she wouldn't get to travel if that was the case. That would explain the title," Varios explained.

With Lorian having no more questions, the two carried on in their search. After traveling what felt like a mile, they came upon a large, hollowed-out cavern where the pathway ended.

The room was large enough to fit a small company and stretched upward the length of three men. It was here that Lord Aaron sat, alone. A small table cluttered with bottles sat adjacent to the lord, who leaned drunkenly in a fine, wooden chair. The lord snored sporadically; his satin garments were stained with wine and, by the smell, piss.

Lorian was relieved to find that the lord was not a prisoner or in other dire straits. But Lord Varios seemed anything but relieved. Sheathing his sword, Varios calmly walked over to the other lord, and after removing his gloves one finger at a time, sent a clenched fist at the drunkard so violently that it threw Lord Aaron from the chair completely.

The wounded noble let out a wail of pain, his long blond hair cascading over his face. In response, Aaron haphazardly attempted to draw a dagger from its place on his thin waist, failing to do so in his stupor.

"You'll not need that, Lord Aaron," said Varios. "Not unless you wish your death to grace us on this day."

"Lord Varios?" Aaron asked with a feeble voice. "Why have you struck me?" He weakly rose from the floor. His attempts to fix his hair gave Lorian a look at the lord's thin, almost feminine features. He had shallow lips that turned downward and a petite nose that seemed too small for his face. The lord bore a single brown eye paired with a brilliant red eye, same as the hanged boy.

"Why are you hiding in the mines, soaked in wine and piss?" Varios asked as he continued his interrogation.

"My apologies. I wasn't expecting you until the end of the week. Forgive me, Lord Varios," replied Aaron.

"Yes, I know. I left early. Your last letter was worrisome and forced my travels to an early start. Now I ask again, why do you hide here like a scared animal?"

"Who is the boy, Sam?" asked Aaron, pointing a sharp finger at Lorian.

"You will address me as Lord Varios, and if you dodge my question once more, I will kill you. Why are you here?"

"I believe you know why, *Looord* Varios," replied Aaron as he stretched the word to antagonize him.

The veins in Lord Varios' neck bulged as his anger intensified. "You knowingly participated in the public execution of a bastard. And not any bastard, but your own son. Do you deny this?"

Fear crawled into the face of Lord Aaron as a dark realization set in. The drunken lord began to sob as he fell to his knees. He began to pound the hard stone floor in anger, breaking the skin on his knuckles. Lord Varios looked astonished at Aaron's reaction, and he lowered his head in sadness. "You didn't know?" asked Varios in a near-whispered tone.

"Strawman said he would solve the problem," Aaron said through tears, "He said he would take the boy away in secret. He was meant to live in the Southlands on an estate I had purchased."

"Why? Why send him away?" asked Varios.

"I was to marry Madaline Strawman, his daughter. Our child was to have all rights to my estate instead of Max. I swear, I didn't know he would do this!" Aaron yelled. Tears and mucus dripped down Lord Aaron's inconsolable face.

"How could you believe something so foolish? As long as your son drew breath, no other children would have as strong a claim. Even as a bastard, royal decree would allow him the naming ceremony where he would've taken yours. And you let them hang him instead. You deserve no leniency, Lord Aaron. I place you under arrest. King Dinivy shall decide your fate, not I," stated Varios as he reached for Lord Aaron's arm.

To his surprise, Lord Aaron had grabbed a handful of gravel from the mine floor and threw it into Lord Varios' face, blinding him. Lorian drew his sword and charged Aaron. Before he could make contact, Lord Aaron vanished with a sound reminiscent of a harsh gale blowing through the canopy of a forest, leaving behind a small statue of a man carved out of wood in his place.

"I'm sorry to do this, Sam," said Aaron from the entrance of the cavern. Lorian turned around expeditiously, shocked to see that Lord Aaron had somehow appeared behind him. Lord Aaron reached for the wall and began to tug on a wooden beam. The beam began to rock back and forth, causing dust to fall from the ceiling.

"Damn you, Aaron!" screamed Lord Varios. After a few tugs, Lord Aaron freed the wooden support, causing a violent tremble within the cavern. The drunken lord vanished once more. Before he could react, Lorian found himself shoved harshly from behind as the ceiling collapsed.

Lorian coughed violently as he forced the dust from his lungs. He had been shoved out of the cavern and into the pathway outside, narrowly evading the collapse. The dim glow of the lanterns beside him showed the aftermath.

Piles of stone covered the once-clear area. A hand shot out from the rocks nearest him, and he suddenly realized that Lord Varios was pinned beneath the rubble.

With every fiber of strength within him, Lorian pulled and removed what stone he could until his lord's head was visible. Once freed partially from the rubble, Varios expelled a mouthful of dust, his lungs gasping desperately for clean air.

"You need to free me now," wheezed Lord Varios, his forehead dripping blood from where his brow had been split.

Lorian panicked. *What can I do?* If Lord Varios perished here, it would be his word against Lord Aaron's. He would be hanged for this crime, same as the lord's son. He could escape or beg Lord Aaron to clear his name, though neither of those options were possible. Not for Lorian. Varios had been too kind to him, too generous. Even if it meant the gallows, he'd help his lord if he could. With a deep breath, Lorian grabbed onto Varios with all his strength and began to pull.

"Hurry!" cried Varios, which sent Lorian into a great panic. *Pull, you useless bastard, pull*! he screamed in his mind. *Why can't I do anything right? My whole life has been nothing but pain, and I refuse to let it end here! Not like this! I am more than my station. I am more than a bastard.*

"I am more!" Lorian screamed aloud as a bright light illuminated the room, blinding him.

Lorian awoke to find Lord Varios hunched against the wall of the pathway, his breathing haggard. "Your Grace," mumbled Lorian, causing Varios to jump. Lorian could see a difference in his lord. Something was off, but he was unsure what. His lord looked weak—not just from the accident, but weaker overall. It suddenly struck Lorian what had changed. "Your Grace, your eye!" announced Lorian as he noticed the magic glow of Vario's white-blue eye was all but gone.

A weak wheeze escaped from the injured noble. His face turned pale, and he softly uttered, "I know. My power is weak." He paused. "How did you do it, Lorian? How did you steal my magic?"

Chapter 5: Try To Understand

"Losing a child is akin to living without a heart. To bear the emptiness of a home, one which is so plagued with memories of fonder times, has led more than one person to an early grave. They say Deaut, mistress of death, welcomes those who have lost children with a smile, for she above all else knows the relief they feel when finally unburdened with the chains of grief."
—Gothic Barkson of the Holy Orphanage in Speral-Lon

Lord Varios shook coldly on the mine floor, his once regal appearance now masked by blood and grime. His brilliant blue-white eye now shone dimly, a sad ember of a once-proud flame.

The bastard and the lord sat quietly for a long while, neither saying anything with their words yet telling one another volumes with their eyes.

Varios could feel the confusion in Lorian, sensing that the event that had just transpired, magnificent and horrifying as it was, had been unintentional. Varios began to wonder if he had played a part in the forfeiture of his magic, assuming something like this would have to occur on behalf of the Wielder, not the powerless. He furrowed his brow in frustration. To his knowledge, nothing like this had ever come to pass before in the history of their people.

As a student in the capital, before his father had died and named him heir over his sister, he had studied art and history at the College of Mainis Fortu. Never in events, current or past, had a transference of power ever occurred.

Legend had taught the young lord that transference into objects of rare metal was possible, though evidence of this occurring was never shown to him, but transference between two people was only possible by birth. Until now.

Lorian's brilliant blue-white eye cut sharply into the lord's mind, into his soul and his heart. *How could this have happened? How can it be undone?* Killing the bastard was an option, but he knew that may only dissolve the power into the collective without returning it to him.

He thought for a long while that Lorian may actually be his son, and that his eye had awoken late, but he discarded the idea as none of the tell-tale signs were apparent. At Lorian's birth, Varios would have felt the draining of power, which would only increase over time. He also hadn't bedded anyone since the passing of his wife, so the odds of him being sired by the lord were nonexistent.

An eye awakening late could be possible, but never past the age of puberty, and certainty not into the early twenties, as the bastard was. Whatever had happened, Varios was certain that it was outside the laws of transference that he'd previously thought to be absolute.

Varios' mind began to wander, searching desperately for an answer to the madness that was this day.

He wished for a moment that he could receive the counsel of his mother, though reality reminded him of her condition. His mother, Lady Varios, was a gifted seer. So gifted, in fact, that lords from all over the world came to her for guidance and insight.

Without his father alive to regulate the lords that came seeking knowledge of future events, her mind began to die from the burden of overused magic. As in all Wielders, their power flows from an infinite source beyond their understanding. The amount of magic one could wield at once was determined by their affinity for it. Those with less affinity would feel the burden of their magic quicker, with more backlash than those more naturally gifted.

His mother had low affinity, and through overuse of her visions, her mind began to wither, and her eye took on the blackness worn by all bearers who overindulged. She now only spoke in rambles, a tired body inhabited by a mind no longer grounded in reality.

Varios had always believed that it was better to be capable in the physical magics, himself being the perfect example, and to feel the sting of sore muscles, broken bones, and torn ligaments rather than the burden of a broken mind when overuse occurred. To feel the spray of fire or the jaggedness of conjured stone was, in his opinion, a kinder consequence than the loss of time or incoherence that followed every fortune told.

Varios smiled as he thought of times past when his family was whole, his mother gardening alongside his sister while he and his father watched.

The spring air in Amphil-Lon always carried the scent of citrus and snowberries thawing on the forest floor, waiting for a soft breeze to carry their seeds to more fertile soil. *What an odd time to reminisce*, he thought. Perhaps with the waning of his magic, the waning of his life may also be occurring.

To welcome Deaut, natural god of death, would certainly be easier than leaving this mine shaft, easier than explaining the unnatural events of the day that could very well see both him and Lorian hung. If the nobility learned that transference of this nature was possible, each of their heads would quickly be separated from their bodies for fear of this information spreading.

Damn bastard.

Varios began to steady himself. He took a deep breath and tried to unburden his mind. His heart slowed, and his thoughts became still. When his eyes did open, he again became aware and determined. Lord Varios knew what had to be done. He opened his mouth for the first time and sang.

The nights are long, the days they bend,
This chance I give you, my friend.
Shall blade not fall, or my life see end,
This chance I give you, my friend.
When the road doth split and the path won't mend,
This chance I give you, my friend.
To stay on course, or return to Farland,
This chance I give you, my friend.
For now, my eyes do close, and my senses blend,
I shall say farewell, my friend.

"A beautiful song, my lord," Lorian replied with a timid voice.

"Aye, it is. My father sung this to me on more than one occasion. And I sang it for my own son, gods rest his soul. It means a great deal to me. Marks events of importance and stands as a placeholder of sorts."

Lorian's eyes went wide at the mention of his son. "A placeholder for what, my lord?"

"Hope, prayers, woe . . . whatever is needed at the moment, I suppose."

79

The two again stared at one another, unmoving and soundless. The lord's voice broke the eerie silence after a few moments. "You and I must now rely on one another, Lorian, if we are to survive. We are two souls intertwined in the most intimate of ways. Whatever our fates may be moving forward, the only certainty we have is that we share the outcome."

"My lord, I don't understand. What has happened?" asked Lorian, the confusion of the situation painted clearly upon his face.

"You must feel the power by now. Yes, you do; there is no doubt. Come, look here," said Varios as he kicked his heel at a small puddle of water that had trickled from the partially collapsed ceiling above. Lorian struggled to his hands and knees, crawling the short distance to the water. He peered deeply into the reflection, the shock and the fear of reality settling onto his face.

"But how?" coughed Lorian.

"I'm not sure. We'll have to investigate when the time is more appropriate. What matters now is how we're going to handle it. We need to leave these mines. I'll need your assistance. My ribs are broken, and I doubt I can walk on my own. Help me to my feet."

Lorian stood and walked toward his lord. Grabbing him by his hands, he lifted the lord to his feet and swung an arm around his shoulder for leverage.

"And what of your eye, my lord?"

"I'll cover it up with some cloth. The real question is, what of your eye, bastard?" laughed the lord, his face twisting in pain at the movement his ribs were forced to undergo. "Listen to me, Lorian. As I said, we are connected now. Eventually, someone will learn the truth of my diminishing. As they will of your eye. We need to get ahead of it. From today, you will openly acknowledge that you are my bastard, Lorian. You are the bastard son of Lord Sam Varios, Baron of Amphil-Lon, and heir apparent to House Varios. Do you understand?"

"But my lord, is that really the only solution? How am I to convince others of this? I am not learned as a noble. All I know are the ways of hammer and steel; I know nothing of politics and magic," Lorian replied pleadingly.

"It must be so, Lorian, for both our lives now depend on this lie. Your eye is my eye. This is not always so, but it can be used to trace lineage. There will be no way around this. You must be my bastard. Say it. Swear it!" shouted Varios, a groan of pain escaping him.

"I . . . I swear it, my lord."

"Not my lord. Father. Say it out loud. Practice it. This is who you are from today—no one else. Our lives depend on it."

"I understand . . . *Father*."

Chapter 6: A Safe Place to Rest

"It was an obvious thing, those with magic rising to power, leading us. Whether we wished for it or not, what could be done to stop them? What good is an arrow, sword, or spear when compared to those who tear lightning from the sky? The mere fact that those who predeceased us did not worship them as gods is the only mystery here."
—Patron-Scholar Godrick, *The First Histories of Magic, Vol. 1*

Together, Lorian and Lord Varios limped back toward the mine lift and returned to the surface of Orion-Lon. Back to the world and to reality. Lorian helped Varios wrap a cloth around his head, masking his dimmed eye and aiding the lie they were about to birth forth.

The journey back to the bell towers that Varios' troops had occupied was arduous and long. Lorian's sore, bruised leg forced him to limp alongside his new father, extending the already grueling journey. The walk back to the lift felt the longest. The dark tunnels seemed to close in on him, the stale recycled air coating his lungs in a layer of mucus.

Lorian swore that, as they passed the chamber where the child-scholar had been studying, her voice was still listing off potential uses for the smooth, oddly shaped stone on which the ancient writing was found.

He was unsure if this ruse would last. How could anyone believe he was the son of such a renowned baron? He already had a father—a good father. *What will become of him? What will he think when he hears the news? Will Lord Varios . . . Will Father allow me to speak the truth to the man who raised me?*

The world was not right—not anymore. Of all those who wished for power and position, Lorian only had ever wished for the means to survive without strife. To be wealthy enough that he and his father could live with dignity and honor. To live without the boot of position constantly on their throats. Yet Lorian could feel the boot press harder than ever now.

He could feel it press the very air from his lungs.

After exiting the mine, the darkness of the second inner ring seemed so bright that Lorian had to squint when compared to the near-total darkness of the mines below. They made quick work of the journey to the outer circle, relief welling within Lorian when he could see that Sebastian was unharmed and ready for riding. Lorian had to hold the reins of the other horse in his hands as they rode together on Sebastian, sharing a saddle lest Varios fall and break more bones.

Lorian and Varios returned to the bell tower to find Captain Bowers issuing orders to the city guardsmen present. Soldiers were running around collecting bodies, ferrying prisoners, and cleaning the debris of the previous scrimmage. Upon seeing the pair, Captain Bowers ordered a small group of soldiers to find a doctor and to secure Lord Varios from the horse. Once Varios had been removed, Lorian dismounted and approached Captain Bowers.

"Captain, he has several broken ribs and has suffered great damage to his eye. He wishes to have the eye mended by a Wielder and has ordered no physician to remove his bandage."

"By the twelve gods, is that you, bastard?" whispered Bowers.

"It is. Father has informed me that I've had an awakening," replied Lorian, matching the Captain's quiet tone.

"Forgive me, my lord. If I had known, I wouldn't have been so informal with you," spoke Bowers, who performed a customary bow.

Lorian was taken aback by the sudden authority he possessed. "Uhm, rise, captain."

The captain rose, waiting to be spoken to or ordered.

Lorian eyed the captain for a moment, unsure what orders he should give. "I'll leave it to you to inform the rest of the company. Please send me Handsir Rikard when you find him."

"Understood, Your Grace," replied Captain Bowers.

Hearing the formality directed toward him caused a lurch within Lorian's stomach. He wished for this to be over soon, as he was unsure how long he could pretend to be nobility.

While his new lord father was being rushed to a doctor, Lorian decided to bide his time in the bell tower, hoping to avoid contact with others while he waited for Rikard to join him. The handsir was the only one he knew well enough to explain to him what he was supposed to do.

Without Varios nearby to give him instruction, Lorian had to make do with what was available. Walking through the large double doors that fed into the base of the tower, Lorian took in the massive damage the building had undergone.

The doors themselves were scorched and caved inward, hanging by their hinges. The oil lanterns within the church had caught fire and erupted, undoubtedly causing the ear-shattering sound he had heard earlier in the courtyard. The pews were splintered and charred, their neat rows now chaotic and upturned. At the altar, Lorian could see the same symbol he saw earlier, the sigil of Gan, lord of stone and gems.

"Ah, the messenger returns at last," groaned a voice from beside the altar.

On the floor lay Magistrate Strawman, bound by the hands and feet, his face wrapped at the midline in oozing bandages.

"And you've changed," the politician wheezed. "It seems we both have undergone a metamorphosis of sorts. Tell me, bastard, how does it feel to embody the power to wield magic beyond comprehension? I imagine it feels better than receiving that magic—the way your lord deals it out, anyhow."

Silence fell between them. Lorian approached apprehensively. On the floor beside the magistrate was a small body bound in linen, the bastard son of Lord Aaron. To Lorian's surprise, huddled over the body, also bound by the hands and feet, was Lord Aaron himself.

Lorian drew his sword in anticipation.

"Leave me be, boy. I'm no harm to anyone. Allow me to grieve for my son," cried Lord Aaron. "How ironic it is. Lord Varios spoke down to me for trying to hide my bastard as I saw fit, and here he had his own hidden heir, the bastard in the dark. And how curious that you should awaken at such an unorthodox age. Makes one wonder." Speculation lingered behind his desolate tone.

Anger overcame Lorian. *How dare he accuse Varios of the same crime when the truth couldn't be further away.*

"You claim to grieve the loss of your son, yet it was by your hand that he met his fate. You're a monster, Lord Aaron. Both you and the magistrate are monsters. I can only hope that whatever natural god oversees your fates ensures your punishment fits the terrible crime that happened here today," retorted Lorian, his animosity palpable.

"Hope all you want, bastard!" laughed the magistrate. "Our punishment will be a fine and a verbal lashing. I know it, Lord Aaron knows it, and if you had half a brain, you'd know it too. Your lord may have marked my flesh, but no cell will hold me. On that, you have my word."

"Your Grace, I believe you summoned me," said Handsir Rikard from behind Lorian.

The anger within Lorian was enough to make him cut the magistrate down, but he relented. Rikard assumed the customary position, and upon Lorian's acknowledgement, rose from the stance.

"Handsir, I require your assistance. Where can we speak privately?" asked Lorian, eager to remove himself from the presence of those horrid men.

"If you'll follow me, Your Grace, I have secured lodging for both you and Lord Varios within a local inn. We have barred patrons from entering and secured the building. Lord Varios is being treated there for his injuries as we speak, Your Grace," replied the handsir.

Lorian was astonished at how Rikard had adjusted to his sudden nobility. It made him feel uneasy to be spoken to like a gentleman, though he supposed this manner of conversation was something he would have to get used to.

The inn was in the lower ring and close to the Western Gate—the one the company originally entered through. The building was old but well-kept. The stone foundation was recently washed and glimmered nicely in the waning sun.

A sign hung over the half-door entrance proclaimed the name 'The Lonely Gem.' To Lorian's mind, it didn't seem suitable for nobility, but given the circumstances, he was sure Varios wouldn't mind.

On the ride over, Rikard explained that Captain Bowers had grabbed a few soldiers and made his way toward the mines. They'd met Lord Aaron near the entrance to the inner circle of the second ring. He had apparently overexerted himself with magic, and when questioned by the soldiers, gave himself up for arrest.

Before they could send more men in to retrieve Lorian and Varios, the two of them had already appeared on horseback.

Entering the inn, Lorian was met with a sight much more lavish than the Canary tavern back home. An assortment of ores and rocks dressed the walls upon display shelves, showing the bounty that waited within the mountain. Chandeliers, large windows, and oil lanterns kept the building brightly lit, and the sweet smell of honey wine and freshly cooked meat filled the air, reminding Lorian that he hadn't eaten in a long while.

"Your Grace, I shall check on Lord Varios and inspect your room. Please sit here and eat your fill before retiring upstairs," suggested the handsir, framing his words as if they were a question but not giving Lorian time to respond before pulling a chair out for him to sit on. Lorian sat and before another word could be said, Rikard had disappeared up a set of stairs that framed the tavern below.

"I thank you for gracing my humble inn with your presence, my lord," said a voice from beside the table. Lorian hadn't heard the man walk up and knew he needed to stay more aware in the future.

The barkeep stood slightly taller than a child and bore two bulging arms that seemed to struggle against the fabric of his shirt for space. The man had a deep voice with dark black eyes, a thickly bearded face, and a dirty apron that hugged tightly to his pot belly. He stood awkwardly bowed over; clearly, he was a man unaccustomed to decorum with nobility.

"Don't bow for me, keep. I'll have a plate of whatever's hot. And a tall glass of whatever's cold," responded Lorian, hoping to make the man feel more comfortable.

"Coming right up, Y'Grace," replied the burly man. Lorian was glad to hear his accent. Many northerners held a particular accent that stretched simple words and condensed longer ones, forcing a more fluid conversation. It reminded him of Amphil-Lon and his father.

Within moments, the man returned and placed a plate of gravied beef with a side of seared vegetables beside him. A tall glass of amber-colored wine accompanied it, and, for the first time, Lorian was feeling content with his new station.

Before beginning to eat, Lorian noticed that the barkeep stood silently by, waiting for his command to leave.

"Would you like to sit?"

"I wouldn't dare, Y'Grace," muttered the barkeep. The man had a funny way of lifting his head to speak with his eyes never seeming to rise from the floor. Curious to know why, Lorian asked.

"Why aren't you looking at me? Have I done something to offend you?"

"No, Y'Grace," he replied meekly.

"Then why won't you look me in the eyes?" he pressed.

"Because y'frighten me, my lord. I'm a simple man who wishes not to be cursed by a Wielder. Forgive me if you find that insulting," he answered.

Lorian's meal suddenly seemed less appetizing. "I'm sorry, uh . . . You may go."

He knew he couldn't blame the man. After all, just earlier today, he would have agreed with him. Lorian felt shame, oddly enough, not because he felt he had done something wrong, but because he knew that others would likely kill to be in his position, and all he wanted was to be rid of it.

Not long into the meal, Rikard summoned Lorian to Varios' room. "He has requested your presence immediately, Your Grace."

Lorian filled his mouth with as much food as he could fit, washing it down with two large gulps of wine, and made for the rooms upstairs.

Varios sat upright in bed, pillows holding his weight against the headboard. "Come, sit. We have much to discuss. Thank you, Rikard. That'll be all."

"Your Grace," replied Rikard with a bow. He gently shut the door behind him, leaving father and son alone.

Varios' torso was wrapped tightly in bandages, and his eye was covered with a clean cloth. He had been washed of grime, and a fresh set of clothes lay neatly folded at the foot of his bed.

"Have you eaten?" the lord asked.

"Yes, Your Grac— Yes, Father," he replied.

"Lorian, I know this isn't easy for you. We must both do our best to play the parts we're given until we learn more about . . . this." Varios continued, "There is much for us to do now. Rikard informed me that we have both the magistrate and Lord Aaron under arrest. I'm glad. The last thing I wanted to do was run through the frost hunting a jumper."

"A jumper?" interrupted Lorian.

"Yes. There is much about magic that you do not know. In the time to come, I will do my best to teach you what must be learned. It will be hard, of course, and painful, but that is how we all learn. Lord Aaron is a jumper, a Wielder of magics bound to the soul. He can swap places with objects he's marked and move through space almost instantly."

Lorian remembered the small wooden figurine that remained in Lord Aaron's spot before the collapse and assumed that was the item he'd chosen to swap with. "Then why didn't he just jump to the capital? Or to Barandor or to his estate? Why just to the second ring?"

"Because he can't. No one can. All magics, regardless of school, are bound by unbreakable laws. One cannot perform an action beyond their capabilities. Could you run from here to Mainis Fortu in a single go? The amount of energy it would require would be too much to bear. He would die trying."

The concept made sense to Lorian, but magic was too alien to him. He feared that fully understanding it would require more knowledge than he had, though he couldn't deny the allure of the power. He felt an odd sense of excitement.

"What is meant by schools of magic?"

A look of annoyance came upon Varios' face. "By the gods, boy, you know nothing. How you're able to read and write is a testament to your father's patience. There are three schools of magic. Mind, body, and soul. Magics of the mind give Wielders the ability to read thoughts, sense the future, and get insight on a person's true intent. Body magics allow a Wielder to harness power in the forms of elements, like me, and soul magics, like Lord Aaron's magic, allow Wielders to jump, among other things."

The mention of Lorian's father forced a sense of guilt into him. A tight feeling in his chest made his heart beat harder, and for a moment, he thought he might cry. Lorian did his best to fight the tightness and listened as carefully as he could.

"Then what am I? What school do I belong to? Body, like you?"

"I'm not sure. We'll have to figure that out as we go. We're going to need an attuning crystal to tell you. You did not awaken normally, and even if you had, your age has progressed further than anyone in history. We'll be writing the rules for you as we go," replied Varios with deep concern. "For now, you need to rest, as do I. We aren't safe in this city, and as soon as the other gentry learn of Lord Aaron's arrest, I doubt they'll allow us to leave the city so easily."

"Are we to return to Amphil-Lon?"

"No. Normally, as arbiter, it would be left to me to punish as I see fit, but Lord Aaron is a noble, and it's a royal law that's been broken. He'll need to stand trial in front of a court of peers in Mainis Fortu. The king will decide on what's to become of him."

Lorian furrowed his brow. He needed an answer to a question burning in his mind. "In the bell tower, Magistrate Strawman said that they wouldn't be punished. That Lord Aaron and he would receive a fine and nothing more. Tell me that isn't true."

"I'm afraid it is the most likely outcome. Nobles don't turn on nobles. I myself may be punished for taking things as far as I have. The king will not appreciate what I've done to Strawman's face."

"That isn't fair! They should be in cells!" roared Lorian.

"I know, but this isn't the way of things. You'll learn, Lorian. Regardless, we need to make for Mainis Fortu at daybreak. I've ordered the men to gather supplies, and Bowers will conscript soldiers from the forces here in Orion-Lon. We've a long journey ahead of us, Lorian. I will teach you what I can along the way, but you must be willing to listen."

"It isn't right."

"I know it isn't," Varios agreed. "Now get some rest. You'll need it for what's to come. Rikard will wake you in the morning. Try and bathe before we leave. You may not get another chance for a long while."

Chapter 7: The Path Least Traveled

Droplets of water fell from the cold stone above, sending frozen jolts of sensation through Lorian's body whenever they landed on him. The bath water created a thick layer of steam in the bathhouse that nestled neatly into the side of the inn.

Rikard had awoken him well before first light. A hot meal awaited him in the inn, and an even hotter bath awaited after. Lorian had never taken a hot bath before—a warm one after his father had bathed, surely, but never one so hot that it could be confused with the searing air of a lively kiln.

His muscles relaxed and his mind stilled as he stewed in the water, relief encompassing him. The past few days of extreme tension he had unknowingly carried in his limbs melted away as he began to doze.

The steam thickened to a point where he could no longer tell where his own hands were, despite being held closely to his face. The rummaging of soldiers and the clamoring of attendants came to a halt outside the bathhouse as the world beyond fell silent.

Lorian could only see the water that embraced him below, not the wooden walls of the tub or the contours of his body that should've been just inches beneath it. Only water, extensive water that stretched from horizon to horizon, leaving Lorian in a void of nothingness, alone and afraid. Where his legs should've dangled now only held the rippling of liquid as something emerged from the depths below.

The hanged boy, the bastard son of Lord Aaron, whose name he learned to be Max, emerged from below, his face the perfect image of his death throes, a morbid reflection of his last moments. His colorless eyes bore no lids, and his purple, oxygen-starved face was stuck in a perpetual scream from which no sound emanated. And then he spoke in a voice that would haunt all of Lorian's days until his last.

"Kill the Raven."

Lorian awoke underneath the cold water in a fit of flailing limbs and confusion. He gasped for air after voiding his lungs of the now stale bathwater, heaving himself from the tub as he did. Handsir Rikard rushed in before Lorian was able to free himself of the water, wrapping him in a towel and helping him to his feet.

"What happened, Lorian? Are you well? Do you need the physician?" yelled Rikard, his voice hoarse and concerned.

"No! I'm all right," heaved Lorian, his senses returning to him as the panic abated. "I fell asleep in the tub. I just need a moment, and I'll be fine," he continued.

He grabbed Lorian tightly by the shoulders, shaking him slightly in anger. "You fool of a bastard! Do you know what would happen to me if I allowed the last heir of House Varios to drown on my watch? And in a tub of your own filth, for that matter! You may be new to this life, but by the gods, you will act accordingly, or I will end your bloodline myself. Am I understood?" the handsir finished, his face red from anger.

Lorian felt small in front of the handsir's rage and, despite his new station, could only apologize for angering the usually timid man. "My apologies, handsir. Forgive me," he replied meekly, his voice still returning from the nightmare.

"You are forgiven. Be more mindful. If a bath can claim your life this easily, I'd hate to see you face an assassin. Perhaps the great House of Varios will fall prey to an overly large wedge of cheese that its last heir was too hasty to chew thoroughly," said Rikard, a hint of amusement in his voice.

The handsir studied Lorian closely for a moment, then offered him a fresh change of clothing. "You must forgive my rash words, Lorian, for I have served House Varios for as long as I can remember, and until your surprising awakening, I was sure the house would fall with your father. I must be overly cautious and blunt with my words because I fear if I am not, carelessness or misfortune may take you."

"I am sorry that it had to be me, handsir. I know you've cared little for my presence since I arrived," Lorian admitted as he prepared for a harsh rebuttal.

"Dear boy, it is not that I don't care for you, but you must understand I've devoted my life to this house. All of my energy must go toward securing and protecting this bloodline. To be fair, your ignorance was a breath of fresh air. All day, I deal with nothing but servants and citizens who look to your father as an object of wealth or power that they can leech from, moths drawn to a flame, and having you around has been a reminder that there are those who wish for more."

"More? I came seeking money as well, handsir," he confessed.

"Ah yes, but to survive, to endure, not from greed but from necessity, and it shows. The lord took to you swiftly, you know, and before you awakened, I was unsure why, but it couldn't be clearer now. You will carry our great house forward, into a future where we can stand proudly."

If only he knew the truth, thought Lorian. "Thank you, handsir."

"Your father wishes you to dress in a hurry. You are to meet with Captain Bowers before departure and make a decision on the soldiers he has conscripted. Meet him in front of the inn as soon as you are able. I shall tidy things here and pack the remainder of your belongings."

Lorian dressed quickly as he had no wish to linger in the bathhouse. He took note of the fine garments left to him, feeling the softness of the long-sleeved shirt as he donned it.

He was given leather trousers that fit him perfectly and a new belt, an overcoat, and a pair of fresh black boots that laced upward from the toes to the shin. Rikard had left a set of gloves for him, but Lorian had never enjoyed the feel of his hands being covered for too long and he stowed them in the pocket of his overcoat.

Finally, before departing, Lorian shifted his necklace, adjusting the trinket so it lay flat against his skin. The gift from Varios was heavy and roughed his skin if left to its own will.

***

"Now don't we finally look the part?" commented Varios to Lorian. He stood tall in front of a large group of soldiers who were standing in file and at attention. "Seems Bowers has outdone himself, and now we need to cull the herd, as it were. Help me dissolve the ranks. We can only carry enough supplies for a hundred men, no more. With all the company we brought included, we need eighty men from the group in front of us. How should we move forward, Lorian?"

Lorian knew nothing of military strategy or how to filter the quality of soldiers and felt unqualified to make that decision.

"I'm not sure, Father. How did Captain Bowers select them?" he asked.

"A great question. Captain, can we have a word with you?" commanded Varios. Bowers had been walking through the formation of the group, inspecting the troops when he was summoned. The captain, who was fully dressed the part of soldier, marched forward, approaching Lorian and his father.

"What are your orders, Your Grace?" asked Bowers.

"Work with my son to select eighty men from the group here. I need to send a few riders ahead of us with news of the arrests. Be quick, captain."

Bowers remarked with a salute, "Aye, commander!"

When Varios was out of sight, Bowers dropped all formality with Lorian as he assumed a normal stance. "So, who's been charged with replacing our former ball fondler, bastard?" joked the captain, a smile stretched across his face.

Lorian was overjoyed that at least one person was going to treat him the same, though he had doubts that it would be this casual when Varios was present.

"Already volunteering for the position, captain? Someone's eager to make lieutenant commander," retorted Lorian, returning Bowers' smile in kind.

"Actually, I was hoping for the cock. Figure it'd be the quickest way to get my own castle," Bowers continued.

The two men laughed, their breath imbuing the air with huffs of fog.

"I've never had to select men before," revealed Lorian, embarrassed of his inexperience.

"Never outside of a brothel, you mean. Worry not. Here's how it's done," replied Bowers. He walked toward the men, stopping front and center. Addressing them, he said, "Men, you have been handpicked by me because I believe you to be the most capable and most courageous soldiers Orion-Lon has to offer. I don't have the food or supplies for all of you, so some must go. Three gold pieces to the first ten men who step forward."

To Lorian's surprise, nearly all the men rushed forward, some even shoving others to gain position.

Bowers then walked toward Lorian, whispering when he arrived, "Did you see that? Money is a great motivator, watch."

Returning to his position, Bowers selected thirty men who had been the fastest to step forward. He then selected the remainder of the men who had either been the slowest or hadn't moved at all. After the selection, he returned to Lorian.

"See, Your Grace? The fastest men to volunteer are willing to kill, even die for some gold. Those are soldiers you want on your side. You need to leverage the avarice of some men. The others were unsure what they wanted, so they were discarded. The slowest men are the most interesting, especially the ones unmotivated by gold. These men see value in other things: their family, their own lives. These men will do anything to keep their lives, and they'll fight just as hard as the fastest men. Play to people's strengths, earn their loyalty, and they'll keep you alive on the battlefield."

"How do you know they won't just flee once paid or abandon their post when conflict comes?" Lorian asked, puzzled by the captain's methods.

"A good question. We pay the greedy men an extra gold coin now, and another when they return home. The slowest men can be bought with gifts that secure themselves or their families. Land, cattle, title, you name it. We now have a hundred good men ready to kill and die for us, if need be," replied the captain with a certainty that he assumed only a seasoned soldier could have.

"Aye, and before I forget, this is for you," said Bowers as he removed a sword and sheath from his waist. "Your father had me purchase it from one of the blacksmiths on the third ring. Said you'd be best at telling the quality based on your background and whatnot. You'll train with a dummy sword, of course, but it's best to feel the weight of a real blade as soon as possible. Use it well, ball fondler. I climbed many steps for that blade." The captain gave a mocking wink.

Without a word, he began to give orders to the men, assemble horses, and make the last of the preparations before dawn broke and forced their journey to a start.

Lorian eagerly tied the sheath to his new belt, fumbling the laces many times before securing it properly. The blade felt heavier than its size would suggest, which intrigued Lorian.

Freeing the blade from its sheath, he held it in both hands, inspecting it with great care. "Handle is slightly heavy on the back end. Need to remove material. The blade is well made—folded steel, and sharp as a razor. Needs a good oiling, though," he said aloud to himself. He inspected the blade further, noticing a shine from the end of the handle. "Small red gem in the pommel for some reason. Why is there always a gem?" he scoffed.

"Glad you like it," spoke Varios, who had approached from behind Lorian, causing him to jump slightly from the scare.

"Damn it all," yelped Lorian in a startle. He had already failed to be more aware of his surroundings.

"It's heartwarming that you've never had to watch your back. You'll get used to it. Life as a noble can be as worrisome as that of a thief on the run. Make a wrong turn or meet the wrong people, and your head may roll," warned Varios.

Lorian's heart sank hearing those words, true as they were. Lorian had grown up in relative safety with his father. Life in Amphil-Lon was as rough as anywhere, but his father, his real father, had made a smart decision to move his shop to the city's outskirts. The hill and the forest that surrounded them offered protection from anyone who thought to do them ill, and trips to the city were usually due to business, meaning he always had a weapon of sorts to defend himself with.

Due to this and either luck or circumstance, Lorian never had to fight—not really. A few times, he was forced to defend himself against the casual drunk or mean-spirited youth, but never in a situation that could result in death. Not until Orion-Lon. Even then, Lorian had felt as if the whole experience was out of body, as if he didn't retain any useful experience from it. He shuddered when remembering the smoothness of the blade as it buried itself in the guard's skull.

"Thank you for the gift, Father. The sword is well made, though it may need some adjusting," he replied, hoping to forget the awful experience of killing a man.

"I think it's you who may need some adjusting. Now that you're my heir, learning to wield your sword is as important as learning to wield your magics. You'll try daily with Bowers. I don't trust the instruction of anyone else."

"Will you teach me to use magic?" Lorian asked hastily. He wanted to deny it, but the thought of actually wielding magic thrilled him. It was every child's dream at one point or another to harness magic like the heroes of old. Fighting monsters and vanquishing evil was an intoxicating fantasy. But that was different for Lorian now. His fantasy had become reality, and the only thing that stood between him and the heroes of old was the knowledge to wield properly.

"We are scheduled to make a stop in Tarns Knoll. An old friend of mine has a castle off the Slate Steps. They have an attunement crystal there that will help us identify your magic. Listen to me, Lorian. It is imperative that you do not attempt to wield your magic before we identify your school. If you were younger, I would be less concerned, but at your age, most Wielders are at their peak. It could kill you."

Fear now crept into Lorian's fantasies of being a hero. The last thing he wanted was to hurt himself attempting to jump or read minds. He felt impatience rise within him, a new yearning to learn and develop his skills. *Sword fighting will have to suffice for now*, he thought. "I understand. I am eager to learn." Lorian could see a hint of annoyance on the lord's face.

"I'm sure you are."

Varios gave Lorian a nod of the head, gesturing for him to follow. Together, they walked toward the Western Gate of Orion-Lon. "When we reach the capital, you'll have to undergo the naming ceremony. Have you heard of this?"

"No, Father. You mentioned it to Lord Aaron when we confronted him, but the term is alien to me."

"When our great king, Marcus Dinivy, outlawed the Bastard Crusades, the noble families were upset. I'm sure you can understand why. This alone wasn't enough to cause issues, as nobles believed that it only made killing their bastard children less convenient than it used to be. When the king learned the nobles were still killing in secret, he passed a law that allowed a bastard child of a noble, if they were firstborn or next in the line of succession, a right to seize the name that belongs to them. The king knew this wouldn't sit well, but his intentions were clear: Don't sire bastard children. When a bastard is of age and can prove his lineage, he may undergo the naming ceremony and lay claim as heir to his respective house. You will do this when we finish our affairs in the capital."

"Will I be taught the formalities? Must I claim your name, or am I allowed any name?"

"You will claim mine. The ritual states that you may claim a name of your choosing, if you can prove lineage. No bastard would forfeit this right as it would remove the surname of Night or Day."

"I've never met a bastard whose surname was Day. What does that mean?"

"Your mother was a lady of the night, yes? So, you are Lorian Night, a title meant to dishonor you and those that sired you. This happens if a man sires a child with a woman of the night, but if a woman sires a child by a man of the night—more specifically, a noblewoman—we call that bastard Day. As you can imagine, that happens less often, and so fewer bastards bear the surname Day," replied Varios as they left the city through the large gate.

The guards atop the wall stopped in their duties, as did the guards on watch at the gate, and saluted both of them. Outside the gate and beyond the drawbridge was the company they had assembled. Several wagons full of supplies and food were centered around a large garrison of both Varios' soldiers and the newly recruited soldiers Bowers had gathered.

Before his eyes, Lorian could see Captain Bowers preparing the company for its march. The company split, and the horsemen surrounded the wagons. The footmen coalesced both behind and ahead of the wagons, forming a layer of defense for the transported goods.

Lorian could see that in the wagon at the very center, bound by hand and foot with metal shackles, were Magistrate Strawman and Lord Aaron.

"Are we safe traveling with another Wielder?" asked Lorian.

"Yes. He's bound and can't imbue an object to switch with. Should be harmless. The real threat is external, I'm afraid. I've sent messengers forward with news of the arrest, but there are whispers already being spoken across the frost. Should those whispers land on the wrong ears, a fight may be inevitable. There are nobles who would see him freed, and there are others who would see me dead, if given the chance. Our advantage lies within our small numbers. If we are quick, then we are safe."

"I thought noble didn't turn on noble. This is because of Lord Aaron, isn't it?" asked Lorian, confused about why there may be danger ahead.

"It is. Would you consider the arrest of Lord Aaron a noble turning on another noble? Perhaps not, but there are those who will. Some may already see it as a declaration of war. You may not know this, Lorian, but even in the world of nobility, grudges form and houses align against other houses. Threats are plentiful; empathy is not. Now that I've claimed an heir, killing me won't end my line. Not with you alive."

"But I'm not your heir. Not really," muttered Lorian.

"And if we do our jobs, they'll never know that," Varios replied. "Keeping our secret safe may put us in danger, though nothing like what we'd face if the truth came to light. Speak no more of this. The sun is rising above the trees, and Bowers is awaiting our orders. Let us proceed."

Chapter 8: A Drop in the Bucket

"The art of war is a very subjective thing. Not in the sense that the forms of battle themselves are subjective, all men die the same, it is to say that the path to victory itself is subjective. The morality of one general may seem barbaric to another, thus creating an opportunity for victory that others may be blind to."
—Lord Commander Hericklen, *A Tale of Triumph*

Orion-Lon had been the farthest south Lorian had ever traveled, until today. Throughout his life, he had many desires, all more or less achievable with hard work and some coin: his own shop, a small vegetable garden where he could grow his own food, and eventually, a wife and children. When he was younger, he imagined his life would be full of adventure and travels, a dream manifested by the tales his father would tell of ancient heroes and places that riddled Centrugard bursting with magic and significance.

Before bed, he would listen to stories of the Saltlands and how no man was ever meant to inhabit them or stories of Farland and how humans had abandoned it against the wishes of the natural gods and sailed to Centrugard.

The most interesting stories were those of the named heroes who fought alongside the ancient peoples that no longer inhabited these lands: elves, dwarves, and dragons that looked like men. Lorian would be wide-eyed the entire time his father spoke, hanging on his every word.

"

If Lorian was lucky, his father would finish the story in one go instead of leaving him to toss and turn, trying to puzzle out how the stories ended to no avail.

Lorian could recall a very interesting story of a man called Ragorn, son of Radall, who allied the broken houses of the dwarves and brought about the first age of inclusion where men and *Dwurn*, the ancients' word for dwarf, would work hand-in-hand, sharing knowledge and secrets of the craft. Lorian could hear his father telling the story to him as if he were a child again.

"Ragorn was one of the first men born in Centrugard after the abandonment of Farland. He had grown up sowing seeds in new soil and hunting game never hunted before, eating fruits never tasted, and drinking from lakes that had not yet been molested by man. Ragorn was the first to embrace the new ways, and this drew the attention of the elves, or Lavel, as they called themselves. The Lavel were a proud people and named themselves the heirs to Centrugard, and to the world, allegedly claiming such as the true children of the natural gods.

"When they came upon Ragorn of the first people, they became enraged at how he hunted game despite the fruit and vegetables that grew abundantly, how he tilled the land and planted foreign crops, and how he tainted the hallowed lakes and rivers with a body that carried dirt, grime, and disease. And so, it was that Ragorn and his people became the first enemies of the Lavel. At the end of the first recorded day, which spanned a month (as in the early years, the shifting of sun and moon was irregular), the proud Lavel sought to rid Centrugard of the first men,

protecting the purity of the land and, more importantly, protecting their inheritance.

"When the sun bent beneath the horizon and the moon began to rise, they attacked. The twilight of the coming night offered protection, for the eyes of men did not adjust well in the growing dark. With whispered secrets to the trees and the brush, the forest surrounding Ragorn and his people shifted and churned until the land became unrecognizable.

"In the land that would become Twilanon, the heart of Lunarson and the bearer of the sacred trees, the first of many battles would ensue.

"The ancient tongue would call this night the Twi blud ul balat, the Battle of the Crimson Twilight, marking the first aggression.

"In the haze of the waning sun, the Lavel struck. Numbering in the thousands, as their numbers were greater in days now past, they attacked without mercy. Their strength and speed were unmatched among the many races of the world, and any who stood before them fell quickly, for the Lavel were cunning and brutal. The weak iron of man was defenseless against the strange metals of the Lavel, and no sword nor spear nor arrow could penetrate their defenses. By total nightfall, no man, woman, or babe was left alive, not even Ragorn.

"In the defense of his people, Ragorn was dealt a fatal blow, a Lavel arrow that pierced his skull through his right eye. Ragorn collapsed lifelessly into the great lake next to which he fought; the lake that today bears the name of Saphers Sea. The current of the lake grew unnaturally

strong that night and carried Ragorn's body southward to the seven rivers and toward the Circlet Mountains.

"It is unknown what transpired before Ragorn's body washed upon the shores of Mount Kladdan, but legend says that Gamil, mistress of water and froth, convinced her husband, Anwah, to ferry the corpse southward.

"When his body reached its destination, she pleaded with Deaut to return his life, which Deaut obliged, asking only that she allow her access to her oceans, lakes, rivers, and streams so no man or beast could evade death.

"Gamil relented and gave permission. Ragorn once again took in air, and life returned to him. The damage from the arrow had made Ragorn less; his wits were confused and his body was awkward and deformed, so Gamil pleaded with Gan to grant Ragorn a new eye, one crafted from gem.

"And so, Gan obliged, but on the condition that his creations, the Dwurn, would be allowed passage through the land and sea. And so, Gamil relented, begging her husband to allow the Dwurn to leave the mountains they inhabited, which angered Anwah, for he detested the creatures born of stone and gem.

"Gamil, wishing not to anger her husband further, schemed. She offered the Dwurn the chance to leave the mountains, but to do so permanently would mean death for the Dwurn, limiting the time they could emerge. Anwah was glad to hear this and agreed, allowing the Dwurn access to the surface, their scheme unknown to Gan. And so, with his new eye, Ragorn's senses returned to him, and his feet became sturdy and his body strong.

*"It is said that Ragorn would go on to make allies
of the Dwurn, aiding them in their struggles, and they, in
turn, would aid the remaining first peoples in crafting
armor and weapons that could withstand the strange metal
of the Lavel.*

*"His eye of gem would grant him the power to wield
the first magics, an unintended consequence of the gift.
This marks the story of the first age of inclusion, and the
first Wielder."*

Lorian soon began to wonder how much time would
need to pass before the feeling of loss and grief would
cease when thinking of the father he left behind. He
wondered if it was even possible to avoid these feelings.
Perhaps, he hoped, there was magic available to him to help
him forget or dull the pain.

As they traveled south, the winds blew increasingly
warmer. The Powdered Roads thickened with snow when
their path bent toward the Bronze Mountains, and thinned
when it curved away.

Their nights and mornings proceeded very similarly
to the schedule they had kept when en route to Orion-Lon,
though the tasks differed greatly. In the morning, Lorian
would be awoken by Handsir Rikard; a hot meal was
always waiting for him. Rikard had not been as casual with
him as they were in the bathhouse, but the tension he felt in
the servant's presence had relaxed and, over time, became
enjoyable.

In their free time, if it ever existed, Lorian would
take instruction from Rikard in secret.

Lorian was still not learned in the ways of a noble
and required extensive tutoring, which Rikard seemed to

delight in giving. Varios attempted to give aid when able, but his duties as lord were unyielding. Most of his time was spent writing and reading correspondence, which Lorian still helped with when he could.

After breakfast, Lorian would spend an hour with Bowers in whatever open space they could find, practicing swordsmanship. If no space was present, either from overgrown shrubbery and brush, or from snowfall that was too dense to move, they would simply practice atop the obstruction, focusing on footwork and balance.

More than once, Lorian rolled an ankle or fell headfirst into a patch of rough roots or thistle, yet he remained steadfast in his learnings. At night, Lorian would eat and practice with his real sword, trying to become intimate with the weight and balance of the blade. Lorian had borrowed a file from a random soldier at the request of the captain, and balanced the blade as well as he could, giving the sword a fresh coat of oil after every use.

After an overly intense session of swordsmanship during the third week on the road, Bowers offered to take Lorian's training to the next level.

"You've learned to hold the blade as well as you'll ever. Keep a not-too-tight grip and tight core, easy enough. Your footwork has also improved, though I'd dare to say it could be better, and you've already got the strength to swing a real blade, so it's time to advance. Going forward, we'll be teaching you basic forms for offense and defense. Once you've got those done, I'll be swinging my own stick at you to reinforce those forms. Right, we'll start with a basic block. Hold your sword at an angle so you can stop and redirect a downward slash from an enemy."

In a makeshift clearing, one free of snow and frost, the two began. Lorian assumed the position, his core tight and his knees slightly bent, like he'd been practicing. When he was fully in the blocking position, Bowers swung his sheathed steel sword downward, knocking Lorian to the ground.

"What in the hell was that for?" screamed Lorian, whose backside was wet with snow and dirt. "I thought you said we would practice before swinging at me! And that's no wooden sword!"

"Aye, Your Grace, I lied," he said, smirking. After waiting for Lorian to rise to his feet, Bowers swung again, all his strength imbued into the blow. Lorian had only enough time to reassume to blocking position, this blow throwing him harder into the ground than the previous.

"What is wrong with you?" Lorian screamed as he rushed to his feet, the defensive position already assumed.

"Good," replied Bowers, his smirk replaced with a seriousness that Lorian had only ever seen him take with his soldiers. "Swordplay is no game, boy. There will come a day, very soon, when you'll be in front of a man whose sword is not sheathed, who is much less fond of you than I. What will you do then? If your answer is anything but 'kill him before he kills me,' then you're wrong. Every decision is life and death on the battlefield, especially for us normal folk without your pretty magic.

"You will kill the men in front of you, or you'll be the one feeding the worms with your bones. When a blow from above is heading toward you, do one of two things: Either get out of the way or block and redirect. When you don't redirect, like you haven't been, all that weight comes down on your shoulders and knees. If you find yourself sitting in the dirt after one of those, you're a dead man. Always assume they're the better fighter; your life depends on it."

"Understood, captain," replied Lorian, his ego throbbing worse than his muscles.

"Wonderful. Now, this is the second defensive form, a block and redirect from the side," Bowers instructed.

For weeks, Lorian spent the better parts of his mornings in this routine, learning the intricacies and subtleties of combat. Long rides would be spent with Varios, learning what he could of the political state of the world he now inhabited. The more interesting topics concerning noble politics were always the ambiguity of personal affairs. Nobles performed their duties—whether baron like his father or duke, count, or knight—and reported statuses of money and goods to their next hierarchical overseer.

He learned that as a baron, Varios reported directly to the crown the figures on everything from taxes to stocks of goods like fish, crops, and manufactured materials such as armaments, building materials, and whatever else Amphil-Lon exported. Other nobles performed their duties, all of them reporting information as directed, yet beyond their station, a noble was free to do what they wished, as long as it didn't impact the flow of information.

He also learned that most nobles saw the new royal laws and decrees as direct interference in their personal affairs, which increased their contempt for the crown.

Lorian was eager to learn as much from Varios about these topics as possible, should he ever be desperate for the information later.

"What could happen if the nobility were to stand against the crown?" Lorian asked after summoning the courage to speak on the topic. The last time he'd openly discussed the issues with noble infighting, Lord Varios had reacted negatively. Lorian hoped that, considering their new predicament, such unsavory conversation could now be shared between them.

"I'm not sure," Varios began. "Something like that hasn't happened in over a thousand years, but . . ." His words were cut short as a call from the front of their company silenced him.

Captain Bowers slowly trotted from the front of the company, urging his horse to turn as he circled back and came to a halt beside Varios. In a faint whisper, Bowers leaned over and spoke softly, ensuring only the two of them could hear. "My lord, I suspect there's an ambush ahead— sixty men, by my count; most on foot, some on horses. What would you like us to do?"

The lord's face sunk, and his lips pursed. "Are you certain?"

"Aye, Your Grace. There are tracks ahead that double back more than once. Last night, I caught a glimpse of some fire smoke, figuring nothing of it considering we were so close to Travul-Lon. But now I'm certain. Should I send some scouts ahead?"

"Yes, send two men. No horses. Have them trek through the woods, then circle around. Are we safe to stop here?" Varios asked.

"It may be wise to get off the road, Your Grace. There's a clearing off the road about a mile back. We can set camp and decide on the course of action."

Varios furrowed his brow in frustration. Before leaving Orion-Lon, he had sent scouts forward, each with the same message, each with different routes in case something like this might happen. Lorian wondered if it was the work of a noble.

Varios thought deeply for a few moments, his eyes glossed over as if some dreadful realization had set in. "Is there any way to avoid bloodshed?"

"I'm afraid not, Your Grace. 'Tis the only path until we reach Tarns Knoll."

"Take us back around. We'll make camp and go from there. Assign more men to guard the wagons while we unload. Nothing is to happen to Magistrate Strawman or Lord Aaron. Am I understood, Bowers?" said Varios in a deadly tone, "If you suspect Lord Aaron of trying to escape, neutralize him; if the magistrate tries to flee, kill him."

Bowers replied with a salute. "Understood, my lord." He heeled his horse and set off to give the appropriate orders.

Lorian had hoped he would not suffer further violence on their journey, though the weight forming in his stomach told another story. "Father, what are we to do?"

"It would seem we have little choice. We wait for the scouts to return with more information, and then we fight."

Chapter 9: The Silence of the Moon

"Can we ever atone for the sin of death? The ancient teachings of the natural gods whisper that if a man falls by your blade, you inherit the burden of realizing his dreams. Yet, this is but a shadow of the true doctrine; a misinterpretation. In truth, the sacred text decrees: if a man falls by your blade, you must bear the crushing weight of extinguishing his dreams."
—Child-Scholar Rafin Storkson at the Battle of the Sky-Bridge

The air ran frigid that night, frost rapidly forming on anything unfortunate enough to stay exposed to the elements.

The dense woods of the north kept the company well hidden from any travelers that dared to explore beyond the road they walked. Though the sun had fallen, the full moon above shone brightly enough that Lorian could see without candlelight, the world turning a grim shade of gray as it rose.

Snow fell softly atop the company, who huddled closely together for warmth while they waited, as Varios had forbidden the lighting of any fires lest they reveal their location. It was an hour after total light fall when the scouts returned.

Varios ordered Bowers, the two scouts, and Lorian into his tent to discuss the next steps. Varios grabbed a candle whose wick was almost spent and placed it atop a round table that decorated the center of the tent. No chairs were yet unpacked, and so the five stood in a circle facing one another, giving Lorian a feeling of being out of place. Varios pinched the wick firmly between his thumb and forefinger, igniting it.

"Worry not, my boy. My tent walls are thick enough to not let the light from this meager flame give us away."

Lorian noted that despite the candlelight's weakness, Varios' face seemed to lose color, and using his magic in his weakened state seemed to exhaust him.

Bowers broke the silence that followed, ordering his men to give what detail they could glean from the enemy encampment. "Aye, captain," replied one of the scouts.

"Your Grace," the other scout began, "they are fifty-five in number. They have ten cavalrymen, and the rest are foot soldiers. They hold only spear or sword, no archers."

Varios seemed pleased with this information, his head nodding softly. "And how far are they from here?" the lord asked.

"Your Grace, they are less than three miles south and a hundred feet off the path. I don't believe they expected us to be here yet," he said.

Lord Varios raised an eyebrow at this new information. "And why do you say that?" he asked.

"They were drinking, my lord, and feasting. Like most the day before a battle."

"How many men were on watch?" Bowers asked, cutting into the conversation.

"Only three groups of two men, by my count. They weren't patrolling—just watching over a tent."

Varios and Bowers both looked at each other, their eyes exchanging information that Lorian couldn't decipher. "You don't think?" Bowers asked as he waited for his lord's confirmation.

"No. Unlikely," Varios said, "but not impossible." He stared off for a moment, and his eyes widened with concern.

"What's not impossible?" Lorian interjected.

"They may have a noble with them, a Wielder," replied Varios.

Lorian's hair stood firm, a shiver running up his spine. "What are we to do if he fights?" he asked.

"We take him alive. We can't afford the scandal of killing a noble right now, even if he is trying to kill us," Varios said before turning to the scouts. "What of their sleeping arrangements? Large tents or individuals? How drunk would you say they are?"

"Very, Your Grace. Piss drunk, even," spoke the scout. "And individual tents, maybe larger, my lord."

"Good," he replied. "Then we take a small group, go by night, and slit their throats while they sleep." There was a chill in his words.

"A good plan, Your Grace. I'll gather some men," replied Bowers. He and the scouts left the tent, leaving the two nobles alone.

Lorian felt the same out-of-body feeling that had plagued him when recalling his first kill. A lightheadedness followed shortly after, making him uneasy.

How could they sit here and discuss the killing of others so casually? He knew the situation was unavoidable, but it didn't mean that empathy had no room to exist. *Or*

*maybe it didn't. Maybe this was the cost of taking lives—
the loss of empathy and concern for others.*

Varios saw through the veil that was Lorian's mind
instantly, reaching out with a firm hand on the shoulder.
"You will need to join us on this, Lorian. They know who
you are and are less likely to target you. I need you to see
this in person. Learn from it; don't run. There is no joy to
be had in killing, especially of this sort, but what and who
we are dictates the burden of these things," he explained,
trying to level with the young Wielder.

"I know I have to go, and I know I should see things
like this, but it doesn't mean I want to. Please don't act like
I had some choice in all this. 'What we are' matters little to
me. I'm only a noble by accident, and now I'm a killer by
choice," Lorian said, his words sinking into the core of his
being.

"And it is a choice you will have to make again and
again, Lorian. We of House Varios are arbiters of justice by
royal decree, and we have a barony to rule. Whether we kill
by order, by sword, or by dagger hidden in shadow, we kill.
I will not allow you to assume that participation is
negotiable. The act of killing by your own hand is optional,
but if you don't swing the sword yourself, you make the
mistake of allowing others to think that you haven't the
stomach or courage to accept the responsibility of your
position, and that puts you, and everyone we rule, in
danger," Varios said, his whispered voice growing in
intensity.

Varios continued, "We have to be accountable for
our actions, and we do this by being present and, if need be,
ending lives. It is always better to save the many by killing

the few. The ends do justify the means. You will do well to remember this." As he finished, the lord left the tent to prepare for the stealthy raid to come.

Lorian took in a few icy breaths before extinguishing the small flame on the round table. He withdrew from the tent to find Bowers waiting for him.

"Here," Bowers said with the hilt of a dagger pointed toward him. "You'll be needing this. Follow me. There are details we must discuss."

As he trailed after Captain Bowers, who walked toward a small group of fifteen men, he realized Bowers seemed different. The jokester Lorian was accustomed to had been replaced by a hardened warrior. "Here are the soldiers who volunteered to accompany us."

Lorian inspected the men who stood silently, only fabric garments covering their skin.

"Why aren't they wearing armor, captain?" asked Lorian.

"Too noisy. The key to success is silence and speed. The snowfall should help hide the sound of our steps as well. That guard in Orion-Lon, was that your first kill?" he asked. Lorian's stomach churned as he remembered the dying guard's death gurgle.

"Yes, captain."

"I thought so. You, soldier, lay down here." One of the fifteen men came forward and laid upon his back, imitating a sleeping guard.

"If we're lucky, each man has his own tent. If we're not, up to three could be camped within a single tent. The key to victory today is this," he said, holding up a dagger similar to the one he'd handed Lorian moments ago. "We cut the throat of the soldiers sleeping within, keeping them quiet until they're done, then we move to the next man, and so on and so forth."

He handed the blade to Lorian. "Show me how you would cut this man's throat."

"I would plunge it in and pull, I suppose," Lorian replied awkwardly.

"There's your mistake," explained the captain as he retrieved his own dagger from his waist. "When we kill a man in his sleep, we mean to do so quickly, efficiently. Use the blade as it's meant; don't stab, slash. Takes less effort and makes it so there's less spray."

He began to mimic the maneuver on his sleeping soldier. "Start here, near the opposite side of the neck, then pull and press at the same time, digging the edge in, not the point. With your other hand, cover the mouth with some cloth. If you've done it right, his vocal cords will be severed, his carotid artery will be severed, his jugular will be severed, and he should die within thirty seconds. It will still spray, so force the wound away and keep your hands clean; last thing you want is a slippery dagger handle," he finished, his tone clear and concise—void of emotion.

"I understand, captain," affirmed Lorian, his voice cracking from grief and nerves.

"Show me. Practice on him. I want to be sure you understand. Keep it sheathed. We'll be needing this man for the raid," he stated, rousing a grim chuckle from his men.

Lorian bent and, as instructed, grabbed the soldier's mouth with his free hand while dragging the edge of the blade firmly against the soldier's neck, end to end. He was surprised at how natural the movement was to him.

"Very good; that will do. If your hands should get wet, use whatever dry cloth you can to wipe away the blood. Can't fumble the blade on the next man, or the whole thing could go to shit, understood?" the captain asked.

Bending back down to practice a few more times gave Lorian the small boost in courage he believed he needed. The reality of the situation came into focus as he pondered his life as it stood now.

Just months before, he'd been prepping charcoal and oiling tools and blades.

Once Bowers was satisfied, he ordered the men to stay warm as they wouldn't be leaving for a few hours longer. Lorian left for his tent to make ready, grabbing spare cloth for the cold and brutal task to come. Sitting on the cot that had been prepared for him gave him a much-needed opportunity to relax.

He asked Rikard to wake him when it was time to depart and fell asleep unnaturally quickly.

The gentle voice of Rikard soon woke him, a warm hand pressing on his shoulder and rocking back and forth. "My apologies, Your Grace. It seems that the men are prepared to leave."

As reality came spinning back to Lorian, the comfort of his dreams dissolved into a hazy and distant memory. He often pondered the peculiar nature of dreams—how they could transport one to such foreign realms, only to snatch away their memory upon waking, leaving behind stale fragments of events that passed mere moments ago.

"Thank you, handsir," he said as he jumped from his cot, donning his cloth garments and tying an extra rag to his waist belt. He decided to leave the overcoat behind as it made his movements feel stiff and instead settled for a long-sleeved shirt.

Before he could leave the tent, Rikard stopped him and held his hand out. "You mustn't forget this, my lord. You'll be needing it," he said as he handed Lorian the dagger Bowers had given him.

"Thank you, Rikard." Lorian summoned what courage he had and left the tent.

Bowers, Varios, and the soldiers stood idly near where the company entered the small grove, none of them speaking as their minds dwelled on the task to come. Lorian's arrival signaled an unspoken order, and the men began to move toward the Powered Road.

Quietly, they made their way back to the pathway, straddling the edge of the road in case they were approached. Moving in single file, the men pushed toward the enemy encampment.

Less than a mile from their destination, Bowers gave a hand signal, and all the men began to creep slowly into the canopy of the frost-covered trees. Lorian was more thankful than ever to Bowers for training him in the conditions he did. This forest floor was less unsteady than the piles of roots and shrubs that he'd been forced to practice on, making movement easier than he assumed.

He noticed for the first time how his body had adapted to this training. He'd always been strong—the fury of the forge demanded it—but he felt more agile now, and his muscles bulged beneath the thin cloth he wore.

The quietness of the world was eerie. No creature was awake at this hour; most were in deep hibernation until spring came. The moonlight echoed through the frozen leaves above and sent an array of shadows dancing before Lorian, their limbs and shapes changing form as the wind blew.

Before long, the group of makeshift cut-throats approached the perimeter of the enemy encampment. *Finding it was easy enough*, thought Lorian.

The enemy's fire still roared despite the cold that challenged it, and its light gave great detail to the camp.

On the southern end was a series of tables with turned-over kegs and leftover food. The western boundary contained the tents in disorderly rows and columns, each vying for close proximity to the fire and the warmth it provided. On the eastern perimeter were the horses, blanketed and tied off. Adjacent to the horses was the guarded tent that the scouts mentioned earlier.

Bowers gave hand signals to the men, Varios included, and the group moved in coordinated patterns toward the soldiers' tents. Lorian was unsure what the hand signals meant but followed Bowers in close pursuit, as he'd been instructed to do before retiring to his cot.

All men approached their respective tents from the rear, peeling the weak fabric back with care as they entered.

Lorian lost sight of the other men as he and Bowers entered their first tent, the moonlight being their only guide in the dark space. The smell of musk and booze filled Lorian's nostrils as he and the captain entered.

Two guards slept an arm's length apart, their thin blankets and garments the only protection against the elements that raged outside. Bowers gave a tilted nod toward the guard sleeping closest to Lorian, indicating the first victim. Lorian removed his dagger from its sheath, a piece of cloth already prepared in his free hand, and froze.

The drunk soldier in front of him was smiling, the result of a pleasant dream, he thought. Lorian's hands began to tremble, and he was unable to follow through. Thoughts of fleeing crossed his mind. *Maybe they would forgive me*, he thought. *Maybe they could leave and find a better option. Perhaps they could bargain!* he rationalized some more, his ideas becoming less grounded in reality.

He felt a tight grip around his dagger hand as Bowers took control of Lorian's arm.

The captain's face was cold and emotionless. With his free hand, Bowers wrapped the man's mouth in cloth. Then, guiding Lorian's hand, he slit the man's throat, accomplishing all three requirements for a good kill.

Lorian attempted to stop the captain, using all his strength to fight against the pull of the soldier, but Bowers overpowered him.

He felt tears wet his cheeks as the dagger pulled harshly against the soldier's throat, a resistance of flesh and blood that failed to stop the blade. The soldier awoke toward the end of the quick slash and flailed helplessly, his severed trachea inhaling gulps of air and blood. But soon, the man perished, his smile erased and replaced by an expression of surprise and horror.

Bowers systematically moved to the next soldier, cutting his throat and covering his cries with practiced precision. Lorian watched, an emptiness consuming him from the inside. Small struggles of other dying soldiers could be heard from other tents, the gurgling and splattering of blood forming a quiet symphony in Lorian's mind.

Bowers forced Lorian from his trance with a sharp tug of his collar, guiding the powerless bastard to the next tent. *Another two in this one.* With a mindlessness he didn't know he was capable of, he slit the soldier's throat closest to him, an observant captain watching all the while.

One tent after the other, he and Bowers performed their dark deeds, until no men were left alive. *Was it eight or nine?* Lorian counted internally. He had no idea how many men he'd just killed.

Varios and Bowers led the assault further as the remaining men ensured their kills were fully effective, stabbing any who twitched or moved to complete their work.

Lorian watched from behind a tent as his father and the captain made short work of the drunken watchstanders, half of whom were nodding off. *The quietness is the worst part,* he thought. It seemed louder than hammer strikes at first, but not to the ears—to the soul.

Varios and Bowers communicated silently to each other before entering the guarded tent. When they were finished, they raced into its contents, a lifeless guard falling halfway through the fabric entrance after a moment. Then, a scream, piercing and loud.

Both men walked angrily out of the tent, a fumbling woman in garb following them, her hands and feet shackled.

"Child-scholar?" Lorian asked aloud, hoping his spoken words would help make sense of the situation.

Chapter 10: But a Pearl in an Oyster

"In truth, the scholardom was established as a way to remove unwanted folk from public eye. It wasn't until the second age that King Mightus Dinivy fully realized the usefulness of their minds. Using their collective wisdom, he ushered in a time of great advancement yet fear of their wisdom grew roots deep within his heart. To keep them from obtaining power, he forbade them from marriage and from siring children who could one day overthrow the rule of magic."
—Patron-Scholar Godrick, *The Formation of the Scholardom, Vol. V*

The morning sun rose promptly, a blanket of warmth lengthening over the vast hills that stretched before the company. Tarns Knoll was a large swath of land that stretched from the western shores of Centrugard to the eastern hills, with plains and obscure deposits of rock and slate that littered everything in between.

Great rivers carried water from the frost, feeding into the lakes and streams of the more southern lands, the current of water quickening as spring approached and the ice melted. Lorian had heard descriptions of other regions of the world, but the difference between imagination and reality was too great. The air smelled of wet grass and flowers.

Despite the cold that lingered, birds chirped harmoniously through the sprinkle of trees that survived in this area, and the cloudless sky was a light shade of blue, a picture of peace. The wind blew gently about Lorian's face, and when he closed his eyes, he could swear he was home again—the sleeping town of Amphil-Lon below and the crackling of the forge as it sparked to life. His father would call him for breakfast soon—bread and a small chunk of cheese they had purchased at yesterday's market.

Lorian was thankful for the company of the child-scholar in the weeks of travel that inched them ever closer to Tarns Knoll. The memories of their dark and brutal night would ring forever in the annals of his mind, a milestone in his sure descent to nobility, yet having the eccentric woman to keep him occupied in conversation was a breath of fresh air.

Both Lorian and Varios were puzzled to learn how she was captured and why. Varios was furious with her at first, cursing the gods for forcing the two together again. His temper worsened when he learned they shared the same destination, Mainis Fortu being the location of her sect.

Custom stated that lords must provide child-scholars with company and resources when requested; it was a service Varios was reluctant to offer. Lorian took great pleasure in watching Varios complain about the child-scholar, the reluctance to help being outweighed by his duty. The whole interaction made Varios seem more human—or perhaps less noble was the proper way to say it.

Lorian's pleasure was cut short when he was ordered to be the child-scholar's guide and companion for the remainder of the journey. It was a quick way for Varios to release himself from the pain and suffering he found in her company and a way to teach Lorian humility. The bastard was anything but upset at this new task; he rather enjoyed the woman and the frantic way she explained the physics and happenings of the world.

During their travels, Lorian came to know her name: Lo. Child-Scholar Lo, to be precise. She was a native of the Maybarn region, born in a small village called Bayan. Apparently, becoming a child-scholar was an irreversible decision. One was branded upon the skin. A sigil of a quill crossed with a chisel was seared into the back of her neck. Her large locks blocked all but her face, keeping the brand out of sight. Once branded, they could own no land, save what was granted by the crown, hold no political station, and bear no children. When Lorian asked how they could keep adults from bearing children, a sad, knotted expression on Lo's face kept Lorian from inquiring further. He could only imagine.

Lorian was always ready with a question, and Lo always had an answer prepared. The two fed each other endlessly in a loop of knowledge. Apparently, Lo had gotten ahead of them while they slept at the inn. She'd left directly from the mines, and because almost no one refused the request of a child-scholar, she jumped aboard a carriage of ore and tin that was heading toward Travul-Lon, where she was abducted.

The entire scenario seemed preposterous to Lorian. Apparently, the group of ambushers overheard her mention Lord Varios when speaking to the coachman, and when questioned by the group, she talked so long and so ceaselessly that they bound her by the wrists and ankles and locked her up. She said it wasn't the first time this had happened, and that she was usually released within a day or two.

"Imagine my surprise when the lord of House Varios arrived with one hundred men to rescue me!" she had said. "The sect will never believe this!"

Lorian felt like he could speak with her about anything and everything, and she always had an answer ready to entertain him or make him wonder.

"Did you ever learn more about the writing on the mine walls before you left?" he asked.

"Nothing more about the writing, unfortunately. It seems to be a dialect similar to the ancient writings we have that speak of Ragorn and the other heroes of the first age. The letters are different, slightly, and the sentence structure differs, but it's related somehow," she explained as she laughed, a curious look in her brown eyes.

"You know what I've always found troubling?" she continued. "The lack of awareness we have—that our people have. We have stories from thousands of years ago that tell us about Dwurn, Lavel, and other varieties of creatures, yet when we question the possibility that the stories may actually be historical events, we're laughed at. How many centuries does it take to fool man into believing that he walks this earth alone? That the magic some of us wield is specific and unique to us, and that gods and science can't coexist? The things we tell ourselves to keep the great lie alive baffle me, young man."

"What great lie, Lo?" Lorian asked, his curiosity piqued.

"That we are special; that we are alone. Intelligence is a curse as much as it is a gift, young lord. We claim superiority because of our great minds, but even animals are able to accept that there is more to the nature of things."

Lorian pondered this for a great while, the light of the fire they sat around fueling his imagination and wonder. *If gods and Dwurn were real, where are they now?*

As was the established routine, Lorian trained with Bowers in the morning, honing his swordsmanship with new forms and practicing battling. The captain never apologized for taking control of Lorian that night, and he never thought to expect an apology. As grim as the event had been, Lorian was thankful to the soldier. Without his influence, Lorian may have upended the entire operation, causing even more death. *What an odd thing to be thankful for*, he thought. Lorian could remember all nine of the men he killed that night, his memories returning in chilling detail after the fog of battle had cleared from his mind. Ten men so far; ten sons, brothers, and fathers. Lorian felt it was his responsibility to remember them, their cries and their fear.

How else could I atone? For every man he killed, he promised to bring twice as many to salvation, for this was the only way he could justify the deeds in his mind. *Whatever salvation may be.*

The remaining hours of the day were filled with travel, the night with study and the reading of correspondence. His conversations with Lo continued whenever possible. After leaving Orion-Lon, Lorian wondered how the lord was sending his letters; then, one morning, while they were still in the frost, Lorian left his tent to see Varios holding a dove atop his forearm. The bird seemed to ferry messages back and forth, making short work of the vast distance that took men weeks to cross. Despite the hardships they faced in recent days, Varios continued to rule over Amphil-Lon, reporting on coin, goods, and crops that entered and left the city, logging all for the crown. Another invitation came for a ball that Lorian remembered from their first reading of letters together.

"Father," began Lorian, his formal greeting when others may be listening, "it seems someone is insistent that you accept this invitation. Would you like me to read it off?"

"Very well," Varios replied with disinterest. An annoyed look spread about his face.

"Lord Varios, Baron of Amphil-Lon and Arbiter of Justice in the Frost, you are hereby invited to attend the engagement of Princess Elia of House Dinivy to Lord Stilfy of House Titus, heir apparent to the Saltlands. The crown eagerly awaits your attendance." He read it once more within his mind and looked toward his lord. "Seems they're not giving you much choice in the matter."

Varios rolled his exposed eye. "They never do. You shall be a welcome surprise, though."

"I'm going as well?" Lorian reacted in shock.

"You are my son, so you must come. The princess is your cousin, after all. In a way."

A gasp nearly escaped him. "What do you mean, my cousin?"

"Her older brother, Prince Drecard, is my sister's son. When she died, the king remarried the princess's mother. Our presence is more or less mandated."

"You're brother to the king?" asked Lorian again, each reveal being more awe-inspiring than the last.

"By marriage, yes. Nobles tend to marry one another, if that wasn't obvious," he replied sardonically.

"What happened to your sister?" Lorian dared to ask. He would never offer the information in casual conversation, so probing his false father was the only way to get answers.

"Died in childbirth, I'm told. I wasn't there," replied Varios, his tone short and to the point. Lorian decided to let the issue lie, hoping to avoid angering the lord.

After midday, the company was approaching the zenith of a rather large hill. The lands were warm this far east, and the wetness of the melted snow mixed with dirt, the resulting mud tarnishing every hoof and wheel that traversed it. The bright sun above blinded Lorian and kept him from seeing over the hill as the terrain's peak formed an eclipse of sorts. The churning of mud and heavy breathing of Sebastian were soon drowned away by a less familiar noise. In the distance and over the hill beat the many tops of drums. Coordinated marching caused the resounding footfalls of soldiers to echo over the hill and swallow the sounds of Varios' company. Something was coming. Captain Bowers brought the formation to a sudden halt.

"Greymoor flags in the distance! An army approaches!" shouted Bowers as he made for his lord's side.

"Your Grace, the Greymoor army approaches from the east, at least a thousand strong. What are your orders?" Bowers asked, a calmness about him that confused Lorian.

If an army of that size were approaching, shouldn't we flee?

"Approach, as we discussed. Didn't think he'd bring that many," muttered Varios.

As the company marched over the hill and out of the blinding sunlight, an army of soldiers clad in steel and gold appeared before Lorian. Five groups of one hundred footmen marched orderly in step. Rows of archers that stretched wider than the footmen, despite their numbers being less, followed behind. Large groups of cavalry trotted adjacent to the footmen and archers, with one smaller group of about five horsemen leading the resplendent group of warfighters. Lorian was amazed by the beautiful design of the soldiers' armor. The full plate metal was composed mostly of steel, except the trim that outlined the steel in a bright gold set on a black backdrop. Each soldier had a crest ingrained somewhere in their armor—a black bear that stood proudly behind a shield and hammer.

"Don't worry, they're here for us. That would be Lord Greymoor and his golden army. Just a show of force for would-be attackers. I asked him to meet us on the way to his castle, in case we ran into any more trouble. This should allow us safe passage to the Slate Steps," Varios explained as Bowers ordered the company to proceed. "Always has to make a scene, doesn't he?"

Chapter 11: From the Cradle

"The Greymoor line can be traced back to the first age, a testament to the strength and vitality of their magic. Few houses can claim such direct lineage to the first men as House Greymoor, and even fewer can match the regard in which they are held as the most loyal to their king."
—Lord Holbitott Varios, Grandfather of Baron Sam Varios

The Greymoor army made camp a mile from Varios' company, the song of shouted orders and hurried soldiers heard from afar. By the time Varios and his soldiers approached, the Greymoors were already set for camp, and the smell of fresh stew and hot bread filled the air. Black tents with golden lace stood in contrast to the grassy landscape that shone dimly as the waning of the sun was underway. Large tents were erected to house the many soldiers, and an even larger tent was set in the middle: the lord's tent. Stitched into the front flaps of the mighty ebony sheets was the Greymoor emblem, an intimidating crest if Lorian had ever seen one.

Fires flickered to life throughout the camp as Varios entered, torches and cook-sites casting much-needed illumination as the sunlight fled. Varios and his men were met by a handful of servants, who saw to the unloading of his supplies and caring of his horses as he and Lorian were led to Lord Greymoor's massive tent. Before they were brought inside, the flaps flipped open from within and a hulking man emerged, clad in the same brilliant armor as the rest of his men. Lord Greymoor stood well over six feet tall, his long white hair tied into a braid that fell between his shoulder blades. His grizzled features were complemented by deep wrinkles and a beard that fluffed out from his square face. Lord Greymoor held a brazen golden eye paired with a normal light brown eye.

Lorian couldn't help but be taken aback by the lord's approach toward Varios. Despite the man's colossal size, his stride seemed overly aggressive. Lorian tensed, anticipating a collision akin to the force of a carriage. However, just before impact, the brutish noble halted, his expression deadly serious. "Ash-Bringer," Greymoor addressed Lord Varios, his tone matching his rough appearance. An eerie stillness settled over the area, and Lorian feared that swords might be drawn, leading to a deadly confrontation between the two men.

"Hello, Uncle," Varios replied, an uncharacteristically wide smile replacing his emotionless face.

Lord Greymoor let out a hearty laugh, spittle flying from his open mouth as he did. With open arms, the two nobles embraced each other like lifelong friends, the stillness in the air replaced with joy and familiarity.

Greymoor grabbed Varios by the shoulder, his massive armored hands forcing a slap to erupt on contact. "How long has it been, Sam? You've gotten old. Look just like your father, I reckon. What in the gods' names happened to your face? Burn your own eye out with a sneeze?" he asked jovially.

Lord Varios returned another smile and answered with practiced deception. "That's partly why I'm here,

Uncle. I'm sure you've read my letters. Lord Aaron and Magistrate Strawman are restrained in a carriage as we speak. Son of a whore dropped a mountain on me," he replied casually. "No offense, son," Varios added, turning to Lorian.

"Ah, I see," Greymoor said, glancing at Lorian and his familiar eye. "Not even a mountain could stop the Ash-Bringer. Surprised you didn't melt him from the inside out. Lost your edge?"

"Lord Aaron remains unharmed and will remain so until the king decides his fate," Varios said with a serious tone.

"Hmm," grunted Greymoor. "Your letters didn't mention the crime. What has our fragile Lord Aaron done to warrant the king's court?" he asked, an eyebrow raised in interest.

"Let's go into your tent first. We'll need some privacy," said Varios. Lord Greymoor gave a nod of approval and retreated to his tent. Lorian followed Varios in, unsure if he was meant to join.

Lavish furniture and decorations filled the tent. Linens of all sorts covered the walls, and the bearskins layered the floor, which Lorian felt was on the nose a bit. A large desk sat near the back of the tent covered with parchment and letters of all sorts. Lorian noted that the same invitation to Princess Elia's engagement sat unopened beneath a pile of correspondence.

"Private enough?" asked Greymoor.

"He executed a bastard in public, Uncle. His own bastard. Maxwell Night. Boy was only ten. Hung him in front of the gentry and used a magistrate to excuse himself of responsibility," explained Varios, his tone sharp and judgmental.

"Ah. The king's court it is. Bloody fool. Had the nerve to attack you, too? Like a rabbit biting a wolf, stupid man," replied Greymoor under his breath. A concerned look caused his brow to furrow, and he examined Varios in great detail. "Does his father know? Is that who attempted to ambush you in the Frost?"

"I don't believe so. We investigated but found no evidence. Not so much as a letter. Whoever it was covered their tracks well. Most of the men were former military. Couldn't determine the houses, but they all bore the scar of helmet-bite."

"Helmet-bite?" Lorian asked. Both lords turned toward him as if they forgot he had accompanied them. He shifted his feet, the sudden attention making him uncomfortable.

"Older soldiers were issued helms that buckled underneath the chin. They would strap them so tightly that the metal buckle would cut into the flesh, leaving a scar," Varios explained, his eye growing unfocused as if he remembered times past.

"Better a scar on the chin than a head liberated from its neck," laughed Greymoor. "And what of the boy? Fathered a bastard after all?"

"It would appear so. Around the time he was born, I felt a dip in power, but that was also around the time of Stenley, so I thought nothing of it. He recently awakened, and there is no doubt he is mine. I have named him heir, and he will undergo the naming ceremony after we've dealt with Lord Aaron."

"This is wonderful news; the family will be glad that the Varios name will not die with you. Though my sons may be upset. They had hoped to inherit your estate," Greymoor said with glee, as if the thought of upsetting his sons tickled him. "You should visit your mother and tell her. She still cries out for you, between the babbling and incoherent soothsaying," he continued. "Let her meet your boy."

"If there is time. I'm afraid we're on a rather tight schedule. I was going to ask for a ship. Sailing down the coast will take less time and should keep a dagger out of my back," Varios said, as if avoiding the topic entirely.

"You'll have your ship and some men. I'll not take no for an answer. But you will meet with your mother first, boy. I'm not asking," ordered Greymoor, his tone rigid and unyielding.

Lorian could see the effect that the older lord had on Varios. In the limited experience he had with conflict, Varios had been the most powerful person he had met. Even now, with barely any magic to wield, Lorian was sure that Varios could overpower most enemies, yet he obeyed Greymoor without question. Lorian was unsure if it was out of respect for the lord or fear, but he assumed it didn't matter.

"Yes, Uncle. I shall see her," he relented.

"Good. My sister will be overjoyed. Your cousin and his daughter are at Castle Greymoor as well. We shall have a feast when we return and introduce your heir," replied the large lord as he bellowed a few laughs. He pulled a few cups from within the desk, along with a large bottle of wine that smelled of fresh berries, filling them to the brim. "We shall leave at first light, but until then, we shall eat and drink until we piss ourselves!" he roared with unfiltered delight.

***

Lorian's head rang loudly in the morning as they rode toward Castle Greymoor, forcing him to stop and expel his breakfast twice before the hangover began to relent. "How can he drink so much and survive the night?" he asked Varios, whose own head was seemingly swimming from the lingering drink.

"I've been asking that question for forty years. I'll let you know when I discover the answer."

Lorian drank as much water as he could stand, and when he was certain that no vomit would follow, ate bread to fill his uneasy belly. "Why did he call you Ash-Bringer?" asked Lorian. The question had been stuck on his mind all night.

A grim look swallowed Varios' face, and he was quiet for many moments after. "It was a name I earned in the War of Forgorn," he said with words so delicate that Lorian was afraid they'd fall from his mouth and shatter.

"It was a bloody awful conflict," Lord Greymoor added. He brought his horse beside the two, his ebony steed dressed in the same splendid armor as the rest of the Greymoor army. "Decades ago, the lower lands tried to overthrow the royal family. War was inevitable. We pushed them over the Great Sky Bridge and back to Forgorn, their tails tucked firmly between their legs like she-men hiding their cocks. Your father earned the title by immolating any

142

who stood before him. He's a hero," finished Greymoor, a certain pride lingering on his words.

Varios remained emotionless, and Lorian could hear the rubbing of leather as his gloved hands clasped his horse's reins tighter. Lorian decided on a new topic to ease the tension. "Lord Greymoor, why do they say your castle is perched upon the Slate Steps? Surely there aren't actual steps made of slate?"

"The castle sits atop five large cliffs, each taller than the last. The sides of the cliffs are composed of slate. From below, their appearance resembles that of colossal steps, but the reality is that they're just very dangerous cliffs."

"Why build a castle upon something so dangerous?"

"Because we can!" he remarked with a laugh that shook Lorian's eardrums and forced his vertigo to return.

"The Greymoor family settled there long before I was born. We found great swathes of gold within the slate and mined it all. Made us the second richest family, just under House Coin. My ancestors liked the view, I suppose, so they settled. Plus, if it's dangerous to live on, it's dangerous to sack. Many have tried; none have succeeded. That's why you'll hear Castle Greymoor called the Golden Hatch. Hah! A fine name, wouldn't you say?"

By the following morning, the Greymoor company had reached the entrance to the Slate Steps. Nestled at the base of the hills, the cliffs offered a stunning view of the marvel before them. Five towering cliff faces stood closely together, their rich slate surfaces reflecting the morning sun onto the surrounding hills, creating a mesmerizing interplay of colors and light.

From below, the cliffs resembled a grand staircase, as if crafted for giants of ancient lore ascending to the heavens. Atop the tallest cliff perched a black castle, its size diminished by the vastness of its mount. Adorned with gold trim, doors, shutters, and statues, it was a testament to opulence. To Lorian, it was undoubtedly one of the wonders of the world. He knew his father would marvel in awe alongside him if he were here. He would make sure to remember every detail he could and write him soon.

A pathway of slate and stone traced the road ahead, its steep angles and absence of rails or ropes signaling the perilous nature of the journey. As Lorian contemplated the audacity of attempting to besiege or assault the castle, he couldn't help but question the sanity of those who would dare such a feat.

Sacking Castle Greymoor seemed a task fit only for a deity. Lord Greymoor further elucidated the fortress' impregnability, revealing its access to the ocean below via lifts and staircases, ensuring swift resupply from incoming ships and rendering the notion of starving the castle into submission nearly impossible. Moreover, House Greymoor boasted one of the largest fleets on the eastern coast, safeguarding their maritime routes against any threats.

This fortress, Lorian concluded, *is built to withstand any assault.*

The trek to Castle Greymoor was grueling and lengthy, the steepness forcing men to dismount their steeds and pull by hand. Most of the army was left below as their presence in the castle was unneeded. Only Varios, Rikard, and a small handful of guards Bowers selected were to accompany Lord Greymoor and his entourage. For an army, traversing the steps would be an unimaginable task, as the narrow roads would force the ranks to thin and leave them vulnerable to attacks from higher ground. The loose stone and slate below created issues for most horses and made travel via carriage or wagon a fantasy. Truly, this was either the worst or the best place to create an outpost like Castle Greymoor.

By the end of the day, a haggard party of soldiers and servants arrived at the top of the final cliff and stood before the great golden gates of Castle Greymoor. Lord Greymoor, seemingly unfazed from the journey, ordered the large gates to be opened, allowing all to access the castle grounds.

Lorian could now see that perception had played him for a fool. Castle Greymoor was unbelievably large when approached from up close. The castle covered most of the cliff's surface and stretched backward toward the ocean. Great walls surrounded the castle, and even greater structures formed of stone and slate flowed over the edge of the cliff and into the sea below.

A massive steel winch carried goods between the castle and the docks below, giving life to the descriptions provided by Lord Greymoor. Lorian felt breathless and in awe of the splendor before him.

"Go now and rest," instructed Lord Greymoor to Varios and Lorian. "Clean yourselves after you've rested and visit your mother. She's in the western wing of the keep, same room she grew up in," he continued with a widespread grin. "Think I'll go wet my tongue with some wine. Wet my cock, too, if there's time! Hah!" He soon disappeared through the large keep doors.

"Let's get this over with," Varios said as he turned to his servants. "Rikard, get the men some food and water. The gatehouse is on the western end. When you're ready, meet me near my mother's room. I suspect she'll want to see you as well."

Rikard gave the customary bow before proceeding with his assigned task. Varios made for the keep doors with Lorian in tow.

"Father, is your mother sick?" Lorian asked.

"You will call her Grandmother out loud. Keep up pretenses. And yes, she's unwell. Has been for a long while," he admitted, a sigh escaping his lungs. "You're about to learn a very grim lesson, Lorian: What happens when you wield your magics without restraint." His words fell dull and lifeless out of his mouth.

As Lorian ventured deeper into the keep, he was unsurprised to discover that the opulence displayed outside was mirrored within. The interior of Castle Greymoor radiated the same lavishness, a testament to the power and wealth of House Greymoor. Chairs and tables crafted from the finest wood adorned every corner, while paintings and murals depicting ancient battles and long-gone Greymoor ancestors covered the walls.

Thick carpets lined the floors, and an abundance of oil lanterns illuminated the castle; enough to rival the brightness of Amphil-Lon itself. The grand hall mirrored the extravagance of the foyer they had entered, save for the imposing presence of a large brown bear, stuffed and positioned at the center of the room, forever frozen in a fierce roar.

Lorian followed Varios through a set of winding halls and stairs that pushed westward and finally deposited them in front of the doors to his mother's chambers. "Listen to me, disregard what she says. She lost her wits long ago, and if you try and look for meaning in her words, you'll find nothing but dead ends and false prophecies," Varios warned, his gaze never leaving the door in front of him. "Her black eye may frighten you, but don't look away. Let it remind you of the consequences of wielding with reckless abandon."

Rikard soon arrived, and together, the three entered Lady Varios' chambers.

The lady's room was far less lavish than the rest of the castle, with only the necessities present. A large porcelain bath sat in one corner, with a fireplace with a dim flame adjacent to it. Against the wall was a large bed, and a few dressers decorated the perimeter. Lady Varios lay peacefully in her bed, covers drawn to her chest. Sleep had taken her, and despite Lord Varios' warnings, Lorian could not detect anything wrong. All he saw was an old lady peacefully resting in the late afternoon. Lord Varios grabbed a chair that was tucked neatly next to the headboard and set it down, sliding himself as close to the bed as he could.

He grabbed his mother's hand from under the blanket, and after removing his glove, he gently clasped it within his. "I'm here, Mother. Forgive me for waking you from your nap," he whispered.

Lady Varios began to stir, her eyes slowly peeling open as she awoke. Lorian could now see what Varios meant about her eye. A blackness Lorian had never seen outlined her once magical eye, an emerald-colored pupil that appeared bright and lively. Veins that fed into the eye and branched outward from the socket and into her face seemed to undulate with darkness. She then spoke, and her voice cracked from the grogginess of her old age and sickness.

"Oh, my sweet Roger. I was just dreaming of you. Tell Halibatt that supper will be ready soon. That girl spends too much time in the garden."

"No, Mother. It's me, Sam. Father and Halibatt are gone. It's just me."

"Oh, Sam," she said as her eyes brightened with the recognition of her son. "Forgive me; I am not well. Stenley was just asking about you. He wants to know why you don't visit him anymore."

Lord Varios' face pinched in sadness. His eye began to well with tears, and his voice grew shaky. "Stenley is gone, Mother. It's just me."

Lorian stood beside Varios, unsure of what to do. Everything Varios had said about his mother was true. She lived in a time that had either passed long ago or never existed. *Stenley must have been his son. How awful*, Lorian thought, *that visiting his mother would force him to experience these losses over again.*

"No, he waits for you on the other side. He misses you. He told me to tell you and Lorian that he knows the truth. He says that lies can only deceive others for a short while but can deceive the liar forever," she said, her words so eerie that Lorian's hair stood on end.

Lorian wanted to speak but found himself unable, his voice frozen from astonishment and fear. *How does she know my name? If she knows that, does she really see into 'the other side,' whatever that could be? Is this the power of a Wielder of mind magic, or is it the product of overuse and madness?* Lorian's heart began to beat wildly, anxiety and fear consuming him. A hand clasped his shoulder—Rikard's hand. It was as if the handsir knew exactly what Lorian was thinking and swiftly took action to ease his nerves.

"My Lady Harfin," Rikard began as he took the customary bow, rising without approval. "It has been too long. You grow more beautiful with each passing day, and I fear the halls of House Varios wither without your presence to keep them lively."

"Oh Rikard, I have missed your sweet words. You make an old woman blush," she responded with almost youthful glee.

"My words are only as sweet as the flower from which they pull their inspiration, my lady," he spoke, charm and wit thick in his tone. "We have come all this way to introduce you to your grandson, Lorian Night, son of your son, Sam Varios. Your son has named him heir to your great house. Will you do us the honor of introducing yourself, Lord Lorian?" he finished, gesturing a hand at Lorian to begin.

"Of c-course," stuttered Lorian, who was still recovering from his shock. "Grandmother, it is an honor to make your acquaintance. I promise to do right by you and by my father as heir," he finished, hoping the training from Rikard was paying off.

"Yes, Lorian. A bastard. A son. You carry within you a shard of the great mother. How unlucky to bear such a thing. Are you the reason my son doomed himself to die? Are you the reason we shall all *burn*? Why do you want us to burn, bastard? Why do you want us to burn? Why do you want us to burn? Why do you want us to burn?" she screamed so loud the room itself trembled.

Her body sat upright in a snapping motion that was unnatural to her age and to her sickly form. The blackness of her eye grew before Lorian until it consumed most of her face. Her discolored teeth appeared filed to a point, and a laugh echoed in Lorian's mind with a voice deep and guttural.

Rikard screamed for Varios and Lorian to leave the room as he did his best to subdue her and calm the intense fit. Varios left without words, his cheeks wet and his head lowered.

Lorian followed moments after Varios, fearful of what would happen if he stayed.

Chapter 12: A Taste of Eternity

"With great caution should he who wields the gift of magic proceed. To misuse the divine connection to the infinite pool is to invite Gan's wrath and the ebony eye that follows it. Suffer not those who practice restraint, but pity those whose souls are lost to the madness of greed."
—Lord Hector Coin on the eve of his son's death

The rest of the evening was filled with a disconcerting silence between Varios and Lorian. After the visit to Lady Varios' chambers, Varios had retreated to his own chambers to settle and prepare for the night's family feast. Javal, Lord Greymoor's handsir, led Lorian to his room, where he sat in silence until Rikard arrived, his business of calming the bewitched noble finally concluded.

"I'm sure you're shaken, Your Grace. Please try to understand her words are not her own. They fall from the lips of a mind now lost to the chaos of unrefined magic and foresight," the Handsir explained, his tone comforting and gentle.

"Rikard," began Lorian as he sat upon the double-length bed, his eyes never leaving the floorboards, "what she said, that I was going to make everyone . . . burn . . ."

"Think nothing of it, young lord. While she's still plagued with visions of events yet to come, her mind lacks the ability to filter and articulate the flow of information she receives. It's like trying to drink the ocean—

impossible. She sees many things, all of them blended together in whispers and fragments, and none of it should be believed.”

“Her voice. Her face. What was that?” he asked in a shaken tone that wavered in volume. Remembering the echoes of laughter within his mind made his skin crawl and his stomach churn.

“We are unsure. Those plagued with this . . . sickness often experience a variety of symptoms. The Wielders of mind magics begin to decay from within their thoughts. This rot often manifests itself physically. All but her eye shall return to normal before long. Lady Varios had never been strong in controlling her abilities. After a reading, she would often become manic—forgetful and even aggressive as well—which took days to overcome and recover from. After your grandfather passed, there was no one to ensure she rested after a reading or to limit the amount of magic she drew. Eventually, this drove her insane and to the state that you see today.”

“Why wasn’t Father there to protect her, Rikard?”

“I’m afraid they had a falling out of sorts. When your father’s wife, Emelia, was pregnant with your older brother, Lady Varios told your father of a prophecy. Your older brother was meant to die in the womb. His death would start a series of events that would one day save all of Centrugard. Save the entire world. It was your father’s destiny to allow your brother to die; the price of being the chosen one. The price of saving everyone,” replied Rikard, who made his way over to the bed.

He sat next to Lorian, his eyes growing distant from the cruel memories that were resurfacing. “Your father rejected this. He went mad for weeks trying to decipher her visions differently, and when Emelia fell sick, he decided to take matters into his own hands." Tears began to fill Rikard's eyes, the wrinkles in the elderly servant's face deepening. "She went into labor soon after. The physicians were powerless to save the babe, and when the time came to make a decision, a decision to save Emelia by killing the child, he broke. They spoke to each other in private, ordering all servants to leave the birthing chamber. When your father emerged, Emelia was gone, and your brother, Stenley, was swaddled tightly in his arms, alive and well. He had ripped the babe from her womb, severing prophecy and, per your grandmother, dooming us all."

"But I thought that Stenley had passed on?"

Rikard began to stiffen, wiping the fresh tears from his face and correcting his half-wrinkled attire. "He did, Your Grace. Three years later, the boy caught fever. He passed within a day of contracting the sickness. The physician hadn't even arrived yet when he drew his last breath."

Lorian was speechless. Varios never carried himself as a man who had suffered through so much. In every opportunity that existed from then until now, he could have given up. Drank his days away, neglected his duty and his people, but he never did. Lorian cursed himself for the few attempts he made at bringing up the lord's past.

"This is why he never remarried," stated Lorian.

"Yes, why he never tried again," replied Rikard as he tapped Lorian's shoulder and stood from the bed. "Until you, I suppose."

"And what of Grandmothers prophecy?" asked Lorian after making the realization that doom may be ever-approaching.

"Apparently subverted with the late death of Stenley. She never elaborated after. The madness was just beginning to emerge at the time."

Rikard resumed his usual professional demeanor. "Ah, yes. On my way to your chambers, I ran into Handsir Javal. Your father requested you be taken to the library before dinner tonight and tested with the attuning crystal. Please follow me, and we can meet him there with a bit of time to spare."

Excitement once again filled Lorian's heart as he contemplated the prospect of Wielding magic.

His thoughts raced as he considered which school he might belong to. Fire magic would undoubtedly be useful, he mused, but so too would the ability to leap great distances. Perhaps body magic would suit him best, though; elements like earth or water might be more compatible with his unknown attributes.

The possibilities seemed endless. However, one thing was certain: Mind Magic would be his last choice. The fear of succumbing to madness, like his false grandmother, made him fervently hope any determining force would prioritize other options.

Lorian followed Rikard through the wealth-lined walls of Castle Greymoor, and, after quite the journey, they entered the grand library which held the attunement crystal. Lorian was never big on reading—due to not having money for books—but always admired knowledge and those who pursued it. Now, as a noble, his own access to literature would grant him opportunity to explore worlds unknown to him before.

The library unfolded before Lorian as a magnificent expanse, its walls towering with shelves upon shelves of books and scrolls. The vastness of the room was awe-inspiring, each shelf brimming with parchment and leather-bound volumes. At one end, a grand fireplace carved from stone roared with warmth, casting flickering shadows across the space. Opposite the flames, a set of fine chairs with ottomans beckoned, inviting visitors to relax in their embrace.

Amidst this scholarly haven sat a young woman who appeared to be in her mid to late twenties by Lorian's estimation. She was nestled comfortably in one of the armchairs, engrossed in a thick brown leather book which seemed as weighty as an ingot. Her eyes moved swiftly across the pages with a fervent intensity. She wore a striking black dress adorned with golden lace, accentuating her slender figure. The intricate braids of her white collar added a touch of elegance to her attire, while the billowing skirt flowed gracefully around her feet.

A silver ornament enhanced with a large green gem dressed her perfectly curled autumn hair. Despite her seriousness, her beauty was undeniable, leaving Lorian hesitant to approach.

"Good evening, Lady Greymoor," announced Handsir Rikard with a customary bow. "May I present Lord Lorian Night of House Varios."

Lady Greymoor started slightly, engrossed as she was in her book and unaware of their arrival.

"Oh, forgive me, Handsir. I wasn't paying attention. You may rise," she replied as she stood from her chair and closed her book, leaving it atop a small table adjacent to her. "I am Lady Jane Greymoor of House Greymoor. A pleasure to greet you, my lord."

"Hello," spoke Lorian, unsure of what to say next. "I'm Lorian."

"Yes, so I've just discovered," she said with amusement in her voice and a nod to Rikard. "Lord Varios asked me to show you the attunement crystal in his stead. He had matters to discuss with Grandfather and won't be free until supper."

"Then I shall leave you both to your business," finished Rikard as he left the great library.

Lorian could see her features more clearly now that the ambient light illuminated her. Her rosy cheeks framed a hazel eye and a bright emerald eye, outshining even the gem in her hair ornament. A small, jagged scar adorned her cheek, concealed from Lorian's view while she was seated; it stretched from her mid-jaw line to her ear. Despite the imperfection, Lorian found himself taken aback by her beauty.

Lorian had never held much appeal for women, being a poor bastard. His only attempt at visiting a brothel ended in rejection, as the working girls had known his mother and felt obliged to protect him from such sins.

Between work and financial constraints, finding a wife was never a priority. As a blacksmith on the outskirts of Amphil-Lon, opportunities to meet women were scarce.

Feln was one of the few women he interacted with regularly, but the fear of ruining their friendship swiftly silenced any thoughts of romance. Moreover, Feln hailed from a wealthier family, making any potential relationship unlikely to gain her father's approval, let alone lead to marriage.

Now, as a noble, Lorian dared to hope for a different life. All he could do was cling to hope.

"Uh, my lady," Lorian said as he bowed.

"Not very accustomed to addressing other nobles, are you? Is it true you're a bastard?" she asked, the bluntness of the question reminding Lorian of what he truly was. Even if he looked the part of a noble, he knew he'd be answering this question for the remainder of his life. Separate from the commoners and separate from nobility, because of a mistake he played no part in.

"It is true, my lady."

"How fascinating!" she said with glee. "I've never met a bastard of noble birth. Your life must be full of so much adventure! Have you been fighting for your right to rule House Varios, or did your father hide you from public eye until you were ready? Oh, the stories you must have!"

Lorian was dumbfounded at her comments. *How can someone look at my life and think it's full of adventure and hard-won battles*? Was she so far removed from reality she sees fantasy in anything not ordinary to her? What a comfortable life she must have to allow thoughts like these to fill her mind. "There was nothing fascinating about it. It was hard. I was always spat at, beaten at times. People used to look at me like I was a rat who carried a disease called misfortune," he replied bluntly.

Her eyes shifted around in shame. "Oh, I'm sorry. I thought—"

"What? A bastard's life would be fun? I'm sorry to say, my lady, it is less than what you may believe to be an adventurous life. My mother was a whore, and my father visited a brothel. There's your story in one sentence," Lorian finished, his voice angrier than he meant it to be.

"I'm sorry, Lord Night," she said with shame on her face.

Lorian felt terrible for having cut into the girl so suddenly. It wasn't her fault she saw excitement in his life. He had no idea what real nobility was like, and for all he knew, she was kept locked away in rooms like this all the time, forced to be called upon when etiquette demanded it. He felt like a fool.

"No, my lady. I'm the one who should apologize. You meant well. Please forgive me."

She nodded in approval, and a still moment fell between them.

"What were you reading, if I may ask?" Lorian asked in hopes to lighten the mood.

"Oh, it's a story about creatures called dragons that used to rule the skies in Centrugard. This was written by Father-Scholar Maverick over three centuries ago, and he stated evidence of these beasts are everywhere and prove their existence! Did you know some of them grew as small as dogs while others were the size of mountains? Isn't it a wondrous concept?" she gushed with enough enthusiasm to make Lorian hope she wasn't overly offended by his harsh words earlier.

"How is such a thing even possible? Wouldn't their bones be larger than a building? Even birds can only carry so much before falling. Wouldn't they drop from the sky?"

Lorian asked in return. The engagement in their conversation seemed to elate her. *Who knows how long it's been since anyone humored her words and was interested to hear more.* "We actually have a Child-Scholar with us at the moment. Her name is Lo. If you have the time later, you should pay her a visit. Bet she'd love to pick your brain."

"How magnificent! Your presence has made my stay at Castle Greymoor worth it! Visiting Grandfather can be boring, but it shouldn't be a concern now that you're here," she said with giddiness and a bright smile that made Lorian's heart skip. Her elation about things others would consider dull or mundane made her a joy to be around. *Not too dissimilar to Lo*, Lorian thought.

"I shall inform her of your interest, Lady Jane."

"Oh! Your attunement. We mustn't forget to perform it before supper. Your father mentioned your emergence happened recently? How interesting, I don't believe I've ever heard of someone emerging so late in life. Is this why you brought a Child-Scholar with you, to study your emergence?"

"No, that's another story entirely. My father wishes to investigate my emergence once our business in the capital is concluded. I'm afraid other matters take priority at the moment. The truth is, I know very little about magic. Even less about wielding it. I don't know what questions I should have or where to begin looking."

"Well, the first step is using the crystal. After we determine your school, we can decide on the best course of action for helping you learn to wield properly."

"What school do you belong to?" Lorian asked with eagerness.

"I belong to the school of soul magics. Though most of our family, the Greymoors, belong to the body magics, like Grandfather. They wield earth as their element."

"What does it mean, exactly? I saw my father shoot flames from his hands. Does the same thing happen with stone?"

"It can, but not always. Some of us are proficient at manipulating the earth around us, some better with manifesting earth, like your father and fire. Grandfather uses his magic to support his body."

"What do you mean, support his body?" inquired Lorian, who was hasty to learn as much as possible.

"As we sire children, our magic wanes. Grandfather has two sons who in turn have their own children. Our magic is split among many people, making it weaker than most. Grandfather is the oldest and feels the loss of magic the hardest. Per my father, when Grandfather was young, he could lift entire slabs of stone and earth above his head. He could make the ground beneath your feet tremble, and he even swears he saw Grandfather kick a boulder clean through a wall once," she said with delight. Her face became sour after a moment, as if she remembered something unsettling. "And so, when Grandfather's magic weakened to a point where he could no longer wield it without great strain, he devised a new method. Within his armor he's placed small amounts of lightweight earth. When he needs to move quickly or swing something heavy, he uses his magic to aid him. By moving the earth within his armor he's able to supplement his strength and speed, to a degree. It's brilliant, isn't it?" she ended, her face turning bright once more.

"That's amazing! I never knew Lord Greymoor was so adept."

"Yes, he's a marvel compared to the rest of us. Are you ready to begin your attunement?" Lorian gave an approving smile, and together they made for the far end of the library.

Set into the wall and surrounded by bookcases was a large cupboard with two walnut doors that swung outward. Lorian watched as Lady Jane ascended the short few steps to the cupboard and opened the doors, revealing a small spherical crystal that was mounted to the cupboard by a claw bracket.

Small metallic handles stood on either side of the crystal, and a stool was tucked within the empty space below.

"Sit upon the stool and grab both handles. Once you're comfortable, peer into the crystal and pour your magic into the sphere. Once enough of your magic has entered the attunement crystal, your school of magic will be revealed."

Lorian apprehensively approached the crystal. His former eagerness began to dwindle as anxiety and fear blossomed forth. He began to wonder if it would hurt, or if the sphere would grow too hot and erupt before him. Perhaps the handles would come to life and dig themselves into his hands while the crystal drained him of life.

He was a Wielder by chance; by accident, not blood. And he was much older than he ought to be for this test. The outcome may be violent or chaotic in some fashion. He dared not let his imagination run any further than he already allowed it.

With a large inhale of air, he straightened his spine and tightened his core. It was time to be brave. He approached the stool and sat, grabbing both handles and focusing all his will and energy at the translucent sphere before him.

"Hmm, that's odd," Lady Jane said. "Usually, it would glow, or fire would ignite within. Sometimes it would get wet if you're more aligned with water," she continued as she rubbed the sphere, checking for liquid. "No, dry as a bone."

"Have I broken it?" Lorian asked, a tinge of worry beginning in his voice.

"No, I just tried it earlier myself. Worked fine. Maybe if we turn the sphere. . ." she said before a violent gale that blew through the library cut her off.

Winds tore books from their shelves, parchment and scrolls shredding into bits amidst the cascading vortex within the great library. Fire surged from the crystal, growing larger by the second as the vortex fed its fury. Beneath their feet, Castle Greymoor trembled, the earth quaking with a force that threatened to split the keep asunder. A blinding light surged forth from the sphere only to be swallowed by darkness. Amidst the chaos, a soft dew descended, calming the tumultuous air. Lorian's fear was second only to his excitement as the magic he had summoned shifted throughout the room.

A stray bolt of lightning pierced the ceiling, showering the room with shards of wood, slate, and gold, peppering the vast collection of literature before them.

Lorian and Lady Jane were sent crashing to the floor below.

Chapter 13: A Shadow Fell Silently

"For centuries, the ruling class of Centrugard has upheld a sacred pact, valuing internal harmony above all else. This agreement has preserved the kingdom through its most tumultuous eras. Yet, it has also sown seeds of discord, creating rifts between those who govern and those who are governed."
—Child-Scholar Kragen, *Political Historiography of Centrugard, Vol. XIII*

Lord Varios and Lord Greymoor descended the black steps of the castle dungeon. During the short visit that Sam Varios had with his mother, his uncle had taken the liberty of moving Lord Aaron and Magistrate Strawman to their own personal cells for safekeeping. In the long days since Orion-Lon, Sam had never taken the time to visit with or speak to either of his prisoners.

The dungeon was a dark and humid hellscape compared to the rest of the castle. The winding stairs from the keep terminated at the southern wall of the dungeon, feeding visitors into a long corridor that housed the cells. Each cell was a small, windowless room locked tightly by large steel doors. Each door had two slits: one for handing food through and the other for checking on the prisoners within. If the guard who stood watch was feeling generous, they'd leave the peeping slit open and allow some light to shine through.

Lord Aaron and the magistrate were kept in the last two cells toward the back of the corridor. Their doors were left open, and a temporary set of steel bars were mounted to allow them more luxury than most.

Sam noticed that a few cells were currently holding other prisoners of unknown crimes and decided to keep his mouth shut on the subject lest his uncle feel the need to relocate him as well. The magistrate quickly fell asleep in a makeshift bed of straw, his once glorious robes now riddled with dirt and torn in several places.

Serves him right.

Lord Aaron was awake and alert when Sam and Lord Greymoor approached. Sam could see someone had placed a book in front of him on the ground, a guard turning the page when Lord Aaron had read through the material.

"Clever way to keep him from imbuing anything, those cuffs," commented Lord Greymoor. The old noble was referring to the metallic shackles keeping Lord Aaron's hands restrained behind his back. A piece of wood was wedged between each cuff so that if the lord attempted to grab an object, the wood would collide first.

Sam muttered under his breath, "No way to escape this time."

"How did you manage to catch the slithery cunt?" Greymoor asked.

"I didn't. Captain Bowers, my company commander, caught him after he overused his magic. Found him just outside the entrance to the mines on the second ring. Lorian saw him jump twice within a few moments of each other. Must've drained his energy," Sam replied, remembering the roof of the mine collapsing upon him. "I would have died if Lorian didn't pull me free that day."

"Hah! Jumped twice and you ran out of energy, Lord Aaron? I remember your father jumping a full mile and still having enough in him to go again. Daddy must be disappointed, no?" taunted Greymoor.

Lord Aaron looked up from his book long enough to cast a smirk at the old noble. "Funny you should mention my father. Can't imagine how he'll feel knowing you kept his only son locked away like a dog."

Lord Greymoor let out an obnoxious laugh after hearing Aaron speak. "Can't imagine how the king'll feel after learning that you broke his law and murdered your own son," he spat.

Lord Aaron's face scrunched sourly in a mixture of anger and sadness.

"To top it off, you tried to kill his son's uncle, an arbiter of justice for your city. Tell me, boy. Where were you planning to run ? All of Centrugard would have been looking for you. You'll face punishment much worse than you think when we get to the capital. Doesn't matter how many friends your father has in that court; I'll flog you myself if I have to," roared the giant man. Spittle and unchewed food flew from his mouth as his rage intensified.

Sam watched as Lord Aaron shrunk in fear before Greymoor. *Who could blame him?* Sam knew his uncle was a man you didn't catch yourself on the wrong side of. They used to call him the stone giant for a reason. Memories of war plagued Sam as battlefields of his past resurfaced, blood and ash suffocating him.

"By the natural gods, Father. Is that Lord Aaron of Orion-Lon?" A face rich with familiarity emerged from behind the assembled nobles. It belonged to a man who stood a foot shorter than the imposing figure of Lord Greymoor.

His garments mirrored those of the stone giant, catching the flickering light of the torches. Sam's gaze sharpened with recognition—it was his second cousin and Lord Greymoor's firstborn son, Bolin Greymoor. Though he shared the same chiseled jawline as his father and the golden gleam in his eyes, Bolin possessed a charm that softened the brute force often associated with their family lineage.

"Good day, cousin," started Sam. "Yes, this is Lord Aaron. He's my prisoner until I can have him judged at the royal court in Mainis Fortu."

"What crimes does he stand accused of?" asked Bolin, his tone full of concern.

"Accused? Nothing. He's guilty of breaking royal law meant to ensure the protection of bastard children sired by nobility." Varios watched as Lord Aaron averted his gaze.

"Is that all?" asked Bolin. "You've jailed the man like an animal for this? They're just bastards, cousin. That law is as new as the shit I took before luncheon."

Sam's face, while calm and emotionless, carried the weight of his anger, causing Bolin to look away from the one-eyed lord.

"He is guilty of pedicide, the killing of a child, and will be judged accordingly. He is also guilty of attempting to circumvent the rightful line of succession and the attempted murder of a noble," Sam finished as he gestured a finger at his covered face.

"I see. Does his father know? I just saw him but a month ago near Twilanon, in Lunarson. Should I send a letter?"

Lord Greymoor roared in anger at the mention of Lord Aaron's father being notified. He approached his son with an inflated chest and a blink-less stare. "You'll do no such thing. Not if you wish to stay heir to House Greymoor. I'll tell Lord Charles Aaron myself after I strip the skin from his son's back with my whip. He'll understand. The king's laws are final, aren't they, boy?" he asked his son rhetorically.

"Yes, Father. The king's laws are concrete and infallible. If you'll excuse me," replied Bolin with disdain as he hurriedly strode away.

Lord Greymoor looked on as his son ascended the dungeon stairs toward the keep. "That damned boy has never had an inkling of sense," he said. "Takes after his mother, gods rest her naïve soul. It's a right shame, Sam, those damn laws of succession. My house will be commanded by that twit of a boy instead of his brother one day."

Sam was aware of Lord Greymoor's strained relationship with his heir, but the degree of disdain apparent in his uncle's demeanor caught him off-guard. Not many noblemen would dare speak so bluntly in the presence of their peers, but Lord Greymoor defied convention at every turn. Just as he was unapologetically imposing in stature, his words lacked the finesse expected of a skilled diplomat. While this forthrightness might serve him well on the battlefield, it posed a significant challenge in the realm of politics, where subtlety and tact were prized virtues.

"Give him more credit, Uncle. He didn't experience the horrors of the Great War. His youth was sheltered, filled with peace, as every man deserves," Sam interjected, attempting to defend his cousin. Yet, he couldn't deny the truth in his uncle's words. Bolin's innocence bordered on foolishness at times.

He was a man who habitually chose the path of least resistance, regardless of the consequences. Sam vividly recalled a childhood incident: Bolin had once destroyed a bust of their great-grandfather, Lord Sirus Greymoor, and pinned the blame on a servant girl who suffered severe punishment for a crime she hadn't committed.

It wasn't until years later, over a round of ale, that Bolin confessed to the deceit without a hint of remorse. From that moment on, Sam had maintained a wary distance from his cousin.

"That child would choke on his own spit if no one was around to tilt his head forward. His brother, on the other hand—a fine lad. Shame my seed couldn't put him first, eh? Hah!" roared the giant noble, his white beard flaring outward as his smile widened.

"Back to business, I suppose. Hope you enjoy your stay at Castle Greymoor, Lord Aaron. I can't imagine the capital being more accommodating than I am. Fair thee well, you fucking traitor," barked Lord Greymoor as he spat at the chained noble.

Sam had nothing to add; simply seeing Aaron made him sick. How a father could arrange the execution of his own child was beyond him. "You're a monster," he muttered as he strode away.

"Oh, I'm the monster?" replied Aaron as he and Lord Greymoor made for the stairs, "Sam Varios the Ash-Bringer thinks me a monster? How many men, women, and children died by your hand, my lord? Is it less evil when commanded? If I'm a monster, then you're in good company, *ASH-BRINGER!*"

Sam hated that damned title. 'Ash-Bringer' hung around his neck like an anchor, an indelible mark that refused to fade. Throughout the Great War, Sam had been entrenched on the front lines, leading his men through a landscape ravaged by conflict. He had witnessed the horrors of battle firsthand, leaving a trail of devastation in his wake. While the act of burning villages to the ground came with a twisted ease, the haunting echoes of the citizens' screams lingered long after the flames had died.

Sam fought to suppress the haunting cries of his past victims, the wails of the innocent threatening to resurface with every recollection of his sins. He was lost in his reverie, but a figure in the last cell before the stairs leading to the keep jolted him back to the present. Lord Greymoor had already departed, leaving Sam momentarily alone.

Through the narrow opening of the cell door, a pair of dull black eyes met his gaze; they were clouded with the unmistakable haze of blindness. The man's face was a patchwork of smooth skin and grotesque scars, a testament to a violent past.

"Is it the Ash-Bringer's voice I hear?" he hissed, his words carrying an eerie chill.

"Who are you?" Sam asked, the man's voice familiar but strangely foreign.

"It is I, my lord. Do you not remember? You gifted me with the blessing of sightlessness on the fields of Forgorn. For this, you have my thanks," he replied, his words crawling from his mouth like a serpent preparing to lunge.

Sam felt a twist within his stomach. Visions of fire and death plagued him as if memories long forgotten resurfaced, only to be suffocated once more into nothingness. "Speak your name!" he demanded, his face growing red from anger.

"I am no one. My name has been offered as a gift to he who anguishes, same as your memories of me. Lord Ash-Bringer, your time draws near. The ancient ones whisper in my ears and give me sight beyond that of the common man. I shall tell you how to recover what was taken from you," said the mysterious prisoner, who receded back into the shadows of his cell. "The church awaits your answer. Follow the stained lamps." Silence hung in the air between them.

"Who are you?" Sam shouted, his fists banging harshly on the steel door. "Guard!" he yelled, alerting one of the two guards standing watch over Lord Aaron and the magistrate. "Open this cell!"

The guard fumbled a ring of keys that hung from his waist and ran toward the lord. He opened the heavy door, the hinges whining loudly in protest, revealing an empty cell.

"Your Grace?" asked the guard in confusion.

Sam felt cold. *Is this a vision? A hallucination? But how? He is no noble. His eyes would have revealed the truth,* he wondered as his thoughts raced rapidly through his head, desperate to find an answer.

Before sense could be made of the situation, the ground beneath him rumbled angrily. The castle swayed with great strain. Sam's feet found it difficult to stay perched on the moist stone below, and he fell harshly to the ground. Dust and light debris fell from the ceiling above as the sound of thunder rang in his ears. A sharp sensation in Sam's mind—a feeling he hadn't experienced since his son's birth—gave him all the answers he needed.

"Lorian," he said with heavy concern.

Chapter 14: A New Way to Wield

"Mind, body, and soul. Together, these three facets of magic create the whole of the spirit. Through centuries of diligent study, we have come to understand these schools of magic and what distinguishes them."
—Lady Selena Bounett, Professor of Magical Physiology at the College of Mainis Fortu

Lorian's body was sprawled awkwardly on the library floor, the smell of burned parchment and seared wood filled his nose. The lingering ring of thunder screeched in his head, and the dust and ash in the air mixed with the dew falling from the ceiling, coating him in soot.

His vision faded at first, clearing only when he was able to stand on his feet and wipe the debris from his face. A hum of energy resounded in the air, and a tingling sensation pulled at his skin and hair.

He took a moment to examine himself for injury and was surprised to see small jolts of electricity dancing around his limbs, each bolt jumping from one spot to the next and disappearing into his body. Small sparks of fire jutted between the electricity, and a sphere of air circled gently around him, clearing the smoke and dust.

"What have you done, you bastard?" screamed Lord Greymoor from the library entrance. "Where is my granddaughter?" he continued as he approached Lorian with red rage painted on his wide face.

"I'm here, Your Grace," said Jane as she coughed through the polluted air.

"Oh, my sweet girl," Lord Greymoor said in a gentle tone that contradicted his personality. "Are you all right, my dear?" He began to inspect her for wounds.

While her hair was disheveled and her dress was tattered, she seemed okay. Jane was lucky enough to be standing in such a way that the blast of lightning missed her. The concussive force threw her and Lorian backward, but she was able to avoid most of the damage by rolling away. Lorian was deeply relieved to see her safe as well, a consideration he regretfully didn't have until his senses returned to him.

"Lorian, what has become of you?" asked Lord Varios, who had entered the room after Lord Greymoor. Varios watched as the hum of magical power enveloping Lorian slowly faded until there was no trace of it left to see. In all his years, Lord Varios had never seen such an intricate mixing of magics. He was as fascinated by his false son as he was terrified. *What happened here?* he wondered. And why had he felt Lorian's first wielding?

"I'll kill him if he hurt you, Jane. Explain what happened before I wring the life from him!" Lord Greymoor exclaimed.

"Grandfather, please. It wasn't Lorian's fault. When he touched the crystal, a torrent of magic poured forth like nothing I've ever seen. It destroyed the library, but it wasn't his doing," she said pleadingly.

"This makes no sense," started Lord Greymoor. "The attunement process is supposed to be controlled, revealing one's school of magic without all this chaos. Are you telling me he's so powerful he shattered the crystal just by using it?"

Lorian quickly turned around to inspect the remnants of the cupboard. Shattered wood and bits of crystal were embedded in anything soft enough to receive them. "I'm . . . I'm sorry, Your Grace," said Lorian, his senses still mangled and unsteady.

The stone giant's eyes bulged angrily at Lorian, the seriousness of the danger he faced only now revealing itself. Lord Greymoor approached him—a mountain towering over a scared child—and embraced him with both hands. "Leave it to my own family to sire a legend in the making! Hah! Javal! Prepare a feast for us unlike any Castle Greymoor has ever seen! Tonight, we shall drink and make merry until our bellies are full of meat and our trousers are full of piss!"

The old noble was ecstatic in a way that frightened Lorian more than his anger. He practically sang with glee as he grabbed Jane and left with Javal, who had been waiting patiently outside the library, to make preparations for tonight's feast. Varios watched from the other side of the room while Lorian stood frozen in thought. Varios was unsure of what the young bastard was thinking but knew that whatever questions he may have, the answers wouldn't be found here. Varios needed to expedite their journey to the capital.

"Lorian, come to your senses. Let's get you cleaned up and ready for supper. I'll walk you to your room," offered Varios.

Together, they proceeded to leave the great library and head to Lorian's bed chambers, where Handsir Rikard was already waiting. The attentive servant helped Lorian out of his dirty garments and into fresh ones while Varios sat at a small desk within the room, his thoughts scrambled and messy.

"What did it feel like?" Varios asked aloud. "All of that power, I mean. When we walked in, you were covered in ambient magic. I've never seen it manifest like that before. So many elements." He spoke as if his thoughts began to wade into his words.

"It hurt a little. I was scared," replied Lorian. The innocence in his voice made Varios' heart drop. Flashbacks to his son Stenley began to populate his mind. A small boy falling onto the hard stone floor of his estate, his knee bleeding. Faint whimpers and two small arms reaching out to him for comfort. "I'm sorry," began Varios ,as he tried to steady his voice. "Are you all right? I should have been there."

Rikard took the opportunity to leave father and son alone. Any burning questions or comments would have to hold steady at the tip of his tongue for a better moment to release them.

"When this began all those weeks ago, I was unsure of a great many things. I still am. We may never uncover the secrets of what happened in the mines, so planning forward is all that can be done at the moment. I meant it when I said you're to be the successor of my house. I have no heir, Lorian. My son left this world long ago, and his absence has haunted my thoughts ever since. I don't know what's happening to you or if it can be stopped or controlled, but I'm on your side," he said as a stream of tears rolled down from his uncovered eye. The lord turned his head to avoid being seen in such a weak state, but Lorian had already seen it.

Lorian walked over to his false father and placed a hand firmly on his shoulder, a weight of tension removing itself from the room. Lorian would never forget his real father, a man who gave his time and love to raise him alone. Nothing Lorian could ever do would be enough to repay him—though coin would come his way whenever Lorian was able to send it—but Lorian had begun to care for Lord Varios. It was something he never could have expected.

Nobles aren't supposed to be so . . . human, Lorian thought. Certainly, the other nobles he'd met had lived up to their egotistical and cruel reputation, but Lord Varios, Jane, and even the overly aggressive Lord Greymoor each had redeeming qualities that made Lorian feel as if they, too, were just victims of fate.

He knew his anger at classism and those who abused their power would never subside, but he had begun to learn that good people existed in this world too.

"Thank you, Father. If there are answers to this mystery, we'll find them together. Until then, I'll do what I can to make House Varios— To make you proud. On this I swear."

Lord Varios grabbed Lorian's hand in return, squeezing it with a desperation known only by those who have allowed themselves to be lonely for too long. Then, he spoke. "Come, supper should be ready. Time to meet the rest of House Greymoor. We leave in the morning, so rest tonight while you have the chance. Tomorrow, we'll practice your wielding when we've set sail."

Lorian and Varios followed Rikard to the dining hall—which was in the easternmost section of the keep—and were greeted with more food than Lorian had ever seen.

Dishes of all varieties covered a long rectangular table. Salted meats such as beef, chicken, pheasant, and more decorated the silver serving plates on the linen-covered surface.

Each meat was accompanied by a set of dressings that complimented the food in ways that Lorian could never understand. Bread and cheese were spread throughout, with wedges of the thick dairy coming in all shapes, sizes, and colors. Mounds of fruit filled in any space between the entrees and acted as samplings for when a guest would tire of savory meat.

Great braziers illuminated the large dining area and forced a mural of gorgeous constellations onto the ceiling, as the firelight sent brilliant reflections off the gold that furnished the room. Slitted windows in the walls gave the room a slight pleasant draft, considering the heat from the food that would be unable to abate otherwise.

Lord Greymoor sat at the head of the table, opposite the entryway. To his left was Jane, and to his right was a lord that Lorian had yet to meet.

Lorian thought that despite the great sea of food before him, the only sight he was able to focus on was Lady Jane.

"There's the man of the hour!" bellowed Lord Greymoor as he ravenously inhaled a leg of mutton. "Take your seat and dig in! We'll all need to be well-fed before we embark on tomorrow's journey, hah!" he continued, grabbing a second leg and shamelessly helping himself.

Lorian took his seat next to Jane, and Varios took his next to his second cousin, Bolin. "What do you mean, 'we'?" asked Varios, a concerned look on his face.

"Didn't know you lost your hearing along with your eye," Lord Greymoor said sarcastically. "We mean to travel with you. I meant it when I said I'd have Aaron's hide myself, with the king's permission, of course. And our Lady Jane here wishes to attend the princess's engagement ball. Bolin will stay here and keep watch over the Golden Hatch, won't you, my boy?" asked the stone giant with an authoritative tone that made it more of a statement than a request.

"As you wish, Father," Bolin replied respectfully.

Lord Bolin Greymoor eyed Lorian from across the table, a familiar look that made him remember the cold glares he would receive from people when they discovered what he was.

Lorian stared back, daring the Greymoor heir to speak the insults that his eyes sang. Now that he was a noble and heir to a great house, Lorian had come to the decision that no man would ever treat him without dignity or respect again.

"It's nice to meet you, Lorian Night," spoke Bolin with a harsh pause on his last name. "I'm told that the tremor earlier was thanks to you. You would be wise not to involve my daughter in anything so dangerous in the future. Am I understood, Lord Night?" he continued with another pause on Lorian's last name.

"Oh, be quiet, you blathering twat," retorted Lord Greymoor with a mouth full of something creamy that rolled down his mouth and into his white beard. "This man's name will pass the lips of every lord, lady, and gentleman worth his salt in the coming days. You'd do well to treat him as such. On another note, Jane isn't promised to anyone yet, is she?"

Bolin's face went sour as he worked through the insinuation. A redness appeared on his face, and spit began to froth at the corners of his mouth as anger overtook him. "I'll not have a bastard wed to my daughter!" he screamed in rage. Lorian was too shocked to receive the insult, his mind focusing on Lady Jane instead.

A disturbing calmness overcame Lord Greymoor. The giant noble set aside the plate of food that he had been charging through and stood ever so slowly. "If you wish to challenge me for control of House Greymoor, you need only ask."

A quiet fell over Bolin, and his face drained of blood as terror overcame him. "Father, I meant only to speak on—"

"On what?" Lord Greymoor interrupted. "As lord of this house, my word is law. If you challenge my words, you challenge my authority. Do you wish to formally challenge my authority, Bolin?" growled the giant.

"No, Father," Bolin replied with shame on his face.

Varios and Jane remained quiet and still throughout the encounter, as if their words or actions would cause the very castle to crumble. Lorian assumed that such a skirmish was to remain isolated between them, and any outside interference or words would only shame them.

Noble customs are strange and unsettling at times, Lorian thought. *If these two are to come to blows now, should we interfere? Or would that make me an immediate target as well?* Lorian didn't know Lord Bolin well, their short interaction leaving a poor image of the man in his mind, but he wondered how a father could speak to his son in such a way.

There must be some awful history between them for an argument to come to this.

"Good," Lord Greymoor began. "Then it's settled. Jane shall marry Lorian. Any opposition from you, Ash-Bringer?"

Lorian's face ignited in shock. Surely Varios would decline. How could he marry someone he'd just met, and how would she feel about this?

"None here, Uncle. It's a fabulous idea. We'll make the arrangements after the princess's engagement party. Wouldn't want to steal the attention from her, now, would we?" Varios said, to Lorian's surprise.

Lorian was about to speak in protest until Varios pierced him with his eye, a clear sign to keep his mouth shut, and he obliged. Looking at Jane gave him no indication of her feelings; her face was still and emotionless, as it had been throughout her family's squabble.

Lorian had never been with a woman, and now he was meant to be a husband. Throughout the dangers faced so far, this conflict was the one that scared him the most.

Lord Bolin could do nothing but stare helplessly at his plate, his imagination surely running wild with words he wished he was brave enough to say.

"Aye, you're right about that. Can't have the king upset with us. I'll have letters prepared and sent a week after the event. We can finally join houses once again—wonderful! Hah!" he announced as he sat down and returned to his feasting and drinking.

The others joined in shortly after, and after supper had ended, Lorian and Varios returned to their respective chambers without so much as an explanation or gripe.

Chapter 15: Deep Are the Sounds of the Ocean

"The Theory of Imbuement is as improbable as wielding two schools of magic simultaneously. While those within the School of Soul, particularly those with the ability to soul-jump, can mark tokens with magic, the true act of imbuement remains beyond our grasp. Henceforth, any further attempts at imbuement are forbidden unless expressly authorized by the crown."
—High-Gothic Calimar Sayden

Rikard woke Lorian before the sun had fully risen, as was custom during long voyages, and prepared a hot bath, a warm meal, and fresh clothes for the day.

Drowsy thoughts pulled themselves in circles within his mind; memories of his youth, of his father, and of the previous night mixed together in daydreams that kept him company in the groggy hours of the morning.

The hot water of his freshly prepared bath decompressed his body and mind, helping him clear his thoughts and refocus on what mattered most. This was a ritual he had developed out of necessity, a mechanism that freed him of the burden of reminiscing about how lonely his real father must be, of Feln—the friend he'd spoken to months ago, before she left for her apprenticeship—and of a life whose direction he no longer steered.

"Your father waits for you at the northern end of the keep, Your Grace. He wishes to accompany you on the lift that will take us to the docks below," said Rikard in his usual monotone voice.

"My thanks, handsir. I'll meet him immediately." He placed both hands on his hips and dropped his head in thought. "Have you heard the news from supper last night? I am to marry Lady Jane Greymoor."

"I have, my lord. A wondrous occasion it will be. You are a man blessed by the natural gods."

"Am I? I know nothing of her. Father agreed to it before asking me, or her, if that was something we wanted. Even among commoners, arranged marriages happen, but I thought that being a noble would grant us more of a choice in these matters."

"When it comes to the succession of great houses like yours and Lord Greymoor's, choice is a luxury that cannot be afforded, Your Grace. Consider yourself lucky to be paired with a woman of such beauty and elegance as Lady Greymoor, for it surely can be worse."

"I see. You're saying if I'm to be wed against my will, it's a good thing she isn't ass-ugly?"

"Your words, not mine, Your Grace. Though the sentiment seems to be there," replied Rikard, who allowed himself a sideways grin at the expense of his lord.

Lorian released a much-needed laugh and finished dressing himself. He donned the usual wardrobe but paused before putting on the necklace—a gift from Lord Varios when he first agreed to join him in service—and examined it once more.

The once-dirty silver chain shone brightly from the constant friction of being worn. The small sphere set within the large opaque ring around it rolled gently along an unseen axis. The ring turned opposite the sphere, as if the two were in opposition to one another, and the dancing of the two objects drew Lorian into a trance.

"Ahh," spoke Rikard, "the thing that began it all. You've been wearing it all this time, haven't you, Your Grace?"

"I have, handsir. I don't think I had ever been given a gift as nice as this in my whole life until that point. It felt like a crossroads of sorts. Take the gift and join the lord in service or refuse it and return to my fath— To the blacksmith's shop. I wonder how different my life would've been if I had refused that day," Lorian asked aloud.

"Not much different, I'd wager," began Rikard. "You'd be in the lord's service again just as soon as you awakened. It's a good thing your eye awoke when it did, I'd say. You saved your father's life in those mines. Not a day goes by that I'm not thankful for that." He finished with a small smile.

"Yes, I suppose you're right."

In his mind, Lorian knew that if he had refused, none of the recent events would have come to pass. He would have no magic to wield, Lord Varios may have died, and Lord Aaron would be a free man.

A reassurance of decision ignited within Lorian as he realized that even though he had to say goodbye to his real father, holding a noble accountable for his actions may end up being worth it. Finally, he could see a light at the end of a mostly dark tunnel—a light that would hold vast potential and purpose for Lorian in this new world.

He would be a true arbiter of justice—one who would hold all accountable to the fullest extent of the law.

Handsir Rikard departed his chambers with Lorian immediately behind him and made way for Lord Varios, who awaited them near the lift. Lorian took in the extravagant furnishings of the keep one last time, unsure of when he would return to Castle Greymoor again.

'Kill the Raven.'

Lorian stopped mid-stride, stunned. His heart began to beat wildly, and sweat glossed his brow.

"Did you say something, handsir?" Lorian asked with a tremble in his voice.

"I did not, Your Grace. Is everything all right?"

Lorian looked around the long hallway they stood in, searching frantically for another person. Recognizing they were alone, he realized that they stood directly in front of Lady Varios' chamber doors. He was so unfamiliar with the castle that he didn't notice the path they'd taken brought him near her room. A rumbling of nerves began to unwind within the young lord, his hands becoming shaky and his spine tingling from a sense of danger that he couldn't articulate.

"Please tell my father I'll be just a moment, Rikard. I wish to return to my room for a short time. Believe I may have left a gift for Lady Jane in the bedside drawer," he lied, hoping to break free of Rikard's watchful eyes.

The old servant raised a concerned eyebrow at Lorian. "I can fetch it, Your Grace. It's of no bother."

"No, I'll grab it. Please tell Father I won't be long."

"Very well, Your Grace," replied the handsir in reaction to the order. With no more to say, Rikard left quickly to carry out his orders.

Lorian felt sorry for ordering the handsir around, but he needed to investigate this darkness he felt. When Rikard was out of sight, Lorian entered the lady's chambers.

The room was ordered the same as it had been during the last visit, and a small fire was lit to keep the old noble warm in her bed. Lorian approached with great caution, watching the rise and fall of her chest as she slept soundly. He pulled a chair to the side of her bed, just as Varios had done, and sat beside her.

Lorian suddenly felt like a mouse that was about to taunt a slumbering cat.

"Grandmother," spoke the frightened bastard, his voice still shaky and his eyes unable to find the courage to look upon her face. "It's Lorian, Sam's son. Are you able to speak?" As Lorian blinked, the old noble once again rose in her bed, her body snapping unnaturally to a sitting position, her eyes wide and overly alert. Lorian jumped in shock, the starling image of the elderly noble forcing his heart to skip.

"Hello, Lorian Night of Amphil-Lon. I see that you have awakened your abilities. Ahh, good. Yes, great power rages within you. How unsightly." She spoke in a deadpan voice. Her eyes lacked moisture and popped forward, intensifying her gaze. Her lips receded around her sharp teeth, and her wrinkled skin scrunched angrily around the frame of her face.

"I know your mind has gone, Grandmother. But I know that visions of the future still haunt you. Please. I feel the grip of something . . . dark beginning to take hold of me. My dreams lately have all turned to dust in my mind. I see only horrible things now; dead things. Something whispers in my ears. What does it want with me?"

"Yes, kill the Raven. I hear it scream inside of your soul, bastard. A dark one has found you. The cries of loved ones drown you in guilt. Why does the Raven mock you? Is it because you are not beholden to the prophecies of man? Oh, what helplessness awaits you. What rage you feel!" she growled.

Lorian didn't understand her ramblings but jumped at the mention of the Raven. How could she know of such a thing if her prophecies were so tattered and broken, like her mind was?

"What Raven? Is it a person? A place? Why does it need to die? Who wants me to kill it and why? I don't understand, Grandmother, please," Lorian pleaded. A foulness had accompanied him since he left Orion-Lon, and he could feel its pressure increasing. Lorian was unsure if this was a result of someone's magic or his own mind becoming lost. He wasn't a noble, not a real one. What if commoners were never meant to wield magic? What if simply having access to it was driving him insane?

"Oh, poor baby," Lady Varios wept, her dry eyes filling with tears. "The bastard baby boy who never asked to be born. The whore mother who died too early to even feed you from her pox-riddled tit. The father who stands childless and betrayed by the only son he ever had. Destiny is cruel when you don't abide by its laws."

"Stop it!" screamed Lorian, who felt transparent and vulnerable at the old woman's words.

She smiled wickedly, her pointed teeth drawing Lorian's focus. "Oh, now you look for relevance in my son, hoping he might see you as the child he lost. Hoping to rise above your station and make a difference. The pity! Oh, the shame!"

"Enough! You wretched old woman!" screamed Lorian as he grabbed her by the throat. He forced her back into her sheets and began to squeeze with a rage he never knew he was capable of. Lorian could feel her windpipe begin to snap beneath his fingers, and only when he was on the verge of ending her life did he release her, surprised by the look on her face.

The blackness of her eye had receded to the point where it was almost gone entirely, replaced by its natural white. Her face grew sad and concerned as clarity came over her. "Where is my son? Sam! SAM! I must tell him. You need to tell him, Lorian! Tell him what awaits him within the cold! So dense and frigid it is! The wrath of the ancients! Oh!" she said as she spiraled. The blackness of her eye returned along with her insanity. She shook violently in bed, laughing all the while.

After Lorian regained control of his emotions, he left. He was afraid that if he allowed himself to linger, her words would force his hand again.

Shame and guilt overcame Lorian as he made his way to the lift where Varios waited. He was no stranger to violence at this point in his life, but that woman had done nothing but speak to him.

Was that enough cause to end her life? Because of her words? She wasn't even in control of herself, and

Lorian had nearabout killed her for it. He was confused and angry. He thought back to when he'd last felt like this.

He and Feln had come across a drunk tanner some years back. Lorian lost control when the man had insisted he was a regular of Lorian's mother's at the brothel. Lorian had attacked him. Feln pulled him off before he'd done any real damage, telling him that a man needed to respect himself if he ever planned on being worthy of it. *What would she say to me now?* he thought. *After what I've done, what I almost did?*

He left like he was leaving with more questions than he had answers. What was coming for Varios? Should he warn him? Should he tell the lord he had been about to kill his mother for no reason other than she'd insulted him? There was no way he could.

No matter what he did going forward, controlling himself needed to be a priority. He could wield magic—powerful magic, by the way that Lord Greymoor and Varios had reacted—and with that he needed to learn control and discipline. Lorian feared what would happen in the future if he allowed himself to lose control. *Who would I hurt, and would they deserve it?*

The only thing he was sure of at the moment was that he needed to keep quiet about this. Maybe Varios knew a seer who hadn't lost her mind that he could inquire with. That would help clear the confusion.

A quick image of Lady Varios' black eye turning white just before her near-death raced through his mind, sending a shiver through his body. *Control*, he thought. *I need to be in control.*

Varios and Rikard looked slightly impatient when Lorian arrived. He had been longer than he intended, and the irritation showed on their faces. "My apologies, Father," Lorian said, hoping to get ahead of a verbal lashing.

"Did you find what you were looking for?" Varios asked.

"No, I didn't. But I will soon, I believe."

"How cryptic," commented Varios. "Let's get to business. Have you ever been on a ship? Out to sea?"

The back of the keep tapered off into a set of smaller rooms that were less decorated than the areas they had previously visited. The room they now entered was dimly lit by oil lanterns—the main source of light being the slit windows that were set into the stone walls—and led to a familiar contraption that Lorian had only ever seen in Orion-Lon.

This lift was made mostly of steel and was twice the size of the ones in Orion-Lon. The safety gate around the rectangular lift made for a safer journey compared to the ramshackle one that the miners used.

Lorian was surprised to see that Lord Greymoor and Lady Jane were already on the lift and waiting. Dozens of crates and leather luggage bags lined the lift, leaving only enough space for the three of them to enter.

"No, Father. I've never been to sea or on any vessel that was bigger than a dock ferry," he replied stiffly. His nerves still felt scrambled.

"Well, you're in for a treat. The Greymoors have some of the largest ships in the world and they're renowned for their beauty."

"You're damn right they are! Hah!" shouted Lord Greymoor. "Aren't you going to say hello to your fiancée, boy?"

"Yes, forgive me, Lord Greymoor. Good morning, Lady Jane. I hope you are well rested for the journey to Mainis Fortu?" Lorian asked with practiced elegance. He was getting better with noble customs as time went on, and it felt like it showed just now. Lorian also felt a hint of nervousness when speaking to Lady Jane. Her beauty always made his words feel clumsy in his mouth, but they hadn't had a chance to speak since the announcement, and he was unsure of her feelings.

"A good morning to you as well, my lord. I am indeed well rested and excited to see the capital with you!" she said with a smile that made Lorian's cheeks run red. *Maybe everything is okay after all?* He allowed himself to believe it.

From behind a series of luggage bags poked a curly-haired woman: Lo.

"Hello, Your Grace!" Lo said with vigor. "Feels like weeks since we last spoke! I can't thank you enough, Lord Varios, for allowing me to travel with you on Lord Greymoor's grand vessel. The rest of the sect will be flabbergasted by my royal treatment. I can't wait!"

Rikard, Lorian, and Varios all climbed aboard the lift and—with the crank of a lever—descended toward the docks at the base of the cliff below. The lift was covered with blackness as it descended through a man-made shaft, with only blips of light shining in from the rising sun through small openings where shaft pieces connected.

"Child-scholar," sighed Lord Varios, "I thought we left you with the rest of the company. How is it you managed to slither your way into the castle?" he asked with disappointment.

"I have your son to thank for that! He alerted Lady Jane to my presence, and I was summoned at her request. It has been magnificent having someone to talk to who is just as eager and willing to learn about the ancient world as I am! We may have a dutiful scholar on our hands in the form of Lady Jane! I'm afraid nobles can't be full-fledged scholars, but you are more than welcome to my sect for any reason!" she said with excitement.

Lorian fought back a smile. He truly enjoyed Lo's radiant personality.

"Oh, how wonderful, Lo! I will have to take you up on that offer if I have some free time between the engagement party and my fiancé's business," she replied with matched glee. Lorian's face went red again after being called her fiancé. Lady Jane seemed unbothered by their sudden engagement, which made Lorian both happy and concerned.

"Oh, did he?" started Varios. "Well, I'll have to make sure my son is properly rewarded for ensuring your company with us on this long, long journey." Lorian could feel Varios' eye burning a hole into the side of his head, and he dared not try and validate that theory.

As the shaft ended, a picture of the open sea illuminated by the rising sun was painted before Lorian. The tumultuous waters below—gray and undefined by the infant sun—churned wildly. The mist from the waters filled Lorian's nose with a salty scent he had never experienced before. The rising sun cast its rays ever so slowly as it rose, lighting the tip of Castle Greymoor first and working its way down the cliff face.

As the light from the morning star met the ocean below, a series of finely-made ships sprung into life and color. The large vessels below carried the insignia of House Greymoor upon their sails. Cannon doors and intricately carved images lined the sides of the ships, and gold-embroidered rails and fixtures adorned the top side of the vessel. A large bear carved from dense wood made up the bowsprit—the front tip of the ship. A large rudder hung from the aft of the enormous ships, complemented in utility by small oar holes that allowed the ship to compensate when wind power was low.

Men hurried along the top deck, moving cargo and cleaning in preparation for the journey. They seemed like ants to Lorian from where they stood in the lift.

The rocky base below was covered in wooden docks that allowed for the movement of men and supplies to and from the castle. *An ingenious design*, Lorian thought. As the lift came to a halt, the largest of the ships—the *High Guard*, it was called, per the writing on the vessel's starboard side—was anchored a hundred meters from the dock. A series of smaller rowboats were stationed neatly in front of the docks and tied to the moorings to prevent them from drifting away.

"Wouldn't it be easier to have the ship itself tied to the dock and a ladder laid out for us to climb? Why make us sail a smaller boat first?" Lorian asked out loud. Lord Greymoor's face soured in disappointment, and Lady Jane let out a small giggle at Lorian's ignorance. He fought against the rising embarrassment.

"The water is too shallow here," explained Child-Scholar Lo, "and turning such a large vessel in this cramped cove would be next to impossible. Moreover, harsh waters could cause the ship to split the dock into pieces and sink her if she scraped along the jagged cliff face. It's safer to take a smaller boat out instead of a large ship in."

Lorian was surprised at the nautical knowledge the child-scholar displayed. Even Lord Greymoor had his mouth half-open in shock. "A woman after my own heart," the stone giant said, causing Lo to blush.

"My family were dock workers in Maybarn. I learned a thing or two before becoming a child-scholar," she replied proudly.

Lord Varios rolled his eye at their interaction. He swung open the safety gate to the lift, and everyone exited with haste. After a few orders from Lord Greymoor to his dock hands, the group set off for the *High Guard*. A set of crewmen rowed the boat forward, and Lorian took this chance to speak with Lady Jane, as they were seated together for the short trip.

"I'm sorry, Jane. I didn't know your grandfather was going to do this, and I'm sure you didn't know either. I haven't been a noble for long, but even this seems sudden. Are you all right?" he asked.

"It's okay, Lorian," she said with a sudden display of shyness, her rosy cheeks deepening in color. "This was always going to happen. Grandfather has always spoken highly of House Varios, and of your father, which is rare of him. Finding out he had a son, and one as special as you, just made his decision that much clearer. To be honest, I'm relieved. We don't know one another very well, but you've been kind to me, understanding. Not all lords are gentle or respectful to their ladies, and Father had prospects for me out of Barandor and Speral-Lon. Men who are much older and much less kind than you. I know this isn't what you wanted, but I'll have you, if you'll have me."

Lorian was taken aback by her answer. *Is married life as a noble really so awful that a kind stranger is enough to satisfy the requirements for a good husband?*

"What about love?" he asked bluntly.

Lady Jane tensed, her face flushed further, and her eyes began to accumulate tears. "Love isn't for people like us. Only the station and the power that comes with it."

"But it doesn't have to be that way. Does it?" he asked. A lump formed in his throat as he tried to gather the courage to speak his mind. "I know we're still strangers, but before we are married, I'd like us to be in love," he said as the strength waned from his limbs and his courage felt depleted. "If that's all right."

"Yes, Lorian," she began with a smile as wide as the ocean itself and eyes that shone brightly in the morning sun. Her features were stunning. "I'd like that."

After a short journey, the small boat reached the starboard side of the *High Guard*, the distance slightly extended by the roughness of the sea. All members climbed aboard with the assistance of the sailors, and when Lorian was fully aboard, he was delighted to see that Captain Bowers and a few other familiar faces from the company awaited them.

"If it isn't the young lord. How has your stay at Castle Greymoor been, Your Grace? Hopefully better than the musty soldiers and sheep fuckers I've had the displeasure of sharing space with," Captain Bowers said with a chuckle.

"To be honest, Bowers, sheep fuckers may have been better company at some points. Ever met Lady Varios?"

"Say no more, Your Grace. It seems I may have had better accommodations after all," he replied in jest. "I've heard of your attunement incident and of your engagement. Congratulations to both. Per your father, training will now consist of both real swords and hand-to-hand combat. You'll train in weaponry with me and in wielding with your father, back-to-back. He wishes you to be in top form when we arrive in the capital. I believe he means to show you off."

"Don't forget about me, captain. Hah!" shouted Lord Greymoor, "I heard you've been training my soon-to-be grandson. I'd like to get a few swings in as well. Test his mettle, and yours. Sounds like you're a good cut-throat when you need to be, but how do you fare against a hammer?" he asked with a gluttony for battle in his eyes that made Captain Bowers shiver.

Chapter 16: The Dance of Iron and Magic

"The path to a hardened body begins with forging an indomitable will. Harden yourself, and soon you shall find the tortures of labor joyful challenges to overcome."
—Lord Ain Greymoor

Lorian crashed onto the deck of the *High Guard* for what felt like the hundredth time that day—his limbs were sore, and his mouth was full of slick blood that seeped from cuts in his mouth and lips.

The strength of Lord Greymoor was unlike anything he had ever experienced—a mountain too tall to climb. Lord Greymoor wore his splendid black-and-gold-trimmed armor. The Greymoor bear roared proudly upon the sigil etched into the metal and arrogantly leaned against his large double-headed hammer, waiting for Lorian to rise once more.

For three hours, Lorian had done everything he could to circumvent the mighty blows of his opponent, watching his footing and deflecting what he could—as Captain Bowers taught him—but it wasn't enough. Every time the stone giant's great weapon came into contact with his sword, his legs buckled and his limbs stung greatly from the impact, draining him of all strength.

Lorian felt like he was doing everything he could just to survive the constant barrage of swings that came from the lord. Varios, Captain Bowers, Lady Jane, and Captain Hrick—Lord Greymoor's commander of the High Guard—watched on as the two went blow to blow, ever observant and analytical of Lorian's mistakes.

With heavy arms and legs that felt composed of lead, he rose once more from the deck, eager to draw even a drop of blood from Greymoor.

He lifted his sword in perfect form, waiting for the hulking brute to charge him.

Lord Greymoor was happy to oblige. With a swiftness unnatural to his size, he sped forward with his hammer raised high. Lorian timed the steps toward him perfectly, and when the hammer was about to fall, he sidestepped around his enemy, faking a deflective blow as the hammer crashed into the deck below. He raised his sword once again, the tip of the blade pointed forward toward the lord's ribs and charged.

To Lorian's surprise, Lord Greymoor released the hammer that had been planted firmly in the planks and caught Lorian's jaw with a backhand that sent him rapidly to the ground. A blackness encroached upon Lorian's vision, the world before him becoming but a pinhole of light, and he faded into unconsciousness with hot blood pouring from his nose and open mouth.

A warm sensation cradled his entire being as the smell of flowers and ocean spray filled his nose. He awoke to find Lady Jane tending to his wounds—her hands placed gently upon his head as she poured faint spurts of magic into him.

"Jane?" he said with a weary voice. "What are you doing?"

"I'm helping you to recover, my lord," she replied with a smile.

"How is this possible?" he asked as his energy returned and the throbbing pain in his jaw began to subside.

"This is the school of soul magics at play. Some of us can jump, some can feel forces beyond our usual understanding, and some can heal. It takes a great deal of energy, but I'm very proficient."

Lorian was surprised to learn that each school had multiple abilities. *Some more useful than others*, he thought. *What a gift it is to be able to heal others. What is the extent of her ability, and what types of wounds can she heal? How does it work, and can anyone from the soul magics learn this ability?*

"Oh good, you're awake," said Varios. "Perfect. Once our Lady here has finished, I'm going to teach you how to wield."

Lorian stood so quickly that it startled Jane, who fell backward. Lorian's excitement was unmatched by any alive at the prospect of finally having the chance to learn to use magic. Ever since becoming a noble, he'd yearned for this moment, and now that it had finally arrived, he was more than eager to hurry things along—injured or not.

"I'm ready, Father. What shall we work on first? Flaming hands? Perhaps I could try to summon some wind to feed our sails or some lightning to test my might? I'm ready for whatever you have in store," he cried with glee.

Varios looked nearly as annoyed as he had when he'd learned that Lo was to accompany them for the trip. His eyelid was half-opened and his mouth was slightly ajar.

"No," he said with a sigh. "First, you shall make me a cup of tea."

"Tea!?" asked Lorian, who couldn't comprehend how this could help him learn to wield.

"Yes, tea," Varios said as he removed a metal cup from his overcoat. He walked toward a barrel of water on the deck and filled it halfway. He then examined it and, when it satisfied him, handed it to Lorian. "Tea leaves are near the aft end in a small brown box. When you're able to get the temperature of the water right, stick in a packet of Forgornian herbs and brew the tea. When it tastes like there's a dash of cinnamon in the water, it's ready."

"But . . . how does this help me learn to use my magics?" Lorian asked.

"You must use your fire magic to warm the cup and brew the tea. Concentrate on the cup and pour your magic into it. Once you learn to hold a steady stream of heat, the tea will brew. Forgornian herbs require a very specific temperature to brew, or they turn the water as sour as curdled milk. Once you master this, we move on to the next lesson."

Varios left through an open door that descended to the lower decks without another word. Lorian stood staring at the teacup long after the lord left, wondering if there was some secret to the training that would help him understand how to wield his magic.

After running through different scenarios in his head—and even some outlandish assumptions that it was some sort of metaphorical test—he began his first lesson in conquering the power within him.

Lorian practiced late into the evening, sailors and soldiers doing their best to ignore the noble boy who sat cross-legged in the middle of the top deck, staring at a teacup. Lady Jane, Lo, and everyone else had already retreated to their cabin spaces below the main deck and were preparing for sleep, leaving him to his less-than-intense training.

The sun began to recede beneath the watery horizon, an amber-red light suffusing the cloud spotted sky, mixing with the lingering oranges and yellows.

Despite the choppiness of the water, Lorian could see a perfect reflection of the great star meeting its doppelganger at the far reaches of the earth, and together, the two celestial giants melted into one and sank beneath the world, leaving a clear, starry night behind them.

Lorian had seen the constellations on many occasions, yet the openness of the sea made the tapestry of twinkling lights seem foreign and titanic in scale.

Holding the cup of water for endless hours made him over-concentrate on what stood before him; the world beyond just now came into view as a blanket of darkness covered the sky. Peering into the infinite beyond above him made Lorian feel small and insignificant but with a strange pleasantness.

He enjoyed remembering that the struggles he faced were only temporary and miniscule when compared to the greatness of the world. For a moment, he forgot what he was even doing, getting lost in the magnificence of the universe, when hot water poured over his exposed hands and burned him.

Lorian winced from the pain and dropped the metallic teacup, a clanging sound echoing out when it struck the ground. Lorian examined the cup whilst rubbing his hands together to soothe the slight sting and noticed the steam rising from the remnants of water that survived the drop. *Wait, I did it? When?*

Lorian picked the teacup up from the deck and swiftly filled it with fresh water from the open barrel that Varios had used earlier. He again sat and focused greatly on the cup.

To his dismay, nothing happened. *What was I doing earlier that I'm not doing now? Looking at the stars? Allowing my mind to wander?* Lorian tried focusing on the stars again, attempting to remove the thought of his task and the cup in his hands.

He felt his focus on present matters slip and allowed his mind to drift—nowhere in particular. A feeling of weightlessness came over him, and he imagined himself floating in a sea of stars, the bright titans of the night sky floating gently past him like driftwood bobbing alongside the current of the water.

A warmth unlike anything he had ever felt surrounded his floating body, like a rush of warm water that enveloped him, and thoughts of joy and happiness danced in his mind.

His skin tightened, and goosebumps came alive atop his body. The warmth of the star-speckled ocean drew him under the water, though no panic coursed through his veins.

He was safe for the first time in his life, completely and totally safe—untouchable to even the natural gods themselves.

Lorian's eyes snapped open, and he was engulfed by a surge of power, reminiscent of the attunement crystal's energy. It felt as though a great dam had ruptured, unleashing torrents mightier than any earthly river. The raging currents sought a conduit, their relentless force seeking release. With unwavering focus, Lorian directed his will toward the teacup once more, each ounce of determination aimed at channeling the unyielding power into the still water.

In an instant, the water began to simmer, then boil, its surface roiling with increasing intensity. Steam billowed forth as the liquid reached a point of no return, its transition to vapor inevitable. The metal teacup glowed with fiery hues of red and orange as heat coursed through it with unchecked aggression. Lorian, seized by sudden panic, released the cup, fearing the searing touch of its scalding surface once more. It fell, scorching the deck with the residual water and charring marks upon the wood.

Reacting swiftly, Lorian scooped two handfuls of water from an open barrel and doused the cup repeatedly until he was certain it no longer posed a threat to him or the ship. After he had a moment to reflect on the events that had brought him to almost burning the ship down, he attempted to brew the tea again.

Lorian's fingers closed around several packets of Forgornian tea from the crate at the aft end of the ship, their scent reminiscent of musky, damp forest debris. He refilled his teacup with water and returned to his place on the deck, returning himself to the beautiful sea of stars in his mind.

As he attempted to channel his magic into the teacup, steam erupted once more; he dropped the cup, scorching the deck and burning his palm slightly. Determination surged within him. *No! I refuse to give up. This is surely something the children are taught to help them level their flow of magic. If I can't control this, I'll never be able to wield properly!* he thought, filling the teacup with fresh water again.

With each attempt, Lorian forced himself back to the mental state that allowed him to access his magic. Gradually, it became easier, the flow of magic growing more constant without needing meditation. Yet, despite his persistence, each refill of the cup ended in failure.

***

It was later than usual when Handsir Rikard roused Lord Varios from his slumber. The sun had just begun its ascent, prompting Varios to crave a stretch of his legs before attending to his bath and meal.

Ascending the ladder wells that adorned the end of each narrow passageway of the lower decks, Varios emerged onto the main deck, greeted by the sight of the vast ocean and Lorian. His adopted son sat upon the deck, legs crossed, amidst scattered scorched sections of wood.

Lorian's hands, arms, and chest bore light burns, evidence of his relentless efforts throughout the night to master the art of making a cup of Forgornian tea. Varios approached him, shock and surprise etched onto his features. "Why didn't you rest? I didn't command you to do this."

205

Lorian looked up at his father, dark circles under his eyes and a stupid, tired grin on his face. He was holding a cup of tea in his hands and sipping gently from it. "Tastes like cinnamon," he said with great fatigue in his voice.

***

Varios and Lord Greymoor spoke softly to each other opposite Lorian's cabin, where the bastard slept heavily from his night of great strain and effort.

"He did it in one night, Uncle. It took me a year to master the Forgornian tea puzzle," Varios said with shock and admiration in his voice.

"You don't say. He displayed great strength at his attunement, but do you think he may be more than an overly proficient Wielder?"

"I'm not sure what he may or may not be. His power is great, yes, but his determination is on a scale of its own. Did you see his burns? He suffered through those all night; that couldn't have been easy," he admitted. Varios had felt a sense of pride in Lorian, but this was quickly replaced with concern. Being skilled in wielding was one thing, but pushing yourself through pain and exhaustion for the sake of greatness was foolish, his mother being a morbid example. He had seen many young men on the battlefield with the same sense of ambition, all resulting in the same fate: a swift death.

"Ah, give him the benefit of doubt. He's new to our world, Ash-Bringer. What son doesn't want to prove himself to his father? At least your boy has some talent to speak of, unlike Bolin. If he wants to push himself, let him. He's got lots of catching up to do, so for his own good, allow him this."

206

Varios didn't agree with his uncle, but he felt no need to vocalize it. Keeping your heir safe from danger was always a priority for nobles, but keeping them safe from themselves was a near-impossible task. Magic kicked back when abused. "Perhaps," Varios relented, hoping to steer his uncle away from the conversation.

"Wake the boy before noon, Sam. My hammer hasn't tasted enough of his skull yet. Hah!" shouted Lord Greymoor with battle-hungry excitement, "We'll be docking at Orco's Island soon, I'll be grabbing a few more men and some ships, and then we can set sail for Mainis Fortu. We'll have the lad nice and presentable by the time we arrive, this I promise you. With the eagerness he's shown to learn, by our arrival, he may be more than you can handle, hah!" he finished as he made his way through the passageway, his large body almost comedic as he squeezed through.

Varios stood outside Lorian's door for a moment longer before following Greymoor down the hall. *If he can control his fire magic quickly, he'll need another tutor for his remaining elements.* Varios knew he wasn't fit to teach him anything outside of his own element, lest he lead the boy to harm himself or others. A proper tutor was required for Lorian, and he believed he knew exactly where he could find the group necessary to help.

Orco's Island was a small halfway stopping point for a series of routes. There, a ship could repair or restock appropriately. Many sailors and soldiers—not to mention mercenaries—stayed there permanently to find work or jump to units and companies needing the manpower.

In the Great War of Forgorn, Varios had led a team of nobles who acted as a forward force meant to cut into the enemies' numbers and reduce them before the main forces could arrive. He was unsure if everyone from the old unit still lingered, except for two. Both had taken up residence on Orco's Island and ran their own mercenary teams.

As low-born nobles, they only held the title of 'sir'—same as knights and higher-ranked military officials—and they often took work under the purview of a high-born noble. Or, in this case, went into business for themselves doing what they did best: war.

It was with them that Varios would find the tutors he needed to try and help Lorian master the other elements. Information about Lorian needed to stay as secret as possible until his naming ceremony for fear the truth of his origin and Varios' magic would come to light. He would need to swear them to secrecy through a blood vow.

More than twenty years had passed since they'd last seen each other, and Varios was willing to bet they would be less than thrilled to see him after all this time, much less to make a blood vow.

Persuading them to join him would not be easy, but it was necessary. Without these two to assist Lorian, another outburst of uncontrolled magic could reveal their secret and lead to consequences worse than just a few injured spectators or a damaged castle.

As Varios ruminated on his thoughts, Handsir Rikard approached, holding a small box in his hands. "My lord, I have been asked to deliver this gift to you. A messenger hawk delivered it mere moments ago; it bore no family crest. Do you wish for me to inspect it before you reveal the contents?" he asked, ready to take the risk of opening a rigged gift.

"No, it's all right, Rikard," started Varios, who felt the onset of nervousness. "I'll take it from here. You have my word I'll take precautions with opening it."

Rikard took a formal bow and left his lord to explore the gift as he saw fit.

Varios began to speculate a great many things while pondering the gift and its meaning. Who in the realm could know of his whereabouts? Lord Handall and his spies, perhaps, or even Charles Aaron, the father of his prisoner. Whatever this gift contained, the message was clear: *I see you.*

Varios opened the gift, and anger welled within him as he inspected the item. No letter or message accompanied the box. The single item within was a newly fashioned eye patch sized perfectly for him.

Someone knows, thought the lord. *I'm not sure how, but someone either knows the full truth or is damn close to figuring it out.* There was less time than Varios had thought.

He needed to get Lorian to the capital and perform the naming ceremony immediately. Only then would Lorian have an unquestionable claim to nobility that would help secure House Varios against threatening scandals like the secret they kept.

Chapter 17: Memories of War

"From the south they came, cloaked in shadow and silence. The armies of Forgornia marched across the Great Sky Bridge and into Centrugard, their footfalls like drums thundering across the land. By sheer will and ruthlessness, our king outwitted and defeated the invaders, taking their princess as his prize."
—Patron-Scholar Godrick, *Accounts of the Forgornian War, Vol. XXIV*

Sam Varios gripped the railing of the *High Guard* tightly as they approached slowly the docks of Orco's Island, veiled by mist. Tension rose within the lord. It had been many years since he last saw his old comrades, and to say they'd left on the best of terms would be far from the truth.

The war had been brutal and long. Sam had done things he wasn't proud of; so had the rest of his unit. They'd come to an unspoken agreement to stay far away from each other—to help them forget the hellscape of war and the sins of the orders they had carried out.

The closer they sailed to the island, the more sulfur and ash Sam could smell in the air, as if his mind was trying to force him away from the encounter he so desperately wished didn't need to happen. He lowered his head in remembrance of the blood-soaked rampage they had carried out.

Ghosts of his past swam just inches beneath the surface of the water below—the burnt bodies of the victims felled by his hand. They all screamed in whispers unheard. *Ash-Bringer,* they cried. *Ash-Bringer.*

The large island was made of a series of stone pillars that stretched toward the sky like dead fingers reaching for help. The base of the pillars arched outward into a gentle slope, meeting the sea with a flat cliff face. Buildings were constructed both on the base and on platforms sitting between the large pillars, held aloft by thick metal supports that dug deeply into the stone.

Unlike the docks near the Golden Hatch, these waters provided a wide enough berth and depth for the ship to dock personally. A series of long docks floated loosely, jutting out at an angle from the nearest collection of buildings so as to allow larger ships to port.

Sailors, soldiers, and large groups of prisoners marched to and from the docks, their dealings and business shrouded in the ambiguity of the flags they flew.

Sam recognized one of the ships shepherding large swaths of prisoners, each linked to the other via thick iron chains. These were men and women being sent to the Shut, an awful frozen wasteland north of the Frost, where prisoners were forced to dig through ancient sheets of ice as punishment for their crimes.

Only once in his lifetime had he ever had the displeasure of visiting the Shut. On orders from King Reynor Dinivy, the current king's late father, he was to escort a particularly notorious criminal who had attempted to raise forces in a coup against the crown but was ousted by his own trusted conspirators.

Beneath the thick blankets of ice was a prison that had been painstakingly carved out by prisoners over the course of two centuries. The large iron doors feeding into the depths below gave the Shut its name. When those doors slammed behind you as you made your descent, all hope and ambition for escape fled rapidly.

Day and night, prisoners toiled relentlessly, carving ice from deep caverns, making more space to accommodate an ever-growing population. Sam wished such a sentence on no man. Orco's Island must be a convenient port on the way there, he assumed.

The striking of swords echoed out from behind Sam as Lorian and Captain Bowers engaged in their morning lessons. Lord Greymoor watched enviously for his turn to spar, impatiently tapping his hand on his double-headed war-hammer.

Lady Jane waited patiently by in case her help was requested with healing Lorian—talking all the while with the child-scholar. *Perhaps about the mysteries of wall scribblings or what the ancients wiped their asses with*, he thought.

Since they'd left Castle Greymoor, Sam had noticed lingering stares and smiles between Lo and Lord Greymoor. It was a fling he hoped wouldn't last long, lest his ears be consumed by her babbling for the foreseeable future.

Sailors were running around the top side, performing the duties required to dock safely at the pier, Captain Hrick Season shouting orders all the while. Sam prepared himself for the upcoming meeting, steeling his nerves as best as he could. He walked over to a sparring area Lorian and Bowers had created, interrupting the lesson.

"Lorian, prepare yourself. We won't be in port long, and there's much for us to do on land. Meet me by the gangway when you're ready," he commanded.

"Yes, Father," Lorian replied obediently.

"What's this about, Ash-Bringer?" protested the brutish lord. "I haven't had my turn with the boy!" he cried in outrage.

"My apologies, Uncle. We have some matters to attend to while you gather more soldiers and ships. We won't be gone long. In the meantime," Sam began as he offered Bowers a wink, "Captain Bowers here hasn't stopped talking about your battle prowess. He doesn't believe you kicked a boulder through your father's war-room wall." He watched Lord Greymoor grow red with anger.

"Oh, do you think me a liar, captain?" barked the lord. "Guess you'll have to find out for yourself when I kick your cock straight through your arsehole," he spat as he charged Bowers, his war-hammer in tow.

Bowers barely had time to summon a flicker of disdain, which he hurled at his lord with reckless abandon. Sam merely acknowledged him with a curt nod before striding purposefully toward the gangway. The wooden bridge awaited them, poised to carry him and Lorian down to the bustling docks of Orco's Island below.

Sam waited for Lorian, who quickly returned top side once he had washed himself, and together, the two descended the gangway and began their march toward the bustling seafarers before them. Their descent was accompanied by a cacophony of Bowers screaming and the energetic symphony of splintering wood.

The flimsy structures past the docks seemed hastily built. Some were missing boards, while others were damaged from either the force of the elements or from lack of care over the years. Men with distant looks in their eyes marched prisoners from one ship to the other. Sam knew Lorian would ask, so he gave the boy a brief description of the prisoners' destination—and of their fate in the Shut.

He explained that while it was possible to serve your sentence and earn your freedom, most succumbed to the cold. Lorian protested about the unfairness of the situation even after Sam had explained it was only the worst criminals who were sent there. Sam agreed.

It was another circumstance of the world they were powerless to change.

Sailors, soldiers, and folk of other professions also resided on the island, and the mixture created a diverse set of stalls and shops that focused on supplying the weary traveler with comforts of the mind and flesh. Several brothels were propped alongside the ramshackle buildings, their bright colors and linens on display to indicate the allure of those inside.

Foods of diverse kinds hung on shelves and racks within the narrow pathways that wound through the structures—everything from bizarrely textured fruits to salted meats and spices with colors that varied as much as the evening sky when the sun began its journey to places unknown.

Not long after they left, Sam and Lorian found themselves facing a large building whose sturdy quality stood in contrast to the decayed buildings between which it was nestled. Above the iron banded door was a sign that hung from thin chains. A sigil of a sword and shield that crossed with a bag of coins stood brightly upon its surface and indicated that this was the business place of sell-swords . . . in other words, mercenaries.

"Allow me to do the talking, Lorian. Keep your words sealed behind your teeth until I say otherwise. I know these men. Until I have them sworn in secrecy, you shall reveal nothing of yourself or your purpose at my side. Are we understood?" Sam asked rhetorically.

"You still haven't told me why we're here, Your Grace. Can I at least know this much?"

"Very well. We are here because I cannot train you to wield properly by myself. You show aptitude for many elements, which is extremely rare. Now be quiet," he replied as he knocked three times upon the door and entered.

The heavy door creaked open, revealing a poorly lit room scented by sweat and cheap booze. A group of haggard-looking mercenaries turned toward the unexpected visitors, their clinking armor and shuffling feet coming to a halt as they inspected the duo. The mercenaries bore dented armor and scarred bodies that painted them as no strangers to combat. Toward the far end of the building sat a pair of mercenaries whose magic eyes pierced Sam through the smog of pipe smoke and humid sea stench.

Sam and Lorian moved silently between the tables and chairs that decorated this berthing of sell-swords. Coins, chinked weapons, and tightly tied purses littered the tabletops as the mercenaries returned to their business. The haggling of items and favors filled the air as chatter resumed. Sam stopped a few feet from the table, the closeness of the magic eyes giving details to their bearers.

One was a tall black-haired woman with brown skin who sat opposite the other magic Wielder. Her large frame carried well-maintained muscle, and the large scar she bore on her left cheek told the story of a warrior who was intimate with violence. Her purple magic eye was alluring. She wore a black cavalier's hat upon her head and had decorated the brim of it with a long red feather from an unknown bird.

Across from her sat a much smaller but equally battle-worn man who had allowed the years to take their toll on his waistline. His rough stubble and foul stench made it painfully obvious that his appearance was only a concern for those who had the displeasure of looking upon him and not his own. He pulled his lips back in a smile that revealed poorly maintained teeth yellowed from excess pipe smoke. He bore a light red eye that seemed to have dulled over the years.

Sam was the first to speak. "Sir Bridgeson, Sir Coalsdottir," he said aloud in a formal greeting befitting their station. "You both look like shit."

The pair of mercenaries sneered with displeasure at the comment.

He noticed as Lorian raised an eyebrow at the woman being called 'sir,' something Sam made note to explain to him later. The man—Sir Bridgeson—was the first to rise from his chair. He grabbed the hilt of a dagger that hung from his waistbelt and took a step forward.

"Lord Sam Varios. Which of the natural gods brought you to our doorstep?" he spoke in a rough voice that held excess mucus.

"Deaut, mistress of death," he replied in an odd cadence.

The air between the four Wielders grew frigid. It was as if Sam had mentioned something taboo that not even those who lurked in dark places would dare to mention. "And what does the mistress wish of us?" asked Sir Coalsdottir from her seat, her voice full of concern. Lorian marveled at the size of the woman, who was almost at eye level even while seated.

"She asks that you whisper your faith into words of blood, may they bind your tongue." Sam said the words in that same cadence.

Both Coalsdottir and Bridgeson looked at one another in shock, their faces losing color by the second. A few silent moments fell between them as they communicated through a series of facial gestures that seemed to dictate their course of action.

"By what grounds do you bind our tongues to the mistress Deaut?" Coalsdottir asked as she grew twice in size when standing on her feet.

"Tower Rand, Calcion, the southern rivers . . . you choose," said Sam in a definitive tone that made both sirs wince as if they had heard something disheartening.

"You dare use those against us, Ash-Bringer? Have we not suffered enough already? You would make us relive those sins?" asked Bridgeson as his eyes glazed over in tears that refused to fall. Coalsdottir squeezed her fists so tightly that the chafing noise made Lorian fear her bones might break.

"Enough, Koh," started Coalsdottir. "He speaks the truth. We owe him this much."

"Thank you, Lya," Sam said softly.

"No! This is not for you. It is for who you used to be, Ash-Bringer!" she shouted. Sam sank his head in despair, his guilt resurfacing from times long lost. Lorian watched on, his face scrunched in confusion at the interaction before him.

"I still thank you, regardless," he said in defeat. "I would bind your tongues immediately. Please, finish what business you have here and meet me at the western docks on a ship called the *High Guard*. Tell them Lord Varios sent for you, and you'll be allowed to board. We have a Wielder of soul magics who can bind us. Until then." He gave a nod of his head.

Neither of the sirs spared Lorian a glance; he didn't seem important enough for them to acknowledge, which Sam was thankful for. The fewer questions they asked before making the blood oath, the less stress and confusion he would have to deal with for now.

Sam left the mercenary building immediately, with Lorian in tow. Fresh sea spray and salt awaited them outside the iron-banded door, and when he was sure no one but Lorian could see him, he let out a series of exaggerated breaths.

Lorian looked at Sam questioningly, seemingly understanding he'd undergone something that caused him great internal conflict. He knew that the sweat accumulating on his brow mixed with the unsteadiness of his steps must have told Lorian everything he needed to know about the exchange which just transpired. The concern on his face told Sam Lorian was unsure if he'd make it through intact.

"Let's return to the ship," said Sam as he gathered his senses. He took a deep inhale and held it before beginning to walk again. Lorian followed after and was extra attentive to his father's movements, visibly relaxing only when Sam showed he had his wits about him again.

The two made their way through the alleys and passageways that would spit them out at the docks, silence settling between them. Sam began to slow after a few minutes of walking, nearly coming to a full stop as he crept forward at a snail's pace.

"Is everything all right, Your Grace?" asked Lorian, his voice full of worry.

"Yes, I'm fine. Tell me, Lorian. How is it I see twice as much as you with only half my vision?" he asked as he came to a full stop.

"I'm not sure what you mean," Lorian replied.

"Earlier, these paths were full of people. Where have they all gone? Where are the merchants, soldiers, and stallholders?" he asked as he reached for the short sword he had sheathed at his hip.

Lorian hadn't noticed the empty alleys. The excitement had blinded him to his surroundings. He drew his sword as well. "Should I be concerned?"

A voice from behind a wooden shed called out in answer. "No. Not if you return what doesn't belong to you."

A man dressed in a black overcoat stepped forward, revealing himself. He had a bearded face with dark eyes void of magic. He stood eye level with Lorian, and his wrinkles put his age around forty years. He had short brown hair curling over his ears and a small scar on his upper lip, which split the beard slightly. Around his waist was a sheathed short sword partnered next to a dagger whose tip was hooked.

"Not another step," commanded Sam as he pointed his blade at the stranger. "As Lord of House Varios and Arbiter of Justice in the Frost, I order you to tell me your name and your business."

The stranger took another step forward in protest of Sam's command. "My name I shall keep for myself, Your Grace," he spat. "As for my business, I believe you're well aware of what I want. Release the heir to House Aaron, that's all. Release him and walk away from here with your boy still breathing," he threatened with a wide smile that contrasted his hostile words. "Sounds fair, doesn't it? An heir for an heir?"

"Lord Aaron will face the king's justice. Not you, nor the men you have atop these roofs, nor even the natural gods will stop me from seeing it through," he said as the men hiding above revealed themselves.

A small group of five men—all clad in the same black leather overcoat as their leader—stood proudly as they were identified, crossbow prepared in their hands. Each man, save the leader, wore a metallic mask that bore no features except a groove for their nose and two eye holes. The men did not speak but pointed their aim at Lorian, as if some unheard order had been shouted.

"Think carefully, lord of snow and fish shit, else your boy leaves this island in a box. Return the heir, now. The boy will stay with us until you've released him," the stranger ordered.

"Listen to me, Lorian," Sam whispered so only the bastard could hear him. "I'm going to create a distraction with my magic. When I do, run to Lord Greymoor and bring as many men with you as you can."

"I won't leave you," replied Lorian, his eyes wandering to each man above him as if some half-witted plot was forming.

"That's an order," he whispered again so as not to be heard by the stranger. "Get ready." Heat began to accumulate near his hands as his magic fought to come through. Leather sizzled audibly as Sam prepared to release whatever magic he was able to muster. Before another moment could pass, four of the men above grunted in pain. They dropped their crossbows and clutched their bellies tightly where a small throwing knife now protruded.

Memories of war forced their way into Sam's mind, and a realization of what was coming dawned on him. "Duck!"

Sam quickly covered Lorian with his overcoat as four large bolts of lightning came crashing from the heavens—each bolt targeting a knife that jutted from the torso of the strangers above.

A familiar roar filled their ears as thunder followed. Static crackled in the air as dust mixed with the crimson spray of the bandits' shattered remains.

A high-pitched siren screeched as he the last crossbowman clutched desperately at his throat. The man's skin ran purple as if he were choking and his eyes bulged forward. His ocular blood vessels ruptured, giving the orbs a morbid gloss of red until he collapsed, dead.

Sam turned his attention to the unmasked stranger in preparation for an attack but was surprised to see that the man had vanished. He was unsure if fear or opportunity made the stranger flee, but regardless of the cause, he was thankful. He stood—the excitement had thrown him to the ground.

"You're quicker than I remember," Sam said aloud as Sir Bridgeson and Sir Coalsdottir approached from behind.

"I already had my shit for the day, so I'm traveling light," Bridgeson said in jest.

"Five minutes, you've been back in our lives, and I've already killed four men. You better compensate us well for this, Sam," Coalsdottir said harshly.

Chapter 18: A Vow Unbreakable

"Secret magics within each school remain undocumented and are rare, even among the most esteemed houses. One such secret, recently revealed, is the blood-vow. Only those versed in soul magic can bind a man by his word, and only those who are bound can free themselves by keeping their oaths, lest their lives be forfeit."
—Unknown

L orian sat beside Varios at a table located in the communal area two decks below the main deck. Across from them sat a disgruntled Sir Bridgeson and Sir Coalsdottir. Varios had ordered all men from the area to ensure their privacy with the upcoming discussion. Upon returning to the *High Guard,* Varios ordered Handsir Rikard to fetch Lady Jane and inform Lord Greymoor of the favor he required of his granddaughter. Varios eagerly awaited approval from his uncle before committing Jane to the duty of performing a blood vow.

Much like the Wielders of other schools of magic, certain capabilities existed across the board—like Varios being able to manipulate and conjure fire, just as Lord Greymoor did with earth. With Lady Jane being a Wielder of the soul magics, it was almost guaranteed that she could perform the blood vow, but he had to ensure that she and Lord Greymoor were aware of the deed without being privy to the purpose behind it.

He would need to take the risk of informing his old comrades beforehand, then swearing them to keep the secret after.

Lorian had taken the initiative of securing ale and bread with a small side of cheese to keep the four of them occupied while they awaited Rikard's message. Sir Bridgeson ate without hesitation, cramming a handful of bread into his mouth, followed by wine and then cheese.

Lorian thought it was disgusting how the man greedily sucked trace amounts of leftover drink from his fingers. Sir Coalsdottir abstained from the feast in front of her, as if she suspected the food to be laced with poison.

Varios wouldn't do something like that, would he? thought Lorian as he remembered the odd way the three spoke to each other in the mercenaries building. *Were they talking in some kind of code? Why did they mention Deaut, lady of death, and what does she have to do with the random places Varios mentioned in response?*

Varios had informed him of the blood vow the two sirs were to undertake when they returned to the ship, but he had never heard of such a thing. And how was his fiancée supposed to help with that?

"Sir Coalsdottir," Lorian began, ending the silence between the four of them. It wasn't the lack of conversation that bothered him so much as the loud chewing and gulping of bread and wine. "How does a woman become a sir? I thought noblewomen were called 'lady.'"

"Who is this idiot child who addresses me so casually, Sam?" asked Coalsdottir in an aggressive tone.

"He is the heir to House Varios. He is my son. Hold your questions about him until my handsir arrives, please," Lord Varios replied bluntly.

This news was surprising enough to force Sir Bridgeson to end his indulgence for a moment as he peered sideways at Coalsdottir with bugged eyes.

"Very well," she replied. "I am called sir because I earned the title in combat. There is no law preventing low-born women from fighting. I was not complacent staying home to rear children and sew doilies. I belong on the road with wine in my belly and iron on my hip, as is the right of any man or woman."

"What is the difference between low-born and high-born nobility?" Lorian asked with confusion.

"How far the silver spoon reaches up your ass, I reckon. Us low-borns only get the tip while the rest of you are trying to squeeze in a second one," laughed Bridgeson as he happily lapped more wine from his tankard. Two trickles of the red beverage traced their way down his chubby face as he failed to form a seal on the cup. He wiped the excess away with the sleeve of his shirt and continued his explanation.

"If you're low-born ,you're either a branch family of a noble house, or you have too many non-magical ancestors that make your magic weak or tainted in the eyes of those puritan cunts," he explained with slight contempt. "Hard to find a wife and settle when the other houses refuse to take you as a caller."

"That's unfair. I'm sorry," said Lorian.

The two sirs looked shocked for a moment that he would apologize. "We don't need your pity, boy. We're better off than commoners, at least. Save your sympathy for them," replied Coalsdottir.

"Why don't your boy know nothing, Sam? Is he actually an idiot? Drop him as a baby, yeah? You're not supposed to hold them by the feet, ya know." He eyed Varios with a sly grin. "And what in the hell happened to your face? Finally catch yourself on fire?"

Before Varios could answer, Handsir Rikard entered the room. The air felt tense as he gave his reply. "Your Grace, I have word from Lord Greymoor as to your request. He approves, but on the condition that you repay the favor, no questions asked."

"That miserable brute always has to leverage something, doesn't he? Very well. Thank you, Rikard. You may leave us. Please ensure no one enters this room until we've adjourned."

"As you wish, my lord," he said as he gave his customary bow and left.

"How is that old man still alive?" started Bridgeson, who wanted to continue his jabs at Varios. "He was old as dirt when we met, and he's even older now. Does kissing your high-born ass grant immortality?" he laughed.

Varios didn't bother to make a reply or counter with a joke of his own. He was in no mood to set a pretense of jovialness and decided to silence both of the sirs by removing the head bandage that had covered the secret he so carefully protected.

Lorian hadn't seen Varios without the bandage in months—not since the incident in Orion-Lon. A scar had formed where stone had struck him above and through the eyebrow. His dimly lit eye was an immediate sign that something was wrong with him.

Before questions could be asked, Varios offered an explanation.

"Lorian Night is my son only in title. The truth is, while my magic does flow through his veins, my blood does not. He was a bastard in my service when an . . . event occurred. Lorian somehow took possession of my magic. Now, my own ability to wield had dwindled to but a shadow of what it once was. I fear I grow weaker by the day, and if my magic wanes completely, my life will too."

Varios spoke in such a straightforward way that Lorian assumed he had practiced it every day since that event occurred. *But who wouldn't?* Lorian had stolen something so precious to the lord, and now he was being forced to lie to the entire world that the boy who stole his magic, and possibly his life, is his one and only heir. *What a torturous way to live.*

"Sam. The implications. How?" asked Coalsdottir, deadly serious.

"I'm aware. Why do you think I'm forcing you into a blood oath? We're uncertain how it happened. Lorian saved my life in Orion-Lon when Lord Aaron caused a collapse of the mines we were in. When I awoke, my power was gone, and the light in my eye was but a glow. As for Lord Aaron, we have him in the brig right now and are taking him to Mainis Fortu, where he will receive the king's punishment."

"So much for nobles not turning on each other," commented Bridgeson.

"He killed a boy of ten years. His own son. For no other reason than because he was a bastard. If he had any sense of dignity or accountability, he would separate his own head from his shoulders, but unfortunately, he's a coward. The king will decide on the punishment because if I chose, he'd be dead, and there would be war," Varios replied with rising anger in his voice.

"What role are we to play in all this? For what purpose have you sought us out? You wouldn't share a secret like this without a reason," Coalsdottir asked.

"You are correct, Lya. Lorian has shown characteristics of exceptional power. During his attunement, he all but destroyed Castle Greymoor. There is evidence that he controls many types of elements as he is also a Wielder of the body magics. I can train him in fire, but for wind and lightning, I'll need you two."

Coalsdottir laughed loudly in reaction. "You want me to believe that this child can wield lightning *and* wind with fire? Look at him, Sam. He looks like a child who just discovered the ability to think, not a prodigy of magics."

"He mastered the Forgornian tea puzzle in a single night."

The room went silent in shock. Lorian inspected the puzzled faces before him, attempting to comprehend why his success in brewing tea was such surprising news to the nobles. "I feel as if I'm missing some important information," he interjected. "Why is it so surprising that I brewed Forgornian tea?"

"I do not believe you, Sam. Show us he can. Prove to me right now that he can brew Forgornian tea, and I will pledge myself to a blood oath and keep your secret,"

Coalsdottir said. Bridgeson nodded in agreement. For the first time, the sloppy noble seemed to be out of quips and one-liners.

"Very well," Varios began as he reached into his overcoat and removed the familiar metallic cup and a small bag of Forgornian herbs. "I thought you might ask, so I came prepared. Lorian, as you did before, brew the tea."

Lorian watched as Varios set the items in front of him and poured fresh water into the cup from the drum of water present on the table already. Lorian felt small before the eyes of the three nobles before him. With practiced effort, he grabbed the cup and imagined himself floating in the sea of stars that had brought him peace previously.

The familiar surge of power came forth—controlled this time by allowing only a steady trickle of the magic through—and with focused precision. His hands began to heat the cup to a temperature he had come across from a night of trial and error.

A sweet cinnamon fragrance filled the small communal area, and when Lorian was sure the tea was ready, he halted the flow of magic and set the cup of steaming aromatic tea in the center of the table.

"Forgornian tea, my lord," muttered Lorian with a sigh of relief.

Bridgeson was the first to react to the spectacle. He reached slowly for the cup, and when he was close enough to grab it, he hesitated. "In one night," he whispered as he lifted the cup to his nose and inhaled deeply. "Unbelievable." He drank lightly from the cup. Without another word, he passed the brew to Coalsdottir, who

repeated the inspection process before drinking from it
herself.

"We are in agreement, Sam. We shall train the boy
as you see fit. We are ready to undertake the blood vow and
swear ourselves to maintaining your secret until you see fit
to release us," she said as she sipped from the tea again.

"Good. We shall bring Lady Jane in and have her
perform the ritual. Prepare yourselves however you'd like,"
Varios replied.

"Why is this tea so special?" Lorian asked. He
desperately wished to be let out of the darkness of
information that they were keeping him in. He felt like he
deserved to know. He was the center of the conversation,
after all.

"Mastering the Forgornian tea puzzle takes years of
work for some," said Varios. "It took me an entire year to
get it right. Channeling the perfect amount of magic allows
you to heat the water to the exact point that Forgornian
herbs need to flavor the liquid. Too much heat, and it sours.
Any less, and it doesn't activate at all. To have such precise
control of your magics so soon is a great feat. Adding to
your already impressive potential and compatibility with
the other elements makes for a very powerful Wielder."

"And very dangerous," Coalsdottir added, her eyes
never leaving the teacup in her hands.

"Why would you give me such a difficult test from
the start? Did you want me to fail?" Lorian asked, concern
rising despite his calm words.

"I wanted you to understand the great challenges
ahead of you. Failing now would humble you and prepare
you for a previously assumed difficult journey of wielding

at your older age. Having mastered it so fast means you're capable of much more. This is why I need Koh and Lya to help you train in the other elements. We need you to have full control of every aspect of your wielding. And, more importantly, we need to understand your capabilities," Varios explained. "Rikard!" he shouted, trying to summon the handsir from the other room. Before the servant could enter, Varios replaced his eye covering; to Lorian's surprise, he used a black eye patch in lieu of the usual cloth bandage he had been sporting.

"Yes, Your Grace?" Rikard said as he strode into the room. "I assume we're ready for Lady Jane to join us?" he asked, anticipating his lord's request.

"Correct. Bring her in and ensure no one attempts to enter. Thank you."

"As you wish, Your Grace," he replied. He grabbed an extra chair, and Jane entered and sat between Varios and Coalsdottir at the edge of the table. Rikard quickly left, as he was instructed, closing the door behind him and staying alert for any who dared to enter the secret meeting of nobles.

"It is a pleasure to make your acquaintance, Sir Lya Coalsdottir and Sir Koh Bridgeson. Handsir Rikard has informed me that a blood vow will be formed between the pair of you and Lord Sam Varios, is this correct?" Jane said as she accurately summarized the situation.

"Yes," the three said in unison.

"I have been instructed that the purpose of the vow is to be kept between the parties. Do any here stand ignorant of the purpose of this vow?" she continued.

Lorian felt like he was observing a completely different person from the kind and eager woman he had come to know. She was more refined and serious than he had known her to be. Shock set in when he once again realized how ignorant he was of the character of the woman he was poised to marry.

"No," they agreed in step.

"Then the purpose of this vow and its requirements are known to all involved. We may begin. Koh and Lya, join hands and place both in mine. Lord Varios, take my other hand. You are all in mutual agreement and will reach out to me with your magics. Once I've established a connection, your agreement will be bound by blood so that if any here break the conditions upon which the agreement is set, their lives shall be willingly forfeited. Once again, do you agree?"

"I agree," Varios said.

"We agree," the two sirs confirmed.

Lya Coalsdottir and Koh Bridgeson did as instructed, joining hands and placing both in Lady Jane's left hand. Varios held her right hand, and in perfect synchronization, the four closed their eyes and made a pact bound by magic and blood. As their eyes opened, their magic eyes glowed in three successive bursts, then faded to normal.

"It is done. You have all been bound and are at the mercy of your commitments," Lady Jane concluded. As she left the communal room, her eyes lingered on Lorian for a long moment, making him blush.

"You had better be worth this, boy," barked Bridgeson.

"I will do what I can, Sir Bridgeson, Sir Coalsdottir. I swear it," Lorian asserted, attempting to reassure them that their efforts wouldn't be in vain.

"You may call me Koh," Bridgeson replied. "I'll not have any of this bullshit formality while we work together. It's already made me tired and thirsty for ale. You fucking high-borns never have any good ale. Why is that? Just wine and other soft liquors that barely sate." He directed his last sentence at Varios.

"And you may call me Lya," Coalsdottir said with more politeness than Lorian thought she was capable of. "You should have told us you were a commoner from the beginning. I wouldn't have pretended to hate you if I'd known," she said with a smile and a wink.

"Calm yourself. He's engaged to Lady Jane," Varios said.

Lorian was surprised. Was Lya showing interest in him that had gone unnoticed until now?

"Engaged does not mean married, Sam," Lya said as she smiled hungrily at Lorian. Being unsure of what to say or how to reply, his cheeks flushed and his hands shook unsteadily.

"So, he is just a boy after all! Hah!" Koh laughed.

"Um, so, when do we begin?" asked Lorian, changing the subject.

"As soon as we leave Orco's Island. I need to speak with Lord Greymoor first about our little encounter in town and see if he has any useful information. Until then, get some rest if you can. You're going to need every ounce of strength going forward. Koh, Lya, Rikard will help with your accommodations and your fee. Be reasonable, please,"

Varios said. He stood from the table, the other low-born nobles standing in return.

He left the three of them alone in the communal area and made his way to the upper deck and to Lord Greymoor. *Someone wants Lord Aaron back, badly*, Varios thought. He had to know who and why. Lord Aaron's father would be the most obvious person, but Lord Handall would have keen interest in their affairs as well. Varios wasn't sure where to focus his attention, but he knew he had to act with care. Whoever it was had shown themselves bold enough to send cut-throat mercenaries after them, and who knew what they would try next.

Chapter 19: The Road Stretches Ever On

The deep blue of the ocean made Varios uneasy. Froth had accumulated near the ship's lower hull along with barnacles and other sea debris unfamiliar to him. Varios stood quietly along the port side of the *High Guard* and leaned lazily over the railing watching the great vessel cut through the rough waves below with ease.

Varios never had an affinity for sailing or water in general. While seasickness was far from what ailed him on these voyages, a certain queasiness did infect his mind. Perhaps it was the isolation of a ship at sea that made him feel unwell, or maybe it was the lack of control if a situation went sour.

He always did feel more secure with earth and soil beneath his feet.

When he was a boy, his father had told him a story of a man named Kylon, one of his ancestors of the ancient world. Men were apparently the first to try and tame the sea, and Kylon was a pioneer of the less-than-modern sail ship. Before man had walked the shores of Centrugard, they lived peaceful lives on the isle of Farland—the birthplace of mankind and all intelligent life. It was said that the natural god Tuli, mistress of nature, gave man life when she and Eruna, natural god of soil and growth, conjured the idea of shaping soil into a living, breathing creature. They toiled for years, shaping the clay and earth into what they believed to be the finest form, giving that shape life and the spark of intelligence thereafter. Kylon was a descendant of these first men, and after discovering that Farland was but a drop of water in a much larger bucket, he set off to explore the many mysteries of the world beyond its shores.

It was said then that Gamil, natural god of water and froth, was angered by the men of Farland and felt that their seafaring vessels perverted her waters. She felt as though dominion over the waters was hers and hers alone. When the men of Farland ventured too far from their shores, she cursed them and forbade them ever return to Farland, shaping the waves of the water and the currents under the sea to carry them away if they came too close to returning. Since those days, mankind had never returned to the island of Farland.

Varios believed this story to be the reason he felt so uneasy upon deep waters. His blood carried with it the curse of Gamil. He wondered how arrogant the ancient men were—thinking they could conquer the realm of the gods, believing they could explore the world at their leisure, forsaking the paradise of Farland. Was it man's destiny to be scrutinized by the beings who gave them life? To always challenge the natural world and bend it to their own image?

Even today, Varios felt humanity did everything it could to seize the powers of the world and shape it to their will. New metals forced humans to destroy the mountains. New farming techniques caused poison to spread to local wildlife and destroy ecosystems. A growing population meant that livestock and fishing industries needed to farm more resources from the sea and earth. If merely sailing was enough to ban humanity from paradise, he wondered, what would mankind's punishment be for all the damage they'd done so far?

A disorienting feeling came over him and forced him to look upon the sea no longer, lest he expel his breakfast into the brine below. He instead refocused his eyes on the small armada that followed the *High Guard*.

Lord Greymoor had gathered more than a few ships and men on Orco's Island. He apparently had a small fleet stationed there, which, when accompanied by the ships that were docked at the Golden Hatch, formed somewhat of a threatening force that followed their flagship. Ten thousand men accompanied them on their adventure to Mainis Fortu, a force sizable enough to draw concern from anyone, especially the royal family. When Varios had probed Lord Greymoor on the decision, he'd merely replied, *"I'm a Greymoor, Ash-Bringer. I shit gold and bleed excellence. Wherever I go, I make a statement."*

Normally, this would be an adequate response for something not too unexpected from the flashy lord, but something felt off. Varios could sense some worry from Greymoor, which he found to be unusual for the otherwise steadfast buffoon that was his uncle. Greymoor was worried about an assault, perhaps. Maybe the force he brought was intended as a deterrent to any who would provoke him or his family. The ambush at Orco's Island must've shaken him more than Varios had thought. His uncle was preparing for war now.

Inspecting the bodies of the masked attackers—what Lya and Koh were kind enough to leave intact—gave little to no information about their origin or employer. The men bore odd scars around their eyes, burns of some kind, perhaps, but no other discernible features or marks that gave context to who they were.

Lord Charles Aaron was Dan Aaron's father and served in Twilanon as the High-Gothic, leader of the church of the natural gods. Since Dan was his prisoner and was being taken to Mainis Fortu to stand trial, Varios knew his father would do anything he could to either intercept them or sway the court to favor Dan and reduce his sentence. It was Varios' mission to see that this did not happen. Lord Dan Aaron would be well behind bars before his father would ever hear word, if it were up to him. Yet, he had to assume that Charles Aaron already knew that his son was taken from Orion-Lon and well on his way to court.

If the lord was the person who discerned his location, he was certain that Charles Aaron would intervene in some manner. But the question was: How did Lord Charles Aaron discover this? It may have been a soldier at Orion-Lon who'd informed him, though there wasn't any way of them knowing where the group were headed. That they would be taking a noble to stand trial at the capital would have to be a very wild assumption on their part, and as nobility refused to hold each other accountable, how did they discover his location and his injury?

"Your mind seems troubled with something, Your Grace," said a voice from behind the lord. He cursed himself for being so distracted that he didn't hear someone approach. When he turned to face the stranger, he was less than thrilled to see Child-Scholar Lo.

"A noble's mind is as restless as the sea, child-scholar. May I help you with something?" he asked, hoping to end their conversation as soon as possible. It wasn't that he hated the child-scholar; he just found her—and all their people—to be overzealous and talkative. He enjoyed peace and quiet when he had the rare opportunity, but with these scholars, that opportunity never came.

"No. I felt as though I might be of some help to you, though," she said warmly. Varios noticed that her usual spunk and energy seemed throttled at the moment, which he was thankful for.

"No, I'm very well. Thank you," he said abruptly.

The sound of metal on metal rang out loudly. Lorian had seemingly started his morning training with Bowers, ending Varios' session of peace and quiet. The two came at each other cautiously. They walked in a circular pattern and studied one another, waiting to see who would make the mistake of attacking first. Varios felt a sense of pride when watching Lorian block and strike at the captain's midsection, deflecting the attack as he had practiced many times before. A small smile crept to the corner of his mouth while he watched.

"He is quite good," started Lo. "Your son has proven to be adept at many things, from what I've observed. Does he know?" Varios' smile vanished as he tried to decipher the meaning of her words.

"Does he know what?"

"That you're proud of him?" she asked. "Tell him every chance you get. Children are precious things, and they should be treasured."

Varios noticed the child-scholar reach for her belly, like a pregnant woman does instinctively, yet Lo hesitated and returned her hand to her side. Varios knew child-scholars were forbidden from siring children, though their rituals for keeping to this oath were unknown to him. He felt a familiar sadness as he watched her. Wanting a child but not having the means to create one or to keep them from harm was an awful and powerless feeling. He sympathized with her.

"He knows. I'm sure he does," replied Varios.

"That's well and good. Be sure to say it anyway," she said again. "He is destined for great things; I can feel it. I'm unsure why, but when we speak, when we're near one another, it's like being near a new discovery of the ancient world. A sixth sense I think I have for identifying the uniqueness of a thing, and he is unique. As are you." She offered a kind smile that made him feel more comfortable around her.

"No wonder my uncle has taken a liking to you. I was unaware that child-scholars were also trained as wordsmiths," he said with a chuckle. Her rosy cheeks deepened with color as embarrassment came over her.

"He's taken a liking to me, has he? Is it not forbidden for nobles and scholars to share a bond?" she asked inquisitively.

"No, not forbidden. Marriage, as you know, is forbidden. But Uncle is a widower and has become rather smitten, I believe. Do what you will with that information," Varios said, feeling an uncharacteristic urge to aid in their affairs.

"I shall take what you've said into consideration, Your Grace," she replied with an awkward curtsey.

Varios watched as she left and made her way down the ladder-well that carried her to the decks below. He figured that she was heading for Lady Jane's room, as the two had been spending ample time together since leaving Castle Greymoor. Varios made a mental note to get to know Jane better, as she was going to be his daughter-in-law relatively soon. The absurdity of that reflection made him chuckle again.

When his wife, Emelia, was still alive, they would spend countless hours imagining what life would be like when they were older, when their children would marry and have kids of their own. He used to joke with her that as soon as their estate was free of children, she would go mad with boredom and force the servants to bring their children to the estate so she could spend time with them.

She would joke in return that he would be the first to go mad, dropping the bravado of being a notorious soldier when, in reality, he wanted nothing more than to be a good father. He loved that about her, how she could take a single glance at him and see through the façade that was

Lord Varios, that was the Ash-Bringer. He missed her so much.

"Father!" yelled Lorian, waking him from his daydream of Emelia and their life before. "I'm about to have my first lesson with Sir Coalsdottir . . . I mean, Lya. Care to watch?" he asked with excitement. Varios allowed himself a small smile.

He made his way over to their sparring circle only to find a winded Captain Bowers on the deck, drinking heavily from a water skin and doing what he could to catch his breath.

***

"Sleeping on the job, are we, captain? Last time I checked, the sparring was supposed to take place on your feet, not your ass," Varios said, clearly toying with the haggard soldier.

"My apologies, Your Grace." Bowers spoke between labored breaths. "Between keeping Lord Greymoor satisfied and increasing the young lord's training, I'm finding myself quite exhausted. Truth be told, my lord, he's gotten very good with a sword. Very fast. Three months we've been training together, I believe. The boy has nearly surpassed me," he observed as he winked at a proud-faced Lorian.

"What can I say?" Lorian started. "I guess it's just in my blood," he said with his chin held high.

Captain Bowers dropped the water skin and rapidly swung a leg at Lorian's ankles, dropping the young lord to his backside with a solid thud. "And what was the first lesson I taught you?"

"Cup the balls?" Lorian groaned smartly.

"Never lose focus," Bowers corrected, awkwardly glancing at Lord Varios.

"Right, I'll have to remember that one more often," he said as he stood to his feet and dusted off his worn training garments.

"Glad to see you have kept the child warm for me, captain," Lya called as she lifted herself from the ladder-well. The large, brown-skinned noble marched toward Lorian with heavy footsteps and a series of metal knives in her hand. Her signature cavalier's hat had been left below deck, revealing thickly braided hair that was previously hidden beneath. Lorian was unsure why seeing her without the hat made him more afraid of her, but it did. She was an enormous person, especially for a woman, and her gentle features betrayed the rough way she spoke and the violence she was capable of.

"He's all yours, Sir Coalsdottir. I shall take my leave of you all now, in case Lord Greymoor wants another rematch."

As if Captain Bowers had summoned the stone giant himself, Lord Greymoor revealed himself from the ladder-well just moments after Lya. "Speak, and the devil himself shall appear, captain. I'll go fetch my hammer. You had better be here when I return," he said as he disappeared beneath the deck once more.

"Fuck," swore the captain. "If you need me later, Your Grace, I shall be hiding in the main cargo bay. Enjoy the remainder of your morning," he said as he gave a formal bow before sprinting for the cargo bay at the aft end of the ship.

"Poor lad," said Lya as she handed Lorian the knives that were in her hand.

"What are these for?" Lorian asked as memories of the battle in Orco's Island returned to him. "Do you use these to summon lightning?" he asked with glee. The thought of conjuring lightning thrilled him. He knew it was dangerous but couldn't help imagining himself wielding a large bolt of lightning like a marble statue of an egotistical deity.

"Yes and no. These are just tools; they hold no magic themselves. Lightning is a very dangerous element to wield, young Lorian. Perhaps the most dangerous of them all. We do not command lightning; we simply help guide it forward. Yes, we can recommend where it goes, but the lightning always has the final say-so," she said in warning.

Like all things Lorian had learned about wielding, perception was only half of the information required to use magic properly.

"This element can and will bite back if you use it improperly," she started again. "Do not confuse the blowback of lightning with the overuse of magic, boy. What I mean for you to understand is that pulling too much magic can hurt you, but mishandling lightning will surely end your life. What I will teach you going forward is meant to do a few things. First, it's to keep you safe while learning to guide the magic. Second, it's knowing the difference between manifesting lightning and manipulating the energy that already exists within the atmosphere. We will focus on manipulation first and manifesting after."

"Lya, I don't quite understand. What does it mean to manipulate it instead of manifest it?" he asked. Lorian had heard these terms before, but no one had bothered to explain them to him. *Does lightning just exist within the air at all times? Do all the elements? And how does one conjure the element versus manipulate what's already there?*

Lya peered at Varios with a look that spoke a thousand different words, all of them chastising him for not giving Lorian a more thorough explanation of the magics. "To manifest, or conjure, is to use your connection to the infinite source and form the element from within. When you brew the Forgornian tea, you are manifesting the heat from within you and focusing it on the metal and, subsequently, the water inside. To manipulate fire would require fire to be present before you. This is different from lightning. The air around us has trace amounts of electrical energy that, when gathered properly, results in a bolt of lightning forming. Do you understand?" she asked with great patience, which Lorian appreciated.

"Yes, I believe I understand."

"Good. This is why I have given you the knives. We are going to manipulate the energy in the air around us and form electricity. Your goal is to guide the bolts toward the knives. These metals are very conductive and will provide the lightning more encouragement to strike where they are placed. To keep the ship from burning down, I have placed small wires that will help disperse the residue energy to the ocean below.

"I will also be here to keep you from harm's way and absorb the energy, if possible," she said with a concerned look. "I have been told that you can summon great power, Lorian. I believe this to be true as you have shown great skill by mastering the Forgornian tea puzzle. But let me be clear. If you summon too much power, you will kill everyone aboard this ship, including yourself. Show restraint."

A great deal of fear filled Lorian. He hadn't considered the downsides to being a potential prodigy. His ego had kept him from stewing on the possibility that he was capable of great harm now. He swore to himself that he would never gloss over the less-appealing aspects of his power going forward.

"I understand. I'm ready."

"Very good," she said as she placed a metal rod on the railings next to Lorian. "Place three of those knives around you in a circle, two arm's lengths apart each. Then, place another between the circle and each of the railings I've rigged. This should help direct the excess energy away."

Lorian did as he was told, ensuring everything was properly secured before he returned to the center of the circle. "All done."

"Good. Now sit."

Lorian sat with his legs crossed, just like he had when he'd first attempted to access his magic.

"Great. Here, take this," she said as she tied metallic wire around the three knives and handed him the knotted ends. "Oh, and this," she finished while reaching out with a small wooden handle that had cloth wrapped around it. Lorian grabbed the knotted ends of the wire and the wooden handles. Unsure what to do with the equipment, he waited silently for more instruction.

She pointed at her teeth. "What are you hesitating for? Bite down on the wood."

Lorian felt embarrassed by his ignorance and promptly bit down, still holding the wires.

"Okay, time for the hard part," she said with an arched eyebrow. Lorian was still lingering in confusion until it dawned on him. She was going to shock him, but why? He didn't need to feel the burn of fire to summon heat forward, so what was the purpose of this? Lya could see the realization set into Lorian's face, and she offered a quick explanation. "It's sort of a rite of passage," she admitted with raised shoulders.

Before Lorian could protest further, the magic hit him. A small bolt came from above and struck the railing. A few sparks jumped from the wires as the current flooded Lorian's body, forcing all his muscles to contract simultaneously. Lorian had never felt such a thing in his life. For what seemed like an eternity, his limbs and face twisted into a ball of tortured muscle as the autonomy of his flesh betrayed him. He bit viciously into the wooden handle in his mouth—now thankful for the thick cloth that kept his teeth from shattering. A series of small grunts and gurgles escaped him, and he collapsed to the deck, convulsing with strained twitches.

When the seizing of his muscles abated and his pain finally eased, he rose. "Why did you do that?" he asked with a weak voice as the shroud of confusion and anguish slowly lifted.

"Now you know what awaits you if you lose control. And that was nothing compared to what I did to those would-be mercenaries. If you are capable of more, imagine what would happen if you lost focus. Be thankful I am here to teach you these hard lessons."

Lorian felt anything but thankful at the moment. He truly believed that, within his short life, no pain he'd experienced had ever come close to what had just happened to him. He looked at Varios for assurance that what he had just suffered was unjust and unnecessary, but the lord's face showed no signs of sympathy. The lord was in full agreement with Lya. And even if he wasn't, Lorian doubted he would reveal it.

"I . . . understand. I'm ready to learn now. Please don't shock me again," he pleaded as he slowly lowered himself to the deck again, his arms shaking. "Do I need to hold these wires again?"

"No, I'll tie those off. Now it is your turn to summon the lightning. Let us begin," she said as she sat opposite him in the circle. He noticed that while she did twist off the knotted ends of wire, she had untied a couple of strands and laid them next to her—in case she needed to take control, he assumed.

Lorian steadied himself as best he could, returning to his place of meditation among the stars. The residual pain made him feel less comfortable and reluctant to reach for his magic, yet he did it anyway. As the great flow of energy entered him, he fought hard to limit what he allowed through, focusing instead on the energy around him. He felt a few mental tugs, and when he was sure he had a grasp on the energy that waited in the air, he tugged back.

He opened his eyes just in time to see the sky grow dark and the winds of a storm blow harshly in. Sailors aboard started screaming and running toward their duty stations in preparation for the incoming gales and rough waters. Thunder roared above, closer than he had ever heard. Lya was screaming at him, but all he could hear was the great bellowing of drums in the heavens.

Lorian looked toward the sky and saw a bolt of lightning streak across the clouds, larger than anything he had ever seen. He knew this was the bolt he commanded. With every ounce of control and focus he could muster, he pleaded for the bolt to land anywhere but the ship. Lorian didn't know if it was by chance or through his will that the bolt struck the ocean beyond but was thankful regardless.

The great stream of energy crashed violently into the sea and sent residual shockwaves of force through the water, rocking the *High Guard*. A wave as tall as a mountain erupted from the area of the strike and threatened to swallow the armada before it.

Chapter 20: Touching Infinity

"He who remained unnamed and secret amongst his divine brothers and sisters toils to this day. While the others remain silent to our prayers, the twelfth natural god remains silent even to those who stand as his equal. It is with him that we pledge our lives and souls, sacrificing our voices in his honor."
—Priest Naman, head of the Silent Order

Lorian drifted serenely amidst the star-studded expanse before him, enveloped in a comforting warmth that embraced his entire being. This peculiar meditative trance he had cultivated symbolized to him the essence of lost elements in his life. The gentle caress of the water mirrored what he imagined a mother's touch would be like. Encircled by the profound depths, he perceived the surrounding abyss as the enigmatic realm perpetually looming to swallow him whole, while the stars offered fleeting moments of solace amid the vast emptiness.

Each celestial body represented a person he had encountered and cherished: his true father, Feln, Lord Varios, Child-Scholar Lo, Jane, even Captain Bowers and Lord Greymoor. In this ethereal sanctuary, the universe divulged its secrets, rendering the intricate complexities of life mundane and comprehensible. Here, amidst the cosmic expanse, the intricacies of existence were unraveled, laid bare before Lorian's contemplative gaze.

As he drifted, awe swept over him as he gazed upon the grandeur of the celestial lights above—or perhaps below; in this ethereal realm, conventional orientation held little significance. To him, therein lay the essence of magic—an inexhaustible font of universal energy, hidden from common view and feared by the elite. It manifested as an unbroken stream of light and vitality coursing through all existence. Trees, grass, flowers, and every form of foliage drew sustenance from it; animals and humans wielded its power for purpose and expression.

The cosmos itself served as its vessel, directing its currents as it deemed fit, while Lorian, in his drifting reverie, stood transfixed in reverence. *Are the ancient gods the architects of this wondrous phenomenon? Are they even tangible entities? Is the boundless flow of magic merely another guise of the divine? Has it always existed, or did it spring forth from some primordial origin? Would it someday cease, and if so, what lay beyond?* These questions tantalized Lorian's mind, offering both clarity and ambiguity when he endeavored to articulate his thoughts.

A figure then approached Lorian—a man who, like him, was adrift within the sea of stars. The man floated toward Lorian until the two were mirroring one another.

"Lorian Night," said the man. His face was stoic; he was both pleased and displeased. For a moment, he resembled Lorian; in another, he held the features of his father, then Varios, and so on. "Of all the creatures to find this place, you are the most unlikely," he continued, "but all things make sense, eventually. Ah, yes. Now it explains itself. You bear her shard, her remnants. An even more unlikely occurrence."

Lorian tried to reply to the entity that spoke to him but was unable to find his voice. Maybe he wasn't supposed to have a voice here. Maybe it was gone for a purpose, he mused. He was meant to listen, not to speak.

"You are a clever boy, indeed. What a hard life you've had, Lorian. Do you ever wish it wasn't so? That things had been different for you, that fate hadn't chosen you to live as a bastard, a man with no claim to his name and no honor? Ah, but you were not chosen, were you? Fate has never granted you boons because fate has never seen you—nor will it, I think," the man said as he floated closer to Lorian, the ever-shifting scape of his features both reassuring and frightening.

"No, you are a boy who fate never discarded because fate never considered you. And so, you live free of these lay lines, adrift," he continued as he placed a gentle hand upon Lorian's shoulder. "Yet something meddles; I feel it. Some believe you are beyond fate and thus free of action and choice, but it is the opposite. Whispers seek to restore you to the cycle, to give you a proper role, assign you. But that too is your choice. Kill the Raven?" he finished, leaving Lorian surprised and wanting to know more. If this person was not the one who whispered to him, then what, or who, was it?

"Do, or do not act. Kill the Raven, or leave it be. Either action is equally available to you, as are all actions. A choice is coming for you, Lorian. One that will decide if you remain absent of fate or become its progenitor. When you leave here, you will retain one truth of things lost and secret. The choice is yours, and I will not intervene. I cannot intervene," he said as he placed his other hand firmly on Lorian's chest and shoved with incredible force.

"Lorian. Lorian. *LORIAN*!" shouted Lady Jane as she treaded water with great strain. Lorian awoke to find himself overboard the *High Guard*, his lungs full of water and salt. He forced the seawater from his lungs with much effort and coughed harshly; his chest and throat ached from the expulsion.

"Jane?" he said as he struggled to inhale fresh air.

"It's all right, I've got you!" she said as she pulled the two of them onto a patch of netting that hung over the hull of the ship. "I saw you fall when the wave hit us. Everyone else was trying to save the ship."

"What happened?" he asked as faint memories of the starry sea still lingered within his mind.

"The lightning . . . There was a wave. I'll have to explain better after we get you top side," she said as she continued to hoist him higher, using the netting as leverage to lift and secure him.

Jane screamed for help, and a small group of sailors climbed down the side and affixed both of them to a rope seat normally used for scraping barnacles. When they were secured, they were both lifted to the top deck and to safety. The entire ordeal was a haze for Lorian. He couldn't remember falling in the water—not until the light rumbling of thunder sounded overhead, the storm receding.

Lorian coughed the remainder of the seawater from his lungs and took in the chaotic scene that was the *High Guard*'s top deck. Cannons, crates, and other secured items had been toppled over; their contents spilled out. Sailors and soldiers alike were restoring the ship as best they could—tying off loose rope that tightened the sails and clearing dangerous debris from the deck.

"Was anyone hurt?" he asked in a panic as he searched for Lya and Varios.

"No, I don't think so. Varios kept Lya from falling overboard, and I jumped in shortly after you fell," she responded as she began to heal Lorian, her emerald eye glowing beautifully.

Lorian noticed Varios and Lya kneeling next to the guardrails on the port side, their clothes drenched and their movements slow and weak, as if they had been battling a hurricane. Lorian tensed as Jane began to heal a few ribs, the pain making him wince. He grabbed onto her hand and forced her to stop the flow of her magic, knowing how exhausted she must've been after saving him.

He sat upright and allowed her a chance to lean on him, which she quickly accepted. He was still unsure what had happened; all he could focus on was the shivering girl in his arms who was to be his wife, and he felt thankful. She truly was a kind person. He looked deeply into her eyes, his own stare lingering between her green eye and her lips. He realized that this was as close as he had ever gotten to a woman, and his heart fluttered.

He pulled her closer, hoping the heat from his body would calm her shivers. She pressed back against him, embracing the closeness. Lorian's eyes danced back and forth from her eyes to her lips. He wanted to kiss her, to give himself over to her completely. She had just saved his life, cared for him amidst the chaos of his magic when no one else thought to. His head inched closer to her, their lips only a hair's breadth away.

She wanted to kiss him too; he could feel it. But something was wrong. Thoughts pulled at the back of his mind, keeping him from embracing her further. He looked into her eyes once more and was displeased with what he saw. It wasn't her; she was perfect. Soaked head to toe, her auburn hair wrapped around the back of her head, and the wet scar on her cheek glistened in the light of the sun. The issue was him. He wasn't worthy of her yet.

Though he was a man, what he saw in her eyes showed him something else. It didn't feel like him. It wasn't. There, in her magical green eye, he saw it. Not the man he thought himself to be, but a boy.

The pounding of Lord Greymoor's massive feet on the hard planks brought him back to reality. He lifted Jane to her feet, saddened to no longer embrace her, and walked her to her grandfather. Lorian noticed the softness that overcame Greymoor whenever Jane was concerned and used this to his advantage to stem the unfiltered anger that was surely to greet him later.

"She's all right, Lord Greymoor. Just tired. She saved my life," he said, hoping to paint a better picture of the events that recently unfolded in lieu of what the stone giant's first impression may have been.

"Come with me, my sweet. I'll have Javal run you a warm bath and fetch you dry clothes," he said as he reassured her. Together, they walked toward the ladder-well that would carry them away.

"Lorian!" Lya yelled as she approached him from the opposite end of the deck. "What about control did you not understand?! There was more magic in that bolt than I've ever seen someone wield at once. It's a mystery how we're not dead right now! It's an even bigger mystery how you're not dead from wielding it!" she screamed. "And when were you going to tell me you could control water as well? We don't have a tutor for that, you damned fool. Warn me next time you try to redirect a wave like that. You nearly capsized the ship!"

Lorian didn't remember the moments before he fell overboard, but he was sure he heard her correctly. When did he control water? He remembered there being moisture present during his attunement but assumed it had more to do with the other elements interacting with each other. Regardless, it didn't matter. He'd lost control of the magic, almost killing everyone. But though the memories of the starry sea were foggy and vague, he remembered something that could help.

"It's all right, Lya. He didn't mean it." Varios spoke in his defense. "This is why I brought you along. Think of how much worse it could have been."

Lya still appeared upset but seemed to relax after considering Varios' words.

Varios was right, after all. Had he not learned to control the flow of ambient magic and energy, everyone here, including himself, would have perished. "I think I know how to fix this issue," Lorian stated, surprising both nobles.

"And how can you do that? Throwing yourself overboard may be the only way to keep you from burning this ship down," Lya replied as the anger overcame her again.

"I can choke the magic before it comes out," he said. From his vision, he recalled learning something that he couldn't put into words. It was like a memory had been planted in his mind that, when he dwelled upon it, made sense, but when he tried to explain it, it wouldn't sound coherent. "There is a way to force my magic into a container and keep it from exploding forward when I don't want it to."

"You're talking about imbuement," Varios stated. "There are tales of Wielders forcing their power into a weapon, but I've never seen evidence of this being possible. How do you know it would work?"

"I . . . just do. I'll need silver. As pure as we can make it. And gemstones as well."

"Here," Varios said as he removed a ring from his pocket. He gazed upon the trinket for a long while, his eyes distant as if some memory played before him that only he could see. "It was given to me by Emelia, my late wife, as an anniversary gift. Take great care." He cautiously handed it to Lorian.

"Why are we humoring this, Sam? He needs to learn control; it is the only way to ensure his safety," Lya said with a frustrated grin on her face.

"Please, trust me. I know I haven't earned it yet, but lend me some favor," Lorian said as he grabbed the ring from Varios. Something stirred within his mind, an answer to a question he had never asked.

The silver ring had an intricate series of swirls Lorian recognized. When the silver would run red hot, a skilled craftsman could bend and twist the soft metal in any shape he wanted as long as material was there. This work had been done over the course of many nights, and by a very skilled smith. A black gem of onyx was inlaid into the singular facet that formed an ovular shape and gave the ring an excellent contrast of colors. Lorian ran the ring down his left index finger, thankful that it fit well enough to not slide or jam.

"I'm going to force as much magic into it as I can. Please alert the men to take cover. I don't want to injure anyone should I fail," Lorian said in a way that caused Varios visible concern.

"This is foolish, Lorian," Lya started. "We can control your power; we don't need to risk your safety any further trying something that dangerous."

"We both know this is for the best, Lya. Should I succeed, I'll have discovered a way to keep myself alive and safe from wild magic. It could take years otherwise."

Lya and Varios looked at each other, communicating silently. At last, they seemed to come to a mutual conclusion. Lya nodded. "Each element is vastly different from the others," she admitted. "If you could cause this much damage with lightning, even under my training, you need some form of restraint. Who knows what else could happen."

"Be careful," Varios replied as he and Lya began to shout and warn the men that toiled atop the main deck. After a few minutes, Lorian was clear to begin. He felt as if he were trying to remember a long-forgotten dream—a faint memory that dared to tiptoe across the boundaries of his knowledge. Then, like a passing scent that reminded a man of a childhood memory, the information came forward.

Lorian felt the flow of his power, his body energizing itself. When he could feel the magic begin to overflow, he refocused on the torrent of power. Unlike fire, where he could focus it through his arms, and lightning, where grasping at ambient energy allowed him to call upon a bolt and direct it, he restricted the flow entirely. He slowed the flow so much that it felt like thick mud coursing through him. He kept opposing the natural force of magic until he felt it condense to a point where he was sure his body contained lead. Finally, when it was solid enough, he began to pool the energy into the ring. At first, the ring opposed him. It fought back, as it wanted to keep the natural structure of energy that currently held it together. Time and time again, the ring refused, denying him the chance to fill it with magic.

He needed to move forward, afraid that the dense magic would tear him apart, but then he remembered. *You do not force magic; you guide it.* He couldn't force the ring to accept the magic. He had to ask its permission. He poured his will and his intention into the silver and onyx, pleading with it to accept. After moments of silence, he felt the ring begrudgingly allow the magic in. The silver seemed to swell and flow as if it were molten once more, the twisted design shifting into a series of jagged shapes that jutted forward until the ring rested again, a hum of power escaping it.

Lorian knew then that he had accomplished what many before him had failed to do. He had imbued the ring with energy, and he could continue to do so as long as he never poured more in than the ring could handle. With this, he could slow the ebbs and flows of his magic as it came out, allowing only what he needed to perform the wield he wanted. With this, he would be safe.

Chapter 21: Who Are You?

"For what purpose do we love? Is it a product of necessity? Born out of a natural urge to survive, to persist? Or is this complex feeling the unintended result of our great intellect? An emotion that lesser creatures are unable to comprehend? For what reason do we continue to love and seek love?"
—Matron-Scholar Hannaly

Lorian sat across from Varios, the two of them resting at a small square table within Varios' cabin. The small room held only a few containers—some for storage of personal items and some for food and other perishables—with the table, two chairs, and a small hammock tied to the exposed beams of the ship's innards.

Varios spun the silver ring in his hand, closely inspecting the familiar trinket with an air of curiosity. By all accounts, the ring was exactly the same in appearance as it had been before he gave it to Lorian. It fit the same, contained the same intricate swirls of silver, and held the same small chunk of onyx in its silvery claws, but now, it was anything but the same.

Within the small ornament was contained a massive amount of energy—magical energy. Even with his connection to the infinite pool of magic weakened, he could feel the familiar hum of magics stirring within, waiting for the chance to explode forward. Memories of his time at the college of Mainis Fortu came flooding into his mind—

lessons on magical energy and what the world knew of it so far.

He watched as his false father contemplated the trinket, his eyes bouncing back and forth between him and the ring. Lorian thought it was odd to see someone he considered so articulate to be speechless and confused.

"Who are you?" asked Varios, catching Lorian off-guard, breaking the complete silence.

"What do you mean?" he replied, his voice slightly apologetic.

"This is supposed to be impossible, Lorian. Everything you're capable of is supposed to be impossible. Never has a Wielder commanded such raw power, never has anyone been capable of mastering all the elements in our school of magic, and no one in modern history has ever imbued an item with magic. So, I'll ask again: Who are you, really?"

Lorian was unsure of how to answer the lord. He had never been anyone but himself. He was always Lorian Night, son of Nord Oslison, a blacksmith, and a lady of the night. He'd never asked for this life, even wishing to be rid of it at times. "I'm Lorian."

"How did you know how to imbue this ring, Lorian? After you summoned that bolt, that monstrosity of magic, and stopped the wave from capsizing the *High Guard*, you fell into the water below. What happened between then and now that gave you insight into something so secret, so incredible, that it could change the very nature of this world?" he asked, waiting for Lorian to give a satisfactory answer.

In truth, Lorian couldn't remember how he knew; he just did. All he retained of the incident were half-remembered moments and vague recollections. Whenever he fought to remember, a mist of the mind obscured the memories, like they were being purposefully hidden. "I don't know how. I just do," he replied, knowing it wouldn't suffice. "Ever since Orion-Lon, things have changed. Not just with how everyone perceives me, but with how I perceive myself. I don't know why my magic is so strong, so wild. I don't know why I can imbue. I don't know what's happening half the time, and I'm tired of being kept in the dark as well. But there is one thing I do know," Lorian said. "Since the night after Lord Aaron's son was executed—after Max was murdered—I've been seeing things. Hearing things, too."

Varios raised his eyebrows in surprise. "And what is it you've been seeing and hearing?"

"At first, it was Max. I fell asleep in the bathtub the morning we left Orion-Lon, and I had a nightmare. He came to me, as dead as the moment you pulled him from the rope, and he spoke to me," Lorian explained as the memories of that hellish dream returned to him. The awful voice that screamed at him. The way Max's face was frozen in fear and pain. "He asked me to kill the Raven. No, he commanded me to kill it." Shivers coursed through his body.

"I don't understand," Varios began. "Why would Max want you to kill a raven? You're positive these aren't just nightmares?"

"I don't believe so. And I don't think Max wants me to kill just any raven—if it's even Max to begin with. I think the Raven is a person, and someone wants them dead. When we were at Castle Greymoor, as we were leaving for the docks below, I heard the call again. Something was asking me to kill the Raven. I was with Rikard when I heard it, but he didn't notice. It was when we passed outside Lady Varios' room."

"My mother?" he asked as his eyes darted back and forth. "You never left something in your room, did you?" he suggested with concern. "You went back to see her? But why?"

"I had to know if she was involved somehow. I didn't think she was, but I thought maybe she had useful information that would help me understand what it is I'm supposed to do," he said as guilt started to overcome him. Lorian remembered what he had done immediately after confronting Lady Varios. He remembered the way he choked her, the feeling of her weak neck in his hands, and the way the blackness of her eye receded as she came closer to death. "My lord, I . . . I," he stuttered as he began to choke on his own words, nervous about how Varios would react when he found out.

"Spit it out, Lorian. What is it you wish to say?"

"I nearly killed her," he admitted in one breath, hoping the quickness of it would keep him from hiding his words any longer.

Varios stared with his mouth slightly open, a confounded expression stuck on his face.

"When I asked her for answers about the Raven, about what haunts me, she told me that a dark one had found me," he continued as he hesitated once more to explain further. "She said horrible things after that, things I think people should never hear from anyone but themselves. I was so angry, my lord. I grabbed her neck, and I squeezed with all my might." Tears began to well within his eyes. "I was going to kill her. I was going to take my anger out on her, for no reason. She only spoke the truth, and I was going to kill her for it," he finished, sobbing at hearing the truth out loud.

Lorian looked to Varios for the first time, wanting to see his reaction. Varios' face was flushed with rage. He squeezed his fists so tightly that he shook. Lorian's fears had become reality. The one person who knew his secrets, who shared this journey with him, hated him.

"Please, Father, forgive me. I was unable to control myself. I just . . ." He attempted to clarify, but Varios, standing from the table and nearly toppling it, interrupted him.

"I . . . need to think. I need to be alone," he said as he made for the door.

"Wait! Please let me explain, Father," he said as the sobs grew more intense. He reached for Varios and grabbed him by the sleeve, hoping that stopping him from leaving would give him enough time to justify what he had done, though he knew there was no justification for what transpired.

Varios ripped his arm away, and Lorian recoiled slightly. He reached out again in desperation; this time, he was met with a shove from Varios that made him trip over his chair and fall onto his backside.

"I am not your father," Varios said as he left the room, slamming the door loudly.

Lorian stayed on the floor for a long while, allowing himself to cry, wishing there was a way to do penance to make up for his betrayal to Varios. He felt so alone, so cold. He wished for nothing more than to be with his father back in Amphil-Lon, eating porridge and bread by the fireplace like they used to. Hearing tales of the ancient gods and the names of things that were lost to history. He cursed the damned Lord Handall for tasking him to deliver that sword, and he cursed himself for accepting the position at Varios' side. His life would have been different if he hadn't. Everything would have made sense.

After he knew there were no more tears to release, he finally stood. He noticed Varios had left the silver ring on the square table. He took the trinket and ran it down his index finger again. The earth felt like it was crashing down around him, with nothing left certain. *Is Varios going to leave me? Force me on this journey alone?* If he did, Lorian needed to be prepared for it. Ready to take the weight of the world unto himself. He would do whatever was necessary to discover the mystery behind the light that had stolen Varios' magic, and he would return what was taken. Then he could go home. Back to the forge and back to his father, where things made sense.

When they arrived in Mainis Fortu, he would escape when the chance arose. The quicker he could begin this journey, the better. And he knew what had to be done. He would seek out the Raven and kill it—*kill him*—if that was what the voices wanted. If it was what would end this miserable tale, he would do it.

Chapter 22: The Main Fortress

—King Marcus Dinivy, in his Founders Day celebration speech

It was hard for Lorian to pretend that everything was all right. He and Varios rarely spoke, only greeting each other when circumstances demanded it or others expected it. For the last week, he had continued his training, spending the mornings learning swordsmanship with Bowers and the afternoons practicing his wielding with Lya with unmatched determination. He knew he would be alone in the days to come and would need every skill he could develop if he were to survive.

The ring he had imbued became an invaluable tool that allowed him to control the exact amount of magic he wanted to release by letting it ebb into the trinket first. He had initially permitted energy to pass through the accessory, and he realized his mistake when the trinket first accepted his magic. He was attempting to use the device as a container when, in reality, he needed it to choke the flow of power as it left his body.

To correct this, he tried slowly allowing the magic to trickle out, but this proved to be too time-consuming.

Changing his approach, he instead held a steady flame in his hand each night, allowing the excess magic to drain away while he conjured thoughts of how to redesign the ring's purpose. When he was certain the ring was empty, he began again. Instead of filling it with raw magic, he asked the trinket to act as a funnel, only allotting predetermined amounts of magic out when he requested. This was the key to him finally wielding lightning.

Two nights before, he asked Lya to sit with him once more, laying the wires down the side of the ship and taking their places within the circle of knives that would serve as targets for the magic and outlets if the power was too much to contain. She agreed, reluctantly, and together, they labored another attempt.

Lorian used the ring to help him feel the tug of ambient energy within the air, and when he was sure he had collected enough, he slowly tugged back, allowing only the power from the ring to direct the lightning. To Lya's surprise and happiness, he only summoned a small bolt from above. It landed peacefully on one of the secondary knives along the railing of the ship and dissipated into the sea, leaving only a light crackling noise behind. Lorian now knew that the application of imbued items could do virtually anything he imagined, so long as the materials chosen and the power applied were appropriate to the desired outcome.

Any free time between his swordplay and wielding lessons was spent deciding how best to construct new devices, each with unique applications—though Rikard and Lady Jane would request his presence for lessons on formality or a cup of tea, if there was ample time. The ingredients necessary for imbuement were an unknown formula to him; guessing was all he was capable of at the moment. He would need access to a great many wares if he really wanted to begin experimenting with the practicality of certain metals and gems, as well as their combinations.

So far, silver could store and restrict magic, depending on the intentions of the person imbuing and how the silver felt about accepting the request. The black onyx was more of a container than an amplifier or augmenter of magic, which interested Lorian greatly. He determined that different gems could, in theory, provide different attributes to an imbued object, with metals acting as the medium through which magic flowed.

Lorian knew that with the knowledge he now had, he could increase his capabilities greatly. After the successful creation of the ring, he wanted to test what else could aid him in his journey to come. *Every hero needs a special weapon*, he thought.

Lorian had been practicing with the sword that Varios had gotten him in Orion-Lon every day since. He practiced with it before Captain Bowers forced him to fight without the wooden swords, and he continued to practice with it during their most recent training. He felt accustomed to the blade now, its weight and balance being more than familiar in his hands. While he had never fought or killed with it, he knew that when the time came, this would be the blade to save his life and steal the lives of others. And so, he decided that if the blade was to remain at his side, it too would wield magics, just the same as him.

Late at night, after he was sure that everyone had gone to bed, he climbed to the main deck, ready to give new life to his sword. Aside from the lingering sailors whose duties never seemed to end, he was alone. His constant training and meditating meant that his presence doing something odd on the main deck was no longer a concern to others; it was simply the casual secret training of a noble. No one would ask or inquire about his business, and he liked that.

When he found a secure spot near the aft, he removed the blade from its sheath on his hip and inspected it. Thanks to the knowledge he'd acquired as a smith's assistant, the blade was in pristine condition, as he was sure to never forget that maintenance was akin to godliness. He sharpened small chips away and kept the blade well-oiled, even shaving bits off the handle when he felt like it needed to be balanced. The handle was wrapped in treated leather to give it a coarse grit, keeping his hands from losing their grip—as well as providing some much-needed calluses. A ruby-like gem he was unfamiliar with was set in the pommel of the blade.

Lorian had always wondered about gems and why rich folk felt the urge to add them to everything they could, except now, as he was thankful it was there. He would prefer onyx, as he was familiar with it, but having a blade forged on a ship like the *High Guard* was nigh impossible. He would need to commission someone to either swap the gem later or provide a new sword with as many facets for gems as could be created without losing the structural integrity of the blade.

He sat cross-legged on the wood and laid the blade directly in front of him. He was curious how it would react, as steel was much less forgiving than pure silver. He placed both hands on the blade and focused intently on the flow of magics within him. His sea of stars ebbed gently, as if a warm breeze blew in from lands unknown, caressing him in a sensation of jubilation. As he felt the coursing of magic, he concentrated it on the blade, eager to see how it would react.

To his surprise, the steel felt more than willing to consume the magic, not needing any coercion to fill the metal with as much energy as it could handle. Lorian felt it was too easy, as if someone were playing a trick on him. If it was so willing to accept his magic, surely anyone who could wield would be able to imbue, he thought.

When he ceased the flow of magic, it made perfect sense. The steel was eager to drink the magical energy but was unable to stop it from flowing out, like a barrel with too many holes.

This was the difference between steel and silver. One would gladly take it but fail to keep it, while the other needed great coercion but would hold fast to what entered.

Lorian then thought of the gem and focused his attention on that instead. He again resumed the flow of magic, allowing the blade to greedily consume what he gave it but continued to guide the energy even after the steel drank it, forcing it to the pommel and to the red gem embedded there.

Lorian could feel the resistance of the gem as it fought against the magical currents, doing everything it could to keep from altering itself in order to accommodate the extra energy. Lorian could tell that coercion wouldn't work on this gem, and he would need to force it instead.

He was reluctant at first, afraid it would shatter the gem and injure him, but he knew waiting for a safer moment, a safer environment, was a sacrifice he couldn't accept, so he pushed on. *Imbuing truly is an art*, he thought. It was no wonder it hadn't been a mainstream practice.

The energy required, the foresight into the materials and the know-how, and the precision to guide magical energy and seduce the metal and gem or force it made imbuing no easy feat.

Lorian was unsure why he'd been chosen to harbor this information, but he was thankful all the same. With him, it would be put to good use. With him, it would be safe. Lorian could feel the gem begin to bend, the dense makeup of the elements that comprised it held desperately to keep their form, to keep from changing.

He pushed in all the right ways, doing whatever possible to keep the stone from adapting—or worse, breaking. Once he felt the will of the stone recoil, he pushed harder than ever, pouring magic into it with all his might. Finally, the stone conceded defeat, allowing Lorian's will and magic to fill its every corner, giving it new life and new purpose.

Lorian could feel a new resistance once the gem opened, a uniqueness that would allow only specific attributes to exist within it. This red gem was more compatible with heat, with the quick churning of magic at the molecular level. It wouldn't tolerate anything else. So, that's what Lorian did. He filled it with the fast, tumultuous magic of heat and fire, summoning the hottest essence he could from within the infinite pool.

The gem shook violently, as did the sword. He knew too much magic would destroy the gem, and maybe him as well, but he needed this to work. He felt the blade resonate with the same internal vibrations that could be felt when wielding fire magic, and then it changed.

The steel began to peel away, as did the gem. Like a newly broken shell, the sword began to shed parts of its outer layers, revealing a new armament. The gem was now smooth, contrary to the jagged appearance given to it by a stone smith, and the blade was different in appearance as well.

Grooves had formed alongside the length of the blade, revealing a docile orange glowing energy beneath the metal that shifted to currents unknown. The entire blade hummed with power, the sharp edges seemingly singing of their greatness with intoned whistles that sliced the air as it brushed by.

Lorian lifted the blade from the deck, in awe of the majesty that exuded from the new sword he had created. He grabbed its familiar handle and gave it a few swings, surprised by how light it felt despite its remaining denseness. Small trails of fire streamed from the sword's blade as it passed by, arches of energy being summoned forth from the gem's stored power. The blade whistled loudly as the arcs of magical energy escaped it, a sound unique to the blade.

Lorian was dazzled by what he had wrought, eager to use the sword in battle, forgetful of the sword's morbid purpose for a moment. "You need a name," he said aloud to himself. "Something worthy of what you are. Something that will be sung for years to come," he continued as he thought deeply for something that would strike awe in others the same way it had struck awe in him.

As Lorian ruminated on potential names, a sailor screamed from the crow's nest above. "Land ho!" he yelled as cliffs appeared on the horizon.

This was Lorian's first glimpse of the eastern cliffs of Mainis Fortu and the destination of their journey.

The sun began to rise, surprising Lorian, as he had unknowingly worked through the night. It casting light upon the foreign lands before him, their rays singing beautifully as the morning light gave depth and color to the world.

As he peered upon the illuminated cliffs, a name spoke itself into his mind. A name he would carry forward through as many adventures and feats this life would grant. He lifted his sword so that the tip of the blade pointed toward the heavens and spoke the name.

"Sun-Screamer."

Chapter 23: He Who Rules

"Since the time of the first men, the line of Dinivy has never been broken. Blood masters who study the art of lineage keeping state that the Dinivy line traces directly back to the first Wielder, Ragorn. The Dinivy surname emerged after Ragorn's passing, as the ruling nobles sought to take power by divine providence, selecting Ragorn's first son as the bearer of this divine name."
—Patron-Scholar Lazzaroos

Lorian observed with keen interest as the *High Guard* and its armada gradually approached the coastline, the imposing silhouette of Mainis Fortu materializing as they drew nearer. Their journey began through the expansive mouth of a fjord, navigating past a colossal statue positioned atop a floating island in the capital's bay.

The statue that loomed over the *High Guard* was that of the formidable figure Rangar, a legendary hero of old, depicted in stone with a sword outstretched defiantly toward the sea—an enduring symbol of Centrugard's indomitable spirit. As the light played upon its surface, Lorian discerned a crimson hue reflecting from the statue's right eye, fashioned to emulate the mystical aura of a noble. Stretching almost as tall as a mountain and situated upon an island rivaling the size of Orco's Island, the statue was crafted from a type of stone unfamiliar to Lorian's eyes. Its texture resembled polished ebony, or perhaps a variant of smooth quartz, imparting upon the figure a subtly matte finish that added to its enigmatic allure.

Lorian watched the statue with awe as the armada of ships went by, curious as to how it was constructed. Despite being awake all night, Lorian found himself full of energy and more than eager to see what the capital of the continent held within its walls.

A canvas of different buildings could be seen in the distance, their details growing clearer as they approached. A port made entirely of stone and metal stood where the earth met the water—dozens of docks sprawling forward like organized roots in search of nutrients.

Staircases and lifts facilitated the movement of people and goods from the dock to the bustling city above, each spacious enough to accommodate a sizable contingent of soldiers. The city itself was nestled between formidable walls, serving as a menacing bulwark against foreign incursions and potential sieges.

Along the crest of these imposing fortifications stood lofty watchtowers positioned at regular intervals, poised to raise the alarm in the event of approaching adversaries. Dominating the heart of the expansive city was a colossal castle, its massive stature dwarfing even the imposing ramparts that encircled it. Six towers flanked the castle in a hexagonal formation, encasing the central structure—a seventh edifice, the castle keep, rising proudly at its heart.

From his vantage point, Lorian struggled to discern the material of the castle's construction, though its pristine white appearance refrained from reflecting the morning sun's rays. Atop the keep fluttered a grand flag emblazoned with the Dinivy family crest—a majestic fire drake with outstretched wings and a sinuous tail, symbolizing the lineage's pride and power.

"It's beautiful, isn't it?" said Lord Greymoor, who approached silently from behind. "It's even more beautiful inside. Between you and I, the Golden Hatch pales in comparison, though I'll deny it if you ask," he finished with a smirk.

"You've been here before, my lord?" Lorian asked, though it was obvious he had been.

"Aye, many times. The royal family is more than just a figurehead, boy," he began as his thoughts seemed to trail off. "The crown's word is law. The crown is law. The capital and its people run the entire world. Best not forget that while you're here," he muttered as he walked away, a brooding tone in his voice.

Lorian looked around him and saw many people had now climbed to the main deck, either to watch or to prepare for the docking of the *High Guard*. Lorian had spent many weeks on the ship, and he was unsure if he was going to miss it or not. Handsir Rikard approached next with information about their next steps.

"Your Grace," he said as he bowed.

"Rise, Rikard."

"Your things have been prepared for unloading. A hot meal waits for us once we make landfall, unless you wish to eat now?" he asked, ready to prepare a meal if need be.

"No, I'll wait. Too excited to eat right now, I think."

"I understand. Your father felt the same when he first visited the capital. Speaking of, I've hardly seen the

276

two of you speak. Is all well?" he inquired, his eyebrow raised in curiosity.

Lorian appreciated the care that the handsir demonstrated. Whether he felt duty-bound or if the feelings were genuine, his concern showed. Lorian couldn't explain the rift that had formed between them, so he decided to act as if all was well. "Nerves, I think. Father has much to attend to here, and I need to prepare for the naming ceremony. It's been distracting us both."

Rikard smiled, his stern, wrinkled face showing more emotion than normal. "Yes, tensions are high considering the cargo we haul. Whatever the reason, he cares for you. Don't make the mistake of thinking you need to face the world alone, Lorian, because you never have to suffer that by yourself," Rikard reminded him before leaving to finish his duties.

Lorian thought it was strange how the old servant always knew the right things to say, and always at the right time. It was a shame Lorian had to ignore his advice going forward. Returning Varios' magic and unraveling the mystery behind why he was able to steal it took priority over repairing his relationship with the lord. Mainis Fortu would be the key needed to unlock everything, hopefully giving him his old life back in return.

"Prepare to port!" cried Captain Hrick as his men scurried across the deck, loosening rope that held the sails taut and securing cargo that wasn't already fastened. Lorian watched as Sir Lya Coalsdottir and Sir Koh Bridgeson came trotting forward with large smiles. They summoned Lorian to the portside of the vessel where the gangway—

the bridge that drops to the pier—would free them from the ship.

"Yer father is giving us charge of you until he can take your fancy prisoner to the castle dungeon," Koh said with a toothy smile.

"Aye," Lya admitted, "but that doesn't keep you safe from my training." She inspected Lorian with great care. "Something's different about you. What have you done?" she asked with more insight that Lorian cared for.

Lorian was thankful he had returned Sun-Screamer to his sheath. He placed a hand on the sword's handle, his subconscious way of keeping track of the magical blade, and responded, "Nothing you need to worry about. What am I to do in the capital while my father brings Lord Aaron before the court?" he asked, hoping to knock Lya off the path of asking too many questions.

"Usually, you'd join him. But he's told us that he wants you training."

Koh interjected, "Getting you ready to take the naming ceremony, too. Can't have his only son playing bastard for the rest of his life."

So, he still wants to name me his heir? Lorian thought. A sense of relief washed over him. *Maybe Varios really does need time. Or maybe he needs the heir regardless. Maybe he's given up trying to get his magic back.*

"Am I to stay on the ship, or are we going to reside within the castle?" Lorian asked with interest. Planning his escape would come easier if he was to be held in port. *Can't be easy leaving a royal castle unnoticed.*

"We're being received as honored guests," said Lady Jane, who joined them from the far side of the ship. Lorian noticed her out of the corner of his eye and did his best to avoid meeting her gaze. He wasn't sure how confident he could be in his escape, knowing he'd have to leave her behind.

"Honored guests!" laughed Koh. "Imagine that, after all these years, we'd return to the capital as honored guests. Fate truly is cruel, wouldn't you say, Lya?"

"Cruel indeed. Last we were here was to deliver the report of our victory over the Forgornians. A victory that was seen as less than honorable. Fate is more than cruel, my short companion. We also carry with us a prisoner of great value, same as last time."

"Don't believe the king will want to marry this one," Koh said, laughing again.

"What do you mean?" asked Lorian with confusion.

Lady Jane came forward and explained, forcing Lorian to look her in the eyes as she did. "When we won the war against the Forgornian Kingdom to the south, we took their princess prisoner. The king married her and sired a daughter, the current princess. He believed this union would keep aggression with the Forgornians to a minimum, but the opposite happened."

Lorian was enamored by Jane's beauty as she explained, so much so that he had to repeat her explanation in his head a few times to really understand it, as he had been too distracted. "I don't know anything about the war. Growing up so far north, all we cared about was getting enough food and work to survive the winter."

"And it's made you a noble worth listening to, I'd bet," noted Lya. "Most of us are too far removed from reality that even pretending to know strife is beyond our capability."

"Always the philosophical one, aren't we? You fight better than you preach, Lya, so stick to fighting," Koh said with an obvious sarcasm meant to keep him safe from her wrath.

A sailor approached the nobles. His posture was too tight, and sweat dripped from his brow despite the coolness of the wind as it carried the spray of the ocean. "Pardon me, lords, l-ladies, and s-sirs," he stammered. "We're approaching the port now. I'll need to prepare the gangway for drop," he finished as he attempted a bow that was more akin to an old man with an injured back. The four of them stepped away to let him work.

"Grandfather said I get to visit Lo at her sect when we've settled in the castle," Lady Jane said as she inched closer to Lorian. "Perhaps you'd like to come with me?"

Lorian's face grew hot, and sweat started to form on his brow—a subtle curse from the sailor, perhaps. "I'm sorry. I don't know how much free time I'll have, my lady," he lied. If he was to escape and set off on his own, he'd need to separate himself from her as much as possible—for both their sakes.

"I see," she said with disappointment.

Crew members began to shout as the ship swung around the pier and slowed. The water was deep enough to shelter the large vessel, which Lorian was surprised by, considering the much smaller ships also stationed nearby. They pulled alongside an extra-long pier, perhaps meant for honored guests, and slowed to a stop. Sailors from the ship shouted to dock workers, and together, they secured the ship with rope, keeping it from drifting off.

As the gangway lowered, Lorian saw Varios and Greymoor approach from the rear with a group of soldiers, Lord Aaron and Magistrate Strawman in tow. They stopped just before exiting the ship. Varios spoke to Lorian for the first time since their fight.

His voice was calm and showed no hints of animosity, leaving Lorian feeling relieved. "After Lord Aaron has been transported to the dungeon, you are to meet me near the Southern Gate. We are to meet the king together. Am I understood?" he asked directly.

Lorian straightened his back as well as he could. "Yes, Father."

He watched as they marched Aaron and Strawman forward and off the *High Guard*. He hadn't seen either of them in quite a while, and that wasn't by coincidence. It took Lorian's every nerve not to send as much lightning as he could at them both. Keeping away was the only reasonable thing he could think of; the alternatives were much more awful. He hated them with every ounce of his being and wished nothing but the worst for them. He knew their sentence would be lenient, and it made him furious. Living by the laws of the land was a lesson Varios had carefully imparted to him, ensuring he knew that if he didn't, there would be death and chaos.

Strawman appeared to have lost a great deal of weight in captivity. By the look of it, he hadn't been washed either—his disgusting tarnished robes reflecting that fact. Lord Aaron, on the other hand, looked well fed and sober, even clean-shaven, which sickened Lorian. If nobles ruled the world, who kept them in check? Lenient sentencing would do nothing for those who suffered under their boot.

Once Varios and his group created enough distance, Lorian followed Koh and Lya as they departed. Lady Jane seemed to stay behind with Child-Scholar Lo and Handsir Javal. She waved gently at him as he left; in return, he offered a small smile and nothing more.

Before they could walk the length of the long pier, a group of twenty armored soldiers bearing the Dinivy crest approached them. Their sudden approach caused Lya to remove her throwing knives from their hiding place in her waistband. Koh didn't seem to prepare, though Lorian was unsure how he fought, considering he hadn't had the chance to train with the man. Lya and Varios had insisted he train in one element at a time.

"Halt!" screamed a soldier. "Do you have Lorian Night with you? Bastard son of Lord Sam Varios?" he shouted.

"Who wants to know?" asked Lya through gritted teeth. Lorian could tell that she was ready to fight. He could sense the ambient energy in the air beginning to form. Lightning was coming.

"Prince Drecard Dinivy requests your presence immediately. You are to accompany us to the castle," he demanded.

The energy in the air dissipated as Lya dropped her guard. She calmed, returning her knives to her belt, and replied, "You may have him, but we shall join as well. This is not a request."

The soldier seemed hesitant to accept but did. He was only a man, after all, and she was a noble.

Chapter 24: Behind the Curtain

"Farland is nothing but a child's fairytale and should be treated as such."
—High-Gothic Aaron

The soldiers escorted Lorian through a series of backways and alleys, all meant to avoid public eye when transporting him to the castle. Lya and Koh seemed to be on guard most of the journey, while Lorian was unusually calm, in direct opposition. He wasn't sure why he wasn't worried. Perhaps it was his lack of experience in battle, or maybe it was overconfidence in his abilities; regardless of the reason, he felt an unnatural mindlessness toward the situation.

During the walk, he made note of specific areas of interest—stairways they took, unique buildings that acted as markers for direction, and any possible spots where he could hide or keep out of sight during his escape attempt. He knew getting out would be difficult, but thanks to these more discreet areas of the capital, he had a better shot than before.

"What does the prince want with me?" Lorian asked the guard who acted as this company's commander.

"That is the prince's business, not mine. You'll have to ask him yourself," he replied sternly and without further explanation.

"He is a lord, and you will show him respect," said Koh with an authoritative tone that was in conflict with his usual carefree character.

"My apologies," said the guard with a hint of resentment. "The prince will inform you of his request, my lord."

Lorian hated the formality and rigamarole that accompanied his position and was left slightly confused as to why someone as lax as Koh would bother keeping up appearances like this. Lorian assumed the customs of the capital, or those who lived here, were the cause of this sudden shift in behavior. He felt as though he was constantly learning the rules of behavior as time went on.

Soon, the six towers of Castle Dinivy came into view as they left the tight corridors that were the capital's back alleys, exposing them to the rest of the city. Much like the well-organized streets of Orion-Lon, the capital felt rich and full of life. The beautifully crafted buildings grew more lustrous and exquisite the closer they came to the castle grounds—their decorative features and polished stones shining brightly in the morning sun—and each teemed with business of some sort.

Stalls held numerous wares and trinkets that satisfied all curiosities. Lorian took note of any stalls that carried with them garments and accessories of more foreign lands. He would need them if he were to escape recognition. He tried to memorize what he believed would stand out the least, as he would like to blend in when he left.

As they approached the southern ramparts of the castle, a series of soldiers who stood watch ceremoniously stepped aside and allowed them trouble-free passage into the castle grounds. The armor the watchstanders wore was magnificent and resplendent when compared to that of the group that escorted them. Each soldier bore silver armor with a carving of a drake sprawled across the breastplate. Their long spears were wrapped in red silk that whipped wildly in the winds. The guards also wore a long cape that draped down their backs and nearly touched the ground, perfectly cut to length based on the height of the guard who wore it. Not a single dent, scratch, or blemish was seen on the armor, a sign of great care, skilled warriors, or extremely durable metal.

As they crossed the long stone courtyards that separated the outer ramparts from the interior castle, Lorian took in the magnificence, eyeing each detail with wonder and appreciation for the craftsmanship that went into its construction. Every stone was either painted or polished to a matte white that kept reflections from the sun to a minimum. The way the stone was layered gave the walls a perfectly symmetrical appearance.

Great statues and gargoyles were placed near corners or overhangs, certainly scaring away any winged beasts that dared to travel too close. The Dinivy drake was carved in the stone as well as embroidered upon great flags that jutted forward from walls at even intervals. Metallic fittings were embedded into the windows, doors, and rails, serving to reinforce those mechanisms and add a finesse that made them pleasing to the eye. The level of effort that went into its design was breathtaking. As a craftsman himself, Lorian felt a deep satisfaction at gazing upon the efforts of thousands of men and dozens, or centuries, of years of work.

"You're drooling, my lord," whispered Lya, followed by a wink and nudge that brought him out of his keen inspection of the castle's infrastructure.

The soldiers marched them forward through a side entrance to the castle keep. Lorian had expected more people to be present within the walls, though the opposite was true. The castle seemed deserted or perhaps purposefully emptied. Once they had gone through a few rooms—whose purposes seemed only to house surveyors of art and entertain guests, based on the never-ending number of chairs and portraits—the soldiers led Lorian to what he assumed was the base of one of the great six towers that he'd first noticed from the *High Guard*.

"The lord must ascend the tower alone, per the prince's wishes," instructed the commander of his escorts. Lya began to refuse, but Lorian stopped her.

"It's all right, Sir Coalsdottir," he began, ensuring to use her title as they used his. "I wouldn't want to surprise the prince with more people than he expected. If I need help, I'll yell." He gave a wink and tapped a throwing knife on his waistband he had been using for practice. She relented with a nod and spoke no more. Lorian gave a nod in return and began to ascend the tower's stairs.

As he approached the top of the tower, he began to feel a sense of nervousness, like threads were being spun out of sight that brought him ever closer to fate. He detested fate. The prince clearly knew who he was and when he would arrive. He even knew to request him once he was sure Varios wouldn't have a chance to object or

come along. For better or worse, Lorian was to be seen
alone and without the supervision of his father—or any
others, for that matter.

He needed to steel himself for what came next.
Lorian wouldn't allow himself to be persuaded into giving
Aaron fair testimony, or Strawman, either. He wouldn't be
a tool for allowing nobles to escape the consequences of
their actions or avoid accountability. If the prince wished to
leverage him in some way, he'd be certain to use that to his
own advantage, not the other way around. *How surreal
things seem now*, he thought as he dwelled on how he'd
gone from forging iron to meeting with royalty within a
few long months.

Lorian took a deep breath as he stopped in front of
the arched door that separated him from the meeting room
that held the prince. He calmed what nerves he could and
knocked three times. He waited for a few moments,
listening for permission to enter or for any sign of life
beyond the door. After deciding to knock once more, a stir
of movement responded. The door swung open without
warning, and a man he had never met pulled him inside and
embraced him.

"It's wonderful to finally meet you, cousin!" said a
freshly-shaven man in gray commoner garbs. He was
slightly older than Lorian and wore a small golden earring
in his right ear. His right eye was bright purple, a sign of
his nobility, and his other was a deep hazel. He was
relatively thin, making him appear lanky due to his tallness.
The man gave Lorian a warm smile and released him from
the surprise hug after a few awkward moments. He realized
after the shock had passed that this was Prince Drecard

Dinivy. Lorian quickly fell to a knee and bowed, as Rikard had taught him during their many lessons.

"My Prince," he said as he waited for the order to rise. Nobles only bowed to royalty, he was taught. And just like servants, they waited to be called to their feet.

"None of that, Lorian! Please, we are family. Get off your knee!" he said with a laugh. He grabbed Lorian by the shoulder and helped him up.

Lorian was taken aback by the lack of formality that the prince showed. As Handsir Rikard hadn't prepared him for this, he was unsure how to react.

"I know this is strange, considering who and what we are, but I abhor the aged customs we follow. Bah! Formality is as useful as a stone wash rag, wouldn't you say? Serves only to further separate us from the rest of the world. As if our appearance doesn't do that for us already," he said as he sat in a large, padded chair.

Lorian took in his surroundings and found a chaotic room vandalized by disorder. Half-read books, plates of unfinished meals, and unwashed clothes were strewn about. A fireplace roared nearby and gave the room a comfortable warmth that kept the bite of the wind at bay, considering all the windows were propped open.

"Oh my," the prince continued as he noticed Lorian inspecting the room. "I hope you'll forgive me, cousin; I've been rather occupied as of late, considering recent events. Afraid I haven't had time to clean or eat, really. Pay it no mind."

"Not an issue at all, my prince," replied Lorian, his voice finally returning to him after the shock passed. He felt oddly comfortable with the prince now that he didn't have to imagine some brooding monarch who held the fate of Centrugard in his hands.

"Ah, very good! Now, I'm sure you're eager to learn why I've summoned you. Truth is, cousin, I've wanted to meet you very badly. Uncle has written to me and father about you. Yes, and about the nasty business with Lord Aaron, of course. I desperately had to speak with you. You've lived your life as a bastard until your awakening, which occurred unusually late, might I note. Not that you're unaware yourself, that is. By all rights, you have lived your life as a commoner, as one of the masses. Tell me, what is it like for them? I need to hear it from the source, not by the sly words of diplomats or advisors. I need to hear it from you," he said with a determination that matched his zealous attitude.

For a moment, Lorian was speechless. Until now, Jane had really been the only one who wanted to know about him, and he had been very cold with her when she asked. Hearing the prince ask about not only his life and struggles but also the struggles of the common man was refreshing. "Where do I begin, my prince?" he said as he started to collect his thoughts.

The prince smiled warmly. "Drecard. Just Drecard. It's just us, Lorian. We don't need to use false titles with one another. When you and I are alone, it will be Drecard and Lorian. Is that all right?"

"Yes, Drecard. I find that more than all right," Lorian said with a smile. "I was raised by a blacksmith, an honorable man who acted as my father for most of my life. We were poor, yes, but never went without, thanks to him. As a bastard, I was treated with contempt in most places I went by noble and commoner alike. They think of us as a blight, a thing to be scorned.

"Most people would be resentful because of this, even angry and violent, but I had the blacksmith. He taught me to write, to read, shared with me stories of the ancient world and of names long lost, and more importantly, he taught me how to be a good person." He hadn't had a chance to talk about his father in a long time, and it felt nice to honor him with words. Tears began to well, though he fought to keep them at bay before the prince. "I was luckier than most in that regard, though he was far from perfect."

"What faults did this blacksmith carry?" asked the prince with great interest.

"Like most, he was beholden to the laws of his station. Always made to cower or bow before those who believed themselves his better. More than once, I had to watch him lower himself to satisfy them, to toss his dignity and pride aside for the sake of survival or fear of retribution," Lorian said, his anger surprising him.

The prince looked more than interested now, a smile growing at the corner of his lips and his eyes becoming wide. "And how did that make you feel, Lorian? Watching the man you looked up to cower before those with more power?"

"Feel?" he started. "At first, nothing. I believed it was my place to stay silent, to lower my head alongside his," he continued as more anger was released from within him. "And then rage. Rage because I knew he was worth more than that, because he *was* more. I was sick of station and lineage dictating his destiny, and mine. Sometimes, I would grow so angry that all I wanted to do was scream, but I couldn't. I would bite my tongue instead, as he taught me. I can still taste the bitter iron of fresh blood."

"And tell me, Lorian. If you could change the world, truly change it, what would you do?" Drecard asked.

Though the question was hypothetical, Lorian knew instantly.

"Burn it all down," said Lorian with a stare that focused on nothing but the feelings that toiled within him.

"I knew I'd like you, cousin. I could tell," Drecard said. "Perhaps now would be a good time to discuss Lord Aaron," he continued, bringing Lorian back from his self-reflection.

"What do you mean?" he asked, already knowing that he could play no part in the lord's outcome.

"The king, my father, is indisposed at the moment. He won't be able to join us for the council meeting and, subsequently, the trial. It falls to me, then, to weigh the judgments of the council and render the verdict on our Lord Aaron. I think both you and I know his sentence will be lenient. They'll demand it. We tend to give reprieve to one another in times of . . . difficulty. They'll be expecting small mercies from me, hoping I refrain from sentencing him to a cell. What would you have me do?" he asked, giving Lorian more than enough to mull over.

"I . . . don't know. He's done something so horrible, so disturbing. How could someone atone for that in a single lifetime?"

"How do you mean?" inquired the prince.

"I saw the boy as he was marched to the gallows, Drecard. I saw the fear in his eyes, and I watched him cry, searching for someone to save him, searching for the very person who damned him to hang. And then I watched as he fell, as he thrashed and screamed through a crushed throat. It wasn't quick," Lorian said with cracks in his voice as he remembered the morbid event. "That boy could have lived a long and happy life, free of pain, and free of the curse of being born a bastard to a ruthless lord. How can Aaron ever pay for such a crime? How could he atone for the pain he caused that innocent boy?"

Lorian waited for a response from the prince, who had fallen silent as he listened. The prince ruminated on what he had said, thinking over every detail. Lorian was surprised when he saw tears had formed in the prince's eyes, genuine tears for a boy he had never known, never met and never would. Had he been wrong about the royal family? *Could genuine care exist with one who holds power the way he does?* Lorian was unsure, but he knew that the prince had, at the very least, a kind heart.

"I thank you, cousin. You have given me much to consider. I would have you lend me your ear and your words as often as you're able during your stay. If it isn't too much trouble," said the prince through calculating words.

"Then you shall have it, cousin," replied Lorian with a smile. They may not truly be related, but he felt he could trust Drecard, and he would, until the prince gave him a reason not to.

"I suspect Uncle would like to meet with me now. He has surely discovered that Father is unavailable and will want to speak with me on matters concerning the trial," he said as he began to dress himself in finer clothes he picked up off the floor. "Oh, I understand you'll be taking the naming ceremony while you're in town. I'm delighted! To take your father's name, and his legacy, is a great thing."

"Yes," Lorian said as he remembered his plan to escape the castle when opportunity showed itself. "It certainly is something."

"Though creating your own legacy is a feat not many can claim. Something to consider, perhaps," he replied as he finished dressing himself.

Lorian took note of his words and was under the impression the prince had just suggested something he couldn't comprehend.

"Care to join me as we greet your father?" the prince asked. "I'll have to gather some men for the arena as well. Lord Greymoor is quite the fighter."

"More than you know," muttered Lorian. "Yes, I shall join you."

"Wonderful. I'll also have to introduce you to my sister while you're here, though she's rather occupied with engagement duties at the moment. Plan on attending her celebration while you're here?" he asked.

"If I am able, I shall. Lady Jane Greymoor has been invited and wishes me to accompany her. We are to be wed, as requested by Father and Lord Greymoor."

"How exciting!" declared the prince as he made for the door that would take him down the tower stairs. "Love is in the air, eh? Perhaps I'll find my bride-to-be as well, one day," he joked as he stopped shy of the top step. "Lorian, truly, thank you for coming to speak with me. I know you didn't have much of a choice," he said with a hearty laugh, "but you've put my mind at peace. My role is a taxing one, playing prince and interim ruler, but my decisions are clear now, thanks to you. Let's change the world, Lorian Night. Together."

Chapter 25: Where the Darkness Lies

"There are evils that stir in the night. Alongside the natural gods, spirits of malevolence and benevolence endured the final expulsion of Navaety. While the gods toiled, the spirits bided their time, waiting for their moment to intervene."
—Patron-Scholar Godrick

Sam Varios marched at the head of his small group of soldiers. Escorting Lord Aaron and Magistrate Strawman was to be made a public spectacle—allowing both gentlemen and commoners to see them in chains. The letters exchanged between the king and himself requested it to be done this way, though he was unsure why, as this was something the crown would usually prefer to keep as quiet as possible for as long as possible.

After ascending the stairs from the port, his group took all the main pathways that led to the Northern Gate—the main gate to the castle. As they marched in the early morning hours, Varios noted who witnessed his group passing by: it was mainly merchants, vagrants, and guards nearing the end of their watch hours.

The large roadways that wound through the city had been modernized over the last few years—all compacted stone and filler meant to keep wear to a minimum from heavy carriages and other damages caused by overuse. The streets were lined with newer-looking oil lanterns hung from freshly polished iron poles, each adorned with the fire drake of the Dinivy crest.

As they approached the castle, a particular lantern whose glass enclosure had been replaced or modified by something peculiar caught Sam's eye. Upon closer inspection, he could see that colored glass had been used to decorate this specific lamp, which hung at the intersection of two paths—one which he was currently on and that led to the castle, and the other which ran perpendicular to it and deeper into the western section of the capital. *Stained glass lanterns*, he thought to himself. Why was that so familiar to him? Why did the sight of it cause the skin on his body to tighten and his hair to stand on end?

"The blind prisoner," he said aloud, prompting Lord Greymoor to inquire.

"What was that, Ash-Bringer?" he asked in annoyance. "Speak up if you want to be heard, nephew."

"Uncle," Sam began as nervous curiosity overcame him, "I hate to ask this of you, but would you do me the honor of escorting the prisoners to the castle on your own?" He brought the group to a temporary halt. "There is something I need to look into, something that may be vital to Aaron's trial," he explained, though his words were only half-truths. "I can't elaborate further. Will you trust me?"

"Aye, I'll see it done. Be quick with your business; I will not greet the king without you. This is your mission, not mine." Greymoor ordered the group to march, leaving Sam by himself.

He waited a few minutes before leaving, hoping to clear some distance so as not to be followed or challenged later about his whereabouts. Sam inspected the lantern more closely, hoping to get some clue as to where he should go or what he should do. Thinking back to his strange interaction with the prisoner in Lord Greymoor's dungeon, the man had mentioned that they were already acquainted. While it may have been true, and the man's blindness could have been caused by him, his face wasn't familiar enough to create a mark on his memory. *It was now, though.* The man had mentioned that Sam's memories of the man were stolen, as was his own name, by the ancient one. Sam hated ambiguity almost as much as he hated tall tales and myths. He would find this man and force him to give answers as to how he knew his shared secret with Lorian and what purpose he had for requesting his presence. Varios shuddered, and his skin tightened as if a cold breeze blew in. Something foul was ahead.

He wasn't aware of any power, any magic, that would allow someone who wasn't of noble birth to vanish like that. The cells were completely closed off as well, so no secret passage or illusion could have hidden the man from his view. Time was of the essence, and keeping a king waiting wasn't an option. If he was to track the mysterious prisoner down, it would need to happen now.

As Sam looked upon the stained-glass lantern, he could see each of the four panels held images that differed from one another. The first panel was that of a white figure who danced upon a dark purple backdrop. The second was of that same figure who spat forth stars and smaller white figures. The third was of the smaller figures tearing the large white figure to pieces. The fourth was a single small figure who wept at the base of the pieces, while the other figures danced upon the dark purple backdrop.

Unable to discern a direction from the glass, he angrily followed the perpendicular road into the western reaches of the capital. The further he traveled, the more run-down the area became. Orphaned children stood at the edges of the road and begged for coin. Shops and street stalls were worn with a patchwork of small repairs. Fruit and meat were either expired or close to expired and carried the smell of decay. Soon, he reached another stained lamp. This lamp contained the same artwork as the last, with one small difference. Within the fourth panel, the small figure still wept, yet one of its arms was stretched out and pointed toward the north. Varios took this as the required direction and moved toward that area.

Lamp after lamp guided his way until, after he came upon the thirteenth lamp, the small white figure pointed him to a decrepit building whose doors hadn't been opened in untold years. The building was two stories tall and came to a sharp point at the top. Large broken windows gave it the eerie appearance of a forgotten cathedral. Its wooden planks were cracked and molded over, and the stairs that led to its double iron-branded doors were slick with moisture and mysterious grease.

Sam was more than cautious of entering the building, but he needed answers. He drew his sword and approached the doors. He saw no point in knocking and tried for the handle. The door was heavy, its hinges rusted and tight. With force, the doors opened, labored screams emanating from the hinges. Sam took in the interior details as he entered.

Pews stretched forward at awkward angles; some faced forward, some sideways, some overturned and shattered. Great braziers hung from the ceiling, and long troughs that stunk of oil lined the walls. Sam removed a glove and stuck his hand in one of the troughs adjacent to him. With desperate effort, he manifested a spark that lit the trough's oil, fatigue making his limbs heavy as it did. The fire ran along the channel at great speed, giving light to the ruins of this ancient place of worship.

To Sam's surprise, the braziers also came to life with fire, as did other fixtures that decorated the room—candles and smaller oil lanterns not integrated into the walls. Figures draped in black robes sat at the pews, as if the light had somehow summoned them forward. At the far end of the room, near an altar of carved wood that resembled thick branches spiraling into one another, was the blind prisoner from Castle Greymoor. He stood proudly at the front as if he was about to give a sermon, and his arms were spread wide as he praised an unknown entity.

"There you are, Lord Variosss . . ." hissed the blind man. "He knew your arrival was inevitable. He knew your curiosity would overcome your sense of safety and bring you to us alone," he continued with a threatening tone.

Sam felt panic overcome him. He brought his sword to a defensive position, keeping his hand ungloved and ready to summon whatever magic he was capable of in this state.

"You offend us, Sam Variosss. We would not do you harm. You are his guessst," he spoke with rasp in his voice. "Mmm . . . you are weak. These things he shares with usss. Your power eludes you; it runs from you. Another has taken it, stolen it!" His arms widened once more in praise.

Sam was taken aback. Someone did know his secret. Someone who wanted to use it against him, it seemed, or wanted to use him. He would not allow that to happen.

"Why have you summoned me here? What is this place, and who are you?" he asked with as much authority as he could summon. *This church, these pious-looking worshippers, the talk of the ancients can only mean one thing*, he thought. *These people must be affiliated with the church of the natural gods.*

"It is not us who summons you; it is he. An audience with you was by design. You are meant for so much more, Lord Variosss. The one in your charge, Lorian Night. He is an anomaly. He must be brought to us. He must return what was stolen!" screamed the blind priest, fire growing in synchronization with his pitch.

"Why does the church of the natural gods want Lorian? Of what use could he be to you?" Varios screamed in return.

Sam had felt fear many times in his life. His first battle, his prophecy, watching Stenley fall sick, but this was different. Though he could see the blind priest speak, he knew his words were not his own. Something was speaking through him, using him as a device to relay Varios a message. Sam shook with despair. He had always hated myths, legends, and tall tales because they weren't real; they were simply an exaggerated tool used to explain the unknown. And if they were real, no one could ever prove it, so what good could they be? But this was real. As real as the sword he held in his hand, and as real as the malice that crept around him. Cold sweat ran heavily down his brow.

"Hah!" cackled the priest, his voice cutting through Sam's confidence. "We do not serve the natural gods, lord!

The ancient one is of the unnatural world, and we follow the unnatural gods. Yesss, he can feel your fear. Humans have always been scared of the unknown, and he is unknown to all, foreign to all. Ender of all. Bring us the one you call son, and he shall reward you, Ash-Bringer," finished the priest as the altar before him erupted in green flames that flickered wildly.

The altar within the flame morphed in shape, slithering wood bending and reforming into a new figure. Screams bellowed forth from the blaze that formed in front of Sam, the crackling of wood mixing with it. A small figure could now be seen from within, its arms stretched forward toward him as if it begged to be near him, yearning for him, his touch, and his protection.

Tears welled heavily from Sam Varios' eyes, streaming down his face and off his jaw. "No, it can't be," he said with sobs. "No, please. This isn't real. It isn't real!" he screamed with rage and confusion. He fell to his knees, his sword slamming to the ground.

A voice called out from the fire. "Father! Save me!" it cried in a child-like voice.

"Stenley!" screamed Varios with rage exploding forward, masking his fear and giving life to his limbs. He sprang forward, grabbing his sword and charging toward the emerald fire burning near the priest. "Give me back my boy!" he screamed with bloodthirsty determination.

As he ran, cloaked figures sitting at the pews jumped from their seats to stop him. Sam summoned forth every bit of magical energy he could muster, calling to the great pool of magic for aid and using the ambient fire from the troughs and braziers to fuel him. Wisps of fire emerged from the ambient flames, coalescing on Sam, shrouding him in a great blaze as he cut through hooded zealots. They singed and dissipated into formless smoke as they fell at his blade, one after the other, until none stood before him and the cage of green flame imprisoning Stenley.

Without a thought, he leaped into the fire, desperate to free his son. As their hands clasped, he could feel his son as flesh and blood before him. Then nothing. Stenley disappeared, as did the priest and every source of light within the church until only Varios remained, isolated in the dark. He grabbed helplessly at the ash speckling the cold wet floor of the abandoned church, his hope and heart feeling as formless as the shadows themselves.

"Stenley . . ."

"Bring us the bastard, Lord Varios. Bring us the false son you've claimed, and free the real heir," the priest said.

Sam felt the backlash of overusing his magic, the pain of his limbs reaching levels he never thought possible. It felt like needles dissecting him from the inside, their many tips stabbing through his flesh. He collapsed into the ash, his legs refusing to obey him. "I can't," he pleaded. "Please, just take me. Take me and release my son, I beg you."

"In the days to come, war will swallow these lands. Brother will turn on brother, father will turn on son. When the Raven falls, you will be tasked with bringing him to the ancient one, he whose presence in this world will mark the ending of all things, the bringer of the end, and then, when all has been made silent and cold, he will rekindle this abandoned existence with an emergence of his own," said the priest with an ethereal voice that echoed through Sam's mind. "Long have the twelve tarnished what she left, what she gave her life for. Now he must right those wrongs, and he will need Lorian to do it. Forget your duty not, Lord Variosss. For if you do, your true son shall pay the toll in your stead. Forget it not," he said as his voice faded away, leaving Sam truly alone.

Sam twitched violently from the recoil, his body failing itself as agony and despair devoured him whole.

Chapter 26: The Council

"And so it was that, after yet another remaking of things, the one who in the ancient tongue has been called Makar, life-giver of all, and who has also been called Lord of Soul and all things orderly, who carried the natural name of Navaety, was the final turn of the cosmic wheel approaching its end. For all things that are considered to be born, or to more accurately say, all things that have been allowed to exist, so too must there be an end of existing and of existence."
—First passage from the *Allos Gignestha*, Book of the Natural Gods

Prince Drecard wound his way through the twisting halls of Castle Dinivy with a speed Lorian found hard to match. Lya and Koh were obviously rattled when he descended the stairs with the prince but soon adjusted and dropped to their knees in formality. Unlike with Lorian, the prince didn't break decorum and simply commanded them to rise before bypassing them and rushing to the door. Lorian followed without an explanation and could feel their eyes burning a hole in the back of his head as they followed.

"Cousin, tell me this while we walk: What kind of man is my uncle? This may come as a shock to you, but after Mother passed, he barely wrote and visited only when commanded. I feel I barely know the man."

Lorian increased the size of his strides so he could come as close to the prince as possible, ensuring he was always at least one pace behind, as Rikard had taught him.

"A difficult question, my prince. He is . . . seldom vocal about himself."

"Ah, yes. Always brooding and full of thoughts yet to be expressed aloud. Then my memories of him haven't failed me," he jested.

"There is more to him, though," Lorian said with haste, as he didn't want to paint Varios in a negative light. "He cares more than the average noble. He has a hard job—arbiter of justice in the Frost. But he takes great care to bring justice to those who deserve it. He always says if a man earned himself a lash or whip or cane, it's the responsibility of the one who oversees that man to dole out its punishment. He's a firm believer in taking responsibility."

"A very just and fair sentiment. Pardon the question. Who was it between the two of you to recommend Lord Aaron be brought to the capital for judgment?" asked the prince as he pushed his way through an arched doorway that led to the castle's inner keep.

"It was his, my Prince. He said if Lord Aaron was to be judged by the local council, he would be reprimanded at worst. He said because Lord Aaron broke a law issued by the crown, then it's the crown who should judge him," replied Lorian, trailing off in his last few words.

Guards and servants alike gave their customary bows as the prince and his ensemble of guests followed closely. Instead of commanding each, he gave a broader wave of the hand, allowing them to resume their duties without further interruption.

"Your tone makes it seem like there's more to the story, cousin. He gave no other reason for bringing Aaron and the magistrate this far?" he inquired with great interest.

"Out loud, yes," Lorian started as he tried to remain as quiet as possible, wishing to limit who overheard his next few sentences. "I believe he was angry as well. Furious, actually. He's very good at hiding what he feels, but . . . he showed it in more than one way. You'll see evidence of this when we look upon the magistrate."

"You mean the oil-lamp accident?" asked the prince with a sarcastic tone. "Uncle mentioned the incident in his letters, of course. Terrible thing, really," continued the prince. "Those oil lanterns are as dangerous as they are useful. The magistrate should have known better when adjusting the light. This is why servants should check for us, clumsy man."

Their strides slowed somewhat as they continued. "Yes," started Lorian, "very bad accident."

"I've been told Max Aaron was executed due to his claim on Lord Aaron's assets. What do you think of all this?"

"I think the reason is unimportant. A boy of ten years was hung by the neck while his father hid in the mines and drank himself unconscious. I don't know how succession works, whether a bastard like him, like me, needs to undergo the naming ceremony before they have a valid claim or if it's inherent to their blood, but I find it less important than what happened."

"Yes, I tend to agree. The naming ceremony is important, but it's not the only way to claim inheritance or act as successor. If Max was the firstborn, his claim was valid. Or, like yourself, if you happen to be the last living heir, your right to those assets is valid as long as your father publicly acknowledges your lineage. Your eye is reminiscent of his, which helps. But that isn't always the case, so accepting you publicly can go a long way. Undergoing the naming ceremony acts as the wax seal in this instance, making the claim irrefutable," explained the prince as he approached a door guarded by two men in resplendent armor matching that of the guards of the exterior castle wall. Without a word, the guards opened the door for the prince, and he and his followers entered.

"He claims ignorance, Lorian," began the prince with a lowered volume meant for his ears only. "Lord Aaron states he had no intention of harming the boy, only of sending him away. He says keeping him from the public eye and keeping him ignorant to the world was his goal, not an execution."

"My prince, respectfully, does it matter?" Lorian asked in matched quietness.

"How do you mean?"

"If Aaron's purpose was only to remove the boy, not kill him, was that not a crime itself? The truth is, we don't know what Lord Aaron wanted or didn't want. What we know is the magistrate hung a child, a noble child, bastard or not, for the sake of siring a new child with the magistrate's daughter, giving the new heir rights to succession that would have been Max's. Whether guilty by the decision to hang his son or guilty by ignorance, he's still guilty," finished Lorian, who found his heart beating quickly from the rage he felt at Lord Aaron.

"You have a fair point, cousin. I'll need to make the council aware of these facts. Undoubtedly, they have already assembled and are absorbing the whispers of those who urge them to give the lord a lenient sentence. I will need to confer with counsel of my own, but still, I'm eager to hear what decision the council comes to. It isn't every day this council deliberates a case of this magnitude. With Father gone, it'll be me who weighs upon the decision. Make no mistake though, cousin; it is my job as monarch, even as a temporary one, to hear all facts with an unbiased opinion and make my decision just and fair. But worry not—I've already taken our conversation into consideration and will share what's important with the other council members. If he is guilty, he will pay accordingly," said the prince as he entered a new room containing a long table with many empty seats.

Lorian and the rest of the followers entered after, the grand council room coming into detail before them. The rectangular table was surrounded by numerous empty chairs, though the table was dressed and ready to receive guests. At the far end of the table sat a large and well-crafted chair meant for the king. The dome ceiling held a mural of the twelve natural gods, each within their own biome. Slit windows gave the room a gentle breeze and much-needed fresh air, the light from the sun helping to illuminate what the oil lanterns could not.

Lorian could see a small handful of people at the far end of the room huddled together closely in discussion. Lord Greymoor was one of those men, and he expressed shock and excitement at seeing Lorian with the prince. He dispersed the group with a command and made way for them, stopping short and dropping to his knee with enthusiasm.

"My prince, it is an honor to be in your presence."

"The honor is mine, Lord Greymoor. You may rise," said the prince with experienced authority. "I was told Uncle Sam would be joining us. May I ask where he is?"

"I beg your pardon, my prince. Lord Varios was to attend this meeting but was pulled away on a personal matter," said Greymoor respectfully. Lorian knew the stone giant didn't wish to lie to the prince, so he must have given what information he could, information he assumed to be true. In reality, Varios was late, very late. Lorian assumed he didn't want to bring this to the prince's attention, so he withheld the knowledge for now.

"May I ask about the king's whereabouts, my prince? I haven't spoken to him in decades and would be delighted to pay my respects," continued Greymoor in a more articulate and neutral tone than Lorian had seen before.

"Ah, yes, I must ask for your forgiveness now. The king is indisposed and won't be attending this meeting. He has given me authority over the matter until he's able to rejoin us. In his stead, I shall assume all roles and authority that would otherwise be his, such as making final judgment on this case."

"Of course, Your Grace," started Lord Greymoor. "If it's of no consequence to you, may I make a request of you, considering your temporary command over this meeting?"

"You may."

"Could we wait for Lord Varios to join us before the meeting begins? I believe his attendance and his experience with Lord Aaron and the crimes in question are vital to this hearing. Missing it would only serve Lord Aaron."

"No, I think we shall continue regardless of my uncle's presence," the prince said. He moved closer to Lord Greymoor to better relay his next words. "The lords of the council are ready to convene, save one. Lord Aaron's father, Charles Aaron, has yet to arrive. While Uncle's testimony would undoubtedly paint a more realistic picture of the events in question, having Lord Charles Aaron here would only further intimidate and, I'm sorry to say, manipulate the vote of the other lords. If uncle should arrive at a later time, he shall be allowed to join, but until then, Cousin Lorian will have to stand in his place."

The prince made his way to the large chair at the far end of the table. He sat calmly and began to review a stack of documents placed before him.

Lord Greymoor accepted the terms of the prince's argument without debate or issue. He instead turned to Lorian and updated him on his father's absence. "Boy, come closer," he whispered, drawing Lorian's attention and curiosity. "While we were en route to the castle dungeon, your father informed me there was information he believed would be pivotal to Lord Aaron's case. Said something about needing to look into it and ran off into the city. It's been hours since then, and I haven't heard from him. I believe something is wrong. I'm going to find Handsir Javal and send out a party to look for him. You need to stay here and do whatever you can to keep things from turning in Aaron's favor. Mark me, boy. This fucking traitor will bleed before the day's end. You have my word on that. I'll return presently," he finished as he made for the door through which Lorian had entered earlier.

Lorian watched as the last familiar face, aside from Koh and Lya, who stood quietly at arm's length from him, walked away, giving him more responsibility in this trial than he felt prepared for. He turned to his tutors and informed them of the situation. "Father has disappeared in the city somewhere. Lord Greymoor is leaving to request a search party. Sir Coalsdottir, Sir Bridgeson, I hate to do this, but will you please assist in looking for him? I fear the average soldier won't suffice if things get bad, and you have a shared history with him. He'll trust you."

"Aye, we can help," said Koh, "but who's going to stay here with you? You're a fledgling noble, an inexperienced Wielder, and an even less seasoned politician. They'll eat you alive if you don't choose your words carefully."

"I have to agree with Koh," admitted Lya, "but I trust you to make the right decisions. We shall search for Sam. Keep your wits about you, Lorian Night. It takes great focus and attention to detail to wield lightning but even greater effort to wield your words and hold true to your virtues." She gave Lorian a final nod and left with Koh.

Lorian watched them leave, feeling as though part of his confidence left with them. In such a short amount of time, Lorian had been given responsibilities and power beyond his understanding. Due to inexperience, he'd nearly killed his friends—and himself. But Lya was right. Through effort, he'd overcome enough small struggles to make a difference in the way he wields and the way he sees himself. This meeting of lords was no different, in theory, than any of the issues he'd faced before. He just needed to stay true to himself and work through the issues as they came. *They're all just small obstacles*, he reminded himself.

Lorian sat adjacent to the prince. The seat at the council was offered to him, so he decided might give insight and clarity to the council members.

***

It had been an hour since Lya and Koh had left to search for Varios—Lord Greymoor having already returned and taken his seat beside Lorian. Prince Drecard waited patiently while nobles from all corners of Centrugard entered and took their proper seats at the council table. Each noble bore a magical eye of various colors—bright reds, oranges, greens, and more—and wore formal attire from their respective regions, each flavored to a certain culture or theme popular among their territories.

He could see a noble with dark skin wearing sandy-brown garments containing flashy gems wrapped around his torso, while another wore a tight-fitting robe with a sash stretched from her waist to her shoulder, the colors bright red and reminiscent of a breathing flame.

Soon, all nobles who would attend were present in the room, though he noted an empty chair was left after everyone retired to their seats.

As the last noble sat, a man dressed in gray silks who had been moving back and forth between the prince and other servants approached the table and made the first announcement.

313

Lorian hadn't known the man's role until now and could see he acted in some advisory capacity to the crown. He was a tall but thin man whose cheeks were sunken in. Dark circles around his eyes and a balding head that desperately clung to what strands it could gave the impression he hadn't seen a break in his duties in decades.

"Good morning, lords and ladies of the realm. It is an honor to serve you during this council of lords. It is my honor to introduce you all and inform you of the purpose for which we have gathered here today. Firstly, presiding over this council in place of his father, the king, is Prince Drecard Dinivy, heir apparent to the kingdom of Centrugard and the Shut, righter ruler of the Farland, son of the Bane of Forgorn, heir to the Emerald Guard, and future Lord of Mainis Fortu," he said with winded breath.

Lorian was surprised at the many titles the prince held, or would hold when his time to rule came. Confused stares and whispers met his introduction, giving Lorian the impression the other lords hadn't been aware of the king's absence either.

"On behalf of the crown, it is my pleasure to welcome you all to Mainis Fortu and to Castle Dinivy. I welcome you, Lord Banish of the Soot Fields. I welcome you, Lady Berall of Mazon. I welcome you, Lord Greymoor of Tarns Knoll. I welcome you, Lord Black of the Foothills. I welcome you, Lord Titus of the Saltlands. I welcome you, Lord Edgar of Pilliny. I welcome you, Lord Fjorn of the Scuttles. I welcome you, Lord, uh . . ." He stopped as he peered at Lorian. "I welcome you, Lord Lorian Night . . . of Amphil-Lon," he said with confusion, forcing all eyes to Lorian.

This was a familiar feeling to him—the stares, the incredulous looks of those who learned of his bastard origin. Normally, Lorian would feel shame and would shrink before the condescending eyes of those who were true-born. But now, Lorian could only feel power and pride. Despite his origins, he was here with all these important lords and ladies, sharing the same table and debating the same case. He held his chin high; he wanted them to know they couldn't make him feel small.

"Continue, Darwin," ordered the prince.

"Ah, forgive me, my prince. Uh, and lastly, we have Lord Charles Aaron, former lord of Orion-Lon and bishop of the church of the natural gods," he finished as the surprise of the lord's attendance forced complete silence in the room. All present nobility looked around the room feverishly in an attempt to identify Lord Charles Aaron, but none could. As if to make a grand entrance, the door to the royal council room swung open, and a common woman dressed in black silks entered. Lorian's heart sank, and his eyes widened in surprise. Feln walked through the doors with determination, making her way to Lord Aaron's empty seat and taking her place at the council.

"Uh, pardon me, but who might you be?" asked Darwin with pursed lips and flared nostrils.

"Oh, my apologies, lords and ladies. I am standing in for Lord Charles Aaron for this meeting. I am his wife, Feln Aaron, and shall be acting on his behalf and on behalf of our son, Dan Aaron," she replied with clear words and a moderate tone so as not to be misheard.

Chapter 27: The Silence of The Axe

"To have a commoner at the council table, how refreshing! This will be a day to remember, I believe," exclaimed Prince Drecard.

Lorian's mind went blank, and his chest became tight. He hadn't seen Feln since she'd left for her apprenticeship with the merchant guild, and now she was married to Lord Aaron's father? *How did this come to be?* he asked himself. *How could she, of all people, the most charismatic, intelligent, and levelheaded person he had ever met, become associated with House Aaron?*

Lorian wanted to reach across the table and shake her until her senses returned. She had to be under some spell, or maybe she was being blackmailed. Maybe someone had her family and was threatening death unless she complied. Lorian was unsure.

The only thing he was certain of was that she was here against her will. She had to be. In no reality was Feln arguing on behalf of a monster like Dan Aaron.

"Ah, yes, I welcome you, Lady Feln Aaron. Now, with the introductions completed, I shall explain the purpose of this council meeting. Acting under the authority as arbiter of justice in the Frost, a position appointed to him by the crown, Lord Sam Varios has arrested and transported Lord Dan Aaron of Orion-Lon under the charges of murder and treason. Magistrate Strawman has also been charged with the same crimes and is to stand trial as well. Are there any who would question the purpose of this meeting or call for further explanation before we proceed?" asked Advisor Darwin.

"Yes," said Feln. "I do not wish for further explanation of this council's purpose, but I do wish to know why Lord Varios isn't here to acknowledge the validity of these accusations."

"I'll answer that one, Darwin," said the prince as he stood.

"Of course, Your Grace," replied Darwin with a deep bow.

"It would seem, Lady Aaron, my uncle has been pulled away for matters which require his immediate attention. For this reason, we have his son, Lord Lorian Night, here in his stead," he explained, pointing an open hand at Lorian.

Feln felt quiet for a long moment after the prince spoke, either in shock at seeing Lorian at the table or in protest of the decision to use Lorian instead of Varios. She cleared her throat shortly after and spoke.

"Forgive me, my prince. But is the statement of a bastard adequate when matters this sensitive are in question?" she asked with words so sharp, Lorian could feel them protruding from his chest.

She had never thrown the fact of him being a bastard in his face. In their youth, she had been the voice of reason, ensuring his station didn't dictate his worth. In truth, his resentment for nobles and others who would demean him or treat him as less stemmed from the encouragement she'd given him in their past, yet now she used this to wound him, to make him seem like nothing more than an unreliable placeholder for Varios.

"She speaks truth!" shouted the dark-skinned noble, Lord Titus. "Bring us Varios or defer this council until his direct involvement can be verified!" Other nobles around the table nodded in confirmation.

"Silence!" screamed Prince Drecard, his optimistic mood taking a sharp turn toward aggressive. "Have you all learned nothing? I, the crown, with all the authority of the king himself, have verified the events you've been briefed on. I appointed Lorian in lieu of his father because he, too, witnessed the events firsthand. His testimony is more reliable than his father's in this case, and anyone who would question the validity of his position or his words on the basis of his lineage will see themselves sat upon the next trial bench with their life in jeopardy. Am I understood, council members?"

Lord Titus scowled in defiance but returned to his chair in defeat.

"Forgive me, Your Grace," said Feln with a slight bow as she returned to her seat as well. Lorian watched her for a long moment, wishing she would return his gaze. He felt numb to her coldness and wished only for an explanation.

"Continue, Darwin," ordered the prince, whose anger had subsided.

"My pleasure, Your Grace," he began as he nervously wiped fresh sweat from his brow. Lorian thought the outburst from the prince could've leveled the thin man based on how he reacted. "We begin now with a recounting of the events in question. Any lords or ladies who wish to question the events or interrogate the accused may do so as long as notice of intent is given. Guards, bring in the accused," he ordered as the council door swung open again.

Both Lord Aaron and Magistrate Strawman were chained and gagged. They were then marched to an area adjacent to the council table where a long bench rested and ordered to sit.

"We shall now begin. First, to provide credibility to the events, I have in my possession correspondence between the crown and Lord Varios about the timeline of events as well as the charges the accused faces. Order of the timeline places Lord Varios arriving a day early to Orion-Lon of the thirteenth day of Shattendar, near noon. Lord Varios was denied entry to Orion-Lon on the grounds of present danger within the city walls. This was proven by spectators to be false and an excuse to keep the arbiter at bay.

"Lorian Night was then ordered to enter the city under the guise of royal tribunary, which the crown has forgiven, considering the circumstances. After arriving at the church of Hamol, natural god of ore, he was restrained on order by Magistrate Strawman. This brings us to our first crime: illegal detention of a noble without prior authorization or reason," he summarized as Magistrate Strawman was brought to his feet by a guard and ungagged.

"Magistrate, how do you plead to this charge?" asked Advisor Darwin without emotion.

"Not guilty!" he screamed, alarming some of the council members. "He did not bear the eye of magic when I had him bound. How was I to know about his noble lineage?" asked the prisoner.

"A fair point," noted Lady Berall of Mazon, her cream-colored face standing in contrast to her blood-colored lips and bright orange eye. "Which is an oddity on its own, wouldn't you agree, my prince?"

Lorian's nerves began to rattle. He had never been asked to address his late awakening and could only explain how it was odd to him as well.

"Yes, though the circumstances of Lorian's awakening isn't what's on trial here, is it, my lady?" asked the prince with a half-smile. Lady Berall simply nodded in return and kept silent. "Though you were unaware of his noble lineage, Magistrate Strawman," began the prince with a sly tone, "he did introduce himself as a messenger on behalf of Lord Varios, did he not?"

"Yes, Your Grace, he did," replied the magistrate with a sullen look on his face. Lorian was unsure if the magistrate was ill or simply so afraid of facing consequences that the blood had drained from his face—a pasty sunken mimic of what was once there.

"And at this point, you had him bound by your guards, did you not?"

"Yes, Your Grace, but I—" he began before being cut-off.

"He was then struck multiple times under your care, was he not? And why was this? Because he attempted to stop you from hanging a child of only ten years? To stop an unjust public execution of a noble child?"

The magistrate's face was full of despair. He realized, perhaps for the first time, there was no help for him in this room or with these people. He looked around desperately, Lorian assumed for Lord Aaron's father, and when he wasn't able to locate him, looked back at Lord Dan Aaron, who refused to meet his gaze.

"That's enough from you for now. Let's continue with the charges, Darwin," the prince said.

"Yes, Your Grace," he began. "Next, Lord Varios forced himself through the gate and into the city, killing seven guardsmen. He then followed the same bells, as did Lorian Night, finding the aftermath of Max Aaron's execution. Varios then removed all opposition from the area, a handful of guards, and apprehended Magistrate Strawman, who then revealed the location of Lord Aaron," he finished as he attempted to catch his breath.

"Varios, accompanied by Lorian Night, traversed the mines and located Aaron, who hid within the lowest level, finding him intoxicated and barely responsive to Varios' probing. After a short discussion and recounting of the execution, Aaron collapsed the mine tunnel onto Lord Varios in an attempt to kill him, then fled the scene. Lord Aaron, do you deny these events?" he asked as Aaron was lifted to his feet and ungagged.

"I deny them. I had no hand in Max's execution. I merely wanted to relocate him for reasons surrounding his safety," Aaron began, his lies slithering off his tongue. "I had suspicions the magistrate was trying to assassinate my son, so I tried to hide him. He wanted me to marry his daughter and wanted our children to inherit my estate and assets. I was in the mines as a diversion to keep the magistrate from discovering my plan, which unfortunately failed. I fled from the mines to get help *for* Lord Varios, not to kill him. The cave-in was not of my doing. I only wanted to help."

The magistrate—now seated and gagged again—screamed through the cloth in his mouth, trying anything he could to refute the lies Aaron spun.

The prince furrowed his brow in deep thought. "I thought this might happen. Cousin," began the prince, "is Lord Aaron lying?"

"Yes, my prince. He admitted to Father, and to me, that it was his plan. I watched as he removed supports from the mine wall, causing the cave-in. He's a liar," Lorian said with as much coldness and hate as he could muster.

"Let's get the full truth, yes? Guards, bring her in, please," he ordered as a robed woman was escorted in, her face kept from sight by a black veil. Lorian wasn't sure why he felt a familiar presence in the woman, a fleeting memory reminiscent of something that made him feel a strange sense of nostalgia. She approached the prince and whispered softly into his ear. He returned the gesture and spoke softly to her, their words only faint whispers in the air.

"I have here a noble whose identity shall be kept secret for reasons surrounding her safety. This ensures a fair and accurate reading of Lord Aaron's mind and shall give us insight into the validity of the events spoken by Dan Aaron. Does anyone here have qualms with this reasoning?" he asked as he peered around the room for anyone brave enough to challenge him.

"This hardly seems fair, my Prince," interjected Feln, whose voice was filled with concern. Her cool demeanor began to crumble, and sweat started to accumulate on her cream-colored face. "As a commoner, I am unable to decipher the meaning of this person's presence and how it will affect the judgment."

Lorian was upset that she'd spoken up, but he agreed. He wasn't aware of any magics that could read minds, at least in his limited experience.

"A fair argument, Lady Aaron," the prince said as he turned his full attention on her. "I won't explain to you the intricacies of magics and how they're separated, but I will allow this explanation. This person is a Wielder of the mind magics and holds a rare skill: thought translation. Through effort, she can analyze his mind, render the events of that day into a format digestible for the rest of us, and play it back to us within our thoughts, like a painter forcing their canvas into the mind's eye. As a commoner, you won't be privy to the reading, I'm afraid, but the other council members will be. Seeing as you're the minority, you'll have to trust the other members of the council. Unless anyone here takes issue with this logic?" he said as he again challenged someone to protest.

After none saw fit to protest, the prince gave a nod of the head to the mysterious noble who approached Lord Aaron—who had been gagged and forced back to the bench again—and placed her gloved hands upon his head, her fingers sinking gently into his temples. Lorian could feel the stirring of magic in the air, a sensation both foreign and familiar. The eddies of magic danced around him, his own magic reacting with excitement as her inspection began. A few silent moments later, Lord Aaron broke out in a cold sweat, his face tired and void of blood. The shrouded woman then turned to the council members with her arms spread wide.

In a flash, all members of the council saw a vision of that day: Dan Aaron conspiring with the magistrate to get rid of Max, wishing not to know of the method. Lord Aaron then hid himself away in the mines when the time came, bottle after bottle drowning away his senses to avoid lingering thoughts on the matter. Hours played for the council members in seconds, the fatigue of the viewing felt by all.

"Well, I believe we now have our answer on the matter, don't we?" asked the prince rhetorically. He gave a nod to a guard across the room, who then saluted the prince and ferried away the shrouded woman. "Now, I think we have sufficient evidence to make our judgment, wouldn't you all agree? If there's nothing else to be said—"

Feln cut his words short. "House Aaron would like to claim leniency on Dan Aaron," she said, silencing the prince and the other council members.

"No one has claimed leniency in the entire history of this council, Lady Aaron. Are you sure?" asked Advisor Darwin.

"I am sure."

"What is she speaking of, Lord Greymoor?" whispered Lorian

"To claim leniency is to render a guilty verdict without further trial. She's doing this to force the crown into the position of keeping their traditional values—as all noble families do—or breaking the unspoken rules that all houses claim to abide by," he replied loudly, his voice making no attempt at discretion.

"Lord Greymoor speaks the truth," an enraged Lord Titus spoke, the vein in his neck bulging wildly. "Nobles do not fight other nobles, my prince," he continued, his anger not subsiding. "If you do not accept leniency here, you will be telling the world that conflict brews amongst its leaders. In-fighting would be the death of order!" he yelled, the ground shaking slightly as his lack of control released bits of magic.

The royal guards began to draw their swords in reaction, but the prince stayed their hands.

"To allow leniency here would force Dan Aaron to admit his guilt, publicly for all to hear. You would allow that of your house? To accept the shame and disgrace of a fallen noble, instead of letting him face judgment, as is right?" the prince asked, his tone deadly serious.

"Charles Aaron doesn't wish for his son to rot in a cell for the remainder of his days."

"Ah, he loves his son very much, that much is evident. It's a shame Dan Aaron didn't love his son the same way. Very well. Take Lord Aaron to the lofted courtyard. He shall admit his guilt to the capital and be granted leniency on behalf of House Dinivy," confirmed the prince as he rose from his chair, the other council members standing in turn. "Oh, as for the magistrate, before I forget. Death would be too easy, I think. You are to be sent to the Shut and made to chisel ice until you either expire or repay your crime in labor," he commanded. Finishing, he walked toward the council doors, the rest of the council members in pursuit.

Lorian watched as guards escorted Dan Aaron from the bench. A weeping magistrate screamed uselessly into his gag, his face left in a state of horror from the sentence given to him. Lorian didn't know much of the Shut, but from what he'd heard, the magistrate would suffer for his crimes, and that delighted him.

As for Lord Dan Aaron, Lorian was furious at his sentence. His cousin had promised him proper punishment for his horrendous crimes. *All there is to show for it is a public confession, and then what? Stripped of his title and sent to live carefree in a villa somewhere? Where is the justice in that?*

Regardless of his feelings, he wanted to see the humiliation on Dan Aaron's face. He wanted to finally see the coward admit he had his own son murdered for no reason other than succession. He quickly followed the others in anticipation of the spectacle.

After walking a short distance, Lorian stood outside the castle and upon a stone courtyard built from the second story of the castle's outer wall. The courtyard had a wooden platform on the far end, which Lorian assumed was for public greetings and other ceremonies.

All council members were present, each accompanied by a guard or two from their personal companies. The guards marched Lord Aaron to the platform and made him kneel before a rapidly growing crowd of citizens.

Lorian thought it was suspicious how many people had already gathered, as if they expected this outcome and were prepared.

"Attention citizens of Mainis Fortu!" yelled Darwin, his voice booming over the crowd below. "As penance for his crimes, Lord Dan Aaron of Orion-Lon has agreed to admit to crimes that occurred months ago, his burdened heart no longer able to bear the guilt. It is for your benefit, great people of Centrugard, that we hold this confession publicly! So that all citizens, noble or of common birth, may be aware that any who break laws set forth by the crown can and will be held accountable!" he finished, his words enticing the spectators to scream and boo accordingly.

"Confess, Lord Dan Aaron. Let your words lighten this weight you carry," Darwin said softly to the prisoner as he removed the gag.

"P . . . People of the capital," Aaron began, his trembling voice playing to a more apologetic character that didn't exist moments ago. "I have killed a boy—a bastard, and my own son. It is with great remorse that I share this with you. I thought I was above the law, that I would go unpunished for my crimes, but I was wrong. In my efforts to flee, I maimed another man, one of noble blood, and for this, I am sorry. May the crown see my woe, my guilt, and forgive me for my crimes," he finished, fake tears rolling down his cheeks. A small smile crept upon his face, like a man who felt relieved after accepting his fate.

Lorian wanted to remove Sun-Screamer and free that wretched smile from its host. He was only a few feet from the prince and doubted anyone, save Lord Greymoor, was quick enough to stop him.

Prince Drecard approached after a moment, the crowd screaming profanities and other unintelligible remarks toward Lord Aaron. "Dear Dan Aaron. It took courage to admit your evils. It took bravery to stand before the greatest capital in the world, full of the greatest citizens in the world, and accept their scrutiny. People of Centrugard!" screamed the prince, their threats and violent words turning to cheers before their beloved liege. "House Aaron has asked for mercy! Asked to claim leniency, an old noble tradition of avoiding responsibility!" he continued, the other council members growing confused. Lord Aaron's self-righteous smile quickly faded from his face. "I say nay! Nay to old, useless traditions! Nay to the age of elitism and consequence free action! And I say nay to House Aaron's plea for mercy!" he shouted, the crowd roaring with excitement and bloodlust.

Lorian watched with glee as Aaron's face went pale. He watched as horrified expressions blossomed among the lords around him, reacting to the prospect of Lord Aaron about to be sentenced to prison before their eyes.

"My prince!" yelled Feln, her eyes wide and full of confusion. "We invoked leniency. You must oblige!"

"Quiet yourself, Lady Aaron, lest you find yourself dangling from this perch. You'd make a pretty corpse," replied Lord Greymoor, who took the initiative to support the prince. He removed his great hammer and stood in front of the other council members, his face cold and ready for violence.

"With his confession," the prince continued, his words gaining momentum with the onlookers below, "we shall see true justice. By the authority granted to me by the natural gods and by the crown, I sentence Lord Dan Aaron to death for his crimes. May he be an example to all those who dare challenge this new world. Death to Lord Aaron, and death to the old ways!" he screamed, the crowd returning his energy.

He turned to the council members with spittle fresh on his lips from addressing the spectators. "And let this be a lesson to all of you. Lord Greymoor, would you do the honor?"

"Are you mad?" shouted Lord Titus, several council members standing beside him in agreement. "This will start a war! Where is the king?" he screamed as he placed a hand on his sword.

Lorian, fearful of an attack on the prince, drew Sun-Screamer, the blade leaving a trail of fire as it arched through the sky. The magic caused a screeching noise as he pointed it toward Lord Titus. "Remove your blade and that will be the last action you take with both arms."

The nobles froze at the sudden display of magic. Lorian's sword caused a panic among the attendees.

Lord Greymoor took the opportunity to approach Lord Aaron, his hammer held high above his head. "I told you it would be my hand, boy. I promised you blood. You want penance? You want salvation? Here it is!" he screamed as his hammer came down with the force to level a mountain. The resounding shockwave from the blow shook the courtyard and sent dust into the air.

Lord Aaron's body lay lifeless at Greymoor's feet, his head reduced to bloody viscera and bone beneath the great hammer. Teeth and cartilage spread forth from the weapon, creating a circle of flesh and gray matter around the newly formed crater.

Lorian sheathed his blade, assuming no further blood would be shed after the execution. Before he could look upon the aftermath of Lord Aaron's body, a burning sensation flooded his magical eye, forcing him to his knees. As the searing pain enveloped him, he noticed that all present nobles—including Lord Greymoor—were doubled over in anguish. A sensation then dulled the pain, and a sense of euphoria and power permeated through his body.

Lorian felt as if he could lift a carriage, run a hundred miles, or summon the very sun itself. The invigorating feeling confused him until he realized what had happened. Lord Aaron's death caused his connection, everyone's connection, to their source of magic to strengthen. *But this could only happen if a family line ended*, he thought. Then it occurred to him.

Lord Dan Aaron was a bastard.

If Charles Aaron was the true father, the magic would've returned to him, but he wasn't, so it returned to all Wielders. Lorian bellowed out in laughter, his voice carrying over the clamor of shouts below. The irony, he thought, was poetic.

Chapter 28: Fallout

"Power and greed, cardinal sins that the natural gods would see eradicated from the souls of man. Bless you all, let the natural ones guide your wretched lives toward ones worth salvation."
—High-Gothic Aaron on last rights for the children lost during the Bastard Crusades

"You've no idea what you've started, boy!" screamed Lord Titus, his dark features twisted in rage. "You are my prince no longer," he spat. Lord Greymoor, now recovered from Lord Aaron's magic returning to the infinite pool, stood in protest, ready to strike down Lord Titus at the order of the prince.

"Calm yourself, Lord Greymoor," ordered the prince, who rose from the ground with strain. Most of the council had recovered from the ordeal, with only a few lingering on the ground in pain. Lord Aaron's body twitched slightly as Greymoor removed his hammer, the remnants of his head falling from the steel in grotesque chunks. "There needn't be any further bloodshed. Lord Dan Aaron got what he deserved. He paid for his crimes in full. I shall adjourn the council now; your services are no longer required. Return to your homes and tell the other noble houses of this day. Let it be a reminder that though we are noble, we must surrender to the rule of law, same as the commoners," he said with dignity.

Lorian stood on guard despite the prince's orders, ready to fight if need be.

"You shouldn't have done that, my prince," said Feln, her fear and confusion temporarily silenced by the realization of what transpired. "Charles Aaron will not forgive this; he will not forgive the crown. I must return to Twilanon and inform my husband." She turned to leave but stopped as the stone giant gifted her information.

"He'll already know," laughed Lord Greymoor. "Every noble from here to the ends of the earth already knows. Send him this message instead, girl. Tell Charles Aaron that House Greymoor supports the crown and let him know that if he dares raise a hand against it in any capacity, he'll be seeing his son again after all."

Without further words, Feln left, her personal group of guards in tow. Lorian watched with grief as she did. He wanted so badly to speak with her, to learn of her recent days and how she wound up as Lady Aaron. More importantly, he wanted to be with his friend, to know she was okay, but he didn't know if she felt the same. *She certainly didn't show it if she did*, he thought.

"Mark my words, Drecard. The crown has made enemies today. I, Lord Titus of the Saltlands, declare you my enemy. You are unfit to wield power in your father's stead, and he is unfit to rule if he trusted you with this. To this council, I propose a new king, a new sovereign who will take power from those undeserving, keeping our traditions alive and unmolested. I will be your king!" he screamed. To Lorian's surprise, other council members began to agree, their guards preparing to draw swords.

Lord Greymoor charged without warning, his hammer swinging aggressively toward Lord Titus. "You dare threaten the crown!" he screamed as his hammer caught an unprepared guard in the torso, crushing the man's armor and bone beneath it.

Lord Titus began to attack, his own sword breaking free of its place at its hip. A man from behind Lord Titus, someone Lorian thought was merely an advisor, removed his hood and grabbed the lord. With his face exposed, Lorian could see that it was another dark-skinned noble, his features nearly a perfect match for Lord Titus. With a breath, he and Lord Titus vanished, remnants of magic lingering in the air as they disappeared.

Other nobles began to flee in response, the ones who stood with Lord Titus being the first to leave. Lorian watched as some nobles disappeared, using their magic to jump, while others ran, ordering their guards to draw swords to keep them safe. Prince Drecard commanded none of the royal guards to pursue, ordering them all to stand down.

"Let them leave! Let the cowards flee, their tails tucked neatly between their legs! Justice has prevailed on this day!" commanded the prince, who solicited more cheers from the massive crowd that continued to gather below. Lorian was unsure why he felt dread slowly encroaching him, like a cold sweat forming on the back of his neck. The world had just changed before him, and he didn't know if it changed for the better.

***

Prince Drecard waited as his servants dressed him in fine ceremonial garments. The purple cloth clashed

333

greatly with the silver trim that laced everything together. The back of his overcoat bore a silver Dinivy drake—posh but garish.

Lorian stood opposite him, waiting. They had gone almost immediately to a room adjacent to the grand hall, where the princess's engagement party was to be held, using it instead to prepare himself and the prince for another event.

"I know this wasn't supposed to happen for a while, but since my sister won't be getting married, holding your naming ceremony will make great use of an otherwise wasted opportunity. I'm sorry about Uncle. I promise we're still searching for him."

Lorian nodded his head, thankful for the care that his cousin showed him. Lorian's original plan to run had crumbled to dust, a war being a relatively inconvenient obstacle to his quest for answers. He was still going to search, but he needed a new plan. Once he was back with Varios, things would be easier to discuss. He wanted to trust Drecard, and his revolutionary attitude toward commoners made the thought attractive, but it wasn't his secret alone to share, and he would need Varios' approval first.

He just hoped that Varios would be able to stomach him long enough to speak.

"Have you thought about what you'll do, cousin?" asked the prince as he finished his preparation and began to leave his dressing chambers. Lorian hurriedly followed.

"About what, my prince?"

He smiled slyly. "The naming ceremony, of course. He doesn't need to be there for you to take his name—not with my approval. This is what he wanted, yes?"

"It is, my prince. He has said so on many occasions. I just hope I can make him proud."

"Pride can be a sin, Lorian. Do what you feel is right. Shame you won't be a bastard anymore. Having someone like you at my side, as my council, sends a powerful message," he quipped, his strides increasing in pace.

Lorian thought about that statement while they walked. He had only ever been a bastard and nothing else. That was to suddenly stop when he took Varios' name? He felt an unorthodox attachment to the name Night, and an odd anxiety about letting it go, letting himself go. It had been a part of him for so long that, if it were to vanish, he feared he would vanish too.

"Did you know Lady Aaron, by chance? She seemed to know you, cousin," inquired the prince, a sly smile stretching across his face.

"I thought I did, but she's different, colder. She's no longer the friend I used to know. Of course, she wasn't Feln Aaron back when we were acquainted."

"Ah yes, Feln," he said as he stopped before the doors that would lead them to the ballroom and to Lorian's naming ceremony, "I knew that name was familiar when she said it. Before she married Lord Charles Aaron, I had heard rumors about her."

"Oh? And what did you hear, my prince?"

"That she rose in power swiftly. Apparently, she's a genius merchant and developed quite a sizable sum in a short time. They say her coffers overflow with gold!" He laughed.

"Now that does sound like her, ever the clever girl," Lorian replied with faint sadness as he remembered all the times she'd had to use her mental prowess to save him from a drunkard or a guard.

"Yes, clever indeed. Except for that black wardrobe. The woman dressed like she was attending a funeral. Suppose that is where she got the name."

"The name, Your Grace?" asked Lorian in confusion. He didn't remember her carrying a title or special name.

"Yes, the Raven, I believe. Ugly bird, in my opinion, but we don't choose our pet names, I suppose."

Lorian felt his mind shatter, his thoughts fleeing his head faster than light. *Feln is the Raven?* How could this be? Was he supposed to kill his best friend? How could he? It was impossible. He needed to find her, needed to speak with her. Why had she fled after the council meeting, and why had she married Lord Charles Aaron? What had she become, and why was he being haunted by entities that wanted her dead?

Prince Drecard opened the doors that led to the ballroom, the bright light blinding Lorian as he mindlessly followed the prince onto the stage meant for his naming ceremony.

Chapter 29: On the Brink

"It has been said that the Bastard Crusades were, in essence, the collective fear of our ruling class incarnate. When the first innocent child was condemned to die, so too was the fate of all nobles who partook in the atrocity. The natural gods wept from their golden towers, their tears sealing the fate of Centrugard."
—Patron-Scholar Yuri Bludson

S am Varios awoke to the gentle pressure of a warm wet rag rubbing against his forehead. He wasn't sure what had happened to him or where he was. The soothing sensation of his head being washed made him want to keep his eye closed for another few minutes, the feeling reminiscent of his mother caring for him when he fell ill as a child.

Pain followed the gentle caress of the moist cloth like a bucket of cold water crashing over him, forcing his eyes open and flooding his mind with memories of his son and the hellspawn that congregated at the church of the unnatural gods. He sat upright, his core muscles screaming at him to relax, though his addled brain and frantic nerves allowed him no such reprieve.

"He's awake! Handsir, he's conscious!" a familiar female voice yelled, her panicked words increasing the tension in his chest.

"Where is the boy?" he screamed, his singular eye failing to adjust to the poor light in the room, leaving the girl beside him with blurred features.

"It is I, Lord Varios!" she replied as she grabbed him by the shoulders in an attempt to keep him steady. "It is Lady Jane Greymoor, Lorian's fiancée, Your Grace. What boy are you speaking of?" she asked, failing to force him back to bed.

"The boy in the emerald fire!" he replied with pained heaves. Sam took in a few long breaths, his body screaming in pain and stiffness "Lorian?" he asked, trying to remember what he needed to tell Lorian. "Where is he? Where is my son?"

"My Lord," she said, her voice going flat, "there has been an incident. I believe it's best if someone else explains it to you."

Handsir Rikard exploded into the room, his face twisted with worry and concern for his lord. Sam could see more clearly now, the blurred figures before him taking shape as detail returned to their forms. He was in a stone chamber barely five meters wide. It contained only the bed upon which he sat, a pail of water beside it, and the door through which Rikard entered.

"Rikard? Where am I?" he asked as he tried to force his senses even despite the pain.

"You are in the capital sect of scholars," answered a voice from outside the door.

Sam watched as two men entered: one he did not recognize and the other Koh Bridgeson. Seeing the already cramped area fill more than it could handle, Lady Jane left, escorted by Handsir Rikard, the old servant's face awash with grief.

"And who are you?" Sam asked through labored breaths, the pain taking its sweet time subsiding.

"Forgive me, my lord. I am Patron-Scholar Godrick, head of this sect," replied the man.

Sam inspected him further now that his eyesight had returned to him completely. Before him was a man of sixty years or more. His waistline indicated he lived a sedentary life, and his voice was pitched higher than normal, like a eunuch's. His nearly bald head and drooped face gave him the appearance of a man whose life had not been easy, though his tone was gentle as could be.

"I am the person responsible for bringing you here, or keeping you here, to be more precise. The truth is, my child-scholars came about you in the old church, drawn there by horrendous noises. I wanted nothing to do with you, in all fairness. Scholars prefer to keep nobility at an arm's length, but Child-Scholar Lo pleaded that you be kept and healed."

Sam thought carefully about the position he was in, how he could attempt to explain his way out. Before he could create an excuse or fabricate a story, Koh spoke.

"Lord Varios, we need to talk, privately, if Patron Scholar Godrick would permit it," he asked, looking toward the elderly scholar for approval. Godrick gave an affirmative nod and then left the room, closing the door behind him.

"I don't know what happened to you, and for the moment, I don't care. Lord Aaron's trial went on without you. Lorian stood in your place," he explained, his voice steady and his words carefully selected. "You were asleep, so you didn't feel it. Prince Drecard executed Lord Dan Aaron publicly. War has been declared, Sam, and I think Lorian has been caught in the middle of it."

Sam's eyes widened in concern for Lorian. Despite everything, he cared deeply for the boy.

Though his mind was still flooded with pain, he knew how grave the situation was. He wondered what events could have occurred within the council meeting to call for the execution of a noble. This was the last thing he had expected, even considering Aaron's crimes.

By traditional laws, Aaron would have been imprisoned, but to execute him, and to do it publicly, was intentional. *Someone wanted to start a war, but his nephew, the prince? Of all people, how could he benefit from a war?* Sam's mind replayed the vile words of the priest of the unnatural gods.

"In the days to come, war will swallow these lands . . ."

"You mentioned I didn't feel it while asleep. You don't mean . . . ?"

"Yes. Lord Aaron was a bastard, unknown to all. When he passed, we all felt it, like a rush of energy."

"Our laws exist for this very reason. Why would the prince do this? Hundreds of years have passed since peace was established, but now that other nobles have felt their own power grow, I doubt his will be the last magical blood spilled," ranted Sam, his anger outweighing the pain for the first time. Despite the return of Aaron's magic, he felt only a small increase in his own connection—the effects of his recent overuse, he assumed.

"We're not sure. Lya was with me earlier when we were looking for you. She ran back to the castle when we heard the news. Haven't seen her since," Koh replied while rubbing the back of his neck.

"And what news of Lorian? What part does he play in this?"

"He was beside the prince when it happened. Lord Titus declared war on the crown and tried to strike the prince down. Lorian stopped him. Whether you like it or not, he's been dragged into this. You should go see him before tonight. He's going to need you."

Sam felt like he'd hit a wall, his emotions more erratic than they'd ever been. He wanted Lorian out of the public eye, away from the turmoil of politics, yet here he was, at the center of one of the most pivotal events in history.

"*Bring us the bastard,*" he'd heard the priest say, remembering the price he would need to pay to see Stenley again.

He didn't know what was right anymore. He had grown to care very deeply for Lorian, even after he had admitted to attacking his mother. Despite where they stood now, sacrificing him wasn't an option, but what about Stenley? If what the priest said was true and his son could be returned to him, how could he live with himself knowing he needed to trade one innocent life for another?

Sam could feel the weight of this impossible choice weighing him down, his soul sinking with every moment.

"Wait, what is happening tonight?" asked Sam, his mind clearing for a moment.

"It's the prince, Sam. Since Lord Titus called for war; his son's engagement to the princess was rescinded. Instead of the engagement party, the prince wishes for Lorian to undergo the naming ceremony instead—with or without you."

"That fool of a boy!" screamed Sam, his legs carrying him from bed in a burst of rage. He quickly dressed himself in the fresh linens waiting neatly by the foot of his bed. "Prince or not, he is my nephew. He is my blood. I will get answers from him, even if I have to hold him by his ankles and shake the damn things out myself. Where is the king?" he asked as he finished buttoning a gray long-sleeved shirt.

"We don't know that either. The prince claimed that he's indisposed, whatever that could mean. I can't imagine him entertaining the idea of war, much less agreeing to it. Something must have happened," suggested Koh, who wiped fresh sweat from his forehead.

"I'm inclined to agree. Lead the way. We need to see Lorian before the ceremony. I must speak with him," he said as the two of them dashed out of the small stone chamber.

Before they could proceed further, a small group of child-scholars blocked their way, their steeled faces awaiting orders from Godrick, who stood nearby.

"Move your scholars, Godrick. I am thankful for the assistance, but do not test me," threatened Sam.

"They are not going to harm you, my lord; you needn't worry," said Godrick, his gentle tone carrying his words peacefully across the divide between them. "I only want a moment of your time. I believe you owe me this much, Ash-Bringer."

Sam was unsure if he spoke the truth about his scholars. Soldiers or not, enough men could bring both of them down eventually. Being stuck in what he assumed was the lower level of the sect gave him a disadvantage. Aside from that, Sam didn't see Jane or Rikard, and someone had taken his sword. He would have to agree, for now.

"Very well, Godrick. I'll grant you a few minutes, but nothing more. Getting back to the castle is imperative."

"I'm sure it is, Your Grace, but calm yourself and follow me. There is much to discuss," Godrick muttered as he slowly walked away, not waiting for either of the nobles to follow.

The child-scholars slowly dispersed as Godrick left, allowing Varios and Koh to pursue the patron scholar unimpeded.

Sure enough, Sam had been correct about their position in the sect; stairs leading to higher levels gave that fact away. Koh and Sam patiently followed the old scholar through a few stretches of hallway, forcing Sam to pace himself. His body felt like it was moments from crumbling beneath him.

They passed rooms filled with trinkets and scientific equipment the likes of which they had never seen, finally ending their journey in a large study.

The room was exceptionally clean, the stone floor highly polished beneath their feet. Shelves of books and ancient artifacts lined the walls, and beautifully designed rugs stretched beneath their feet. An assembly of chairs was stationed atop the rug and in front of a roaring fireplace. Koh, who was already sweating greatly from the walk, wished to sit farthest away, afraid he would melt. Varios sat directly across from the old scholar, who sank slowly into his cushioned chair, releasing pain-filled groans as he did.

"Now, can I interest you in any tea or biscuits?" the patron-scholar asked politely.

Koh raised his hand in excitement, ready to indulge himself. Nevertheless, Sam refused the snacks with a wave of his hand.

"Figured I'd ask," he said as he adjusted himself in the chair. "When my scholars found you, a sort of deliria had set in. You were speaking nonsense, the pain or something else keeping you in a trance-like state," he explained as a scholar came in with a single biscuit and kettle of fresh water. He waited patiently while the child-scholar brewed his tea, smiling all the while. "Thank you, dear," Godrick said as the child-scholar left. "You spoke of the unnatural gods, raving that they wronged you in some way. This is what I wish to speak about."

"Unnatural gods. What in the hells is that?" asked Koh, his eyes never leaving the last bits of biscuit that remained on Godrick's plate.

Sam grew nervous at the inquiry, afraid that speaking too much would reveal facts that he'd never be able to silence again. He remained quiet, not wanting to divulge any information.

"Wise to remain silent, my lord. But in some cases, silence can make one seem guilty. I shall explain what I know of the unnatural gods. If you feel inclined to speak up or ask questions, I shall happily oblige," Godrick began as

344

he cleared his throat and downed another sip of steaming tea.

"Through research of the ancient world, we have come to know of another religion, one whose roots are so embedded in the annals of time that we can no longer discern where they began or if they're true. When Navaety, mother of all, birthed the world, she left twelve gods, who we've come to call the natural gods, in full control of creation. When the gods created our world and sowed the seeds of their interventions, they were forced out—cursed to never return to what they had wrought.

"This is the truth that we all know today; the origin of everything. Through rigorous study and translation of ancient languages thought dead, we've uncovered information that contradicts this story. There were *thirteen* gods, not *twelve*. Tevan, the thirteenth god, cursed the other twelve, forbade them from returning to this world out of hate and jealousy. In their absence, spirits of old claimed the vacant thrones of these gods for their own, each claiming lordship over their respective domains.

"These came to be the unnatural gods, perverters of the natural order." Godrick paused, coughing up phlegm that had lodged itself in his lungs and sipping the remainder of the tea. "This information I give freely to you, with one stipulation."

"And what would that be?" Sam replied, breaking his silence.

"That you remember this conversation, this information, ever should you need it repeated or explained. I have always welcomed all to my sect, despite opposition from the other nobles, and will continue to do so. Whispers are going around the kingdom, Lord Varios, speaking of war. Death will come, whether we wish it or not. I leave the fate of the scholars to you. We can stay neutral, as we always have, or you can finally open your eyes and accept the knowledge we carry has uses beyond our comprehension. This is all I wish to say," finished Godrick as he stood from his chair, waddling away without further words.

"He has a point, I think. If there is war and they could help us, it may be in our interest to hear them out," Koh said.

"No, I will not have the death of innocent academics on my hands. These people exist only for research, for purposes that the crown finds useful. I'll not make decisions on behalf of the royal family," Sam replied.

"What was all of that about? Why was he telling us of unnatural gods? Feel keen on sharing?" Koh asked, his interest genuine for the first time.

"It's nothing. I'll explain later, after we find Lorian," he replied calmly, though his thoughts were anything but calm. Something was off about Godrick, though he couldn't place what it was. The man didn't seem malicious, but there was something in his eyes that made Sam believe he had a motive beyond what he revealed.

"Then let's get moving, you secretive cunt," he replied with a smile.

***

The day progressed much faster than Sam had hoped. The sun was already well beneath the horizon.

It was evening when he and Koh arrived at the castle. Before leaving the sect, he'd had a moment to speak with his handsir, agreeing that Lady Jane and Rikard were to meet them here after attending to their own personal business within the sect, which he neglected to ask about.

Sam was horrified to find that the ceremony was well underway already. He watched as Lorian and Prince Drecard finished their vows. Sam could only stare in desperation as Lorian swore his oath at the prince's feet, his voice echoing across the great ballroom upon which the ceremony was held.

He watched as the prince honored Lorian with his sword. Lorian then stood, facing the nobles who were brave enough to stay and the gentry who were duty-bound to attend. Each noble, gentleman and commander present bore an air of discomfort. The entire room was waiting for something that couldn't be spoken into words, like a looming cloud of despair that hovered just out of sight. A slender man then spoke to the crowd, his voice carrying news that cut Sam deeper than any blade.

"By the power of the crown, Lorian Night, son of Lord Sam Varios, has completed his vows and finished the naming ceremony. By all rights, this name now belongs fully to him. May its greatness be carried by his descendants until the natural gods reclaim us all. In front of the prince, and witnessed by all, I give you, first of his name and heir to Amphil-Lon, Lord Lorian of House Night!" he screamed. The crowd reacted with gasps and incredulous looks.

Lorian had done the unthinkable and taken his own last name, making him the first lord to ever bear the surname Night.

***

347

Lorian looked down upon all who were present, his dead-eyed glare announcing a warning to those who thought themselves above justice and order. A question echoed in his head—one that held more significance than he'd been aware of when it was first asked.

"And tell me, Lorian. If you could change the world, truly change it, what would you do?"

Lorian smiled to himself. His answer remained true: *Burn it all down.*

Preview of Book 2, Chapter 1: Flight of the Raven

The cold winds whipped through Lorian's tattered tent, its ragged sheets the result of weeks of neglect and constant travel. The other three men in his company shivered in vain, their bodies' meek attempt at generating heat to fight the bitter weather turning their lips blue and their ears an angry red. They huddled close to him, hoping to siphon the lifesaving heat that he emitted through his magic.
Through his adventures with his false father, Lord Sam Varios, he had acquired many useful tricks for surviving. A passive release of heat he had witnessed during their expedition to the mines of Orion-Lon gave birth to the idea for a shroud of flame that kept his limbs warm during nights like this.

Lorian waited patiently in his tent, the chattering teeth of his personal guard a small distraction to the purpose of this quest. He had staked this tent high upon a hill that overlooked a hidden road forking between Twilanon and Granar; an outpost for Titus' army just north of the Holy City. He would need this vantage point to accurately estimate the incoming garrison that protected essential cargo supplying the rebels this far north.

This shipment was important to him, it didn't just carry weapons, rations and armor, it carried the Raven. Reports from the crown's survey corps stated that she'd travel with this envoy, though he didn't know why. Since the Great Returning, her whereabouts had been elusive to say the least. She was practically a ghost -a phantom that only surfaced when transactions of great importance would occur. *Is that what this is?* He pondered, his thoughts going awry with possibilities that continuously painted her in a grim light. "Lord Night," whispered one of his guards as the front flap to his tent was pulled aside. "There in the distance; it has to be them."

Lorian stepped from out of the tent, his eyes already adjusted to the dark swirl of snow that danced around his head. Far down the road, coming from Twilanon, a series of torches came into view. Their light, though meagre at first, soon painted a picture of the convoy that carried Feln. Two large carriages, each with a four-horse tow, slowly rolled forward. A group of twelve soldiers headed the group while another of equal size followed behind. A litter of spearmen marched alongside the cargo and a single soldier led the entire ensemble upon horseback. As they grew closer, Lorian could see the hazy glow of the lead soldier's eye. He was a Wielder. Though the reports didn't indicate the presence of any nobility, he had already prepared himself for such a scenario. He had become diligent in these war-torn months, something this obvious would not take him by surprise.

"Where are Bladesdottir and Lord Greymoor? Bring them to me now." Lorian ordered. He never let his eyes leave the company below. His determination felt like fire in his stomach.

A tired looking woman in thick leather armor approached him from the side. Her face held the wrinkles of age and the pink glow of her right eye stood in contrast to her graying black hair. She kneeled beside him as another noble approached, kneeling adjacent to her and awaiting orders. His golden eye and defined jaw were obvious indicators of his lineage. If it weren't for the youth that shimmered upon his smooth skin, one might mistake him for his grandfather.

Lorian looked the both of them over, ensuring they were prepared for the fight to come.

"There's a Wielder at the brow of the caravan. I'll take him on. I'll need you two to handle the other soldiers," he ordered. He had fought alongside these two for the last few missions and was more than pleased with their capabilities. Jenon Bladesdottir was a low-born noble and an excellent sharpshooter. He had witnessed her remove the petals from a daisy at no less than one hundred yards. She used the elemental power of wind to carry her arrows farther and with more accuracy than could be managed otherwise. Johnathan Greymoor was, in all contrast to his gentle face, a heavyweight hammer man, like his grandfather, and his stamina seemed to have no limits. Both were as dependable a soldier he could ask for.

"My lord," began Johnathan as he struggled to keep his voice low. "What would you have us do if we encounter the Raven?"
Imagining any harm befalling Feln made Lorian's mouth twitch. "She is not to be harmed. Restrain her if possible or leave her to me and I'll do it. Prince Drecard has deemed her essential to disrupting supply chains to the frontlines and it's imperative she's apprehended."

Both Johnathan and Jenon replied with a nod of their heads.

"We've no idea what the Wielder is capable of. I'll call down lighting on the soldiers grouped towards the back when they pass. Jenon, use the chaos to take out the men steering the carriages. Johnthan will engage the other group while I remove the Wielder from play, any disagreements?" He asked, knowing they'd never second guess his judgment.

Once they had huddled together, Lorian turned to the men and gave his orders. "Wait until Bladesdottir and Greymoor have engaged before you lot head in. Attack from the rear and make your way forward. Restrain any who surrender only if it doesn't put you in harm's way, am I understood?"
The exhausted men slammed a fist into their chests in salute. Despite the frigidity in the air, a spark of excitement and nerves flooded his body, as it did before any battle. He could see the desire in his men's eyes, they wanted to succeed. Not just for their own sake, but for his. They wanted to honor Lord Night and bring glory to his house.

Now in place, the soldiers under his command waited eagerly for the signal he'd give to commence the start of the battle. Time slowed around Lorian in the last moment before his hand gestured forward. He watched the flakes of snow fall gently before his eyes before landing onto his leather armor and melting away. A foggy exhale escaped from his mouth and filled in the air before him.

The time was now, his hand lifted into the air and squeezed into a fist. The men began to slide gently down from the top of the hill, the enchanted earth erasing the noise of their descent. Lorian had a clear view of the caravan below him; a thicket of bare pine trees served as a wall blocking the carriages from escaping off-road.

When the men were halfway down the slope, Lorian pulled two throwing knives from his waist band. He thanked Lya Coalsdottir internally before taking aim at the group of soldiers following behind the last wagon.

He only had to wait a moment before he sensed the energy in the air. Months of practice and practical use gave him the control he so desperately craved. He could now control, with effort, the amount of power called forth. With the ring he imbued with magic, he was more than capable of a precise and moderately charged attack. With more power, his precision waned, though the attack he had planned would be weak enough for him to direct how he saw fit.

He saw Johnathan reach the bottom before the other soldiers; his notoriously large warhammer already withdrawn. Jenon was next to him, her longbow notched with two arrows pointed towards her targets.

The moment arrived and Lorian tossed his knives with great force, their serrated blades digging into the frosted armor of two faceless soldiers. They yelped in pain and confusion. He waited a moment, then slid down the hill, his command of lightning causing the clouds above to swirl like whirlpools of energy. When he reached the bottom, he released control of the magic he stored in the air above. Bolts of lightning traced along ethereal lines and unto their targets, his throwing knives.

Light and sound erupted forth, blinding and deafening those nearby. The whistle of arrows followed the thunder and Lorian watched as both carriage drivers fell lifelessly in their seats. He and Johnathan leapt from their spots and began to engage their own targets.

Lorian was first to approach his enemy – a noble whose heavy armor sat atop broad shoulders. His magical eye glowed a distinct yellow and softly brightened the rigid features of his face. He was at least a head taller than Lorian and bore scars alongside his neck and head that gave him the air of a man experienced in violence.

Getting into a battle of attrition with this man would be a costly mistake.

Dashing towards the horse, he removed *Sun-Screamer* from its sheath - the familiar screech of magic followed by a trail of fire sung forth. Many men had seen his enchanted sword at this point, and it had grown famous amongst his men and infamous in the eyes of the enemy.

On several occasions Lorian had been interrogated as to the origin of the blade, some even going so far as to tempt him with money or position for its secret. He never once surrendered its answers. The power of imbuement was lost for a reason - at least he assumed. Whoever that faceless man was that revealed its truth did so for a reason, and he wouldn't allow anyone else access to such powerful knowledge. He would keep it safe.

In lieu of attacking the mounted noble, he instead aimed for the horse, slicing through its thickly muscled neck, forcing its rider to the ground where they could fight as equals. A flash of sadness passed through him, as it always did when he took a life.

He couldn't help but hope that Sebastain, his father's horse, was well and happy back in Tarns-Knoll. He had to leave the steed behind when he and Varios first made their way to Mainis Fortu. He vowed to ride him again when the war was over.

The enemy Wielder jumped from his saddle, rolling away from the thrashing beast as its life drained away. His foe stood and removed a longsword that had been secured on his back. Lorian was never a fan of two-handed weapons. He knew the force behind armaments such as this could devastate an unprepared man, even shatter swords too feeble to withstand a parry, but having a free hand for Wielding proved too useful.

The two Wielders circled each other slowly, waiting for the perfect moment to strike. The world fell silent around Lorian as he prepared to kill this stranger. He heard only the beating of his heart. In battles now past he had made the mistake of allowing anxiety and fear to control his actions. Even empathy would stay his hands in moments that, without the aid of his men, would have resulted in his death. He felt the rise of those feelings and subdued them as he had learned. All emotions had their place, but that place could never be the battlefield.

He analyzed the Wielder in the short seconds before their blades met. He was obviously stronger, nimble too based on how quickly he recovered from falling off his horse. With a weapon that required two hands, Lorian was sure that this man didn't belong to the School of Body Magics like he did. Otherwise, he would need a free hand to fight him off. "I've heard tales of you, Lord bastard," the noble said, his eyes darting between Lorian's feet and sword. "Some think you're a god. They say you piss lighting and shit fire," the man laughed hysterically, as if he was relieved to see the rumors about him were false. He readied his blade, pointing the tip at Lorian and leapt forward with great speed.

Lorian readied Sun-Screamer and titled the blade away from himself, the perfect position to deflect. He knew from his time training with the Stone Giant that a forward thrust with such a large blade forced the attacker off balance, and he would use this to his advantage. As the two blades met, Lorian braced himself and allowed the Wielder's blade to slide alongside his own. When the blade glided far enough, he pivoted around the noble whose momentum carried him forward, leaving him vulnerable. Lorian planted his leading foot firmly in the ground and lunged forth, his speed amplified by his will to see Feln. He pointed his flame wrought blade towards the sky and swung down on the off-balance brute before him. The sword met no purchase and slammed harshly into the slush below, his enemy a phantom in the wind.

Fuck, he's a jumper.

The familiar awe he first felt when watching Lord Dan Aaron vanish within the mines of Orion-Lon returned to him, as did dread. The whirl of magics stirred within the air and had only enough time to lift Sun-Screamer when a flashing pain tore through his back.

Battle-hardened as he'd become in the war-ravaged months, he was unprepared for the awful pain that exploded through his senses. He felt as if someone poured molten iron alongside his back, the searing pain spreading quicker than wildfire to his limbs.

In all the battles he had been in thus far, the thought of fighting a jumper was something he foolishly believed he would be prepared for. He examined the battlefield as thoroughly as he could and saw no totems or other items that could act as a jump-point for his enemy's magic. Dan Aaron had used a small carved figurine for his but no such item could be seen in this instance.

How did he do it? What have I missed?

Lorian's legs buckled from the pain, and he felt himself losing control as he fell to a knee. Words from Captain Bowers rang through his mind as he recalled one of their first training sessions.

"Every decision is life and death on the battlefield... If you find yourself sitting in the dirt. . . you're a dead man." He couldn't let all of his hard work end here. He suffered too greatly and for too long for such a trivial and forgetful death. He needed to rise again; forget the pain that swam through his

veins like the jumping cod in Mellomirror; ignore the dizziness that dulled his senses.

His control over the earthen element was weak, unpracticed, and clunky, but he would need it now. After training with Lord Greymoor six months prior, the Stone Giant let him on to the advantage he carried in his old age - something Jane had told them at their first meeting. Small, concentrated pockets of earth had been inserted into his armor. As his magic weakened with every child born into his house, he needed a way to sustain himself and keep appearances that his wielding hadn't waned or lessened. By controlling the pockets of earth within his armor, he could move faster, lift more, and stem the draining of stamina through supplementary magic.
He called it his Iron Skeleton.

Lorian was thankful now most of all for this insight. He had been gifted a set of armor similar to Greymoor's in hope that he too could master this hidden technique. While he couldn't consider himself proficient by any means, he would use this now to save his life. He reached the pockets of earth with his magic, as he had been taught, and tugged them harshly like a marionette forcing his puppet forward, propelling his tired body out of harm's way.

The crash of his enemy's sword came only moments after his desperate maneuver, leaving both the battling Wielders surprised and momentarily frozen. He steadied his trembling body using the Iron Skeleton technique and took in what details he could of his opponent. The man's forehead was fresh with sweat and his skin was paler than the moment prior. His exhales were quick and heavy and his posture was sluggish. Lorian knew these were clear signs of magical exhaustion.

Hot blood poured from the wound that stretched from his back to the side of his hip. The slick liquid coated his greaves and steam rose from where it met the snowfall. He wasn't sure how deep it was or if anything critical had been struck, but this was no time for triage. He'd either die of the wound or by this man's sword and he knew which of the two took priority.

The noble was jumping somehow, and he needed to discover the method. He wouldn't survive another slash like this one. Lorian wasn't sure how much stamina the man had, but based on his haggard appearance, it couldn't be much. He could jump a half-dozen times, maybe more, by his estimate. He'd need to charge him, force him to expose his method, then counter.

He refocused his Iron Skeleton and supplied more magic in the areas that began to grow numb and lifeless. He steadied his sword and took in a sharp breath, then lunged forward once more. The pain from his wound pulling open and shut with his movements was akin to barbed hooks yanking him in different directions. He pushed through regardless.

The enemy noble went on the defensive, his exhaustion apparent. He deflected what he could from Lorian's barrage of swings, but the sheer volume was quickly becoming too much to bear. Lorian knew that he'd either have to jump, or be impaled by Sun-Screamer.

A powerful thrust of the magical blade forced the noble to lose balance. *This is it*, Lorian thought. *He is going to jump. Focus, see what he does, how he moves.*
He watched his opponent's body, analyzing what he could as he went in for a killing swipe that would cut the man's throat. A twitch of the noble's fingers gave Lorian the information he

needed. He watched as the jumper pointed the pommel of his sword to the side. When his aim was true, the noble activated a previously unseen trigger within the handle of his blade by twisting two halves in opposite directions. A small shard sprang forward from a slot in the pommel; his totem. Lorian used his Iron Skeleton to change the direction of momentum that carried Sun-Screamer forward. The pain was overwhelming. Changing the direction of such a furious swipe would normally be taxing and uncomfortable.

Changing it whilst an open wound drained his life away was another story entirely. His flesh tore as the direction of his force changed from the enemy before him to the new location of the jumper's totem. He rotated his hips quickly and slashed towards the open air, praying to the natural gods that his timing was true.

The jumper's eyes widened in disbelief as Lorian vanished. When he reappeared, Sun-Screamer was ripping through the jumper's throat, its flames dancing along the tattered skin that once connected his head to his neck. In the span of an exhale, Lorian killed his opponent. The noble's body thrashed helplessly as its nerves searched desperately for salvation, hot blood squirting from its seared, stumped neck. The head rolled a good way from the battle, landing face up in a shrub of tangled weeds and wild winterberries. The glow from his eyes dimmed as his mouth mashed opened and closed, searching for a breath that couldn't be pulled in.

Lorian had won. He collapsed to a knee, the sound of his own heart beating wildly above the clamor of Johnathan's rampage just meters away. His vision dimmed and he had to steady himself on Sun-Screamer. A hand grabbed him by the shoulder, though he hadn't the energy to protest or inspect its owner.

"Lord Night!" Screamed a familiar voice. The anguish in their words made him think that death's approach was imminent. Flashes of Feln's face flooded his mind. Suddenly, they were on the graveled shores of Mellomirror again, searching for silver laced shells that they could pawn for extra coin. Lorian never found any, though Feln could spot its glare from a dozen meters away. She was always better than him. "How bad is it?" He asked, not knowing to whom he questioned. Whatever the answer was, it was sure to be grim. "You need a physician my lord, now," they replied as they hoisted him to his feet. He turned his head to inspect his savior Jenon. He should've known.

The voice of one of the soldiers screamed out, bringing Lorian back from purgatory. "Your grace! It's the Raven! She flees!"

He couldn't believe it. Feln. She was actually here. He watched as she jumped from the leading carriage, her black garments contrasting against the white of the snow. She eyed him for a long moment, her blue eyes piercing his soul. She turned and ran, weaving through the brush and trees, she disappeared from his sight.

Lorian stood and began to pursue but was forced back by Jenon.

"My lord, if you take chase you will bleed to death. Send the men, she can't outpace them forever," she said. He knew she was right, but it didn't matter. He needed to be the one to catch her, to have her explain herself. He tried again but was met with the same force. "If you don't let me stitch this wound, I'll kill you myself. Sit down!" Jenon ordered - her nostrils flaring with rage.

"Damn it! I don't have time for this!" Lorian protested. He unbuckled his plate armor and let it fall to the ground. He lifted the tattered undershirt and placed it around his wound. As before, he called forth his magic. *Like Forgornian tea*, he thought.

Heath came forth and poured into the wound. The pain was dull at first, the lack of blood and frigid air keeping his flesh dull, until it wasn't. *A curious thing*, he thought, *to smell the cooked flesh of oneself.* The wound drank the fire until he was certain it was no longer in danger of killing him.

He would still need stitches, but he prayed this would hold for now.

"You're mad!" Jenon accused, her face scrunching into a look of disgust and sadness.

He ignored her, time was of the essence. Faint as he was, he pursued Feln through the thicket of foliage and leafless trees. He was slow, but the thick snowfall made it easy to follow her tracks. Torn pieces of her ebony dress sat perched upon thorned bushes and sharp branches. Her escape was sloppy and careless. It wasn't long before he saw her in the distance, her darkened form a silhouette hidden among the shadows of the woods. She made for the eastern marches, a desperate attempt to reach a garrisoned unit outside Twilanon, he assumed. Twilanon was still miles from each of them and, as Lorian saw it, she would never reach the garrison before he caught up to her.

He was closing in on her, her footfalls leaving perfect imprints in the powder below indicated that she'd slowed somewhat. When he cleared a grouping of trees, he learned why. An abandoned cabin stood before him; the hollow insides glowed gently in the firelight.

Why did she light a fire? Is she giving herself up?

He approached the cabin doors with caution, his wound stinging him with every beat of his heart. In his stupor, he had left his chest plate and sword on the battlefield. If she was to attack him, he'd be defenseless. He had his magic but knew he'd never wield it at Feln. After all this time, the thought of harming her still made him sick. He knew he was a fool but in his heart, he wanted her to be the victim of some nefarious plot. He wanted to save her.

He swung the rotten wooden door open, the hinges moaning in protest. The gentle smell of roasting nuts filled his nose and upon the ground was Feln, basking in the glow of a growing fire. Her legs were exposed and cut from her dodging through the unforgiving forest and her skin was a hot pink as the blood in her limbs searched for any heat they could find. Her dress was in rags now and it hung loosely from one shoulder. She bore no weapon.

"I always knew it would be you, Lorian," she said as she added tinder to the pile of burning wood. "To find me, I mean. To force me into a cell, to have me tried by jury and hung from the rafts." Her words were filled with sadness, but her face was straight and unforgiving.

"Why did it have to come to this, Feln? How could you take the side of monsters like house Aaron? How could you marry that man?" He asked, not fully aware that he'd approached her from the side and sat next to her. "Tell me there's a reason that we stand against one another; that you continue to help those that seek to overthrow my cousin; that you don't write me. Please," he pleaded as she turned to him with tears freshly falling from her face.

"The world is not so simple, Lorian. And you're an idiot. You've always been an idiot. And I've never been so jealous of you for it." A stream of tears now fell continuously down her face, though she stifled any noise that threatened to escape with them. "I am here of my own will. I married into house Aaron of my own will. I don't need rescuing and I never have. Consider for a moment that you're the one on the wrong side," she continued as her fingers crept underneath her naked thigh. "Maybe it's you that needs to be rescued." She stabbed at him with a concealed dagger, the blade stopping shy of his neck.

Lorian began to weep along with her, his hand bloodied from grabbing the blade to stop her thrust at his throat. She was the enemy now; it was clear and certain. *Maybe it had always been so obvious*. He thought. Maybe he had been blind. Blinded not by some unseen force, not even by love. Blinded by his own ego, his own self-righteousness. He could never see her for what she was, nor could he humor the possibility that she had done this of her own volition. She was someone to be saved because that's what he needed her to be. She was right, he was truly an idiot.

He wouldn't allow her to be kept in a cell for months, or years. Treated like a savage and abused. He wouldn't allow her to be prostrated through the streets as a traitor and stripped naked before the masses before being hanged. If she was to die, he would be the one to do it. It was right, it was just, and Varios had been the one to teach him this.

He threw her dagger into the fire and grabbed her by the throat. They sat upright for a moment, her surprise keeping her from fighting back. As she started to thrash, he squeezed harder, forcing her onto her back. Her blue eyes were bright in the firelight, each a reflection of the cloudless skies they had sat beneath in their youth.

Feln's face twisted in anger, and she grabbed Lorian's neck in return, an attempt to subdue him before he could end her. The two struggled against one another in vain, neither able to overcome the other. Feln's face soon softened and her hands released and regrouped on the back of his head. She pulled him in with force and pressed her lips against his, causing him to release as well. Their lips broke free as they both gasped for precious air; their eyes locked in disbelief.

They reconnected once more, their oxygen seemingly less important than their desire to touch. Lorian began to rip away the remaining shreds of her blackened dress, the fibers coming undone effortlessly. She returned the gesture by unbuckling his greaves and sliding his trousers down just enough to expose his cock. They shared a sharp inhale as he entered her, his hips pressing into hers as his inhibitions spirited away. She ripped at his blood sullen undershirt and tossed its remains into the fire – the flames growing brighter in reaction. He pushed himself upright and drank in her form. The shadows danced around her naked breasts and fled with each thrust he gave. He traced her collar bones with his lips as he matched the rhythm of her own movements. Her eyebrows curled upward, and she looked at him in exasperation, as if she was unable to express herself with words. She pulled him in aggressively, her legs locking around his waist. She wrestled control from him, forcing him to roll to the side, her body stuck to his as they fell. She sat upright on him, and she ground her hips down and in swivels. He touched her everywhere he could, desperate to make these moments last forever. She grabbed his hands and directed them to her nipples, showing him how she preferred to be touched while squeezing his member with her own. Together, the two fell into a euphoric rhythm of ecstasy, each touch, kiss and thrust building momentum. Sweat glistened from their bodies and made their movements slippery but efficient. The climax built and Lorian surrendered himself to her completely, letting her decide where he would deposit. As the sensation grew more

intense, he closed his eyes and awaited the moment of joy that
he would share with Feln.

Kill the Raven

Lorian's eyes shot open in fear. Atop him, Feln's body
twitched in orgasm as her head shifted to that of a nightmarish
Raven who squawked ferociously at him. "Kill the raven!" the
monster demanded.

He awoke with a startle; his body covered in sweat.
Lorian peered around the room, his confusion slowly
evaporating as the details of his bedchamber came into focus.
Beside him was Jane, she awoke with him and held him
tightly, waiting for his senses to return.

"Another nightmare?" She asked, innocent to the details
of the dream that haunted him.

"Yes, love," he replied. "Forgive me, go back to sleep."